Malitu Book One

No Heart For A Thief

JAMES LLOYD DULIN

G & D Publishing

Copyright © 2023 by G & D Publishing

First paperback edition January 2023

Cover Illustration by Felix Ortiz
Typography by Michael Dulin
Map by Gustavo Schmitt
Copy Edit by Amy Vrana
Proofread by Victoria Gross

ISBN: 979-8-9871736-0-2 (paperback)
ASIN: B0BLGPMNZG (ebook)

www.jamesldulin.com

CONTENT AND TRIGGER WARNINGS
As a note of caution, this story contains depictions of graphic violence, violence towards children, derogatory behavior towards marginalized characters based on skin color and gender identity, colonialism, death of family members, drug addiction, slavery, survivor's guilt, and religious manipulation.

For my sons Sonny and Dominic,
and my best friend, wife, and partner, Aneicka.

ENNEA

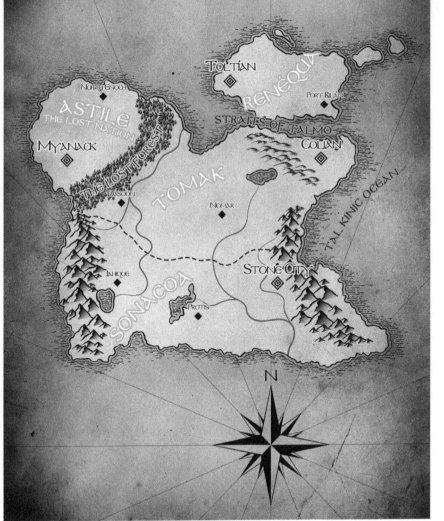

CHAPTER ONE

Below the bluff where Kaylo stood, small oddities peeled away the veneer of peace overlaying the forest. Figures darted through the trees in blurs of color. Sunlight glinted off the helm of a soldier. None of it had anything to do with Kaylo, but when the spirits screamed, their anguish broke open everything he had locked away. The past had returned, and the hiding—as all things did—had ended.

A young girl raced through a clearing back into the overgrown brush, two soldiers following close behind.

The scene fell silent beneath the ambient noise of the forest. Violence felt like it should announce itself with a bang, but the turns had taught him otherwise. Blood had ways of spilling in the quietest of moments.

Wisdom said to let the girl die. Kaylo hid from trouble for a reason.

Flashes of the girl broke through the trees, her ashen gray hair flaring out behind her before the forest swallowed her once again. Her cedar-brown complexion matched his own. Too few Tomakans roamed freely these days. Those who had survived lived under occupation or escaped into some dark corner of the countryside.

The soldiers ran through an outcropping moments after the girl. She had done an admirable job cutting through the dense wood, keeping distance between her and her attackers. But she was a child. The soldiers would outlast her. Or she would trip. A myriad of things might happen, but no matter the details, in the end, they would spirit her away like so many before.

Kaylo stepped over the edge of the bluff before he admitted to himself what he was about to do. His foot sank into the loose soil below, and the steep slope of the land drove him down the hill, the summer breeze kissing his cheeks as he ran against its current.

In the moments it took to reach the base of the hill, Kaylo abandoned pretense. There would be consequences if he survived, and plenty of time to regret his decision, but the decision had been made.

At the base of the bluff, he skidded to a stop and shut his eyes to the world. Vision only served to distract the mind in times such as these.

Kenke Forest, his forest, spread out like a map in his mind—the proud ironoak trees and stubborn underbrush, the dark soil, the sloping hills, and the Sanine River that cut the forest in two. This land had sheltered him for a dozen turns. If he meant to catch his prey, he had to cut through the dense brush rather than go around it.

Without a second thought, he launched himself forward.

Rough roots and wild shrubs lashed against his exposed ankles, but the pain would make itself known later. His knee ached with an old wound, and his chest burned for lack of air. Though his ligaments strained, he was still young enough—or stubborn enough—to call on his strength.

At one time, he could have run blindfolded through the forest and still found his mark, but no longer. He had grown too comfortable and set in his ways. Trees jumped out in front of him. He bore down on the moment—the forest, and the earth—as he pushed the pain and judgments from his mind.

"Seed and Balance," he muttered in repetition between heaving breaths, a mantra to his ancestor spirits.

The forest showed no signs of disturbance apart from an old set of animal tracks. Birds chirped. Wind rustled the trees. Everything carried on as it should.

He stopped.

In his rush to be the man he had been, he misjudged the path. The girl could have veered away in infinite directions. If he hadn't intercepted them by now, with all likelihood, the soldiers had caught their prey.

"Seed and Balance," he muttered again.

The Gousht no longer took prisoners, and Kaylo owned some measure of that change. Now the bastards cut strays open and hung them as warnings.

Kaylo closed his eyes to listen, and the spirits wailed. He whipped his head towards their cries, but before he could take in the sight, something slammed into his side.

Pain crawled along his ribs, back into his shoulder blade. His head rebounded off the ground as the child he meant to save tumbled over him. Dirt kicked up into a cloud, and they both lay groaning, sprawled out on the forest floor.

He should have listened to wisdom.

The dust settled, and the girl scrambled off the ground as soldiers broke through the trees. She made it to her feet as the taller of the two soldiers strode over and slammed his fist into her gut. The sounds of her coughing, gasping, and retching mixed together as she collapsed to the dirt.

Clad in green, padded armor, the soldiers loomed over their prey as they caught their breaths through self-assured smiles. The very image of Gousht soldiers—young, lean, and pale.

In their rush, they had yet to pay Kaylo any mind. The curve of his belt knife peeked out from beneath the dirt just beyond his reach and glinted in the sunlight. He shot his hand towards the weapon, like a man of lesser experience. Situations like these required patience.

The shorter soldier clamped her boot down on his wrist as his fingers brushed the knife's hilt. She leaned her weight over her foot as she bent down to pick up Kaylo's knife. His skin stretched, and his bones rebelled against the pressure until a small moan escaped his clenched teeth, and the soldier eased up, like she had been waiting to hear his pain.

"*Looks like the konki found a friend,*" the soldier said in Gousht, her accent thick and heavy.

Whoever decided to turn konki—a delicious fruit—into a slur, deserved a slit throat and a shallow grave. As a boy, Kaylo loved konki with its bright red flesh and thick brown husk. They must have thought themselves terribly clever.

The soldier removed her helm and wiped the sweat from her brow, letting her silver-white hair fall to her shoulders. She looked young. War hadn't had a chance to ugly her unblemished skin.

For all their reductive thinking, the Gousht didn't mind sending women to die in battle, not as long as they served as infantry and followed the orders of their assumed betters.

Her face twisted into a mask of exaggerated disgust. "*Ehh, this one is old and ragged. We should put him out of his misery.*" The repulsive language slurred its consonants and elongated its vowels, like someone speaking with a full mouth.

She twisted Kaylo's blade in her hands. "*But he does have a nice knife.*"

"*Let me see that,*" the other soldier said, reaching for the blade. He held it to the light and admired the well-crafted tool before slipping it into his belt. "*A keepsake to remember you by, old man.*"

Old? Kaylo thought.

The patches on his robes had overtaken the original thread long ago, he hadn't bathed in at least a span, and tendrils of his matted curls hung in front of his face, but none of that made him old. Thirty-four turns only counted as old to the young.

"*You enjoy this too much, Kels,*" the second soldier playfully rebuked as he reached into the pouch at his waist. He appeared older than the first soldier, but only slightly, standing tall and proud, his pale skin glistening with sweat.

"*Jauk, if we have to be in this shit-pile colony, we should enjoy ourselves.*" Her lips spread into a wide-mouthed grin.

The Empire loved this type of soldier—confident youth in love with power and violence, the type of person who bantered over death.

Jauk returned her grin as he pulled out a palm-sized crystal from his pouch. He flipped it back and forth in his hands, as if admiring the clarity of the perfect jewel, but something deeper than admiration flickered in his eyes. Hunger. His stance, his focus, his grip on the jewel spoke of a man who didn't just enjoy what was to come; he needed it.

The Tomakan girl squeezed her eyelids shut as if straining to hear something in the distance, a young dancer searching for The Song. A novice. Even the soldiers recognized what she was up to, dense as they were.

Kels kicked the girl in the side, and she broke into a second fit of coughing.

The soldier leaned over her victim. "*Your little lullaby is not going to save you. And look at what you did. Some old forest hermit is going to die because you ran.*" Kels's smile widened. "*At least your parents were smart enough to stay put.*"

Kels seized the collar of the girl's robe and dragged her towards an ironoak tree. The girl kicked at the dirt and cursed in common tongue, but it meant nothing to Kels. The soldier slammed the girl into the tree as if she weighed nothing, then bound her hands to the trunk.

The dancer's soft cries tore at Kaylo's shame, but rushing through moments like these was a good way to die a bad death. An opening would present itself.

With every passing second, Kaylo's reservations about killing these soldiers dissipated. As a rule, he valued life regardless of its trappings, but these green bastards deserved to meet their god.

If the soldiers had known who they had encountered or if they hadn't fallen as deeply into the lure of their small power, maybe they would have had a chance. Not likely, but maybe.

As they said in Tomak, the soldiers focused on the trees and got lost in the forest. Neither of them had given Kaylo a second glance since they disarmed him. To them, he was an old, unarmed man in ragged clothes living in the forest.

Jauk stretched his arm out towards the girl as he clutched the crystal in his palm. The young dancer's eyes widened. She thrashed against her bindings to no avail. The beads on her braids rattled about like a child's toy as her wails carried into the emptiness of the forest.

As the crystal began to glow, the girl's back arched away from the tree trunk, she bared her teeth to the sky, and her screams pitched upward.

The soldiers were enthralled with their own power, the glowing stone reflecting in their pale blue eyes. It called to them, and the rest of the world fell silent behind it.

It took every remnant of Kaylo's lapsed discipline not to rush the soldiers. Time ran thin for the girl, but a wasted opportunity would mean both of their lives. Slowly—near silently—he crept towards the soldiers.

Jauk turned his head at the last moment, a moment too late.

Kaylo planted his foot behind Jauk's legs, reached across the front of his chest, and rotated, slamming the man to the ground and forcing the crown of his head to strike first.

The glowing crystal fell from his grip and tumbled into the dirt beside him.

Still clear. Still empty.

The girl stopped screaming. Kels squinted at Kaylo as if to test the truth of her eyes.

Unfortunately, her shock didn't last. She reached into her green padded armor and retrieved a dull red crystal, which hung from her neck. The color churned beneath the crystal's surface like a living thing. She raised her other arm towards Kaylo, and the crystal glowed a brilliant red.

The air in front of him shimmered before igniting and popping in a small explosion. He swerved from the heat.

Ten paces separated Kaylo from his target.

Light refracted through another pocket of air, then another, and another. Kaylo veered to the side just before the air pockets burst in a succession of bright flashes.

When he looked up, Kels's wicked smile shined in the light of the crystal. Then he raised his hand into the air, and the light vanished.

Her smile disappeared with the crystal's light. She gripped the gemstone harder and stretched out her arm like she had before, but nothing happened. The crystal had gone clear. Her face contorted—almost comically—with confusion.

The air surrounding her shimmered, and realization dawned on her face. Her expression grew slack with horror as she whispered, "*Thief.*" Then the air around her erupted in cascading explosions that sent her tumbling backward.

Jauk didn't waste any time once he regained his footing. The soldier clutched a tawny crystal and raised his free hand to the sky before slamming it to the ground in a dramatic gesture. The earth rippled and cracked.

For all the power they wielded, most Gousht didn't take the time to understand the spirits they controlled.

Kaylo simply stepped aside and reached into the air to grab something no one else could see, and the ground steadied.

The green bastards always looked confused when Kaylo took away their toys. Jauk gripped the jewel tighter and desperately stomped his feet, but the earth remained still.

Why do they always think that will work? Kaylo thought as he approached the soldier slowly, but with purpose.

As soon as he was close enough, Kaylo lunged forward and jabbed Jauk in the throat. The soldier fell to his knees, coughing, his hand clutching his crystal rather than the hilt of his sword. Kaylo pulled his purloined knife from the soldier's belt and plunged the blade into his quilted armor. The layered fabric resisted Kaylo's knife and then gave way to the force.

Without malice or righteousness, Kaylo gripped the back of the soldier's tunic and lowered the dying man to the forest floor.

His work was not finished.

The young dancer's gaze followed Kaylo as he walked past her to finish off the other soldier. Her mouth hung agape. He must have been a fearsome sight, ragged and covered in blood.

He shook his head and muttered, "Seed and Balance." This wasn't the person he wanted to be, not anymore.

Kels moaned and kicked her feet into the dirt, pushing herself farther from Kaylo. The flames had scorched her pale skin red, black, and gray, yet she still clung to life. He bent down and held her in place as she begged for mercy. Then he offered what little mercy he had for her with a quick death as he thrust the blade between her ribs into her heart.

He had not always been such a capable killer, but as with most things in life, his skill had grown with time and experience. His blade slid free of her wound, and blood followed, turning her green uniform brown.

Kaylo wiped his blade on the Emperor's seal stitched onto the dead soldier's armor—the serpent strangling the lion, now covered in blood. He sheathed his knife and went about gathering the crystals, including the stone that had fallen from Jauk's hand.

The stones rattled against each other in his cradled arms. He closed his eyes and listened until he found what he needed. The young dancer gasped as the crystals turned to dust and fell through Kaylo's arms like sand, the colors trapped within dispersing into the air. She had probably never seen anyone destroy a spirit crystal before. Few had.

Killing came easily, but now he had to deal with this stray Tomakan girl.

A red streak of blood ran from a cut on her forehead, accenting her brown skin. She was young. Twelve turns, maybe fourteen, no more. Her lavender and green robes hung loose, tied at the waist over a pair of homespun pants. Despite the dirt and ripped fabric, her clothing bore the signs of his people.

Her bottom lip stuck out and quivered with the rise and fall of her chest. She would never forget today. It would define her as all his violent days had defined him.

There was nothing he could do about that now, but he could free her.

He approached her as he would a startled animal, with a slow gait and averted eyes. She yanked against her bindings, looking back and forth as if searching for an escape.

"What is your name?" he asked with as gentle of a voice as he could find.

The girl continued to struggle against her bindings, saying nothing.

"I'm not going to hurt you." He bent down to untie the rope lashed around the girl's wrists. A knife would have been quicker, but she probably wouldn't have reacted well to him brandishing a blade this close to her.

"Is there anyone else chasing you?" he asked.

The girl remained quiet.

He adjusted his ragged robes, knelt to her level, and placed his hand on her shoulder. "I won't force you to answer. But for both of our safety, is anyone else chasing you?"

She shook her head.

With one last jerking motion, he freed her of the rope. "There you go. That's better. Do you have somewhere to go? Is there anywhere I can take you? Where is your family?"

The girl shook her head, tears streaming down her face. He met her eyes. Trauma changed a person in ways varied and unpredictable, but it always settled in the eyes.

She shook her head again, and her beaded braids clattered against the tree behind her. Cries erupted from her lungs before she threw her body against Kaylo's chest. He flinched as she clutched him tighter.

After twelve turns without touching another person, this little girl sought comfort in his arms, arms covered in blood and gore. He hesitated for a breath or two. This wouldn't end well. People met poor ends when they lingered in his company.

Yet again, his nature overtook his wisdom, and he wrapped his arms around the girl as she sobbed into his shoulder.

"Family knows," he whispered, holding her until she gave into sleep.

Hopefully, her dreams would allow her to escape for a few hours. She had learned too much about the nature of The Waking today. The land of the living was a wicked place, and she deserved a space to hide from it, even if only for a short time.

Chapter Two

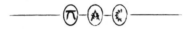

As Tayen woke, a single candlelight carved out a small refuge from the darkness encircling her. A wall of interwoven trees grew out of the place beside her, where her sister should have been. Since her family escaped their occupied village—in the early days of her memories—they had moved more times than the seasons had changed. New surroundings became common, but Nita, her sister, always slept on her right.

"Nita." Tayen's whispers carried into the room past the edge of the candlelight, but no one called back.

Tayen pushed herself up, and the bedroll beneath her bunched up in an unfamiliar way. The bedroll, which was not hers, wore its age with stains and pieces of straw peeking out from small tears.

Despite the warmth of the summer night, a chill raced up her arms and teased the side of her neck. The insides of her head swirled as her vision blinked in and out. Her head stung like she had run dead on into an ironoak. She reached for the injury, but it had been pasted over with a poultice which stunk of soggy grass.

"Mommy," she said, a bit louder than a whisper.

The light from the candle only spread so far before it dissipated. It brushed over the wall where Nita should have been. If this were a cabin wall, she had never seen its likeness. One sturdy tree entwined with another and another, each still very much alive.

Where am I? she thought. *Where is everyone?*

She closed her eyes and grasped after her memories, and the world tittered beneath her, making her stomach churn.

Tayen's mother had been after her to sweep out their hut, so she ran off and hid in the forest. She threw rocks at a target she marked on a tree, and the day passed over her. No one had come out to find her, not even to scold her. Every additional moment she waited would only deepen her parents' anger.

The hides covering the entrance to their hut glowed with the fire inside. When she pulled the furs away, smoke rushed through the opening. It smelled of charred meat and stung her eyes.

When her vision adjusted, she found her family, laying atop one another in the fire—a pile of brown limbs in a tangled mess, splashed with blood and ash.

Her mother's eyes remained open but empty.

Time stopped as Tayen gazed into her mother's eyes through the flames.

Then something stirred in the corner of the hut, and she ripped her attention from the bodies that used to be her family, finding a figure obscured by the smoke and shadows.

She had run, and the air had burned her lungs as she gulped it down.

The memory unraveled and repeated over and over in her head. Tears washed over her face. Had she been home, her body would have fed the flames as well.

I should have died with them, she thought.

Air soured on her tongue with each breath. She had saved herself, ran from the soldiers who killed her family, and now her family had crossed into The Mist, leaving her here.

Where am I? she thought, then froze at the recollection of the man in ragged robes. *He must have taken me.*

The light didn't pierce far enough into the darkness, which could have concealed any number of threats.

She held her breath for fear of the sound and then took hurried swallows of air when she could no longer hold out. Her blood raced through her veins. That man had slaughtered two Gousht soldiers like butchering livestock. He had moved like a spirit, only to come back wearing their blood.

The Song whirled in the blackness all around her. She threw her arms wide and brought them back together in a loud clap that drove the shadows from the room. The dim candlelight spread out to fill the void the shadows left behind, expanding in every direction into a room at least four-fold the size of her family's hut.

Trees, bushes, and vines tangled into a vast dome that met at a giant stormwood tree in the center of the room. Her father once told her that stormwoods got their name because of a lightning storm that caused a forest fire. Only the stormwoods remained in the ashes the fire left behind. She had seen one before, only once.

Awe replaced fear.

Trees shouldn't have grown this way, and yet the curves of the walls moved as if any other shape would have been unnatural. The simplicity of the form and grandness of the space helped settle her breathing into a steady rhythm.

A vibrant garden of fruits and vegetables lined the perimeter, save for one section lined with books, actual books. Tayen hadn't seen more than three books in her life, and here the tomes that didn't fit on the shelves lay on the ground in stacks.

She walked towards the book collection with a hunger, then stopped as she came to the stormwood tree.

The tree's trunk stretched wider than she could from fingertip to fingertip. It encased two figures carved into the heart of the tree. As hard as stormwood was, it must have taken a lifetime to chip away the bark and wood, and still, despite their massive size, every surface of the figures had been carved with fine detail.

Their beauty and peculiarity drew her in. Nearly human, yet entirely not.

Neither of the figures had a mouth, but they had been carved with too much care for this absence to have been a mistake.

A horizontal line cut the woman's face in two, the top half stained black and the bottom white. She loomed like a threat whose beauty could not be denied. Every curve of her face flowed in perfect symmetry, clashing with the man's face on the right. A mess of jagged angles, his asymmetry mirrored the natural shape of the tree structure around them, exuding a calm manner regardless of his harsh edges.

"Neat trick," a voice called out from behind her.

Tayen whipped around. The old hermit—the man who had saved her, then taken her—sat on his bedroll near the far edge of the room.

Now that things moved slower, he wasn't very old. His tangled, bird-nest hair framed his expressionless face. He looked like he probably smelled bad, but he didn't look scary.

Without another word, he curled his forearm slowly and deliberately, then grasped something Tayen couldn't see from the air. The Song went silent, and the shadows slithered over the ground and crawled back to where they had been before she sent them away, covering the ragged man in darkness yet again.

The sound of her own breath filled her eardrums as her hands shook at her side.

"Go to sleep, shadow dancer," he said.

Her feet refused to move.

How? she thought. The Song returned like waters breaking through a dam, and the shadows sung to her once more.

The ragged man didn't speak again, and if he had moved, he moved as silent as the darkness itself. Only her breath and The Song disturbed the silence.

Moonlight outlined the furs draped over the exit. There wouldn't be another opportunity. She dug her boots into the swept dirt and ran.

As she threw the furs to one side, she stopped.

The ragged man hadn't stirred, hadn't made a sound. No one would stop her from leaving, but then, she had nowhere to go.

The forest stretched out before her, encased in the light of the moons. No matter where she ran, her family wouldn't be there. She would be alone.

Behind her, candlelight flickered over a bedroll. The blanket she had slept under lay strewn to the side. This man didn't owe her anything, and yet he had saved her.

Her hand brushed over the poultice pasted over her head wound. Any decision she made would make her a fool. At least this decision came with a candle and a blanket.

The furs swung back into place as she stepped away from the opening and walked back to the candlelight.

The forest held more threats than the ragged man, but that didn't mean she trusted him. She lay awake as wax dripped down the length of the candle. The flame wavered as it ate away at the wax and her resolve. She blinked despite herself, and eventually, sleep took her.

───────────────

Sunlight spilled into the treehouse and stirred Tayen from her dreamless sleep. At least the spirits had offered her that small kindness.

The scent of coriander and anise filled the air, and, for a moment, she expected her father to be huddled over the griddle, cooking frycakes like he did on special occasions. Instead, a solitary bowl of spiced porridge waited next to her bedroll, topped with berries and drizzled in honey.

The remains of a fire flickered away on the other side of the stormwood tree. Other than the flames, she was alone.

Steam rose from the bowl into the cool summer morning. Its warmth spread along her fingertips as she picked it up. She dipped the spoon into the porridge, brought it to her lips, then paused.

The ragged man shared her father's generous hand with spices. It smelled like her father and his frycakes, a tacky dough he fried, then covered in honey and crushed berries.

What if the porridge tastes like daddy's frycakes? she thought. *What if it doesn't?*

She set the bowl down and slid it away, spilling the contents onto the swept dirt floor.

Even if she wanted to cry, Tayen didn't have the water, especially not over a stupid bowl of boiled grains.

She swallowed, and a scratch ran the length of her dry throat, which made her laugh. Not even her body belonged to her anymore. It was just a medium for her pain.

"Blessed Mother!" She ripped the blanket that didn't belong to her off her legs, stood up, and threw it to the dirt. "You left me nothing!"

Her voice reverberated through the treehouse.

"Nothing. There's nothing left."

In the fullness of daylight, the ragged man's home was more spectacular than it had been the previous night, which made her hate it all the more.

The ironoak trees that made up the walls twisted around each other so tightly that one became indistinguishable from another. As they rose and curved towards the center of the dome, shades of brown transitioned into splashes of green leaves glowing in the sunlight.

Her mother's eyes had been the same shade, and the leaves stared down at Tayen like her mother had the night she died.

Most of her features were a gift from her father—her smile, her sharp jawline—but her mother gave her the color in her eyes.

Despite her dehydration, her tears fell once again.

"You should have taken me too," she said between heaving breaths.

She screamed with all her rage, but even her screams turned into cries. Then she threw herself against the borrowed bedroll and let her tears soak into the worn fabric.

Her family had been her whole life. Without them, Tayen couldn't be the person she had been. She jerked with each sob until she surrendered to exhaustion.

Tayen cupped her hands and dug into the cool earth. She had been nine, maybe ten, and it rained the day before.

A worm burrowed through the disturbed soil and brushed over Tayen's fingers. She giggled. The little squirmers made such intricate paths in the dirt. Nita found them disgusting, which only gave Tayen another reason to love them.

Nita had gathered all the autumn leaves, covering the ground into a pile beneath a sequoia tree. "Come on, Tayen. Jump with me."

"You do it," Tayen said. "I'll watch."

Her little sister had always loved to move. She climbed anything climbable, and several things not. If she could run somewhere, she didn't think twice before sprinting away, whereas Tayen enjoyed her quiet and studied the world around her. Their mother liked to call Tayen her little observer.

Leaves exploded into the air as Nita threw herself into the pile, then fluttered back down to the ground, catching the sunlight as they fell.

Her sister's giggles called out from beneath the cluttered leaves. "Did you see?"

"Of course. You don't have to scream when you jump."

"The next pile is going to be even bigger," Nita said as she climbed from the remnants of the mound.

Behind her, the forest darkened despite the sunlight.

Tingles squirmed between Tayen's shoulder blades as if someone was lurking in the woods watching them, as if she was the one being observed.

The darkness crept closer. She peered into the shadows and found an empty forest.

"Nita, maybe we should start going home," Tayen said.

"No, I'm having fun. You should help me. We could make a huge pile."

The darkness continued closing in, and the presence grew more pronounced. "Nita, there's someone out here. We should go."

Nita looked up and all around, but she didn't react as the shadows came closer. Her face contorted into a mocking gesture. "Very funny. You can't scare me."

Shapes and silhouettes of people formed in the darkness. Everywhere Tayen looked, the figures returned her gaze.

"Nita, please!" Tayen grabbed her sister's arm, but Nita slipped from her grasp.

"Stop it!" Nita yelled.

The figures were almost within arm's reach. Tayen's chest constricted. She reached for her sister, but again, her sister yanked her arm away.

"Nita! We need to leave!" Tayen screamed, but the darkness was upon them.

Hands reached out of the shadows. One grabbed Nita's leg. Another grasped her shoulder. A third arm wrapped around her neck. Then, all at once, they dragged Nita into the darkness.

Tayen reached for her sister, but she couldn't do anything now that Nita had become another silhouette lost in the dark.

"Take me!" Tayen screamed as the shadows receded. "Take me!"

Tayen gulped for air as she jolted awake. It had only been a dream. The walls of the treehouse surrounded her once again. She loosened her grip on the blanket and took a slow breath.

The treehouse had grown dimmer. On the far side of the stormwood, the ragged man sat next to the fire, turning a rabbit over the flame. The smell of greasy meat clung to the air, and her stomach rumbled in response. She clutched her small belly with both hands.

He met her glance, and she turned away. "If you want to eat, you'll have to come closer," he said, then carved a piece from the rabbit and held it out to her.

What does he want? Tayen pulled the blanket tight over her shoulders.

Her parents taught her to avoid strangers. Runaways. Rebels. Her family stayed away. They had only traded with other groups a handful of times. Even then, her mother made her stay out of sight and watch from a safe distance with Nita.

The muscles in her jaw clenched. It hurt to think about her mother, but every memory she had connected back to her family. They had been her whole life, and the Gousht had taken them from her.

For so many turns, the war seemed like a daemontale. Violence happened in stories. When Tayen's parents taught her how to be small, run, and hide, it felt like a game. If only it had been.

Every muscle in Tayen's body told her to run from this stranger. He continued to hold his hand out with a bit of rabbit meat, but he was dangerous. He may have washed the blood from his skin, but he had killed two soldiers with ease.

He saved my life, she thought, then saw the knives at his hip. *And he could end it just as easily.*

She moved hesitantly towards the fire, the smell growing stronger. She loved rabbit, but she forced herself to concentrate on the man's eyes. At the first sign of danger, she needed to run.

Slowly, she reached her hand out. Her fingers barely grazed the meat as the ragged man snapped his hand back.

He smiled like he had done something clever, and all her fear vanished, replaced by annoyance. Nita used to do the same thing. People who played with food were aggravating.

He gestured to the stumps surrounding the fire. "Sit," he said. "I'm not one to share food with strangers."

Then why did you offer? she thought, but kept her words to herself and sat down on one of the stumps, careful to leave one in between them.

"My name is Kaylo. What do they call you?"

He had an annoying smile. If she wanted to tell him her name, she would. That had nothing to do with food.

She took the size of him. If she drew her nails across his skin, he would probably be five shades lighter beneath the dirt. His hair looked like a bramble patch of weeds, and if his robes shed a few more threads, they would probably fall apart. And yet, he had a kind face.

Instead of waiting for a response, Kaylo went back to his meal, turning the spit and carving off another bite before taking a handful of berries from a large wooden bowl.

Tayen's father used to do the same thing when she needed time to think. He went on with whatever needed doing and gave her space. But this man wasn't her father. They murdered her father.

She considered walking back to the bedroll. She could outlast him, but then her stomach groaned again, louder. She sucked her lip. "Tayen."

Kaylo didn't bother to turn towards her. Instead, he nodded, carved off the rabbit's hind leg, and held it out for her.

"Tayen, huh?" He said her name like he was considering if she had lied to him. "Good name. There was a Tomakan warrior named Tayen during the Hundred-Turn War. Stories say she was fearless and kind. Stories also say she killed enough Sonacoans to fill two villages. So much for relying on stories."

He placed the bowl of berries in front of her. "So, Tayen, what are you doing in the forest?"

"We never stay in one place very long," she said with a full mouth. "My family..." Her throat closed around her words, and she trailed off. She focused on chewing instead.

Kaylo sliced off another chunk of rabbit meat and offered it to her. She snatched it from him, too hungry to remember her wariness, then they finished their meal in silence.

When he finished eating, Kaylo handed the bones to the girl to pick clean. She already ate most of the rabbit; might as well let her finish her work.

Cleaning up was a small task—a rag, a basin of water, the wooden bowls, and the rotisserie spit. Life slowed down as he ran his rag over the surface of the bowls, making them shine and leaving a light trail of water against the grain of the wood.

"How'd you do it?" Tayen asked.

"Do what?"

"When you fought the soldiers, you called The Flame and The Mountain."

"Nothing stopping me from being twice-marked."

"You live in a treehouse, and last night, you called the shadows back," she said. "No one's marked by four spirits."

"A treehouse? A treehouse?" Kaylo said in ascending volume and fake outrage. "This is a hallow."

She pursed her lips and glanced to the side. The look, presumably meant to chastise, only made him laugh.

"How do you think I did it?"

She went quiet and turned her gaze towards the stormwood carvings, and her eyes jumped wide. "You're a thief."

"I don't like that term." The words came out harsher than he had intended, right when she had started to open up.

Whatever skill he had with people faded away around the same time he stopped shaving. He was wandering through a strange forest with his eyes closed, running into every tree in his path. He needed to be gentler.

"Sorry," Tayen said with a bowed head.

"It's more like borrowing," he said, aiming for levity but missing his target.

Tayen smiled weakly at his attempt and fumbled around with the bones in her hands. "What do you call it?"

"I would say I'm a spirit dancer."

"Oh, okay." The bones clinked in her hands. "What happens now?"

Kaylo sighed. "You make it through today, then you move on to tomorrow. It won't be easy. I've seen enough death to know the ache. On the best days, it's numbing."

As he heard himself speak, he looked down at the child in front of him. Everything about bringing her here had been a mistake.

"Am I supposed to stay here?" she asked

"I hadn't thought on it much. You're welcome to."

"Why?"

"What do you mean, why?" he asked.

"Why? Why would you take me in? Why did you save me? What do you want?"

"Look, I didn't plan any of this out," he said with far too much force.

At her age, conflict had scared him. Even though war had a way of aging children beyond their days, he had to take more care with his words.

He pulled the rabbit carcass from the spit, collected the bones, and carried them over to the stormwood carvings. The bones made a hollow clicking noise when he dropped them into a stone basin at the foot of the idols. After a bit too much firestarter and the flick of his knife against a flint stone, flames filled the basin.

As he sat on the ground in silence, staring at the carvings in the tree, feeling something between hatred and duty, the bones started to crack as the fire grew hotter.

"What are you doing?" Tayen asked from over his shoulder.

"If there is one thing I know in this world, it's that the spirits are real, and they are fickle as anyone under the moons."

The bones continued to crack in the background. "To the sixth—The Seed, who gives us food and shelter. I ask that you calm angry hearts with forgiveness. I mean, that's what you're supposed to do, right? Not that it has worked all that well, but, you know, maybe try harder." Kaylo shifted his gaze to the two-toned carving. "To the seventh—The Balance, who started this whole mess. Why don't you get off your vestigial ass and do something about this war?"

Kaylo brought three fingers to his lips, then touched them to the ground before pushing himself up from the floor and clapping the dirt from his hands.

The girl's jaw dangled from her face like it might fall to the floor. He chuckled. "I said the spirits were real. I didn't say I liked the bastards."

"You can't speak to the spirits like that," Tayen whispered, as if she expected the spirits to appear.

"Why? What are they going to do, take away all that's dear to me?" Kaylo asked with a wide gesture to his empty home. "Listen, little shade, at the end of the day, the spirits will do what they're going to do. No prayer is going to change that. And right now, they seem content with letting us all kill each other over land and their so-called gifts."

"Why pray then?"

"I don't know. Tradition. The Empire tried to steal our culture. They tried to force us to be more obedient versions of them. I hold on to what I can."

"If you care that much, why are you hiding from the war?"

"Who says I'm hiding?"

The girl looked around and spread her arms wide, mimicking his earlier gesture.

Kaylo chuckled. "Fair point, but trust me, it's better this way."

"But yesterday...you killed those soldiers so easily."

"They had the cleanest uniforms I've ever seen. I was probably the first person they ever confronted who fought back," Kaylo said.

"Liar," Tayen said.

"Excuse me?"

"You could help a lot of people, but you're hiding in some treehouse."

Kaylo took a deep breath. "You really shouldn't speak to your elders that way. And it's a hallow."

"I'm fourteen, and you're not that old."

"Anyone ever tell you your mouth is too smart for your age?"

"What's wrong with being smart?"

Kaylo ran his hands through his thick mess of gray curls and let out a heavy sigh. "It's been a long day, little shade. You can stay up if you want to, but I am going to go to bed."

"Thank you," she said in a much lower voice. He raised his eyebrows in a question, and she continued, "You saved me." Then she turned and walked back to the fire.

"For now," he mumbled to himself as the flames cast her in silhouette.

CHAPTER THREE

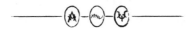

Smoke filled the hut like a thick fog, stinging Tayen's eyes and making
them water. The scent of burned meat and something slightly metallic
clung to the air. Her senses told her to run, but she couldn't move.
She tried to turn her head or close her eyes, but her body would not
respond, as if she were merely an observer being forced to stare into the
acrid fog.

The hard edges of shapes solidified in the smoke and formed into
silhouettes. Her mother's arm reached behind her head unnaturally, like
it fell out of socket as she tried to scratch her back. Patches of her flesh
hung from her body, blackened with soot and scorch marks. Her braids
had been singed or burned to her scalp. But her face...her mother's face
remained unblemished, the same face that would kiss Tayen goodnight
and wake her in the morning.

Her mother lay there, atop her father and her sister, nothing more
than a pile of flesh, bone, and sinew. Their bodies were strangers,
hollowed out. Nothing of her family lingered. Then her mother's eyelids
popped open, irises faded to a muted and dim green, a distant relative
of what they had been. They fit poorly in her mother's face. Her skin
tightened as her lips turned into a smile.

Her mouth moved, but she made no sound.

Tayen called to her, "Mommy, I can't hear you. What are you trying to say?"

Again, her mother's mouth moved, still nothing came out. Tayen cried and cried for her mother to speak to her, but her mother could only form her mouth around the words. Her lips moved too quickly. Tayen only made out one word.

Blood.

She squinted, but the smoke became opaque. Then the smoke filled her lungs as she screamed.

Suddenly, Tayen became aware of other people in the tent, wading through the smoke, staring at her. They closed in around her as the clouds of grayish fog became thicker and thicker until she could no longer breathe.

The girl tossed and turned in her sleep. Slight moans and whimpers crossed the hallow. Kaylo should have gone to her, woken her up and comforted her. But what would he say? Place an arm on her shoulder and tell her everything would be okay? She didn't need platitudes. The words she needed to hear didn't exist. If they did, she needed to hear them from someone else.

As Sokan, Ennea's first daughter, the sun, made her presence known, light began to slip through the hallow's entrance. No matter how he readjusted himself under his blanket, sleep refused him. No use lying there staring at the walls.

In the early turns, when the isolation threatened to overwhelm him with the worst of his thoughts, routine offered him a sense of structure. The simple task of tending to small necessities saved him.

Of all the species of wood he had stacked along an edge of the hallow, he habitually reached for the maple logs first. It burned subtle and sweet, making the air smell of sap. He arranged the logs in the firepit with care, not that it mattered. He had plenty of firestarter, though the oil often tainted the smell of the wood.

As the handful of wood shavings in the center of the stack lit up in a flash, the fire sprang alive, filling the hallow with a gentle crackling.

Tayen tossed about under her blanket. She would need to eat when she woke up. That he could handle.

The oats rattled as he added them to the pot, followed by a couple pinches of salt, a healthy hand of ground cardamom and anise, and water. Even before he set the pot over the flame, the smell mixed with the maple wood in the air.

The girl snapped up in a coughing fit, turning this way and that, as if she expected to be somewhere else. Then she stopped on him. Her eyes peered into the heart of his spirit, and her face stilled and hardened.

"Good morning," he said. It felt like a ridiculous thing to say, given how she had woken up, but the silence unnerved him in a way it rarely had before. "Breakfast will be ready shortly. There's fresh water over there if you need it."

She followed his finger towards the water. Without saying anything, she walked over and filled a small wooden bowl before splashing water over her face and running her hands through her braids.

While she calmed down from whatever nightmare haunted her, Kaylo focused on the pot in front of him. She hadn't told him what had happened yet, but he could fill in the gaps. The way she avoided talking about her parents told him enough not to ask.

He plucked ripe blueberries, strawberries, and blackberries from the bushes around the hallow walls. Extra blueberries. She had eaten a lot of them the night before.

When the oats absorbed enough of the water, he stirred in a handful of berries. Cardamom and anise kicked up into the air again, and the sweet, floral pepper notes filled his nose.

Good food allowed him to show the care and respect his words could not, so he hovered over the pot. Taken off the flames too soon, and the oats would have too much bite. Too late, and it would become a soggy mess.

When he pulled the pot from the stand, he found Tayen standing over him. A small yelp escaped his mouth, and he nearly spilled breakfast.

For the first time, she smiled, and her cheeks puffed out.

"Hungry?" he asked, and she nodded. He ladled out two bowls of porridge and topped them with honey and fresh berries.

She took her bowl, and for a long while, stared at its contents.

"Too hot?" Kaylo asked.

Her gaze found him, but she didn't say anything. Then she lifted her spoon to her mouth and closed her eyes before taking a bite. Her cheeks pulled back into a grimace like she had to hold back tears. A moment later, she took another bite and another.

"Good?" Kaylo asked.

"Exactly like my father's frycakes," she said. Her lips turned into an expression that could have been a smile, or maybe a broken heart.

He nodded, and they ate in a silence laden with unasked questions.

After breakfast, Kaylo offered his antagonistic prayers to the absent spirits. He held back a few graphic suggestions on what they could do with his burned offering. Young ears listened in. On top of that, he wasn't even sure spirits were physically equipped for his suggestions.

Tayen knelt next to him and offered more conventional prayers to Ennea and The Shadow. Then, at his suggestion, she distracted herself with the books on his shelves.

In keeping with routine, Kaylo tended his plants from where he had last stopped. He knelt on the swept dirt and ran his knife methodically through the plants, peeling away the overgrowth and shearing any dead or dying branches.

The world stopped in these moments between his knife and the plants. Occasionally, he would scrutinize a single plant for hours, only to make a few cuts. If the plant would be healthier for it, time was a fair sacrifice.

The leaves of the moonlight hazel felt like velvet beneath his fingertips. He cradled the branches as he searched for the next cut. The shrub had grown too large. A shame to stunt such a beautiful plant, but a balance existed in the hallow. Each plant shared the small ecosystem with the next. After he severed a few branches, he stripped the bark and leaves for later. Good medicine in moonlight hazel.

———————

Morning became midday, and still the two dancers occupied their separate worlds underneath the bowed trunks of the ironoak hallow. Tayen tried to focus on the book in front of her. Something about the spiritual connection of dancers to The Mist. All meaning faded from the words until they became nothing more than black ink on off-white pages.

Only days before, she would have been ecstatic to read a new book. Her parents had only ever owned three—a collection of daemontales for children, a historical accounting of Tomak before the great war, and a strange story about a woman who built her home at the bottom of the ocean—the books her mother used to teach her to read. They most likely burned in the same fire as her family. Imperial policy dictated all texts not written in the language of their god be destroyed.

Tayen tottered on the edge of sleep when she sensed a presence lurking. Kaylo stood above her like a nervous child. It seemed silly that she had once feared this man.

"I'm going hunting for dinner," he said, then turned to grab his bow and quiver.

"Can I come?"

"You don't have to. You can stay and read if you like."

"No, I'll come."

Kaylo nodded, his expression still uncertain. He unsheathed one of several knifes hanging from his belt, flipped it in the air, and caught it by the blade. It took an awkward glance and a moment of silence for Tayen to understand he meant for her to take it.

Outside the treehouse, the forest felt familiar and strange

simultaneously. Tayen had lived in one forest or another most of her life, but in all that time, she had never been with anyone other than her family.

The fearsome thing Kaylo had been when he killed the soldiers came alive again as he stalked through the brush. The flora seemed to make way for him as he crept along, scanning the forest with every step.

He sniffed the air, and Tayen followed suit, but it smelled like the forest to her—damp soil and a pleasant mixture of plants, but nothing worth note.

"What do you smell?" she asked quietly.

"Nothing yet. We are getting closer to the river. Keep watch for tracks."

"Why do you live out here by yourself?"

"For the quiet," he said in a flat, serious tone.

"No, really, why?"

Kaylo straightened up, turned, and met her eyes. This wasn't the same nervous man from the hallow. "Hunting is best done quietly."

"You know there's a war going on."

"I know all about the war, little shade."

"Is that why you're hiding out in your treehouse?"

"It's not a treehouse..." Kaylo stopped himself and let out a heavy sigh. "Blessed Mother, you are annoying. I don't know how your parents raised you, but..." The tension that had been building in his face went slack.

"Why is it important to you?" he asked in a softer voice.

Pressure welled up behind her eyes, but she clenched her teeth. He didn't get to make her cry. "Because they're dead. Because the Gousht killed them. And I'm left with a stranger who hides away in a treehouse."

Kaylo walked over and sat down on the trunk of a fallen tree. He patted the spot beside him, like he had the right to tell her where to go.

"I'm sorry they're gone. I'm sorry you're stuck with me, in the hallow." He emphasized the last phrase, and his lips curled in a pained smile. "If you haven't noticed, I'm not too good with people, so I stay away. I wasn't any good at war either."

"What does that mean? You killed those two soldiers the other day."

"War is about more than fighting," Kaylo said. "When I was your age, a little older, my friends and I thought if we killed enough Gousht and freed enough slaves that we could end the occupation. Instead, we started a war."

"You were part of the Uprising?"

"We didn't understand. We didn't think the Empire could do any worse than slavery and occupation. Then they showed us how wrong we were and started slaughtering whole villages to prove that they could."

"You think slavery was better?"

"Better alive than dead."

"I doubt the rest of Ennea would agree with you."

"The dead might," Kaylo said and stared off into the forest like he was looking through the past. "This war is my fault, little shade. I don't have the schooling to count all the blood I owe."

When he stood, the forest hermit didn't look as strong as he had a few moments ago. He walked deeper into the forest, his shoulders limp, his gait small and slow. A man hiding in his own skin.

The observer in Tayen watched as Kaylo forced his way through the routine of hunting. He knelt to analyze a snapped stem and a tuft of fur, but he didn't move like the predator he could be.

A light babble from the river whispered underneath the rest of the ambient noises. Kaylo waved her over, and they crouched behind a cropping of bushes. An arrow softly scraped against leather as he pulled it from his quiver. He adjusted himself, readied the bow, and settled in to wait for whatever might cross their path.

"Are we just going to wait here?"

Kaylo didn't answer. He simply looked at her, his eyes wide and glaring.

"What did you mean when you said you started the war?"

"What is it that you don't understand about quiet and hunting?"

"Were you at Anilace?" she asked.

"Oakheart."

"What?"

"Oakheart Mountain," he said. "The Gousht named it Anilace after one of the Emperor's consorts when they turned the mountain into a mine."

"Wait, you're not just a spirit thief, are you?" Tayen squinted at the man in front of her. Tomakan. Spirit Thief. Part of the Uprising.

He couldn't be, she thought. He smelled like he hadn't seen water in several moons. *But then again, how many spirit thieves were at Anilace?*

"You're Ennea's Thief," she said. "The Hero of Anilace."

"I'm not a hero." Kaylo spat the words out.

"What are you talking about?" Tayen asked. "You freed all those people."

"And sent them out to die in a never-ending war."

"My father used to tell me stories about you."

"Daemontales."

"You gave Ennea hope..." Tayen started, but Kaylo clapped his hand over her mouth. His eyes narrowed as he stared into the dense wood of the forest, searching for something.

"Get down," Kaylo whispered. "Slowly."

The tone of his voice said more than his words, and after everything, she was inclined to follow his lead. Each crunch of the leaves as she lowered herself to the ground made her heart pause. Every muscle locked in place.

A stranger held her life in his hands. And again, she was too defenseless and weak to do anything.

When she ran from the bastards who killed her family, she proved what a coward she was. A hatred swelled in her chest, and yet for all her hate, she lay prone on the forest floor, hiding from something she hadn't even seen.

Trees fluttered in the wind, and birds sang into the silence. Nothing that didn't belong. She strained to hear what Kaylo had, then, at the edge of her reach, a slight noise went against the grain of the forest. It started as a rustling that struck against the rhythm of the wind before the quiet cadence of voices emerged in the distance.

Kaylo continued to stare into the woods. *How did he hear them?* She followed his eyeline into the forest. Blotches of yellow and green moved through the trees, then flashes of light catching metal.

If she ran now, she could escape. They hadn't seen her yet.

Kaylo placed a hand on her shoulder. He gestured at his ear and whispered, "Listen for The Song. Reach for it."

"What?" Tayen whispered back. The sound barely formed in her mouth.

Kaylo met her eyes. "I don't have time to explain. Reach for The Shadow."

Does he want me to fight?

Her hands began shaking. Then, her breath felt like it wasn't enough. *I don't want to die,* she thought.

She closed her eyes and tried to slow her breathing, which made her feel like she would run out of air.

No one ever trained her to shadow dance, not really. Her parents taught her what they could, but their spirits were bound to their bodies. The spirit-bound didn't know anything about The Song outside of stories. "The Song is elusive and ever-changing," they used to say, like it meant something.

She tried to focus on the darkness behind her eyelids, but her family met her there, piled on the floor of their hut, her mother's dull green eyes wading in the dark.

She gasped for air but still needed more. She gasped again and again, trying to fill her lungs, but it still wasn't enough. Her head felt light. *Too loud.* She gasped. *Calm down.* Again. *Calm down.* And again. *CALM DOWN!*

Then a steady rhythm of air moved beside her as Kaylo breathed in and out. He placed his hand between her shoulder blades. "I won't let anything happen to you."

Maybe because she had seen him fight, or maybe because she had grown up listening to stories about Ennea's Thief. Either way, she believed him.

In and out, she matched her breath to his. She closed her eyes again and listened. There it was, so near she could touch it. The Song.

For all its closeness, The Song hummed softly, like the beginnings of a fire, a flame that would go out if not fed. She reached towards the sound, but as soon as she got close enough to call The Shadow, The Song vanished.

The absence differed from moments before. Over the turns, she'd had difficulty finding The Song at times, but it simply went silent, an empty void where there should have been connection.

She turned to apologize to Kaylo, but the ragged man pushed himself to his feet, leaving his bow and quiver beside her.

Tayen lay flat against the forest floor as he swept his arms inward, one after another, like beckoning someone towards him. Shadows crawled across the ground, leaving nearby trees and bushes. They scurried like animals towards Kaylo, and when they reached him, they curled around his legs in a thick, dark haze. Tayen had never seen anything like it.

Casting the shadows from a room or completely blocking out the light was different. She could push the shadows away or pull them closer, but each of the shadows moved towards Kaylo as if they had a specific role to play in the dance.

Shadows continued to leave their places until they covered Kaylo in a dark cloud. She strained her eyes, but the cloud shuttered like a mirage, and he faded away the more she focused on him.

"Stay here," he said from within the darkness.

When he moved, the shadows moved with him. The dark mist crept towards the soldiers, stopping behind a tree for a moment before moving to the next. She didn't dare to blink.

No question. She intended to stay right where he left her. She couldn't do a damn thing to help him.

———————

Kaylo moved through the forest with single-minded purpose. Each time he stopped behind a tree, he planned his next set of steps through the uneven terrain. If the soldiers looked his way, they would only see a dark haze moving through the woods. Inexperienced soldiers might dismiss it, but seasoned fighters would know to trust their eyes when they saw shadows moving against the sunlight.

Slower is better than clumsy.

Several minutes passed before he could hear and see the soldiers clearly. When he did, an icy chill ran the length of his body, followed by a fiery anger.

Blood banner.

Four of the soldiers were pale as a cloud, the Emperor's own through and through. But one of them had skin as dark as the soil, a Sonacoan woman wearing the enemy's uniform, her head shaved smooth.

The Church of Gousht had declared the natural red curls of Sonacoans deviant under the eyes of The One True God after they laid claim to Ennea. They forced every Sonacoan to shave their hair or bind it under a head wrap.

Kaylo hated the Gousht, but soldiers followed their people, their church, and their emperor. Their place made sense. Enneans who lifted blades against their own people—blood banners...he hated them in an intimate way.

The Empire had ways to turn blood against blood. They promised life, freedom, and coin. They stole children from their homes and filled their heads with lies. Then the Gousht used their blood banners as harshly as they used everyone else they subjugated. The traitors were disposable, but Kaylo couldn't find pity for them in his spirit. Maybe he should have tried harder. Choices didn't come easy when it came to the Gousht.

"*They probably got lost after they killed the little konki,*" the blood

banner said. Kaylo snarled at her slur but held his silence. She spoke
Gousht with a coarse accent that made the words sound unnatural. *"Kels
and Jauk love the hunt, but they aren't the sharpest sticks in the forest."*

A towering soldier squared his feet towards the blood banner, cracking
his knuckles. *"You'd be wise to mind your place, zeze,"* he said.

Were Kaylo a younger, rasher man, he would have killed the giant of
a soldier for the slur alone. The Gousht liked to dirty Ennean words and
aim them like weapons. Zeze was an old word meaning black, like soil
or the night, but the Gousht turned it into a reminder that darker skin
made Enneans lesser.

The large soldier stared down the blood banner until she relented and
lowered her head.

An older soldier stepped forward, his metal chestplate marking him as
their commander. *"We'll cover more ground in two groups. You three..."*
Crack.

Kaylo's bad knee buckled under him, and he slammed forward into
the tree he hid behind.

The soldiers fell silent. Their heads swiveled back and forth, searching
for the noise as their hands reached for their blades and bows.

It hadn't been a large noise, but it didn't have to be. If they found
him, he wouldn't be able to run, and five on one equaled dangerous odds
under the best of circumstances.

The pain cut from his left knee to his thigh. He bit his tongue and
waited, hoping the dark cloud of shadows would keep him hidden.

The Sonacoan woman looked directly at Kaylo, like she could see
through the dark veil. The smooth curves of her cheeks and her sharp
eyes unnerved him. He had known those who might have called her
kin. This was not the face of the enemy, and that made her all the more
dangerous.

When a warrior spilled blood, they had to move on and kill again.
Seeing a loved one in the enemy's face could lead to a quick death.

After several moments that lasted too long, she turned away.

The blood banner had chosen her side. If it came to it, he would have to send her into The Mist with the rest of her brood.

Still stiff and alert, the commander continued where he had left off. "*You three head north,*" he said and pointed at the three Gousht soldiers. "*Move slowly. Slower than you think you should. It's better to be thorough and slow than quick and careless. I want you back at camp before you see the first moon. If you make me come out here and search for your worthless hides, I'll make sure you regret it.*" The soldiers nodded at their orders in near-unison and turned north.

"*Zeze, you're with me,*" the commander said. He said the slur without malice, like he believed it was what she was and had no feelings on the matter.

She nodded and followed him west.

Kaylo grasped the tree as they walked away, his knee still throbbing. For the time being, they would be safe in the hallow, in the east of the Kenke Forest. It would take turns to search the whole of the forest with five soldiers.

Once the heavy footfalls of the soldiers faded away, he shifted some of his weight to his left. It hurt and he wouldn't be moving quickly, but he could make the walk home. He returned to where he left the girl, even slower than when he approached the soldiers.

Tayen looked up as Kaylo moved closer. "Why did you do that?"

He unwrapped the shadows surrounding him, and they tore from each other like strips of fabric, one after the other, revealing him to the world a piece at a time. Then the dark patches glided over the forest floor to find their rightful places.

"I had to know what they were saying. Some risks are a necessary part of staying alive."

"No. Why did you let them live?" she demanded.

Kaylo looked at the anger-shaped girl in front of him and sighed. "In less than a day, you have gone from terrified of killing to craving it."

"I lost everything in less than a day!" Tayen yelled.

He knew her anger like he knew himself. Her fear and rage were not separate entities, just the loudest parts of her trauma. She would discover the quieter parts in time—loneliness, mania, guilt.

Empathy kept his words from being too unkind. "First of all, they may have walked in another direction, but that doesn't mean they can't hear you screaming. Second, if five soldiers came searching for two missing comrades, how many do you think they will send when another five go missing?"

She met his eyes and set her jaw. The young, angry child he used to be stood in front of him. Even if she knew he was right, her anger wouldn't allow her to admit it.

Kaylo knelt to level his eyes with hers, and the pain in his knee flared. "I know what you're feeling, but following your anger is a good way to die."

"You have no idea what I'm feeling!" Tayen yelled, not quite as loud, but loud enough to show her defiance. Then she stalked towards the hallow without looking back.

Pain rippled through Kaylo's leg as he followed. If he rested, he would lose sight of her. *I'm not ready for this,* he thought. She needed more than he had to give.

As he walked, the pain accented his misery. The girl needed care, yet the spirits gave her a broken man. *They really are a bunch of irritating bastards.*

The walk back to the hallow seemed much longer.

———

The silence that Tayen and Kaylo shared over dinner was becoming familiar. Kaylo ladled a second share of the vegetable soup into his bowl. Soup on a hot summer evening wasn't particularly appetizing, but that's what happened after a failed hunt. The strips of dried saltmeat he added made a poor substitute for fresh meat.

"I need you to teach me to fight," Tayen said.

Kaylo sighed as he mourned the silence. "No."

"If you train me, I can take care of myself."

"I can't do that."

"Why?" Tayen asked, her tone sharpening. "Show me how to bend the shadows like you did today. Show me how to fight."

Before he could say no again, she continued, "What am I supposed to do, hide from the Gousht for the rest of my life? They killed my family, and I ran away. Do you know what that's like?"

Her pain consumed her. Even now, it changed her. *Who had this girl been before?*

"I know exactly what that's like," he said.

"I promise I'll be a good student. I'll listen to whatever you say."

"I am sure you would be, but I can't," Kaylo said, then stood up and began cleaning up after their meal.

"Coward!" Tayen yelled.

"Killing Gousht won't bring your family back."

"And hiding from the world won't fix anything either."

"The answer is no." Water swished in the pot as he rinsed out the remnants of their meal. After he wiped his bowl clean, he reached out for hers. She looked at his hand, then met his eyes. Her lips formed a firm line. Tears started running down her cheeks, and still, she glared at him.

He turned away, unable to tell her no again. *I am a coward,* he thought as he got up and walked towards his bedroll.

CHAPTER FOUR

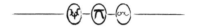

Growing up, Tayen's father told her stories. The characters who focused on revenge continually made selfish, simple-minded decisions. They seemed silly and petty. The right decision practically called their name, but they always ignored it to pursue vengeance.

She hadn't been completely wrong. After dreaming of her family's murder for the second night in a row and being unable to turn away from the gore, vengeance still felt like a petty motivation. However, her mother called for blood. Petty or not, she owed her mother her due.

Blood for blood.

I should have died too, she thought as she stared up into the domed ceiling of the treehouse.

When she stopped shivering from her nightmare, she wiped her cheeks dry. Tears were wasted water. She spread the ragged blanket on the ground and gathered what she would need into a pile—the belt knife Kaylo had given her, a waterskin, a whistle that Nita carved, several loose beads for her braids, and an obsidian stone she found the morning her family died.

The rock had been precious then, shiny and smooth like glass. Now it seemed like a childish indulgence. She placed it in her meager pile all the same.

Her hands moved easily, pulling each corner of the blanket over her possessions and tying it in a knot as she had done every time when her parents decided to move. The process had become ritual, but this time, her family wouldn't be joining her.

In a few short days, this treehouse had become a safe place. A garden of food grew around the perimeter. She slept in a dry bed. When she closed her eyes, she only had to fear the dreams that lay in wait.

Blood for blood. The old words whispered in her head like a mantra. Her mother called to her from the other side of The Mist.

She slung the bundle over her shoulder and walked towards the exit.

"You're free to leave if you want, but give me a moment," Kaylo said from the firepit. He did not turn to look at her, he just sat stirring his breakfast.

Had he tried to stop her, she would have run. Had he begged her to stay, it would have been easy to ignore. But he asked for a moment, and Tayen was her mother's daughter—she couldn't repay his kindness with rudeness.

"No matter what you say, I am leaving."

"If that's what you want," Kaylo said. "I have traveled my share, and while every journey was different, food rarely came easy. Sit with me and eat something before you go."

She did not answer. Her head tilted towards the treehouse entrance, not knowing where to go, only that she had to.

"The choice will always be yours," Kaylo said. "I don't keep those who would not be kept."

Perhaps it was foolish youth, or perhaps she needed someone to trust—either way, she believed him. He hadn't lied to her, not yet, and her stomach had been growling since she woke.

Her father always said, "There's wisdom in a full stomach." Tayen walked to the firepit without another word.

As soon as Kaylo handed her a bowl, she spooned out her first bite. The porridge burned her tongue, but she chewed and swallowed regardless. The quicker she ate, the less time Kaylo had to change her mind, but he didn't interrupt her.

A blueberry popped in her mouth.

Whenever she and her father found blueberries, he let her smuggle a handful away before they got home. The next morning, he would make a batch of frycakes and wink at their shared secret.

She took a long sip of water to keep herself from crying over the memory.

Her spoon scraped the wooden bowl, and she shoveled the last honeyed bite into her mouth. "Say what you have to say," she said with a mouthful.

"As poorly as I show it...I mean, when I was your age..." Kaylo stopped and took a deep breath. "I know loss. My loss wasn't the same as yours, but I understand what you are feeling more than most. I know how angry you are. I know how much it hurts to remember, and how remembering is the only thing that comes close to comfort." His hands shook slightly while he spoke.

"What I'm trying to say..." He paused as if he were searching for the words.

Tayen met his eyes—brown like her father's, like her sister's. But he wasn't them.

"I will train you," he said. The words came out rough, like he had to force them from his throat.

"You want to train me?"

"No, but I will."

"That's encouraging," she said sarcastically.

"Tomak is a dying nation. A handful of occupied cities and scattered refugees trying to survive the war. I don't want to see you die. Our people have to outlast..." Kaylo stopped himself and shook his head.

"No, that's not the reason. It's true, but not the reason," he said. "Little shade, the truth is that I feel responsible for you. Not because we wear the same skin, although that might be a part of it. Not because I saved you once. And not because you remind me of myself." He idly fiddled with his knife as he spoke. "I can't bear another spirit. I've collected too many dead."

"I remind you of yourself?"

"If you leave now, you will die," he said, staring into the fire. "You'll go looking for a fight and, if you're lucky, you'll take one or two soldiers into The Mist with you. That might be enough for you right now, but I don't want you to die.

"So, I will train you. I'll teach you how to fight with a blade and how to dance with The Shadow. I'll teach you to kill, if that's what you want to learn. But I have one stipulation: I am going to try to convince you not to. I am going to try to change your mind. All you have to do is listen. Pacify an aging man by listening to his tale."

"You want to tell me a story?"

"Don't dismiss the power of a story."

"You won't convince me."

"Maybe not." His shoulders hunched as he leaned towards her.

The crackle of the fire accented the silence that fell between them as the walls of the treehouse closed in. Tayen sat on the stump, staring at Kaylo. He had changed. He wore the same ragged robes, and his beard and hair overwhelmed his face, yet a subtle look of hope shined in his eyes.

Ennea's Thief, she thought. *Older and dirtier, but still Ennea's Thief.* The man from her father's stories was offering to train her.

"I'm not afraid to die," she said.

"But are you willing to live?"

Tayen turned to the fire, and her mother stared at her from the flames. "You'll teach me how to kill the Gousht? And I can leave anytime I want?" Tayen asked.

He leveled his gaze and nodded. "Yes, but when you go, you're gone. Your lessons will cease the moment you decide to leave. Do you understand? I won't have you come back with blood on your hands, looking for more."

He extended his hands towards her.

She had a belt knife and a tentative connection with The Shadow. The soldiers had swords, bows, and, most likely, spirit crystals. She couldn't kill them all. Not yet.

Hesitantly, Tayen grasped his right hand between hers, and he did the same. She said the words her parents taught her. "On the spirits, great and small, old and new." Kaylo smiled and repeated the phrase.

He could have this promise for now. Whatever pledge she made, her promise to her mother would always come first. *No matter what it takes, I will give you your blood.*

———

Kaylo couldn't say whether he had made the right decision. At best, he delayed the inevitable. People around him died. This girl would be no different.

He allowed Tayen the space she needed—or rather, took the space he needed.

He had trained others to fight, but he had been young and stupid. A true kana required a kind of patience and a thoughtfulness he didn't possess. Even talking to the girl wore on him.

Denial and avoidance had become part of his routine, and so, he moved about the hallow as if she weren't there. He washed out the pot and the bowls. He poured a handful of dried oats and scraps of maple wood into the offering basin. Then he knelt before the stormwood carvings, and as he did so, Tayen knelt beside him. She placed an obsidian stone beside the basin and offered her prayer to The Shadow.

After turns of paranoia, it felt strange to have someone following his footsteps, watching his every movement. The hair on the back of his neck stiffened. He placed his hand on the hilt of his knife, took a breath, then released it slowly.

The leather grip of his knife fit his hand, the weight of the blade balancing perfectly.

He found the spot where he stopped yesterday and began to tend his garden. Routine quieted the warnings in his mind. His hands moved nimbly, tracing each stem, branch, and vine. As he cut the overgrowth away, his knife moved as deftly as his fingers.

Tayen watched as he worked in silence. "How will this help me fight the Gousht?"

"Try it. You may see," he said without raising his eyes from his task. It sounded like something one of his kanas might have said.

"I'm not here to garden your treehouse."

He stopped his blade mid-cut. "For the last time, this is a hallow, not a treehouse. The Seed built this home. I pulled the trees from The Song myself. Give it the respect it deserves," he said.

The branch in his hand cracked as it cut. "Blessed fucking Mother," he said under his breath.

The child-sized pit of anger glared at him with green eyes as bright as they were sharp. *If Munnie were here, she would know what to say,* he thought.

"Do you know where the term kana comes from?" he asked.

"The moon."

"Correct," Kaylo said. "When I was about your age, I met my first kana. She told me about the sister moons, the teacher and the student. Unfortunately, she isn't here. So you'll have to settle for me."

He smiled. She did not smile back.

"Since the beginning of time, before the spirits, before the nations, before Ennea gave the first human life, Sokan, the sun, traveled through the sky with Kana, the first moon. One night, Ennea's youngest daughter, Toka, asked to follow her sister through the sky, and Kana agreed. Kana streaked across the sky and showed Toka the way. Each night Kana coaxed her sister along until Toka knew the night's sky as intimately as Kana. Eventually, Toka learned to shine even brighter than her older sister, but Kana was not jealous. She took pride in her sister."

"And you believe that?"

"It is how the story goes. Stories don't have to be true to contain truth," Kaylo said.

"What does that have to do with cutting up plants?"

In the wake of Kaylo's touch, the leaves and stems of the bush in front of him sprang back into place. "Do you see this barberry bush? Most things in life grow out-of-balance; this plant is no different," he said. "Overgrown and undergrown, depending on where and how you look.

"My first kana, Munnie, taught me to look closely, to know the needs of the world around me—not that I understood at the time. Some lessons take a lifetime to learn," Kaylo said. "Plants were always easier for me to read."

"I thought you said you would train me," Tayen said.

"Munnie was trying to teach me patience," Kaylo said with heavy enunciation. "Without her lessons, I would be long dead. Although, some might see that as a failure on her part." He smiled at his self-deprecation.

Shifting his weight, Kaylo held a stem of purple-red leaves to give Tayen a better view. "Where should we cut?"

"How should I know?"

"Fair question," Kaylo said, swallowing his annoyance. "The truth is, there isn't one right answer. Cut this bush in a million ways, and it will grow despite or because of you. The trick isn't to find the answer but to search for an answer. Look at the bush and weigh its balance in your mind. Don't look to make it pretty. Make a cut that helps the bush find balance and flourish."

"It doesn't matter," Tayen said. "I stayed to learn to kill couta, not to do your chores." She stood up and dropped her belt knife to the ground.

"Okay, first lesson: surviving a fight is about more than wielding a blade or releasing an arrow. You have to be able to think your way through a problem," he said, forgetting all of his patience. "Second lesson: Don't soil our language. Not in my home."

"You're defending them?"

"This isn't about the Gousht. This is about our culture, our way of life," he said. "They came here and tried to take everything from us. Don't give them anything. Not even the ugliest of our words."

Blood swelled under Kaylo's cheeks, and his face darkened. His heart beat in the back of his jaw. She had sapped the little patience he had.

He settled his gaze and met Tayen's eyes. "Little shade, if you continue to stare at me like death, you will find me an unkind man," he said. Though he spoke softly, the volume couldn't mask his fury.

When she looked away, she dipped her head low and became the little girl she was. Somehow, he continually found new ways to act foolish. This girl deserved better, a kana who could be a guide, a waypoint.

"I'm going to leave you with your thoughts and your gardening." Kaylo got up, slung his bow over his shoulder, hung his quiver from his belt, and left the hallow.

"Seed and Balance," he muttered to himself.

He didn't have to go back. If he left, he could find another patch of forest somewhere to hide. He had played the coward before; nothing would stop him from being one again.

In the course of a morning, he became the worst parts of his three kanas—cryptic, mean, and distant. Munnie would have lectured him for letting his anger rule him. "When you've found a path in anger, you know which path not to take," he could hear her say.

The forest sung with all of its familiar sounds, but the notes ran flat.

A fallen ironoak blocked his path, simple enough to walk around or climb over, but instead he stopped. Rot had set into its trunk. For all the tree's strength, time poisoned what it was meant to be.

He sat on the withering tree, reached down, and cupped a handful of soil. As he shifted the black grains back and forth between his hands, the coarse earth rubbed over his palms.

Soil and trees came easy to him, like people never had. Trees tended to last longer. Ever since he first met death, people came and went. Yet, for some reason, he persisted.

Maybe it could be different with her, he thought.

"Time is not a path we walk; it is the wind that rushes about us on our journey," Kaylo muttered to himself. Munnie had been full of riddles, and, for reasons unknown, they had started to make sense.

The forest sounded much like it had for the last twelve turns, but the winds were changing. The forest whispered. Kenke Forest wouldn't be home much longer. Past the noise of the forest towards The Song, he closed his eyes to listen, but nothing came. He let the dirt fall through his fingers before brushing off his hands.

As the evening air surrendered some of the day's aggressive heat, Kana and Toka reached over the horizon. Kaylo headed home with two rabbits swinging from his belt. The moons chided him from the sky, Toka ever brighter than Kana.

After how he had behaved, it wouldn't have surprised him if Tayen had left. *Maybe it would be easier.*

He peeled back the hides from the entryway and walked into the hallow. Firelight flickered off the walls, and there, on the other side of the stormwood, Tayen sat hunched over a bush. Kaylo's chest felt like it would tear open.

He walked over to the young shadow dancer and asked gently, "What are you doing?"

She didn't turn around. She didn't speak. Her shoulders continued to move as she worked the knife through a rosebush she had badly over-pruned.

Kaylo stepped closer, expecting the angry child he had left behind, but when he turned her shoulder, tears wet her face. Blisters and cuts crawled over her fingers.

She let her knife fall from her hands to the ground between them. "I'm sorry," she sobbed and repeated again and again, never meeting his eyes. "I don't want to be alone."

Some people fought hardest when they felt like they might break. It was what he had always done.

He knelt and placed a hand on both of her shoulders. "I am a poor teacher and even worse company, but you have a home with me as long as you like."

He walked her over to the water basin and washed her cuts with care, pausing when she winced and waiting for her to nod permission to continue. After all his mistakes, he allowed the silence to settle between them. Words always flipped the wrong way in his mouth.

The basin turned murky pink by the time they finished, and the firelight had dimmed.

A few more logs stirred the fire, and Kaylo set to dressing and cooking one of the rabbits he had caught as Tayen sat eating berries.

"Earlier," Kaylo started, then searched for the right words. "That wasn't you're fault. It was mine. I chose to be angry instead of scared."

Tayen looked up, her eyes puffy and red, and asked, "Why?"

"Because I don't know what I'm doing," Kaylo said with a sigh. "There are many reasons I ended up alone in a forest, not the least of which was my lack of communication skills."

They ate and their conversation paced like a shy animal testing a person's temperament. "Why do you tend the plants with a knife when you could control them with The Song?" Tayen asked, interrupting a particularly drawn-out patch of silence.

After a moment's hesitation, he found his answer. "Because it's how I was taught. And when I was on my own, it gave me something to do while I lingered in my thoughts.

"My first kana told me The Song is the connection between all life. Just because we can pull on that connection doesn't mean we should. Freedom that relies on controlling others is hardly freedom."

"What are you talking about?" Tayen asked, giggling.

Kaylo broke into a smile. "Sometimes I don't even know." The moment dissipated like the others before it into another uncomfortable silence. As the fire cracked, Kaylo tossed another log into the pit.

The shadows cast by the fires danced against their nature as Tayen waved her hands in her lap. They flickered and stretched farther than the fire would account for.

"What does it sound like to you?" Kaylo asked.

"What do you mean? It sounds like The Song."

"In my experience, The Song sounds different to everyone," he said. "What does it sound like to you?"

Tayen closed her eyes. "When night falls in the forest," she said. "You know how the forest sounds right before the first moon rises and the sun sets? It's quiet, but not silent. Like there's a lot of noise somewhere far away, but the world is calm around you. I don't know. It's not really a song."

"No, I suppose it's not, but I can't think of a better word for it. Can you?" Kaylo asked, and Tayen shook her head.

Their conversation lulled. Kaylo searched for the right words. His teachers always knew what to say next. If they had carried this many doubts, they had done a better job of hiding them.

He stared into the fire, trying to decide where to start. "Earlier I told you I was going to tell you a story," he said. "Tonight is as good as any other to start.

"This is not a happy story, and I can't tell you what to do with these words. That you must choose for yourself."

Chapter Five

You see, little shade, a story is a peculiar thing. Change a word—the emphasis of a word—and it can become something it was never meant to be. A hero can become a tyrant. A tyrant can become a great uniter. And a boy who makes a lot of stupid decisions can become a myth.

I have heard the stories about Ennea's Thief, the Hero of Anilace. They are closer to daemontales than the truth. Besides the details, which are greatly overstated, those stories begin and end in the wrong places. They ignore the context and aftermath.

My mother taught me how to tell a story properly. The most important decision is where to begin.

I could start my story with The Song. After all, if it weren't for the spirits, I wouldn't be worthy of a story.

When I first heard it, I was barely four. Not that I remember it much. After this many turns, what I think of as a memory might be little more than a combination of what I've been told and embellishments I added to fill in the gaps.

However, I do remember The Song.

The rhythm crept towards me, a distant thumping in crescendo, until it surrounded me. Since that day, The Song has sounded like a thousand different things. That day, it sounded as if I were a seed searching for light from beneath the soil. People who haven't heard The Song will never understand it, but that was how it sounded.

Apparently, I sat on the ground playing in the dirt, then went silent. I was never silent. My parents rushed to see what had gone wrong, and I waved my little arms through the air, like I was grabbing after fireflies that weren't there. I giggled, and the dirt at my feet bulged until a green tendril of a dandelion sprouted and bloomed in front of me. The sight might have scared other children, but I smiled.

My parents were shocked. Being spirit-bound, they never thought their son would be a dancer. Most people think spirits follow bloodlines, and they often do, but the Great Spirits don't care about blood. They're looking for complements—spirits that fit their own.

My parents told anyone who would listen about my gift. Back then, a descendant of The Seed meant a promise of healthy crops and fertile soil. The Song was an honor, but that was before the invasion. Ironic to think of it now; they considered me a good omen.

That would be one place to begin, although I do not think that would be the right place, not for the story I intend to tell.

I could start with the Gousht. Everything changed when their ships arrived on the southern coast. I was seven and enthralled by the idea of strangers from across the ocean.

Anything that took me outside of my small world and its routine excited me. When the rumors started, I clung to every story, every word I heard about them.

The outsiders came from a land without The Mist, an entire nation of spirits bound to their bodies. They were giants, pale as the moonlight with hair white as snowfall. They wore robes of metal and spoke an unknowable language. So many rumors passed around they began to run at odds. The outsiders prayed to one god or hundreds. Some were said to hide their faces from the world. Their emperor was a spirit taken to human form. Each half-true or contrary tale only added to the mystery.

In a different time, all of Ennea would have met them with a sword

and a spear—a time when four nations carved out territory in blood.
But by the time the Gousht arrived on our shores, it had been over two
hundred turns since the Conclave of Spirits, when a group of refugees,
who took to the land to avoid the fighting, mediated a peace to end the
Hundred-Turn War. Borders were drawn, and the four nations became
five as the refugees, known as the Jani, formed a nation of Nomads
dedicated to serving The Blessed Mother, Ennea.

After nearly a hundred turns of one war followed by another, often
overlapping or running in parallel, these nomads helped our people learn
to coexist—or isolate depending on the version of history.

Time and peace made us complacent.

It started out small—stories about missing dancers and small villages
burning. Most people dismissed it as idle talk. My mother wasn't one of
those people. She studied history and expected the worst.

In the middle of the night, my parents woke me up, and we walked
for three days through the forest to Nomar, a city large enough to be
lost in. We built our home on the outskirts of the city, and my mother
forbade me from calling on The Seed. If the rumors were true, no one
could know I could hear The Song.

The invasion started abruptly. When the warships arrived, the Gousht
overran Sonacoa. Several moons passed before Tomak and Renêqua joined
the war. Neither Astile nor the Jani could be persuaded to fight.

The three nations had nearly driven the invaders back to the coast
when the Gousht discovered what lay beneath Oakheart Mountain.
Whatever advantage we had vanished. The war ended when they pried
the first spirit crystal from the soil.

The nations resisted for almost two turns, and then the Stone City fell
and hope with it. After that, everything from the southern coast to the
island nation of Renêqua belonged to the Gousht.

Sadly, my mother had been right. The Gousht laid smaller towns
to waste. Sunador, the village where I was born, burned down to a
memory. They chained up anyone who survived and put them to work

in the mines. Larger cities became occupied territory, assimilated into the Empire.

My family, like many others, held on to what we could of our ways despite everything that changed.

But this is not a history lesson. If it were, I would not be the right person to tell it.

If I am to tell the story of how I became the person I am today, there is only one place to begin: my first true loss. At the time, I mourned my freedom, but I quickly learned there were greater things to mourn.

CHAPTER SIX

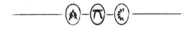

IN THE SMALLEST DAYS of autumn, not long after my sixteenth turn, I waited for Sokan to fall before I climbed from my bedroom window. The metal latch squeaked into the night, and I held my breath before lowering myself to the tuft of grass below and easing the window shut.

The lodestone marked the northernmost point of Nomar, at the edge of the tree line. A straight line ran from my home to the stone, but I chose a more indirect route, one more densely covered in buildings. If the Gousht caught me out after curfew, they would make my punishment a spectacle, not that they needed the excuse. Any soldier with a whim and a whip could do as they pleased.

No matter how many times I walked the same path, my heart thundered inside my chest. I ran my hand along each building as I moved, feeling the changing textures of clay brick, stone, and wooden walls. They steadied me.

Both Kana and Toka shined small in a cloudless sky.

Thick Gousht accents cut through the silence, and I threw my back against a cold brick building and crouched down. Lantern light peered around the corner of the building as the voices grew closer, and the accompanying boots tromped over the dirt path.

If I moved, they might hear me. If I stayed put, they would only have to turn their heads to find me.

I swallowed and focused on my breathing like Munnie taught me. In and out. In and out.

The light grew stronger.

"*Can you believe that? The Commander said I wasn't leadership material. Bastard.*"

"*What the fuck does he know? His asshole is tighter than a konki drum,*" the second soldier said. They both chuckled, and the smell of cheap barley wine filled the air.

The light flooded around the corner and crept over the dirt towards my feet. I couldn't stop my hand from shaking. Two soldiers clad in their green and yellow padded armor stepped into the gap between the buildings. The bigger one dragged the shaft of his spear in the dirt as he stumbled by, the tip of which caught the lantern light with a blade sharp enough to cut the night.

One step after another, they crossed the gap between buildings. I clenched my fist to keep my hand still. Then they passed by, neither glancing my way.

A small laugh escaped my lips, and all the air in my lungs rushed out. *These are the warriors who defeated my people?* I thought.

Once the smell of their barley wine dissipated, I thanked The Mother and pushed myself off the ground.

Nomar was a common city, bigger than most in Tomak, especially of those left standing. The city radiated out from the town square, trade shops closer to the center and homes on the perimeter. Despite the city's size, The Gousht never bothered to run heavy patrols. Maybe they figured their public punishments would keep us in our place.

At the edge of the city, a fifty-pace gap separated the last building from the tree line. The forest represented unlimited possibilities. Another fifty paces and the land stretched for days. No occupied cities. No cities at all.

If I could convince my mother, we could leave. The Jani lived out there, surviving off the land. As long as we knew Ennea better than the Gousht, we could hide.

But my mother would never leave. She believed we needed to outlast the occupation. At least that's what she said, but I think she was too scared of losing me to risk running.

The lodestone stood tall in the distance; the little bit of moonlight reflected off the boulder like a beacon. As I approached the marker, a burst of fire broke the darkness, then another and another. Shay danced along the forest's edge. Small pops of light accentuated her movements where anyone near the outer rim of the city could see her.

Typical, I thought.

Shay carried herself like nothing could break her. No matter how many times I lectured her, I had to stop and watch in awe. She moved like the fire itself, delicate and dangerous. Her blue cloak flapped in the air as she twisted. The deep copper of her skin burst to life in the small pops of firelight.

Suddenly, she stopped, and darkness filled the space between us once again. I felt her eyes on me, even though mine had yet to readjust.

"You were staring," Shay said. "See something you like?"

The darkness disguised my blushing cheeks. As much as I wanted to deny it, I couldn't. Shay was gorgeous. Her Sonacoan father's red curls fell loosely against her face in lovely contrast against her mother's warm brown skin and sharp features. The nights I dreamed of her were the nights I didn't want to wake.

"Why don't you start a pyre and call every soldier in the city? You could put on a show for them before they steal The Flame and send you to the mines," I whispered at Shay, closing the gap between us.

The sliver of moonlight caught her smile. "There aren't enough bucketheads in all Nomar to take me to the mines," she said in her full voice.

Shay always talked about fighting back and joining the Missing's rebellion. If she ever did, I could never follow. She could call fire. Even if I wanted to fight back, the best I could do was grow an abundance of shrubbery.

I learned to walk away after a while. As my mother liked to say, sometimes words can only encourage someone looking for trouble.

The forest canopy quieted the moonlight. Every step I took deeper into the forest helped my muscles unravel a little more. The forest felt more like home than any house ever had.

Shay caught up, and we walked our usual path to Munnie's hallow. Conversation always moved easily between us. We could talk about endless nothing, so the hour trek never lasted as long when we walked together.

We stopped beside a rock formation, which jutted up into the air like a pair of broken arrowheads. Rocks cluttered around the base. A gash separated two slabs of stone. The formation could have been older than the forest itself, as natural as any tree growing from the soil.

If anyone passed by, they wouldn't have a single reason to scrutinize the stone structure.

Shay disappeared through the jagged opening, and I followed. The floor angled deeper into the earth, and the walls began to flatten and smooth.

"Auntie," I called out, and the sound echoed through the antechamber into the main room of the hallow. The world expanded within those walls, like the hallow had outgrown the rock that contained it.

Tapestries ran along almost every wall, colors bounding off the slate gray backdrops, but the wall at the far end with no color to break apart the endless gray held a far greater treasure. Large sections of stone had been chiseled away from the middle of the empty slab, revealing a woman in the rock.

The carving stood in the stone as if the surrounding rock had weathered away of its own accord. Smooth lines transitioned into jagged peaks at each of her joints, and the light faded to black in its failed attempts to reach the deep trenches of the sculpture. As her shoulders narrowed, trails of stone-carved foliage created a mane of wild hair. Yet, amongst all the intricacies, she didn't have a mouth, and Munnie would never tell me why.

This was what a master earth dancer could accomplish. I could call forth a sapling from the soil, but Munnie weathered stone into a cave and crafted a sculpture from solid rock. The first time I walked into the hallow, I doubted my own eyes. Even now, I had to run my finger along the cold rock to remind myself the sculpture wasn't real.

"Incredible, isn't she?" a voice called out behind me.

My whole body jolted, and I whipped around.

Munnie stood there, grinning like a child. Despite nearly seventy turns in The Waking, she didn't look a moon past fifty. Her long gray braids dropped to either side of her shoulders, tied off with two pieces of red fabric, which matched the color of her textured robe.

"Shit, Munnie!" I yelled out. "Don't scare me like that."

Munnie's grin went flat. "Even a conquered people can take the time to respect their elders."

"Sorry, Auntie."

Shay chuckled, then Munnie grabbed me by the sleeve and pulled me into her. Her warmth brushed over me as she wrapped her arms around me. No matter what happened beyond these walls, we were safe with Munnie.

When she finished with me, she grabbed ahold of Shay.

We met Munnie in the thick of the wood two turns before while we were dancing with the spirits. Shay almost set the forest on fire when Munnie announced herself. She smiled and told Shay to continue. After several nights of meeting in the forest, she invited us back to her hallow, and we came almost every night thereafter.

"Come, enough of this," Munnie said. "We have work to do."

She led us towards the firepit to start the night's lesson. Shay and I sat cross-legged in front of seven crystal prisms protruding from the dirt floor. Shay drew her knife from her belt and started shaving scraps of cherrywood into a stone basin.

The rocking chair squeaked as Munnie took her seat, and then the gentle tune of the wood moving to and fro filled the hallow as we waited for our kana to begin. Munnie valued tradition. Even Shay learned to remain silent, regardless of how much she despised waiting.

When Munnie finally nodded her permission, Shay sighed as if she had been holding her breath for this moment. Relenting to tradition didn't keep her from reminding us how annoying she found it.

Sparks jumped off the flint stone as Shay scraped her blade across the surface, but the shavings didn't catch. "The Flame would be easier."

Munnie continued to rock back and forth without a word, and Shay went back to her flint rock until the wood shavings caught fire.

"To The Mother, the Daughters, and the Great Spirits—to their Song, to their gifts, to our ancestors and our descendants we give thanks." Shay recited the words coldly but clearly.

The smell of the burning cherrywood filled the air with a sweet musk.

"To the first—The Shadow, who gave us a way out of the darkness. We ask for your wisdom and your blessing." I enunciated every word so the spirits could hear me.

"To the second and third—the twins—The River and The Flame, the diviners of water and fire. We ask for your patience and strength," Shay said, emphasizing each reference to The Flame.

"To the fourth—The Mountain, the life of earth and stone. We ask you to steady our hearts for what is to come," I said.

"To the fifth—The Wind, the current that moves through all. We ask your sight to guide us," Shay said quickly, already bored.

"To the sixth—The Seed, the caretaker of life," I said as slowly as I could to annoy Shay. Munnie smiled knowingly. "We ask that you calm angry hearts with forgiveness."

"To the seventh—The Thief, the last one. Stay away." Shay touched three fingers to her lips, then to the ground.

Munnie smiled at her obstinate pupil. "That's not how I remember the prayer ending," she said with a small chuckle. "Why do you think we pray to The Thief, Shay?"

Shay rolled her eyes and groaned at the question. It wasn't that questions were rare. Shay just had the uncanny ability to sustain irritation. "Tradition. It's the reason we pray in the first place."

"Is it now?" Munnie asked. "You don't think the spirits can hear your prayers? You hear their Song, don't you?"

Shay fell silent, bowed her head, and pouted her lip like a chastised child. Her performance lacked any true signs of remorse.

"When you hear The Song..." Munnie touched her finger to her ear and paused. "You hear all spirits, not just the seven Great Spirits, but all spirits who have passed into The Mist. Without The Thief, The Song would be incomplete, flat."

"Burn The Thief and her descendants and give their ashes to the sea," Shay said. "There's a reason they're outcasts."

Munnie's belly laugh filled the room. She never could resist Shay's rudeness. The girl's spirit could not be tamed, and it warmed Munnie to her core. "Customarily, one would wait for their elders to leave before blaspheming," she said. "But I guess I'm not one to hold on to every custom. Shall we dance?"

Shay stood up without further prompting, then took slow steps into the open floor by the firepit, stretching the moments as we waited to see what she had planned for tonight, how she would make the fire contort. If not for the occupation, Shay would have danced with the fire for all to see. As it was, she had to settle for us.

All sound fell away, except the crackling of the firewood. She lunged forward towards the firepit, extending her clasped hands. The flames surged up from the fire, and light bounced off the slate gray surfaces of the hallow walls.

Her arms cut through the air in sharp motions. She twisted away from the pit and moved wildly, like untouched nature, life without walls. The air shimmered and popped around her.

It wasn't precisely a dance, just as it wasn't precisely a song. The balls of her feet anchored each step to the ground. As she moved, pockets of air wavered, then exploded into momentary flames. Light erupted, catching her joyful expression in one flash after another.

Flashes of fire flooded the dim hallow and left spots in my vision, but I couldn't look away. Her loose curls swirled around her head like the fire itself.

I could never do anything that powerful.

In daemontales, fire dancers could throw fire or make it wash over their enemies like a tidal wave, but real dancing wasn't the magic of stories. Shay could heat the air or anything that would burn until it burst into flames. As long as she had focus, time, and oxygen to feed the fire, she could ignite her fiery ancestor.

The Song allowed the elements to do what they naturally did, and dancing gave the elements direction. Trees grew. I could make them grow faster.

After several minutes of dancing, Shay stopped, and the hallow settled to its dim equilibrium. She plopped back down next to me, sweating, breathing hard, and smiling. When I looked at her, I saw the fire. She was as wild and free, as beautiful and dangerous as any flame.

She patted my knee. "You're up, grass guy."

I flashed her a rude hand gesture as I got up and walked into the open space.

After turns of nightly humiliation, I should have grown used to it. Shay never had to fight to find The Flame. It waited for her call. But after several turns of ignoring The Song, The Seed eluded me. I pushed through my barriers and groped in the darkness, but The Song didn't reach back. On the occasions when I found it, we shared a tenuous connection.

Munnie had tried to help me learn how to control my bond with The Seed, but something always stood in the way.

Even with my eyes closed, I could feel Shay and Munnie watching me. Too much time had passed. The Song refused me again. My chest deflated, and the air rushed out of my lungs.

I'm not a dancer, I thought. *A dancer needs The Song.*

Then a low rumble of discordant tones trembled beneath my feet. The Song shuddered in and out of focus. I reached my consciousness towards the fragile noise. It withdrew for a moment, then burst to life, and The Song seized me.

My body obeyed The Song. My knees bent and my feet ground into the dirt. Nothing existed beyond the noise and my movements. I swung my arms wide and wove them through the air in a chaotic pattern.

The earth bulged within The Song before the dirt moved. Then a seedling broke through the ground and spat soil into the air. The seedling unfurled and split time and time again as it found its shape. Small stems thickened and branched out. I continued to dance, and buds opened into green leaves and ripe berries in mere seconds.

Sweat beaded down the side of my face. The bush in front of me was small, but thick with dark blackberries.

Sure, I couldn't call flames, and I couldn't hold back an army with a bush, but this plant hadn't been there a moment ago. I called this life into existence.

I found my place next to Shay and smiled.

"Nice work." Shay got up, walked over to the blackberry bush, and plucked a berry. "Thanks for the snack," she said with a wink as she popped the berry into her mouth.

My lungs dropped into my stomach as I stared at the bush. It hadn't grown completely. Large gaps spaced out the stumpy branches.

In that moment, I hated Shay. Heat swelled under my cheeks. I looked towards the exit, but I couldn't run from this.

I used to be able to touch The Song without any effort. The Seed reached for me, and I pulled life from it as easy as taking a breath.

The rhythm of my heartbeat thumped in my temples, and then The Song rushed over me like it hadn't in several turns. It crashed through whatever barriers I built to control it and took me. I shut my eyes to the world, and my body moved freely into The Song. Colors flared up behind my eyelids. By the time I opened my eyes, I couldn't gulp down air fast enough, and a thicket of bushes surrounded me.

The bushes reached my shoulders, all of them full and lush. Large berries bloomed from every branch. Munnie and Shay stared at me overtop the large plants, Munnie with a slight smile and Shay wearing a blank stare.

"How did that feel?" Munnie asked. I shook my head. "Take a moment and think about it. Describe The Song. How did it compare to when you called the first bush?"

"With the first bush, I had to reach for The Song. It was distant, and I had to search through it. The blackberry bush was the first thing I could make sense of," I said. "But just now, The Song called to me. It crashed into me and pulled me under an ocean of sound. I had no choice but to move with it."

"You let your emotions get the best of you," Munnie lightly chided.

"Auntie?"

"The Song is a constant ocean, to use your metaphor. The spirits are in constant motion around us. If we let ourselves get taken by the current, we can wield tremendous power, but we could also lose ourselves," she said.

"Let me drop the metaphor, if I may." She paused, reading the blank stares on our faces. "The Mist and the spirits within it surround us, everywhere and always. Ennea gifted some of us the ability to hear a small part of the spirits' call. If we isolate ourselves from The Song, it may be difficult to find. If we allow The Song to envelope us, we may lose ourselves to The Mist, never to come back to The Waking.

"I'm trying to say be careful. You need to work to understand The Song before you can fully wield it. The more you know about The Song and the spirits, the easier it will be for you to call on it and control it. Otherwise, it will control you."

I nodded, but I couldn't help staring at the thicket of bushes. It had been too long since I felt The Song envelop me.

Munnie continued the rest of her lesson. She lectured about Ennean history, and I listened, but my mind wandered.

What did she mean, we could get lost in The Song? She spoke about The Song, The Mist, and the spirits like they were the same—different thing. It didn't make any sense. *How could The Song be The Mist?*

Munnie was the type of kana who let us wander when we needed to. She always said, "Some thoughts are more important than listening. Be wise enough to know which."

As we got ready to leave, Munnie called me over to speak privately. Shay practiced dancing while we spoke. "Kaylo, The Seed and The Flame are both Great Spirits," she said. "Neither greater than the other."

"But Shay can..." I started to complain, but she cut me off.

"Shay can do wonderful things. She can call on The Flame with such ease, but she doesn't seek the deeper melodies. She could be a master with your patience. And you could be a master with her freedom."

"Yes, Auntie," I said, but a noise nagged at me like a fly buzzing around my head. It almost sounded like The Song, but somehow different.

Munnie walked us to the entrance, and the sound stopped. I walked out into the forest, dazed and tired. The moons had crested past the sky's highest point and begun to fall again. If I got home soon, I could sleep for a few hours before school.

"What did Munnie say to you?" Shay asked.

"You need to be more patient," I said. "Then you could be a master."

"Bullshit," Shay said, and a bubble of air burst in a small flash. "I could take out all the guards in Nomar, but you both hold me back." The air continued to pop periodically until we reached the tree line.

I kept my distance as she passed the lodestone. The weird noise came back again, and as soon as she stopped dancing, it went away. It was like I could hear when she called for The Song, but it sounded different than when The Seed sang to me, muffled and muted—like an echo.

CHAPTER SEVEN

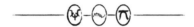

NO MATTER HOW I shifted, the bench cut into the back of my thighs. My father would have gone on about the poor craftwork had he been there, but the Gousht didn't care for our comfort. Every morning, they packed Nomar's children into their church to fill our minds with their nonsense. The younger children had already come and gone.

My heartbeat pounded at the base of my skull.

I hadn't slept at all last night. Every time I got close, the echo of Shay's Song crept into my mind. The Song didn't work that way. A dancer couldn't hear another dancer's connection to the spirits.

At the front of the church, the city priest knelt in prayer under the broken circle before he began his sermon. Remnants of the old town hall peeked through the green and yellow drapery. The clay brick walls and ironoak floorboards hadn't changed, only been covered by new adornments.

Morning light poured in through the windows and reflected off the iron symbol of their god. The seam where the vertical bar divided the circle in two blended in near flawlessly. Nomar's smiths had done good work, which no one begrudged. We all had made compromises to survive under Gousht rule.

The bell chimed the hour overhead, and my muscles contracted with each brass clang. The soldiers slammed the door shut, and the sound reverberated through the hall. I, and the couple hundred other children packed into the surrounding benches, straightened up.

Clad in his customary crimson robes, the priest made his way to the raised platform. The hooded veil that covered his face made him an ominous figure, despite his small, round stature.

"*May the light of The One guide you,*" the priest said in Gousht, as he did every morning.

"*For light, we look to you,*" I said in disarrayed unison with the other children.

I blinked several times and struggled to keep my eyelids open more with each blink.

"*Today, I would like to talk to you about why,*" the priest said. "*Why did we come to your shores? Why do we ask you to come to this church every morning? And why do I stand before you and speak of The One True God?*"

Shay sat several rows ahead of me to the left. The Song or whatever I heard last night remained silent.

"*For the answer, I need only turn to the text. In the beginning, The One gave men free rein. With our freedom, we warred endlessly. We bore children and left them ignorant of their creator. We wasted our freedom. Only after The One took the form of a man and bore twelve sons to guide us did we find our way. 'And on to each of his sons, he bestowed a sliver of his wisdom. To the last son, he conferred a mission. Where there be men of flawed nature, he would be their correction.' Chapter three verses ten to twelve of the Book of Josian.*" The priest raised a large leather-bound copy of the Writ and shook it for emphasis.

As direct descendants of The One True God, each crowned emperor contributed a new section to their holy book. It documented their version of history and interpretation of the path their god left to them. Even for a holy book, there was quite a lot of killing.

"*The youngest turned to his brothers and bid them to create an army*

*worthy of their father. It was thus that Gousht became a nation that
would become an empire. Their descendants became the priests of the
church that would lead an army all across the world, always in service of
the youngest son in the line of the youngest sons before him. What does
this have to do with you?"* The priest waved his arms over us and paused,
as if to let us ponder the question.

I pinched my thigh between my fingernails to keep myself awake.

"That is simple," he said. *"You squandered your free will on civil
wars and daemon worship. The One True God sent us to save you from
yourselves."*

Every sermon rounded out in the same conclusion: Ennea needed
saving. He found countless ways to come to the same conclusion day after
day. Although he did occasionally repeat himself.

*"You have the chance to be the grace of your people. Help them to
see the power of The One True God or they will fall before it."* He raised
his fist in the air and then slammed it down into his free hand.

Even though his veil hid his face from me, I imagined him smiling. He
had to know how ridiculous his words were.

"Seek power, and you will find The One True God."

I rose from my seat with all the others as the priest walked from
the platform, down the aisle, and out of the heavy ironoak doors. They
slammed shut, and the clatter rattled through my head.

Ms. Hanack nodded from the raised platform, and we all sat back on
the uncomfortable benches.

She wore her silver-white hair in a tight bun, which nearly blended
into the paleness of her skin. Everything about her spoke of discipline.
From her posture to her impeccably clean clothing, Hanack set herself
apart. Her icy eyes held a threat, one that she often fulfilled with the
cane she carried as she taught.

Somehow, Hanack managed to craft lessons worse than the priest's
sermons. She called it a civilized education, complete with inaccurate
tellings of history and instruction in their 'superior' language.

To the Gousht, our language proved our inferiority. The roots of common tongue reached back into the tribes that existed before the nations of Ennea. Dozens of languages merged into one over centuries of tribal dealings and war. No self-respecting Gousht would dirty themselves speaking it. And if there was anything they respected, it was themselves.

"*Good morning, class.*" Hanack's shrill voice carried through the hall with ease. She raised a small book in her left hand. "*Today, we read from 'The Treatise on the Savage Continent.'*"

She stepped down from the platform and paced the aisle with the book in one and the long, thin length of wood in the other.

Her cane clicked against the floorboards as she walked. When it stopped, she stood in front of Wal, one of her favorite victims.

Better him than me, I thought.

I liked Wal well enough, but his mouth was smarter than he was. His arms and legs bore the marks of his constant missteps. She handed him the book. "*Second paragraph, page thirty-two.*"

The book shook in his hands as he read through the text in butchered Gousht. "*Emperor Candor IV gathered his closest priests when the scouts returned from the sunrise...*"

Thwack. Hanack rapped his knuckles with a swift swipe of her cane.

Wal jerked back and breathed in sharply. Then he continued, correcting his error. "*When the scouts returned from the north. The Emperor turned to his eldest brother, the High Priest of the Church, and asked for his thoughts.*

"'*If the barbarians can truly wield evil spirits, they will be too costly to subdue,' the High Priest said. He suggested they treat with the enemy rather than charge into battle.*

"*Then the Emperor turned to another priest and asked the same question. The second priest spoke simply, 'If the One True God is with us, we have nothing to fear.'*

"*The High Priest was executed before the warships set sail.*"

The more Wal stumbled his way through the passage, the harder it became to keep my eyelids open.

I allowed myself a moment. My headache dulled when I closed my eyes. Someone else continued on to the next section, but their voice lacked definition. Colors floated in the darkness. Each color began to buzz, louder and louder. The sounds took shape, and each one mimicked the others, almost harmonies. Distorted versions of The Song called from every direction.

Crack. Crack. Crack.

I jumped in my seat as Hanack smacked the floorboards with her cane again. A crowd of children's face angled towards me from every direction.

"*Welcome back, Mr. Kaylo,*" Hanack said with condescension. Our names were the only thing she knew about any of us. "*Now that you have seen fit to rejoin us, can you tell us about the God Caves? Ms. Rena read all about them, and quite beautifully, I may add.*"

Rena smirked from a few seats down the bench, gratefully lapping up the kind words like a puppy after spilled milk. She must have run a hot comb through her hair every morning to get it as straight as she could, like the pale bastards would forget her brown skin if she tried hard enough.

It took me a moment to translate and understand what Hanack had said. She tapped her foot against the floorboards.

"*The God Caves,*" I repeated. "*The One called down to the...*"

I couldn't remember the damn word for priest. Wal just read it aloud. What an awful fucking language.

"*The One called down to the men who attend him,*" I said, feeling a sudden heat in my cheeks. "*He told them where to find a weapon that would help them defeat the Enneans, a crystal that could steal our spirits.*"

Hanack inhaled sharply and tilted her head. "*Steal?*" she repeated. "*Are you calling The One True God a thief?*" She bounced her cane against her palm.

"*I'm sorry, no, I meant...*" I said, but she interrupted me.

"*Silence, Mr. Kaylo!*" she yelled. "*Blasphemy against The One True God will not be permitted in my class. Is it stealing to take something dangerous out of the hands of a child, Mr. Kaylo?*"

Each time she said my name, another pin pricked my patience. She didn't even mean to insult us. To her, we simply were wild children in need of strong guidance. I bit my bottom lip. The Song roared in my ears, forcing the church to fade into the distance until only my anger and Ms. Hanack remained.

"*My people aren't children,*" I growled at her.

The silence in the church hall deepened, as if I peeled back a layer to reveal a quiet that existed beneath the silence that was already there.

Hanack arched her eyebrows.

Usually, I minded my mother and Munnie. I blended in and kept my eyes down. No one expected me to lash out. The Song battered against me, and I threw up my barriers to muffle its roar, but it insisted on being heard.

Hanack gathered her stoic demeanor. She swung the cane through the air and the sound of it hitting the floorboards broke the silence. "*Here, Mr. Kaylo.*"

I stood up immediately. Waiting showed fear, and she didn't deserve the satisfaction.

Rena grinned as I passed her, Wal met my eyes and winced in sympathy, but I didn't want sympathy. I straightened my back. If Hanack was going to beat me, she wouldn't hear me beg. I wouldn't cast my eyes to the floor.

When I reached the aisle, I faced her and waited. I had never been caned before, but she had her routine. Every day, she found at least one victim. The waiting dragged on as she toyed with the cane in her hands.

When she met my eyes, she smiled. "*Book of Emperor Amaralis, Chapter Twelve, verse Twenty-One—'Mercy lies with the rod,'*" she said. Her satisfaction seeped into her voice. She raised the cane high above her head and brought it down against my right thigh.

At first, I felt the pain everywhere except my thigh, and then it exploded in a line where she struck me. I ground my teeth and winced.

She struck me again and again. The pain crisscrossed as her cane landed at a slightly different angle each time. On the fourth strike, my leg buckled, and I collapsed to my knees in front of her. She struck me once more on the shoulder for good measure.

The Song slammed against my barriers. I could have let go and given myself to The Song. A few simple movements and an ironoak would have crashed through the floorboards into the rafters of the church. If I wanted to, I could have brought their church crumbling down to the ground. I only had to let go.

The other children strained their necks to stare at me with wide eyes. I found Shay in the crowd, took a deep breath, and exhaled slowly.

Hanack straightened up and looked around the church as if surprised by her indulgence. Several strands of her hair had come loose from her bun, her glasses hung askew, and her shirt was slightly untucked from her long black skirt. She looked untidy.

"*I hope you've learned your lesson,*" she said as she adjusted her glasses. "*Now, take your seat, Mr. Kaylo. There are further lessons to be learned.*"

Hanack passed the text to another student who continued where I had not. The passage became noise in the background. The whole left side of my body felt like one long bruise ready to bloom from my thigh to my shoulder.

Part of me enjoyed standing up to Hanack for once. My father constantly told me that survival didn't require pride, but at this moment, pride felt necessary.

Maybe that was why Shay talked about joining the Missing or fleeing the city. Despite the pain, the sliver of freedom I took reminded me of what life had been like before the Gousht, when I didn't live in fear.

The day I began pushing away The Song, I started becoming a smaller version of myself. I didn't have shackles around my ankles, but I was still a prisoner.

Prisoners are still alive, I reminded myself.

My mother and father had given up so much to keep me alive and out of the Empire's slave camps. They left family behind. They left the life they had built to keep me from harm. Maybe my father had been right—pride was an indulgence. We had to survive, even if that meant sacrificing the things that made me feel like a person.

When Hanack dismissed class, I waited behind and limped to the front of the church. I apologized for my outburst. Hanack's mouth curled at my humiliation. She had shown me my place, and it hurt more than if she had struck me a dozen more times with her cane. I lowered my head and focused on my breathing.

If she reported me to the priest, he might make an example of my family. The thought sent a shiver through me as I limped down the aisle towards the doors.

Rena and her cronies waited for me on the church steps. All of her teeth stood on display as I walked by. They pitched their voices for everyone to hear their conversation.

"*Ms. Hanack shouldn't have stopped at five.*"

"*Blasphemy deserves blood.*"

"*Stupid konki.*"

I balled my fists and walked away with my chin tucked against my chest. Then the stairs behind me thumped loudly. When I turned, Rena lay face down in the dirt.

Shay stepped over her. "Oh, Rena, I'm so sorry. You really should pay better attention."

Rena rushed to her feet and screamed, "You'll regret that, *kunnit!*"

Gousht had many ugly expressions, but *kunnit,* sour blood, stood amongst the worst. They used it interchangeably for blood infections and people of mixed-race heritage.

Beneath the smudges of dirt, Rena was the perfect image of Gousht assimilation. From the green and yellow embroidered tunic and trousers to the broken circle pendent hanging from her neck, she painted herself like one of them.

Shay rounded on her and came face to face with Rena. They stood there for a moment, staring at each other, only wisps of air separating them. "What are you going to do?" Shay asked.

I had sparred with Shay often enough to know that look on her face. She wanted to punch Rena squarely in the jaw. I also knew from experience how painful that would be.

Rena smiled and backed away. "Fighting is such a brutish way to solve disputes," she said. Then she walked off with her friends in tow.

The crowd disbanded, then Shay and I began our journey home like it had been any other day. I didn't thank her, and she didn't call me an idiot for bringing attention to myself. It didn't need to be said, and it would have been a strange role-reversal for us.

In all the city, we only had each other to confide in. A bond like that said a lot in silence.

As we approached the town square, the mass of people grew thicker. We wove through the crowd until we couldn't move any farther. Shay and I shared a glance, then pushed our way into the thick of the commotion. We both stopped when we caught sight of the caller's stage.

Communities built caller's stages as a means for elders and other leaders to address the people. The Gousht turned it into a spectacle, a wooden platform where they could make examples of dissidents.

Soldiers stood on either side of a Tomakan woman strapped to a pillar. Tears in her robes exposed portions of her chest to the chilled autumn air. Dark bruises speckled her brown skin. They had sheared her hair, leaving rough patches over her scalp. Even as her head hung, there was nothing to cover her tear-soaked face.

I had seen her before, but I didn't know her name. I should have known her name.

The priest stood next to her with open arms, addressing the people, "... *threatened the Empire by concealing her true nature.*" His voice rung out over the horrified crowd and, even though most of them didn't understand the language, they understood his meaning.

"*This woman before you is an abomination in the light of The One True God. Good people of Nomar, you know the spirit-marked are enemies of the Empire. Evil spirits must be purged from this land. Their very existence is an obscenity to God's rule. Their violence and cruelty must be met in kind.*"

The priest, with his veiled face and assumption of power, embodied the Gousht. During combat training with Munnie, I pictured him. His voice often interrupted my dreams.

He might have stood shorter and stouter than most of the soldiers, but he had the power. He commanded the soldiers from behind his cloaked robes, wearing that medallion from his neck like a mandate directly from their god.

The woman wailed in front of hundreds of us, and no one did a thing.

The priest slowly reached into his robes and withdrew a translucent crystal the size of his palm. He held it over his head for everyone in the crowd to see.

His footsteps clanged against the wooden platform as he ambled towards the dancer. She strained against the ropes that bound her to the pillar. Panic washed over her face. She screamed.

And I did nothing.

She begged for us to help her as the priest stretched his hand towards her.

"*By the God of power, by command of the Emperor, I cleanse you of your soiled spirit!*"

My heart pounded in my chest, and The Song drummed in a contrasting rhythm.

The crystal glowed blue, and a faint aura left her body as she thrashed against her bindings. It only took a few moments, then she slumped against her restraints—not unconscious, only defeated.

Tears ran down my face, and my jaw ached from clenching my teeth.

The soldiers lifted the woman back to a standing position. Her mouth hung agape, and she turned from soldier to soldier.

"No," she begged. Her head shook back and forth. "No more, please."

The priest ignored her and turned to address the people. "*The mercy of our Emperor is only matched by that of The One True God. I have cleansed this poor soul, but the Crown cannot absolve her of her crimes without proper punishment.*"

The crystal glowed a brilliant blue in his hand. A broken ringing emitted from the crystal, like the sound from the night before. Not The Song, but an echo of it.

The priest grabbed for the prisoner's hand, but she pulled away from him.

The soldier on her left gripped her tighter and forced her hand forward. She wrestled in his grip like a rabbit with its leg caught in a trap.

The priest reached out and encircled her index finger in his hand. He paused for a moment to make sure he had the crowd's attention. The echo grew louder in my head, and the dancer cried out before I understood what happened.

He froze her finger solid. Then, in one jarring motion, the priest snapped her finger off at the large knuckle. It fell to the wooden planks below them, and he settled his boot over the finger and crushed it under his heel.

The crowd fell silent. The woman's head dropped to her chest, and the soldiers slowly untied her. They carried her away with her feet dragging behind them.

"*The righteous call of God's justice has been answered, and the mercy of the Crown has been offered. We saved this soul so that she might still be of service to the Empire,*" the priest announced. He bowed his head. "*To the God of power, we pray. For he, and no other, is the offer, the answer, and the way.*"

CHAPTER EIGHT

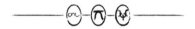

AN OPAQUE GRAY HAZE gathered around me and blotted out the world.
The crowd in the town square vanished. Shay disappeared. The water
dancer's screams repeated in a cascading chorus, one scream layering upon
another until the sound reached a peak and broke into utter silence.

Dark silhouettes formed in the gray cloud all around me. The priest,
only a shadowed outline in the haze, reached forward and grasped the
water dancer's finger before he snapped it free from her hand. She didn't
make a sound this time. A slight shade of a finger fell through the fog to
the floor. When the priest crunched it beneath his boot, the sound of
her frozen digit cracking into countless pieces reverberated through the
haze in every direction.

I rushed at the priest, screaming a soundless scream, and his silhouette
dissipated as I passed through him. Even here, I couldn't fight back. That
sadistic bastard lived beyond my reach.

The haze darkened, and another presence joined me. A figure cloaked
in the darkness itself walked through the void. The shadows surrounding
it billowed in the windless dark. For all the figure's strangeness, it exuded
an air of familiarity.

A muffled noise filtered into the emptiness around me.

The closer the figure came, the more translucent the cloak of shadows became.

A muffled noise grew louder and took form, but it reached to me from a great distance.

The figure moved to pull back the hood of its cloak.

Pain broke through my cheekbone, and pressure built up behind my eyes as I fell to the ground in the middle of a fogless town square. Shay stood over me, smiling and rubbing the knuckles on her right hand with her left.

"Ow!" I reached up to my cheek.

"You didn't leave me any choice."

"What are you talking about?"

"You went blank. It was weird," she said. "I tried shaking you, but that didn't work."

"So you punched me in the face?"

"I stand by my decision." She offered her hand to help me up. I took it begrudgingly. "No need to thank me."

"You're an asshole," I said.

"And you say the nicest things."

The crowd in the town square scattered, carrying the story of what had happened with them. The blank looks on their faces reflected numb parts of my spirit back at me as we joined the exodus away from the caller's stage. We had to be home, and no amount of mourning would change what we had witnessed.

Flares of pain crawled through my thigh from my earlier punishment and my cheek pulsed, ready for a new bruise, but my pain felt insignificant. Small cruelties had become commonplace. I barely reacted when the soldiers referred to us as konki or pilfered from the few possessions we had left. But what the priest did to the water dancer lingered.

The idea of being torn from my spirit, only to have it turned against me, twisted my insides into knots.

"Have you ever seen...that before?" Shay asked.

"No."

The soldiers with spirit crystals liked to wear them in plain view, like a warning, but seeing a colorful crystal hanging from a chain and seeing a spirit fragment ripped from someone stood oceans apart.

"That'll never happen to me," Shay said. "I'll die before I give them The Flame."

"Then we'll die," I said like surrender.

Every day added another layer of exhaustion. No matter what task I set myself to, part of me worried about being discovered or dying, or someone I loved dying. I never seemed to be able to take a full breath. The Gousht hadn't even left me my dreams.

Pain slammed over my shoulder.

Shay stood there, glaring at me with her hand still balled into a tight fist. "If you're done fighting, then I'll go. I'll leave tonight. I'll find the Missing. At least they fight back."

"Blessed Mother, Shay! Rumors don't fight back," I said. "People go missing all the time. That doesn't mean they became freedom fighters. It means they're dead, or the Gousht sent them to the camps. Between the two, the dead have the easier road."

Shay bit her lip, and her nostrils flared. "You might as well join them if you've already given up."

She walked off, and I said nothing.

Our relationship revolved around fighting. We physically and verbally sparred, then one of us stalked off. But something about this fight settled differently in my chest.

If I ran, I could have caught up with her, but I kept my feet planted in the dirt. *She's not going anywhere,* I thought.

My mother's voice rattled in my head. "Regret is the promise of stubborn people."

I turned towards home and limped off.

When I staggered into the house that evening, my mother demanded

to know what had happened. I told her I got into a fight with Shay and
didn't want to talk about it; the caning would only worry her. She shook
her head and joined my father at the stove. They fussed over the pot and
exchanged easy words like every ill in the world stopped at our doorstep.
They escaped into each other.

My father set the bowls around the table like he did every night, and
my mother offered prayer. They did the best they could with the rations
we received. We ate soup most nights because water stretched the food
into a meal.

"How was your day, 'lo?" my father asked.

"Apparently, he and Shay have been fighting again," my mother said.

"Fighting is how you find your way, isn't that right?" he said.

"That reminds me of a story," she said.

"Of course it does." I rolled my eyes.

Her brown eyes turned hard, and she stared me down. "Stories are
our people," she said. "They might seem like words, but they are far
more. You know better."

"I know," I said. "I'm sorry."

"As I was saying, that reminds me of a story. In the time of the Great
War, more than two hundred turns past, a pair of warriors met at a
pond. Each had lost their companions and were searching for a way back
when they found the watering hole. It had been days since either of
them had fresh water. Dehydration and exhaustion had begun to set in,
but still they drew their weapons when they saw each other.

"The Tomakan warrior charged across the water with his spear, but
the Sonacoan warrior had clever feet. Over and over again, she dodged
the Tomakan warrior's attacks. Whatever disadvantage her size and reach
left her, she countered with speed. She pivoted and spun this way and
that, always quicker than the tip of his spear. The Tomakan warrior's
attacks grew slower as he continued to press his advantage.

"He lunged forward with all his might, but he had grown too slow.
The Sonacoan warrior slipped past his wild attack and buried her sword

in his gut. He fell to his knees and collapsed lifelessly into the pond.

"Having soiled the water with his blood and bile, the Sonacoan warrior left him there in search of another source of water, but the skirmish had left her just as tired as the fallen Tomakan. Her quick feet grew heavy as she traipsed through the forest looking for water. Hours passed, but still she hadn't found any. When she no longer had the energy to continue, she took refuge for the night. She could find water in the morning. As sleep took her, it took her for the last time. The Mother wrapped her in The Mist and took her before morning light."

"I feel like you're reaching for a deeper point here," I said.

"Watch the tone," my father said.

"Sometimes fighting is the best way to poison the water for everyone, even if you win," she said and shook her head. "I love you, but you can be denser than a clay brick."

I didn't say anything through the rest of the meal as my parents chatted about inconsequential things. People outside our home thought of my father as a quiet man but put him at a table with my mother and he found more words than he had in a span.

We cleaned up after the meal and each retreated into our solitude. My mother worked on her writing. After the Gousht burned all her books, at least the ones they could find, she chose to work on replacements. "The future will need the past," she would say.

Even though my father toiled away at the workshop all day, he sat by the fire and whittled away at a length of wood.

I walked out to the back of the house and sat on a patch of grass outside the window of my room. Over the last few turns, it had become my place. It wasn't hidden or secret, but it was mine.

The day had been a collection of threats, and each one placed another weight over my shoulders. If I considered any specific incident too deeply, the whole pile of consequences would come crashing down at once.

The church bells rang the call to prayer as Sokan fell and marked the end of the day. All over the city, soldiers bowed their heads before their

god. For some reason, the Gousht believed they existed in subservience
to The One True God, not in harmony with him. They also seemed to
think he needed prayers to be scheduled.

I tried to meditate like Munnie had taught me. I concentrated on the
air as I breathed in. *This is the air Ennea gave us; it is a gift.* I shifted my
hands through the grass, the work of my ancestor spirit. *Life continues.* I
steadied my focus and tried to slow my heartbeat.

Snap.

A twig crunched under the boot of a neighbor walking by, and the
sound of the water dancer's finger breaking reverberated in my head.

The image of her frozen nub of flesh as the base of her finger flashed
in front of me. She hadn't bled. I fought the bile back down my throat.

They could do the same to me, take away what made me who I was,
break my body, and still not be done.

As the brutal event played out in my mind, I remembered the crystal
singing, like when Shay danced the night before.

I shook my head. I must have imagined it.

When the moons finally broke above the forest, I snuck out of my
window. Kana had grown a day fuller, and Toka crept towards a moonless
night. It took all my willpower not to run through the darkness in a
straight line to the lodestone.

Shay wouldn't have run off, I told myself. *She's not that impulsive.*

So I followed my less-direct path through the buildings on the
outskirts of Nomar. The muscles in my thigh protested every movement,
but my limp gentled.

Autumn's chill hung heavy in the air. The Song walked with me at the
edge of my concentration. It would have been a pleasant night if not for
the day that preceded it.

At the edge of the city, the lodestone waited for me, but Shay didn't.
She didn't tempt fate by dancing just beyond the tree line. She didn't

glare at me like I had been holding her up for hours.

Shay ran late all the time, but not tonight. She had gone off to find the Missing and left me behind.

For her sake, I hoped they existed. She deserved to find everything she wanted—a cause, a place she didn't have to hide, and peace, even if it came through violence.

A strange sound buzzed through the forest. *The echo,* I thought. *She didn't leave me.*

I took off running towards the sound. The echo grew louder. I hadn't lost her. Then the echo tore off into pieces. Not one, but several echoes wailed into the night.

No!

I pushed my legs harder. My breathing couldn't keep up with my need. I stumbled over several exposed roots, but my legs found pace again. The echoes grew even louder and more distinct.

"Blessed Mother, let me be wrong," I prayed between gasping breaths.

Flames and smoke jumped out of the night. Shay darted between trees in the distance. Pops of light followed her. The smell of singed forest and overturned earth consumed the air around me.

How did they find her?

In the chaos of the scene, the Emperor's seal, which had been embroidered into the soldiers' padded armor, leaped out at me. The snake coiled around the lion's throat.

In the clearing, two snakes circled around one lion. They maneuvered through the trees, searching for an advantage.

A tree caught fire, and Shay rolled to the right. Smoke clung to the air. She called The Flame, and a pocket of air flickered and exploded, throwing one of the green silhouettes to the ground. The soldier regained her footing, and the two of them worked their way to either side of Shay.

Their movements lacked a dancer's finesse. They wielded their crystals like weapons, not pieces of themselves, whereas Shay moved like fire itself, and still she hadn't gained any ground.

She and the pair of soldiers had reached a stalemate, waiting for someone to make a wrong move.

I pulled my belt knife and charged at the back of the soldier closest to me. Fallen branches and twigs cracked under my boots. My breathing howled in my ears. I pushed out every bit of air from my lungs, yelling into the night.

The soldier turned to face me and, without hesitation, brought her dull brown crystal to the dirt. The ground cracked and broke unevenly in front of me, capturing my foot in the open earth. As I stumbled, my knife tumbled off into the darkness.

The firelight flickered over the soldier's face, and the world stopped. She was young and thin. If not for her icy blue eyes, she would have appeared fragile. But a dark desire glimmered in her irises. She rolled her crystal back and forth in one hand as she reached for her sword with the other. Her helm painted a dark shadow over her brow.

I tried to yank myself free of the chasm, but I couldn't anchor myself. My hands slipped through the loose dirt.

She crept closer. I had seen this soldier walking through the city countless times. She only carried a few more turns than I did. When she patrolled the city, she almost looked pleasant, but that false gentleness didn't exist in her now. She wanted my blood.

Despite all the turns I had spent learning their cruelty, the change in her baring shocked me.

The dull brown crystal began to glow. The ground shook, and then Shay appeared over her shoulder.

Shay shifted her stance and made a series of jabbing motions in the soldier's direction. The air around the soldier shimmered. Her eyes widened, then the shimmering around her ignited. A gust of wind rushed over me to feed the flame before the force of the explosion threw me back, ripping my leg free from the earth.

The charred remnants of the soldier's body dropped to the ground, smelling of burned hair and roasted meat. Shay smiled over her kill.

A bright red light glowed in the darkness behind Shay—the captured spirit of The Flame turned within its crystal prison.

The second soldier took advantage of his comrade's death.

Shay turned but didn't move fast enough. The soldier charged at Shay with his crystal extended in one hand and his sword ready in the other.

It was only a small burst of fire. Shay clutched at her face as the flames spread through her curls and the soldier drove his sword through her chest.

The world lost all sound.

Shay's body wavered, then fell, the sword still buried in her flesh.

My body moved on instinct. I pulled myself from the dirt and charged the soldier. The air between us popped with small flames until the echo broke through the silence and I snatched it out of the air.

A new spirit boiled in my chest—frantic to escape, clawing at me from the inside. As the echo roared, I danced with its anger. Trees all around the soldier burst into flames.

The Flame's desire to consume fueled my rage. The spirit wanted to claim the whole forest.

My arms carved into the night, and the fire spread all around the soldier. He screamed as the flames enveloped him. His dark shape floundered in the fire. Then he collapsed, and the silence returned.

I pulled on The Flame, and the fires all around me hushed to a whisper of smoke rising from the forest floor. Soot scarred the trees. Some few embers flittered in the night. The captured spirit still raged against the prison within me until I stopped fighting to restrain it, and it disappeared, taking all of its pain and rage with it.

In the night's stillness, the brush beyond the battleground rustled in the darkness. I snapped towards the sound and squared up, ready to fight, but there was no one left to fight.

Shay groaned and coughed. I rushed to her side.

The patch of flesh around her right eye had blackened like a pit of ash. Her chest heaved up and down arrhythmically. Her good eye remained wide open, staring at me. Blood pooled around the sword and sank into the soil beneath her. Too much blood.

"I'll get help," I said. "Munnie, she can fix this." Tears streamed down my face.

I reached for her hand, and she recoiled.

It was instinct, I told myself, but she looked at me as if I were a stranger. She knew what I was. A malitu. A corrupt spirit. A thief.

Even as she lay dying, my only friend feared me.

I didn't know if I wanted the moment to last forever or to end immediately. I would never lay eyes on her again.

She was beautiful. Forget the blood and burns, my love for her hadn't changed. Still, I couldn't say the words.

Her soft green eyes watered and coated her face with streaks of tears, blood, and ash.

In the distance, heavy boots stomped through the forest. Muffled shouts grew closer, but I couldn't look away. The soldiers must have seen the fire and smoke rise above the treetops. Or maybe they heard the screams.

My heart raced. I had to leave, but I couldn't.

Shay opened her mouth to speak, but the words wouldn't come. "It's okay. I won't leave you, Shay," I said.

She shook her head slightly and tried to speak again. The sound barely formed in her mouth. "Run."

"No, I can't. I won't leave you."

"Run," she repeated with more force and grimaced at the pain.

Clattering metal cut through the night. The soldiers would be there soon.

I stared at her, shaking my head. "I'm sorry," I said. "I'm so sorry, Shay."

She traded her life for mine, and it wasn't a fair trade. I didn't deserve her sacrifice. She didn't deserve to die in the middle of the forest with only the Gousht for company.

I pulled myself from her side and ran into the forest.

If the spirits had a fraction of the power they had in the stories, then I hated them more than the Gousht. For all their power, they left us powerless. They abandoned us.

Tears blurred my vision as I ran through the dark wood. My feet moved of their own accord. My body ached, and my lungs burned, but I couldn't stop. If I stopped, the truth about what had happened and what I was would catch up with me. So, I ran home like a child, where I thought it would be safe.

CHAPTER NINE

THE WALLS OF MY house quieted the wind and the ambient noises of the night but did nothing to still the pounding in my chest. The hearth had gone cold and dark. Gentle sleeping sounds came from my parent's room.

I fell back against the thick wooden door and slid to the ground.

Shay died, and the city slept through it.

Every time I closed my eyes, she stared back at me—her face burned and afraid, her hand recoiling from my touch.

She shouldn't have died afraid. It went against everything she had been.

Cold spread through the door and down my back. I sobbed because my friend died. I sobbed because I killed her.

Candlelight flickered awake in my parents' bedroom. Feet scuffled on the floorboards, but I didn't move. I couldn't. My mother appeared in the doorway and gathered me up with one look, my torn clothing, the dirt and blood on my skin, the tears streaking my face, and she rushed to me.

She set a hand on each of my shoulders and tried to meet my eyes, but I couldn't. I didn't want her to see me.

"What happened? Where were you?" she asked. I could only cry and shake my head. Her hands gripped my shoulders more firmly, and she asked again, "What happened?"

"Shay's dead," I said and wept even harder, having said the words aloud.

My mother pulled me into her, and I abandoned myself into her arms. Her hand brushed the nape of my neck, and my body slowed under her touch.

When I looked up, my father stood in the doorway, watching us. He slowly walked over to the dining table and sat down. "I need you to tell us what happened," he said in a low, steady tone. Then he waited. He didn't repeat himself or rush me, instead he lit a candle on the table and waited.

My mother helped me into a chair. For several moments, I sat there, unable to find the words to describe what had happened. I stared into the flame to avoid looking at my parents, and I saw the forest burning. Then, the story came spilling out of me.

As I told them what happened, it all played out again. Shay fought off the soldiers. She saved me, and then the couta bastard thrust his sword through her gut. The fire surrounded him, and he burned to death. His screams rang in my ears. Shay's rough and cracked voice told me to run. By the end of my story, my sobbing overwhelmed my words.

I told them almost every crude detail, but I couldn't bring myself to tell them about the echoes or what I was. *A thief who lies.* I couldn't bear to see Shay's horror on their faces.

My mother's hand rested on mine. They allowed me to calm down, then my father asked his questions. "Are you hurt? Did anyone else see you? Are you sure the soldiers were dead before you ran away?"

I answered each question as best as I could, but the world didn't make sense. My body felt like a home that belonged to someone else.

My head pounded, and I had wiped the skin around my eyes raw. *It should have been me. I should have died.*

Our home had never been large, two small bedrooms, a hearth, and a table, but it shrank in the silence of that moment.

The soldiers did what soldiers always did. Blaming them was like blaming a rabid fox for biting. They were the circumstances, but I let Shay die.

The Seed sang a mourning song, full of windblown trees and roots reaching in the depths of Ennea. I yearned to be outside, lost in the forest and The Song.

"Tonight, we are going to clean you up," my mother said. "We will burn your clothes, scrub the soot from your hair, and cover your bruises. Tomorrow, you are going to go to school like every other day. Nothing can appear out of place. Then, the next day, you will do the same." She pressed her thumb into the palm of her opposite hand like she always did when she got anxious.

"Two soldiers are dead. The Gousht aren't going to let that be," my father said. "They will punish someone."

"As long as it isn't Kaylo," my mother hissed. Her eyes leveled like a blade at my father's throat. She would never let anyone hurt me. She would allow the whole of Nomar burn to the ground for my sake.

"I can't let someone else..." I started, then whispers of The Song filled the night. No, not The Song—echoes.

I pushed myself from the table, and my chair crashed to the ground. A soldier carrying a lantern led a group of his comrades down the row of homes next to ours with the priest in tow. A spirit crystal softly glowed in one of their palms.

I pulled back from the window. "We need to run," I said.

"What is it?" my mother asked.

"*Come out, boy,*" the priest shouted in Gousht. "*We know you're a dancer.*"

The soldiers drew their weapons and awaited the priest's orders. Then a small figure came into view beside them. Lantern light washed over Rena's face as she stood there with her arms folded across her chest.

All my shame evaporated in the rush of hatred that swept over me. The rustling in the brush. Rena must have been there, in the forest, watching as they killed Shay. She probably led them to Shay, and now she led them to my home, to my family.

The Song bellowed all around me. Everything that sprouted from the earth connected like an unending web, and I stood the center of it all. I could pull on any of those threads and they would bend to my calling. I wanted to see her die in agony.

My father's hands fell on my shoulders and pulled me from The Song. He shook me, and I returned to the four walls of our home. My mother had been saying something, but I couldn't remember what.

"You have to go. You have to run," she said.

I blinked. Her words didn't make any sense to me. Rena was outside, covered in Shay's blood, just like me. Blood owed blood, like the stories my mother always quoted.

"*Come out now, and you will live,*" the priest said.

"Now," my father said. "You have to leave now. We will give you as much time as we can."

The soldiers approached the door and a second echo flared up in the darkness to meet the first. The noise surrounded me. I clutched at my ears and shook my head, but it did nothing to block out The Song or the echoes.

My mother thrust a canvas sack into my hands. She pulled me close and kissed me on the cheek. When she released me from her grasp, she ran her hand over my braided hair. Tears rushed down her face as she smiled at me. "You're the greatest gift Ennea ever gave me," she said. "I love you."

Her words didn't make sense. They couldn't stay behind. I wasn't a gift. If they only knew I was a malitu, they wouldn't sacrifice themselves.

I tried to give her the bag back, but she clasped her hands around mine and said, "You carry our stories now."

My father barricaded the front door with our table and whatever else he could find. It wouldn't last long.

Rena must have told them how I called The Flame in the forest. They wanted to steal my spirit, which kept them from burning our home to ash for the moment.

My father turned towards me and met my eyes. Tears crawled down the hard-set lines of his face.

People confused his stoic nature with a lack of care, but my father loved deeply. To know his low, calm voice was to know him. Calluses covered his hands from crafting metal and wood every day, but he had a gentle touch. I had never been scared of my father until that night. He looked like a battlefield.

He pulled me into him and enveloped me. "Make me proud. I'll be watching," he said. "Family knows."

I squeezed his torso as tightly as I could. When he stepped away, he reached to his belt and placed his knife in my hand.

The stormwood handle wrapped with leather filled my palm. It was larger than my knife had been and sharp as a summer sunrise. I gawked at it. My father always carried his knife, whether in his belt or in his hands. Anytime he didn't have a project, he worked the blade over wood or sharpened it against a whetstone.

The door slammed against the barricade.

My father had built a solid home, but no door would last long against Gousht soldiers. "Go," he said as he grabbed a hammer from his toolkit and waited for them to break through.

I looked to my mother, but she wouldn't meet my gaze. She stood next to her husband with a kitchen knife in her hand. They stood upright and proud, and somehow that made me feel more ashamed.

I turned, ran towards my room, and leaped out the back window. The echoes rose in sharp crescendo behind me. I couldn't bear to look back and see my home in flames. If I did, I wouldn't be able to move another step, and so I ran. I ran until my legs went numb, then kept running, my father's knife heavy on my hip.

The edges of my vision faded first, followed by an opaque gray haze blotting out patches of the world. The rolling ache that reminded me my body was still there waned, and the sound of the forest and my heavy footfalls vanished. Then, the haze consumed everything until nothing remained but a heavy fog surrounding me.

CHAPTER TEN

The fire dwindled and crackled into the air in spits of sparks and ash. As the silence drew longer than comfortable, Tayen's fingernails scraped back and forth over the frayed hem of her robe.

They both had outlived their families; maybe neither shouldn't have.

Kaylo's wrinkles sat deeper, and his skin looked paler. He hunched towards the fire like he didn't have the strength to hold himself upright. This many turns past, and his story weighed him down as if he had to relive every word of it.

"I think that's all for tonight," he said. A hollow sound crept into the timber of his voice.

The firelight fluttered over Kaylo. The things that he survived had broken him.

If he couldn't move past what happened to him, can I? she thought. *Do I deserve to?*

"Sleep," Kaylo said. "Your training starts tomorrow, and you'll need your energy." He stood up and walked into the darkness where his bedroll lay.

They had both run away and left their families behind.

Tayen reached into her robe and pulled out the whistle her sister carved for her. The light rolled over its uneven surfaces. It really was ugly.

Her fingers traced the three holes her sister bore into the hollowed-out length of wood.

The last time she spoke to Nita, Tayen hadn't said anything important. She didn't tell Nita that she loved her. Instead, Tayen asked her not to tell their parents where she went. Their mother had told Tayen to sweep out the hut, and she hated sweeping. No matter how many times she swept it, dirt was still dirt.

Am I going to turn out like him, full of sad stories? she thought. *I should have died with them.*

She put her lips to one end of the whistle and blew lightly. The air flittered through the wood and pitched high like a shrill bird call. It sounded as ugly as the whistle looked. She offered a sad smile to the night.

When Tayen woke up, Kaylo was already sitting over the pot next to the fire. He greeted her with a smile. The weight and the depression that he wore the night before had vanished with the morning sun.

It didn't make sense. Even the happiest memories of her family dropped her to the ground, breathless. Maybe she could learn to smile through the pain too.

Tayen took her seat by the fire, and the smell of cardamom and anise lifted from the pot as Kaylo stirred the porridge.

"Do you eat the same thing every morning?" Tayen asked.

"When you cook, you can choose what we eat." Kaylo held an apple over the pot and sliced pieces of it into the oats.

A silence of hard memories and hesitant questions enveloped them and held them as they ate.

When Tayen found her family surrounded by soldiers, they had already been dead. But Kaylo had to leave his parents behind while they were still alive. The guilt of it still hung on his shoulders this many turns later.

She stole glances at him as he ate, and if he caught her attentions, he ignored them.

When they finished their meal, they each knelt in front of their respective idols. Kaylo prayed in profane offerings to the figures he carved into the stormwood, but The Shadow hadn't killed Tayen's family. Those responsible walked on this side of The Mist.

Blood owed blood. Tayen's mother called for it in her dreams, so why did her hands shake when she thought about honoring her debt?

Praying had always been a habit. She never considered the words to be anything more than words, until now. Maybe the spirits were listening.

The obsidian stone stared back at her in black reflection. "To the first—The Shadow, the wisdom offered to The Waking," she whispered so Kaylo wouldn't hear. "Help me find the courage to do what I must."

Despite the words, her hands quivered at the thought of the soldiers, so when Kaylo moved to the next routine instead of her training, she didn't complain.

After all, Munnie had spoken about patience in Kaylo's story. This could have been a lesson, and she played along as if it was.

They tended to a section of the hallow's wall. But when she asked questions about how to trim the plants, he responded with some version of, "There is no right cut, but the cut that the plant needs."

The only thing that restrained her temper was his smile.

He wore his mask well, smiled with his entire face, but when he turned back to the plants, his eyes softened and his cheeks slackened. The man from the previous night, who buckled beneath his own story, sat beside her.

While he trimmed the plants, he moved slowly and deliberately, holding each branch in his hands, searching for the cut. His movements were too practiced to be random and too random to be anything else.

"Let go," he said. He turned and caught her staring. "If you make a mistake, the plant will still grow. It will take what you've done and make something beautiful out of it."

Tayen had made enough mistakes to know they didn't always grow into something beautiful. Still, she nodded and drew her knife through the branch in her hand.

"Why didn't your parents go with you?" she asked.

Kaylo's hands continued to move as if he hadn't heard her question. She shouldn't have said anything. Even if he insisted on telling her his story, she didn't have to pick at the old wounds.

"I don't know," he said after what felt like too long. "I've asked myself the same thing many times. I think they believed they were giving me a better chance to survive." His knife continued to move but slower than it had before.

The skin on the pads of Tayen's fingers went raw by the time they broke for lunch. Blisters grew on top of her blisters.

Kaylo charred some vegetables with the coals in the firepit and shared out a bit of saltmeat. It hardly amounted to a meal, but it felt like a feast after a full morning.

"*How is your food?*" Kaylo asked in Gousht.

Tayen's lips curled in disgust at the sound of Gousht.

"Do you know their tongue?" he asked.

"A little," she said, letting her distaste poison her tone.

"You obviously know your letters," he said, nodding in the direction of the pile of books next to her bedroll. "That's a good start. A shadow needs to hear all and be heard by none. You will start learning Gousht tomorrow. If you had grown up in the cities, they would have forced you to learn it by now."

"How long do you expect me to stay here?" Tayen asked with a mouth full of saltmeat.

Kaylo shook his head at her. "For as long as you would."

Tayen hated the idea of speaking their tongue. The Gousht assumed everything belonged to them and made everyone fit into their version of the world. She didn't want their language infecting her thoughts. If they had their way, every Ennean would be dressed in trousers and a tunic, speaking Gousht, and praying to The One True God.

But if she wanted to fight them, she would need to know more about them. That didn't mean she liked the idea. Then again, she didn't have to like it.

With a mouthful of charred squash and saltmeat, she asked, "If we're studying their language tomorrow, what are we doing today?"

"Teaching you manners if you continue to speak with a full mouth," Kaylo chided. "Swallow, little shade. Swallow."

Tayen chewed at the tough meat until she gave up and swallowed the too big chunks. She coughed to clear her throat and asked again, "What lesson shall we learn today, oh, great kana?"

Kaylo smiled at her and shook his head. "Well, my young toka, today you are going to try to kill me," he said.

She sneered at him. "So, the Hero of Anilace has a sense of humor?"

"Children of Ennea can call the spirits, but the most effective tool you carry with you into a fight will always be a blade. A shadow cannot kill a soldier, but it can get you close enough to slit their throat. Shadow dancers have to become the shadows themselves—noiseless and unassuming—then strike out of the darkness.

"If you are serious about wanting your revenge, you need to become an illusion until the very moment you become the blade. Do you understand?" Kaylo asked with a quiet intensity.

The idea of dragging a blade across a person's throat made her own throat tighten. Her hand climbed up to her neck, and a chill rushed over her skin. She had never tried to hurt anyone before.

"Meet me outside." Kaylo placed his knife on the stump between them, then walked out of the hallow, with no further explanation.

The blade of his knife ran nearly twice the length of her belt knife. A strip of leather wrapped around the deep brown wooden hilt. The color of the wood matched the tree in the middle of the hallow.

She picked it up and studied it. For the knife's size, it should have been heavier. The metal wore marks of age, but Kaylo had cared for it. She brought her finger to the knife's edge and pulled it back immediately, a thin red line marking the pad of her finger.

The knife reminded her of the way Kaylo described his father's knife, but this blade couldn't have been the same one. Kaylo never would have given her his father's knife.

The weight of the weapon grew with each step she took out of the hallow. This blade had known plenty of blood through the turns. Her hand shook slightly. She grabbed the hilt tighter.

He won't scare me away, she thought. *I won't abandon my family, not again.*

Tayen walked into the dim light of the afternoon. He told her to stop when she got within thirty paces. A flat stretch of ground ran between them with ironoaks cluttering the land, the canopy masking what little sun peaked through the clouds.

Kaylo stood there for a moment, and then he raised a long piece of gray cloth to his eyes and knotted it around his head. "When I tell you, you are going to try and stab me with that knife."

"No, I'm not," Tayen said. "Why would I stab you?"

"I know you won't. I said you would try."

"This is stupid. I see what you're doing, but I'm not going to give up on my family because I don't want to kill you."

"If I thought it would be that easy, I would have handed you a knife right away and skipped story time," Kaylo said. "You expect to kill a small regiment of Gousht soldiers, but can't find the heart to bring a knife to one man? I'll make it easier for you." Kaylo slowly turned his back to her.

That's it. The blisters on the joints of her fingers threatened to burst the way she gripped the knife. She took a deep breath. *I'm sick of this game.*

The wind lapped against her cheeks as she sprinted through the trees.

The distance between her and her kana disappeared. He stood still as a rock. She reached her arm forward with the tip of the blade aimed just below his shoulder blades.

At the last moment, he stepped to the side. As she passed by, he caught her arm and twisted. The forest floor drove the air from her lungs as she crashed to the ground. Spots of color and black blinked in and out of her vision as she coughed, trying to recapture her breath.

"You are a noisy shadow," Kaylo called out from elsewhere in the forest.

She balled her hands into fists, and her blood turned hot in her veins. The debt she owed her family wasn't a joke.

She swept her hands through the forest floor, searching for the knife she dropped. It bit her on the forearm and blood dripped from the slight wound. But she didn't jump at the pain. Her anger served as a quick scab.

He hadn't gone far, maybe another thirty paces into the forest. Still facing away from her. Still blindfolded.

Tears of warm blood trickled down the length of her arm as she gripped the knife. If he wanted her to attack him, she would. She looked around the forest and plotted her route. This time she wouldn't be taken off-guard.

The sun lowered by the width of two of her fingers as she closed the distance between her and her kana. She paused for long stretches behind trees to throw him off. Her anger urged her to move faster, but she was too stubborn to let it rule her. She made it within five paces of her target before she leaped at him.

Again, he stepped to the side, but this time, he let her fall to the ground without touching her.

Variations of the same scenario played out five more times, and each time Tayen's new approach failed. She tried to go as slow as she could, then the exact opposite. She threw rocks to distract him with the sound. Nothing made a difference. He evaded her with ease, and it gave her blood to the spirits. By the end, she truly wanted to bury the knife in her kana.

"That last time, you were closer," Kaylo said.

He stood over her, smiling, with his blindfold slung around his neck, and his eyebrows arching in a smug expression.

The weathered leather of the knife's hilt dug into her skin. She pushed herself to her feet and jabbed at Kaylo. He shifted his stance and caught her wrist.

"Your anger is working against your goal," he said.

He twisted her arm slightly. Blood and dirt covered the curved metal blade.

"What happened to this blade? Your blade is your responsibility. There are times it will be your life. Treat it with more respect," he said evenly, but the sharpness of his rebuke carried through, regardless of how subtly he spoke it.

For some, anger lent voice, but Tayen's seething resentment stole the words from her mouth. His eyes betrayed his enjoyment. This was a game to him. She made a low growl and ripped her wrist from his grip before stalking back to the hallow.

***

The cut on her arm stung as she washed the dirt and dried blood away with a bowl of water and a rag. The firepit blazed, far too much heat radiating from the flames. An acrid smell stung her nostrils as the heavy hand of firestarter she used burned into the air.

Kaylo didn't say anything as he sat down beside her. He placed a stone mortar on the ground and filled it with several leaves, a strip of bark, a handful of dirt, and some water. The sound of stone grinding against stone challenged the silence. Then it stopped.

"Let me see your arm," he said and held his hand out.

The thick paste looked like slightly greener mud and smelled like wet grass. "What is that?"

"A simple poultice, but it should keep the wound clean of infection," he said.

Tayen relented and held out her arm. He worked the paste over the long, shallow cut on her forearm. It was cool against her skin.

"You remind me of Shay," he said softly. "She hated failing. She needed to be the strongest in every room, and usually she was, but whenever she made a mistake, she would get furious." Kaylo shook his head and caught his quickening breath. "We train so that we can make mistakes when it is safe to make them. Shay never got that. Maybe if she'd had more time...."

"You bring your pain and anger everywhere you go. They are your first enemy in a fight. They gave you this cut." He spread the thick paste evenly over her forearm and turned her wound towards the fire. "Hold your arm like this and let the poultice dry."

She shifted closer to the fire, and her skin chafed under her sweat-drenched robes.

"Focus on your breath," he said. "In and out."

He demonstrated beside her like she didn't know how to breathe.

"Remember, a shadow cannot cut down a soldier no matter how fierce. Learn from the shadows. They don't charge in with anger. A shadow is a silent mimic," Kaylo said, then sighed. "I can only train you like my kanas trained me. Maybe it isn't the right way, but today you strategized and struggled to trick your opponent. You never repeated a failed tactic, which tells me that as much as your anger betrays you, it doesn't control you."

"You are either silent for hours at a time or you don't stop talking," she said.

"You did well today," he said with a slight smile.

She couldn't smile back, but she stopped glaring at him.

"You think I train you hard? I had to spar with Shay." He said the words like a joke, but a sadness crept into his eyes, and he turned to the fire.

The silence that fell between them had a different weight, full of vulnerabilities like it could shatter with a touch.

Tayen cradled her arm and looked at the hardened paste covering her wound. It barely hurt. She was safe here. But she had been safe before.

He can be taken away too, she thought. *And when he's gone...* The fire lit up his face as he cleaned his mortar and pestle. *I'll be truly alone.*

CHAPTER ELEVEN

As sunlight streamed through the forest canopy and landed across my face, I stirred from my sleep. I couldn't recall falling asleep outside. If I didn't get home soon, there would be trouble. A heavy pressure throbbed behind my eyes and the bridge of my nose. The muscles in my legs and back rebelled in pain against the slightest movement.

Autumn's breeze disturbed the surrounding air. It smelled of pine, even though there wasn't a pine tree in sight. Instead, thin, pale trees with bark like sheets of grayish-brown paper layered over each other filled the forest.

Home didn't look anything like this.

Rich, red soil replaced the deep brown earth upon which I grew up. Grass grew in strange thick patches in the rocky landscape.

My chest tightened. It grew harder and harder to keep my lungs full. Then the beauty that surrounded me clashed in stark contrast to the slow flood of memories.

The crack of the water dancer's finger snapped in my ears.

Shay's echo broke into several parts, and I couldn't catch them fast enough.

A soldier screamed as the flames consumed him.

Shay writhed in pain, her face badly burned.

I left her to die.

My mother kissed my cheek. Holding imperfect weapons, she and my father stood in front of the barricaded door.

I left them to die.

"No! No! No!" I screamed and grabbed a handful of red soil and threw it into the air, only for the wind to scatter it. "It's a dream. It has to be a dream."

But the earth felt like earth, despite its color, and my body ached in all the ways that told me I hadn't been dreaming.

As I pushed myself up, the ground tilted under my feet. My head throbbed at pace with my heart. I lifted my hand to my forehead, and it came back sticky with blood. The dark red sheen on my fingers glinted in the sunlight. This was a stranger's body.

My breathing drowned out all the sounds of the forest. *Slow down,* I thought, and focused on my belly like Munnie taught me. In and out. Rise and fall. *Control your breathing. Breath comes before everything else.*

Every time my diaphragm expanded, it pulled against the muscles in my lower back. The pain rooted me to the moment; Munnie taught me how to solve these kinds of problems.

If I intended to clean the cut on my head and calm my aches, I needed to find water.

The world slowed, and I noticed a strange sproutling—an ashburn, unlike any other tree in the forest—sheltering the patch of dirt where I had slept. At the base of its immature trunk, it curved unnaturally out of the earth and unsettled the soil.

I laughed, and my abdomen contracted painfully.

In my haze, I had pulled this sproutling from The Song and curved the tree trunk to shelter myself.

No matter how I tried, I couldn't remember calling the tree. My cheeks grew taut and pulled my lips into a smile as I stared at my ingenuity.

They are dead, and I am smiling over a half-grown, bent tree. My face fell back into place, and I bit my lip. Tears would only be a waste of water.

"If you find yourself lost, take care of your body first. The fear will be there when you're ready for it." Munnie's voice rang out in my head as if she stood next to me.

I shut my eyes and let the forest wash over me. The wind rustled through the autumn leaves that still clung to the trees. A flight of swallows twittered away to the south. In all the ambient noises of the forest, The Song didn't sing, and its absence called out louder than any creature that called this wood home.

The Song never stopped its melody. If I couldn't hear it, my walls had blocked it out.

As I reached for my self-imposed barriers, Shay flashed in front of me, her hand failing to cover the burn across her face. Blood traversed the cracks in her skin like rivers.

When a dancer opened themselves to The Song, they opened themselves completely, and too much waited on the other side of my walls. I could find water another way.

At the base of the sproutling, the sack my mother had given me lay bundled up. I pulled the tie loose from the sack and peeked inside the leather as if it contained a trap. Instead, I found most of a stale loaf of bread, two empty water skins, a small pot, a few Gousht coins, and a handful of root vegetables—whatever had been in mother's reach at the time.

A strip of blue fabric stood apart from the rest of the contents. As I reached for it, the smooth material glided over my hands. The moment I felt it, without needing to peel back the fabric, I knew what my mother had given me.

My mother's research diary grew heavier after I saw the leather binding beneath the cloth. For turns, she collected all her notes and stories on these pages. She had been determined to capture a true history of our people to help replace what the Gousht burned.

She would never write it now.

As if it were a relic left by The Mother herself, I folded the fabric back in place and returned the book to the sack without even prying open the cover. The ink within those pages could have destroyed me.

All of it could wait for later. And though it took all my willpower to return the bread back to the sack, water had to come first. Bread would only worsen my thirst.

Munnie taught me how to track water. At least, she had tried, but I never took it seriously. My whole life, I never lived more than a handful of steps from a drink.

My tongue felt drier than bark, but my body hadn't slowed down yet, which meant I could keep moving at a normal pace until Sokan set. After that, if I didn't find water, a new level of danger would find me—one more immediate than my memories.

The sun fell the width of four fingers into the sky, passing the hour, before I found a clear set of deer tracks. Signs of the animal hid amongst the wood, heading east, and the forest shrank into focus as I stalked under Sokan's heat.

Maybe some of what Munnie had taught me had taken root more than I thought.

Every step I took revealed another strange plant, but this forest moved like any other. Each plant and animal under the canopy lived in balance with one another. Disruptions and disturbances meant the same thing here as they did in my forest. The bent branches of a nearby bush, a tuft of fur caught in the dusting on the ground, even the remains of the creature's last meal told a story.

Sweat ran slick on my forehead, and my thirst grew louder. It had already been too long. I lifted my hand to the sky and measured the sun's descent—only three hours remained before the light faded behind the horizon.

"Blessed Mother, selfish prayers find quiet replies and all that, but I could use a hand," I said. "A pond. A stream. Something."

A brown tuft of fur clung in the broken stem of a ninebark bush. It was longer than deer fur. Maybe a rabbit.

Beyond the bush, several animal tracks marked the soil. I kissed three fingers and touched them to the land in thanks. Where animals gathered, water would be close by.

As I ran after the markings, my father's knife bounced against my leg. Water babbled to the east like a promise, and my thirst drove my legs with more insistence.

"I learned something, Munnie."

The sound of water grew into a light roar, but I still couldn't see it through the trees. I had hoped for a small brook or creek, but the rush of the water grew too loud.

My hope died as each new cluster of trees opened up to rockier and rockier earth. To be this loud and still out of sight, the river had to be enormous.

If I didn't reach the water soon, my body would find ways to conserve what little energy I had left. I would be as good as dead if that happened, and, despite my grief, my body and spirit were determined to live.

Past the promise of another grouping of trees, the crash of the rapids overwhelmed and overtook every other sound the forest had to offer. The trees parted and gave way to a clearing.

White-tipped water crashed through the rocky terrain. Enormous boulders and jagged rocks lined the river. Water rushed and turned with the rough bank, down the rocky channel, and over a series of small falls.

It made no sense.

Across the river, a range of mountains rose out of the forest. Mountain ranges in Ennea ran along the east and west coasts. The rivers in Tomak flowed through the rolling hills and thick forest.

Munnie had sat me down in front of crusty maps for hours, memorizing every river, valley, and mountain of Ennea. None of the rivers in Tomak moved like this. The Tampir River snaked through the rocks near the Conca Mountain range, but it never crossed the border.

My headache returned stronger than before. I couldn't be in Sonacoa. It took days to reach the border from Nomar.

But the soil, the trees, the rapids, and the mountains told a different story.

How many days had I lost?

I had spent my entire life in Tomak, every night under the same roof as my parents.

As reality crashed against me like the rapids over the rocky bank, my body began shaking.

Flames consumed my home. My parents' screams pierced me through the chest. Shay's lifeless body hung from the gallows in the town square.

My stomach wrenched, and I buckled at the waist. What little I had in my stomach splattered against the rocky soil before I collapsed into the tall grass on the riverbank. My body lurched violently with each sob. And, even though everything had been my fault, I spat breathless curses at the world.

Sokan gave the sky over to her sisters and left me there curled in the tall grass.

I prayed for the spirits to take retribution on Rena and the priest. I prayed for the soldiers who killed my parents to burn as they took their last breaths. I prayed for death, but sleep took me instead.

———————

When I woke, Kana and Toka hung high above me. The walls of my mouth felt as rough as sand, and, as much as I wanted the pain to be over, I crawled to the edge of the river.

I was grateful for the small rocks scraping my knees—the small, bright pains distracting me from the larger ones.

My skin tingled as I reached into the cool river and lifted a cupped hand to my mouth. The few drips that passed my lips weren't enough. I dropped myself unceremoniously to the rough river edge and dunked my head into the water, letting the current wash over my sun-brushed skin.

When I lifted my head, I coughed up more water than I could drink down. I couldn't even drink from a river without fucking it up.

With a deep breath, I leaned down to sip at the rushing waters. And once I drank my fill, I submerged my head again to feel the coolness of the river lapping at me.

I must have lain on that riverbank for hours.

If I followed the river north, then turned west with the sun, I could find my way home. I could find Munnie. But she didn't need the kind of attention I would bring with me. Soldiers would be on the lookout.

No, better she thought me dead. She would never have to know she taught a thief. And she would never look at me the way Shay had.

My waterskins sloshed in a reassuring rhythm as I walked south with the river. If I had ended up where I assumed I had, the Stone City would be about a day or two walk away. The Tampir flowed right past Sonacoa's capital city, the city that withstood. All I had to do was follow it.

After hearing my mother's countless stories about the impenetrable city that fell, I had always wanted to see it. It would hide me as well as anywhere else. No one knew my name.

The sparse collection of trees along the riverbank offered little cover, so I stuck to the thicker brush within the tree line. My muscles strained and pulled as I hiked the rocky terrain, but at least I had water now.

I helped myself to a fistful of stale bread as the morning light spilled through the trees. Light danced over the choppy river, and its serenity struck me as odd. The world didn't feel capable of beauty, yet there it was.

As Kana took back the sky from her sister, I reached the valley's edge. Below, the Last Wall connected one mountain to another, and with it the Stone city awaited, still over half a day away.

I never thought I would see the fabled wall.

As the story went, three dancers prayed to The Mountain for

protection after the Hundred-Turn War, none of them believing the peace could last. They walked into The Mist and spoke with the spirit, and she offered to surround their city with a wall unlike any other as long as they honored her.

When they returned from The Mist, the Great Spirit worked through the dancers and called a mountain from the earth, bridging the gap between two others. Over the next turn, they danced and weathered the stone until it formed a seamless wall with but one gate. Within that wall, they built the Stone City.

For as many times as I had pictured it, nothing could have prepared me for the scale of the wall. And still, it hadn't kept the Empire out.

A jagged-edged gap broke the towering giant in two.

When every other city had fallen to the Gousht, the Stone City withstood. Their food stores and farms would have outlasted any siege, but a group of blood banners brought down the wall from inside. And as it fell, the nations of Ennea fell with it.

The city had an air of foreboding, like a grave marker. As I descended into the valley, the city took shape. Stone buildings towered above the streets like rows of corn in a field. The entire city had been a monument to The Mountain.

My mother had moved us to Nomar because we could lose ourselves in the crowd. Well, the Stone City was large enough to lose a hundred children. I could find a way inside the wall, a safe place to hide, and eventually, it could feel something like home.

If I kept pace, I would reach the wall not long after dawn. Soldiers weren't looking for people breaking into the city. Only fools broke into prisons.

The weight of the metal coins in my sack felt reassuring, like a warm meal.

Then I stopped.

From atop the tallest building in the city, the broken circle stared at me. The Emperor's green and yellow seal hung from the eaves. The banner waved in the wind; the serpent's fangs protruding, ready to strike.

My mind flashed to the soldier rushing at me with her blade drawn, then to Shay's broken body lying in the dirt.

The ground clung to my feet.

I whipped my head back and forth, searching for a soldier in the forest, but I was alone, and the earth lay flat underneath my boots. But when I lifted my foot to take another step, I couldn't stop shaking.

Shay's scream rang out in my ears, and I crumbled to my knees.

Whether it was a step away or ten thousand, I couldn't bring myself to walk towards the occupied city any more than I could return home. The broken circle, the Emperor's seal, and the shattered wall promised death of one sort or another.

Even though part of me longed for The Mist, to see those I had lost to it, I didn't have the courage to seek it.

The forest tore against my clothes and skin as I ran deeper into the woods, away from the Stone City. When my lungs threatened to burst, I fell to the ground, panting. No amount of air could calm the burning in my chest. I closed my eyes to reach for The Song, something familiar, but it refused to come to me.

The spirits had abandoned me like everyone else.

Each breath was too shallow. I panted. The world blurred. I tried to focus on the trees. The forest had always been my escape, but the image of Shay met me there, surrounded by burning trees. I collapsed into the dirt, and everything went black.

Shay stood in front of an ironoak tree.

As I watched her from the darkness, she ran her fingers over the bark, and it stripped from the ironoak. Large sections of the tree's husk shed. She pulled more and more from the trunk, like she was looking for something buried in the tree.

Piece after piece, the old bark crumbled in her hands, revealing rotten flesh beneath. Then she started clawing into the rot, to the dead hollow of the tree.

Nothing was as it should have been. The rot ran from bark to bark.

As I looked out over the forest, a field of lifeless giants climbed into the night sky, each as rotten as the next. Smoke rose from deep in the forest. The trees were kindling, waiting for fire.

"Shay! Shay, you need to run!" I screamed. "Come with me!"

She didn't move from the tree. She didn't even look at me.

In my fear, I ran to her and reached out, but she stepped beyond my grasp. When she turned, a burn sprawled over her face. The flesh peeled back from the wound around her eye, colored with ash and char. With every step I took towards her, she edged back. Her brow arched. Her bottom lip trembled as her tears ran streaks of blood down the remnants of her face. Then I spoke her name, and she ran.

Deeper and deeper, we raced through the forest towards the fire.

"Stop, Shay. Please, stop. Please, don't leave."

The closer I got, the faster she ran. When I screamed for her, my lungs filled with smoke, and she pressed farther into the forest. Fire surrounded us, and still she ran into the heart of it, until everything, everywhere flames and smoke leaped into the sky. In the distance, her silhouette fell to the forest floor.

———

When I sprang up from the dream, tears glazed over my eyes. Instead of a fire, thriving trees grew under the autumn sun. No sign of Shay. The new day broke around me, and I was alone in the forest.

"What are you doing here, boy?" a voice called out.

A chorus of fevered drums and screaming chords rushed over me, and, in my fear, The Song took me. I scrambled to my feet and stomped against the earth, raising my right arm like a twisting claw. As my arm rose, thick razorthistle bushes sprouted from the soil in every direction.

CHAPTER TWELVE

"SHIT, that really hurt."

The trees remained empty despite the voices. No green. No yellow. No sunlight glinting off steel blades.

Razorthistle bushes sprawled out for at least ten paces in every direction, the stiff leaves ending in sharp edges. The Song radiated in the background with echoes weaving through it.

Dancers.

"That was impressive," another voice said.

"Impressive? I'm bleeding. Did the kid think he could protect himself with a bush?"

The echoes radiated from behind a heavy thicket of trees and bushes. A shadow shifted under the cover of the forest. "What do you want from me?" I demanded, staring straight at whoever lurked behind the trees. My voice felt rough from disuse.

A man stepped out from behind a tree followed by a second younger man. They wore nearly identical sand-colored robes, water skins draped over their shoulders, short swords hung from their waists, and colorful chani cloth wrapped around their heads.

Jani nomads.

The nomads didn't share any similarities apart from their matching coverings. The older of the two barely rose to the young man's shoulders. His thick red beard contrasted his dark skin and framed his overly-familiar smile.

Between the blade dangling from his belt and his smile, I trusted the blade more.

His companion carried the tall and lean frame of a warrior. His fair, golden brown skin marked him as a northerner. As no one left the Lost Nation, his people must have hailed from the island beyond the Strait of Talmo, Renêqua.

Blood speckled the torn hem of his robe, and he stared at me like a death promise. But, given that he hadn't tried to kill me yet, he was one of the nicer people I had encountered recently.

I held The Song close to me and rested my hand on the hilt of my father's knife. If my history lesson were to be believed, the Jani dedicated themselves to nonviolence, a nation of nomads who lived in harmony with The Blessed Mother. But the occupation changed many things, and now the peaceful nomads wore swords on their hips. Principles bent easier than iron or steel.

The echo around the older nomad crested as he began swirling his arms in front of him. Before I could reach for The Song, the razorthistles started to mature all at once. Their leaves turned to brown, then the branches of the bushes followed until the plants crumbled to the soil, brittle with age.

"You have nothing to fear, boy," the Sonacoan nomad said. "Our spirits are brothers. Why shouldn't we be?" His cheeks spread ever wider, and I tightened my grip on my knife. "My name is Jonac, and this irritable young man is Torrel. What is your name?"

"Leave me alone." My voice lacked the strength of my demand. After everything that had happened—how alone I felt—I wanted to trust him.

Jonac stepped forward, holding his palms up as if approaching a startled animal. "If that is truly what you wish, we will, but I could not pass by a brother spirit and not offer my help. Are you hurt?" His eyes scanned over me, and my eyes followed.

For the first time since I woke up in this strange forest, I looked at myself. A mixture of blood, soil, and ash stained my clothing. A tear ran down my right pant leg, and small gashes and holes marred my robe, each rip matching an accompanying abrasion.

My robes would better suit a corpse.

"Go away!"

"What happened, little brother?" Jonac asked, still walking closer.

"You heard him. Let's go," Torrel said, but Jonac waved him off without breaking eye contact.

He stood within arm's length as my hand shook on the hilt of my blade. Then he reached out and pulled me into him.

For all my walls and anger, his embrace caught me off-guard, and I didn't have the will to push him away. Instead, I sunk into his soft robes and wept as he gripped me tighter.

"Torrel, get some firewood." Jonac held me and patted my shoulder blade.

The young nomad kicked up dirt and muttered to himself, but he walked into the woods as Jonac instructed.

Once alone, Jonac sat me down. His hands moved from one small wound to the next as he fussed over my scrapes and bruises. If he had questions about how I had collected my injuries, he kept them to himself.

I sat in the grass and let him apply poultices to my burns and cuts. The effort it would have taken to fight him was more than I had to give. By the time he finished his examination, he had slathered most of my body with a rough green paste. It quieted the pain like cool water on sunburned skin, but it stunk like rot.

"Thank you," I said—almost whispered—too hesitant to be friendly, yet too much my mother's son not to be polite.

When I looked up at Jonac, he smiled like neither my fear nor my suspicion had affected him in the slightest.

Once every season or two, both the moons disappear from the night's sky. They called it a thief's night because of the mischief people made in the darkness. His irises reminded me of such a night, black as any I had ever seen.

Wrinkles mapped his face when he smiled, but I couldn't judge his age. He acted like a young man, but the traces of gray in his beard suggested otherwise.

The echo shook me from the moment.

Jonac danced over the earth, each step flowing into the next. His body spun and weaved, and the echo followed.

An uneasy feeling crept over my skin. I had heard other spirits sifted through the sieve of The Thief, but hearing The Seed distorted like this sickened my stomach.

He continued his dance, and a small garden grew in his wake. Each step he took, every twist of his arm pulled another plant from the soil or ripened its harvest.

His precision reminded me of Munnie; maybe because I knew so few dancers. Most learned to hide themselves. The Gousht dragged the rest away to the mines after stripping them of their connection to their spirit ancestors, like the water dancer from the caller's stage.

A dozen different plants spread out over the ground between us. It would have taken me hours of reaching for one species of flora at a time.

When Jonac stopped, and his echo subsided, he dabbed sweat from his brow with a piece of fabric and smiled at me. If he hid anything devious in his grin, he hid it well.

"Little brother, make yourself useful and dig up those carrots." Jonac didn't waste any time. He pulled a pot from his pack and rinsed it with a splash of water before collecting his harvest.

Turns of lessons, and constant reminders from my parents, worked against any rebellion I may have felt. We respected our elders, and so, with little thought, I dug into the red soil around the newly risen crops.

When Torrel stomped back into the clearing, we had busied ourselves pulling vegetables from the dirt, and he muttered something under his breath. His words didn't carry the distance between us, but the scowl permanently etched on his face indicated it hadn't been pleasant.

The firewood he collected clattered to the ground, breaking the silence before he set to work. His hands moved without hesitation or pause. He stacked the wood meticulously and worked his knife along a length of kindling until he had a pile of shavings. It only took a moment for him to catch a spark from his flint. The shavings burned quick and hot, and then the stack above burst to life.

Its flickering light made his soft brown skin glow in the autumn evening. His headwrap slipped to one side and exposed the coarse brown curls of hair beneath.

After the Hundred-Turn War, the Lost Nation walled themselves behind a forest of stormwoods, and the Renêquans kept to their island. I had never met a northerner before.

"You don't have an accent," I said.

"I was born Jani," Torrel said. The edge to his voice was a blade itself.

A long scar ran from his jawline past his clavicle, straight, like he had been cut open. He adjusted his robe when he caught me staring. His brow furrowed deeper, and his anger aged him.

When he finished working the fire to a steady blaze, he retreated to a nearby tree and rested his back against its trunk to glare at me from a comfortable position.

"Little brother, come here and help me," Jonac said.

When he called me brother, he spoke with an earnestness that drew my spirit towards him.

This man is a stranger, I reminded myself. *A smile is not the same as safety.*

Jonac fumbled around in his pack before handing me several items, one after the other—a large wooden spoon, a pouch of seasonings, and a waterskin.

As he needed them, he called for the pouch and the water. The lines in his face deepened, and his smile faded. He called for the spoon and added another pinch of seasonings to the pot.

When he looked back, my expression had grown as intent as his, and he chuckled. "A proper meal is as serious as prayer."

"Why are there only two of you?" I asked.

"Ah, you've noticed," Jonac said. "Our home and our people are always moving, but you can never be too safe these days. So we're scouting ahead for the rest of our clan."

"Jonac, we don't know this boy," Torrel said in a grizzled voice.

My belly grumbled, and Jonac handed me some blackberries from the bush behind him. "He doesn't look like a spy to me. Tell me, little brother, are you a spy?"

I shook my head, and Jonac continued to tell me all about their clan.

The Jani didn't share much with outsiders, and I had my mother's curiosity, but he didn't shy away from my onslaught of questions.

Their clan moved with the seasons, which kept them hidden from the Gousht, but more than that, it honored their way of life. And, although Jani clans moved independent of one another, they knew the signs to look for should they need to find a friendly fire.

"Ennea hides us from harm," he said. "The Gousht don't know her like we do."

"That hasn't stopped them," I muttered, and his smile softened.

A question saturated the silence that hung between us. Maybe it was unfair to ask, but I had to. "Why did the Jani hide when the Gousht invaded? Why didn't you fight?"

Jonac's face went slack, aging him by a decade. He sighed, then spoke with a heavy voice. "The elders counseled patience. Our people chose to dedicate our lives to Ennea, to forsake violence. During the Great War, we arose as a voice for peace.

"When the invasion began, our people maintained the ways of our ancestors. The elders disavowed those few who left their clans to fight. 'War passes by the land, and the land remains,' they said. I don't know if that is true anymore." Jonac stared into the flames and went quiet.

The guilt spreading across his face was my fault. I shouldn't have said anything. After all, my family hid from the war too, and he didn't owe me an explanation.

An uncomfortable quiet fell over us as the soup finished cooking, and then the sounds of our eating filled the gaps.

"This meal is delicious," I said, hoping to lighten the mood.

Jonac nodded, but his smile did not return. "Herbs and spices," he said. "Give me herbs and spices, and I'll eat the bark off an ironoak if I have to."

I slurped the last of my broth and smiled. After going days without a proper meal, it felt odd to be full. "My father always said, 'A meal without company is only food.'"

Jonac grunted with a full mouth and gave me a wink, but the gloom still hung in the air.

"This is ridiculous," Torrel said. His voice carried a sharp edge. "Our people survived. The Jani don't owe anyone anything—not this kid, not his father. We are nomads, not warriors. If we fought, we would have died like the rest of them. You know that better than most."

Jonac's expression turned darker than the night surrounding us. His brow furrowed, and his mouth went tight. Within the outward wrappings he showed the world, he contained a storm. As he locked eyes with Torrel, the storm subsided as quickly as it came.

"Ennea is not only the land or the spirits who reside here. Ennea is our mother, and she has many children. She weeps with them. She dies with them," he said. "The Jani let our brothers and sisters die." Anger tinted his words, not anger like that of his young companion, but an anger that grew out of grief.

"The Jani do not take sides," Torrel said. "We chose peace."

"Sometimes choosing peace means choosing a side."

"But during the Great War...."

"The Jani chose not to spill Ennean blood. Ennean blood," Jonac said. He sighed and closed his eyes. "Does this look like peace to you?" His voice settled to a whisper.

The rage in Torrel's eyes thinned. He slumped into himself, like he aimed to hide from his shame.

"My mom tried to hide us," I said softly. Speaking about her felt strange now that she had passed into The Mist, but I couldn't think about that. "She moved us from our home in the middle of the night. She thought we could hide in a bigger city, and we did, for a while."

Torrel didn't look at me as I spoke, but the rigidity in his muscles softened.

"We would have hidden if we could have," I said.

For a moment, I thought I might have reached through Torrel's anger, but he turned away, clapped the dirt from his pants, and stalked off into the forest.

"We all have our burdens. Pride is one of his," Jonac said.

He started moving about, cleaning up after dinner. He gathered the three wooden bowls and rinsed them clean, then wiped down the pot and stowed away his spices.

"You have more questions in those eyes than they have room to offer," he said. "The routine helps me find calm, even if peace is too far from reach." He paused his busy hands and faced me. "You could come with us if you wanted."

"You don't know me. You don't even know my name." My belly twisted into knots. If he knew—no one would invite a malitu to follow them home.

"Ah, that is true, but you could fix that," he said with a smile returning to his face.

Five simple words, I thought. *I am a spirit thief. Say it. Say it!*

"We all have our stories, little brother," he said. "And as you can see, we all have our shame."

"This is more than shame," I said.

"Brothers can bear heavier burdens together." Jonac reached his hands out to me.

An unknown, unending forest surrounded us, and no one in all of its expanse even knew to look for me. I had nowhere to go.

Forgive me, I thought.

I clasped his right hand between both of mine. "My name is Kaylo."

CHAPTER THIRTEEN

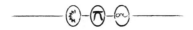

THE NOMADS SLEPT IN shifts. I didn't sleep at all.

The campfire blazed beside me as I stared into the night's sky, trying to block out the echoes emanating from Jonac and Torrel. Whether or not the nomads slept, the distorted glimpses into The Song whispered to me from every angle. As one echo faded, the other would crescendo.

When The Gousht invaded, I struggled for several turns to close out The Seed, and still he slipped through my barriers from time to time. If things continued this way, the echoes would drive me insane before I learned how to control them.

As Toka crested over the highest point in the sky, I stoked the fire and took out my father's knife. It slipped through the segment of birchwood without resistance, and the shavings fell to the ground at my feet. Indentations in the leather wrapping around the knife's hilt marked where my father had held the blade, but my fingers didn't fit the grooves he left behind.

The blade jumped as it ran over a knot in the wood and bit my finger. Blood trickled from the small cut. I didn't deserve his blade, so I set it beside me with the blood-smeared scrap of birch.

Over the latter half of the night, while Torrel held watch, he glared at me. The whispers from his echo sounded like a threat. As unpleasant as Torrel had been, he had read the situation correctly. I was dangerous. Over the course of one night, my decisions had killed three of the people I loved most in the world.

When Jonac woke up, I had dug myself deep enough into my self-loathing that I barely heard him call my name. He put me to work, and I helped pack away the camp.

I shouldn't do this, I thought. They didn't deserve the troubles I carried with me.

"Boy, get moving," Jonac said. "You're going to have to get used to a faster pace. This isn't the city."

Even though he spoke far more and wore his expressions in plain view, Jonac carried the same calm in his spirit as my father.

I nodded and set to finishing my tasks.

Once every last knot slipped into place, we each hefted our loads and turned our backs to the sun. I had made a decision—even if it was the wrong one.

While I walked, the noises of the forest carried on as if nothing had changed, but The Song didn't join in the commotion. I lowered my barriers and reached for The Seed for comfort, but only the bastard versions of The Song greeted me.

No matter how far I fell behind the nomads, their echoes clung to the air around me.

Maybe I deserved the torment.

We walked from the first glimpse of the sun to the rising of the second moon. When we stopped, I nearly collapsed on the ground and passed out in the dirt, and we still had two more days of hard walking in front of us.

Autumn's chill had set in, and the moons had climbed above the canopy by the time we finished our supper. The quilt Jonac gave me did little to keep away the cold. So, I lay close to the fire, searching for sleep, only for Torrel's snoring to fill the forest. The lucky prick.

Eventually, even the snoring faded into the background. Nothing could keep me away from sleep, not after two days without, not even The Song and its offshoots. Then, as sleep spread over me like welcomed warmth, Jonac jostled my shoulder. He hovered over me, grinning like a child.

"What's wrong? Is it my shift?" Only a lifetime of my mother's rearing kept my voice respectful.

"Do you want to play a game?" he asked.

"A game?" The last remnant of my willpower kept me from tossing dirt in his eye, but I couldn't keep the barbs from my tone. Yet, he continued to smile, and the genuineness of it broke my irritation. "Sure, why not?"

He sat cross-legged on the ground and pulled out two leather pouches from his travel sack. The fire flickered next to us as he carefully drew his belt knife through the dirt, three lines one way and another three across.

As he sorted things out, he explained the game. I must have nodded off once or twice because when he finished, I had no idea what I had to do. He tossed a pouch to me and told me to pull out five runes.

Five pebble-sized pieces of ironoak stained black sat in my palm, each identical to the last, save a marking carved into one side.

What am I supposed to do with these? I thought. *If I throw them at the nomad, I can go to sleep.*

The rough markings had a touch of something familiar as I ran my fingers over them. Maybe I had seen them in one of the old books my mother kept hidden away.

"Spirit marks," Jonac said. "Runes from before the Great War, before the nations brought together our disparate dialects into one common tongue."

Jonac pulled out one rune of his pouch after another and identified each of the six runes, each great spirit, except The Thief. "There was a time when children of Ennea marked their flesh with these runes as a symbol of their connection to The Song," Jonac said. "Luckily, those days are beyond us."

"My mother said they used hot iron to burn the symbols into their arms. I was a bad student, but that made an impression," I said and smiled. "She said our knowledge would outlast the Gousht, even if we couldn't."

As I spoke about my mother, my chest constricted, but the pain carried a strange comfort as well. If my memories of her could hurt me, she couldn't have been completely gone.

"Wise woman," Jonac said.

He continued to explain the game. Each player tried to claim five of the nine crosspoints. During their turn, one player could place a rune face down on an empty crosspoint or challenge an opponent's facedown rune. If a challenger won, they would replace the rune with one from their hand. Then they could play again or end their turn. If they lost, they lost the crosspoint permanently to the defending player.

"So, you can only claim a crosspoint when you're defending?" I asked. "That doesn't make any sense."

Jonac shrugged and smiled. "I didn't make up the rules," he said, though I wasn't sure that was true.

The game required luck and memory. Both pouches contained two of every spirit rune, and each spirit would win against half the others and lose against the rest. It was simple and utterly complicated at the same time, which is to say I didn't understand the game at all.

He gave his pouch a shake and drew out five pieces of whittled ironoak stained white. We played several games over the next hour or so. I could barely stay awake, let alone remember which spirit defeated which. Even as Jonac kindly reminded me, he didn't hesitate to take advantage of my stupid mistakes, smiling and winking at me every time he won another game.

None of our matches lasted longer than five minutes, except for our final game of the night. I held him off for twenty minutes, exchanging one rune for another. He had claimed four crosspoints, but I refused to allow him to take his fifth. When he challenged one of my facedown runes with The River, I turned it over to reveal The Shadow and won my third crosspoint.

One facedown, white marker lay on the map, awaiting my turn. I looked at the runes in my hand, picked one, and slid it forward to challenge. The Flame rune shined in the fire's light, and Jonac smiled as he slowly turned over The Wind.

"Nice game, little brother," he said with a taunting smile.

I sucked my teeth. "Why are we playing this game anyway?"

"That is a good question," Jonac said and started collecting the runes into the two pouches.

"Are you going to answer the question?"

"Now, what kind of kana would I be if I did that?" he asked.

Kana? My breath stopped halfway to my lungs. *He doesn't know me. He found me wandering the forest alone. Why would he want to be my kana?*

"No, little brother, if I gave you all the answers, you wouldn't have to search. Answers are worth more when you seek them out," he said. He didn't even think twice about calling himself my kana. "Why do you think we are playing Runes?"

I sat there speechless, staring at this man I met a day ago.

"Kaylo, why do you think we are playing this game?"

"I don't know." My voice sounded breathy and odd. "You're trying to teach me a lesson."

"Not a bad answer. Technically correct, and if that's all the answer you need, then it will do," he said. "You are tired. Sleep, and maybe you will find an answer in your dreams. At the very least, you will stop yawning every thirty seconds." He collected the pouches, swiped his hand over the lines in the dirt, and retired to his bedroll.

Lying beside the fire, questions and echoes surrounded me, but my exhaustion conquered them both.

———

A field of black surrounded me. Three rows of boulders lay on a deep gash in the ground, each stained black or white, the grain of the ironoak wood creating patterns along the surfaces.

As I walked along the chasm, I dragged my hand along the smooth surface of a boulder. It stood taller than me and was cold to the touch.

At the end of the row, a glossy, black boulder waited for me. The ironoak had been perfectly finished, smoothed until the oblong carving created a line of absolute symmetry. My distorted reflection warped around the surface.

He grinned at me, though I did not smile back.

When I blinked, he disappeared.

A shiver ran through me as I stepped towards the stained surface. It took a hold of something in my core and pulled me closer. I reached out a hand, and my fingers slipped into the surface as if the boulder were made of liquid. Cold fire tingled along my skin.

This was wrong.

Every instinct screamed, and I tried to pull my hand away, but the boulder clung to me. No matter how I yanked backwards, I only sank deeper into the boulder. A shimmer crossed the surface, transforming into my grinning reflection.

The lines of his braids mapped his scalp in the same pattern as mine, strains coming loose in the same places from abuse and neglect. He had a matching scar at the far edge of his eye from when I dropped a clay pot when I was five. Spatters of dirt accented his skin, and, in every other way, he was me, except for how his cheeks pulled back into a gentle smile.

"What are you?" I asked.

His mouth faded away, leaving the rest of his features undisturbed. Then the glossy surface jerked me into the blackness.

Icy fire crawled over my entire body. Every direction I turned, black nothingness stared back at me.

When I looked down, a smattering of markers lay on a grid of intersecting lines, and a shadow-cloaked figure sat on the opposite side of the game.

Where the figure moved, the shadow followed. They reached forward and left behind a facedown rune on an empty crosspoint. My opponent's white runes far outnumbered mine.

I reached into my pouch and drew five oblong pieces of ironoak. Each time I challenged, my opponent flipped over their marker and won another crosspoint. In a field of white runes, I laid down a final challenge.

The glossy white pebble of ironoak lay face down. Yet, somehow, I knew what rune would be etched into the other side. The shadow-cast hand slowly turned over the rune, revealing The Thief's marking.

My eyes snapped open as the light of the new sun poured through gaps in the canopy, and, for all the passing hours, my exhaustion clung to me still, the dream another weight to weigh me down.

Off in the distance, The Song sang in the forest. I rubbed the crust from my eyes and tried to pull my senses about me.

Torrel leaned against a tree, humming to himself. He hadn't looked in my direction since I stirred. For the first time, he looked content. *Probably thinking about strangling a kitten,* I thought.

When I turned to look for Jonac, I met his eyes, and his smile spread as wide as it always did. Sleep had taken a dozen turns from his face. *How old is this man?* I wondered for the dozenth time. Even if I guessed, I couldn't be sure I would get the decade right.

He waved me over, and I joined him in breaking down the small camp. As I emptied my waterskin over the last few embers of the fire, the smell of wet ash touched painful memories, but I shook them off and focused on the next task. Someone had to fill the waterskins.

Our path ran parallel to Clear River, so water was never too far away. When the camp fell out of sight, the echoes faded until they finally disappeared. My mind unraveled. The pressure in my head dissipated, and my body became my own once more.

Twittering birds, gusts of wind, and The Song filled the forest with a familiar melody. Nothing else.

Taking my fill in the process, I filled the waterskins one by one, the brisk river water stinging my skin in a pleasant way. When I finished, I soaked my feet in the river and let the current lap against my calves. The moment lingered on too long, but going back meant wading into the echoes.

"When a thing must be done, waiting only adds weight to the task," I said, and my father's words stung in a pleasant way. So, I pulled my feet from the water and laced up my boots.

As the echoes returned, they were less abrasive, like a nagging horsefly rather than a swarm of hornets.

Torrel stiffened when he saw me, settling back into his usual welcoming demeanor, a mixture of stoicism and contempt. I met his glare in turn. If he wanted to be adversarial, I could accommodate him.

We could have spent the entire morning locked in silent battle, but Jonac walked up to me, cast his arm over my shoulder, and turned me to gather my things.

As I took inventory of my travel sack, my mother's book sat at the bottom, still in its wrapping. My spirit settled, knowing that I had her words with me. I brushed my fingers against the blue cloth before tying off the sack with everything in its place.

As we started out, we settled our stomachs with saltmeat. Jonac and I walked out front, with Torrel glaring at me from behind. When I made to face him, Jonac placed a hand on my shoulder, steering me forward.

"Why does he hate me?"

"Torrel is a good man. A young man, a stubborn man, but a good man. The invasion cost him as much as any and left him the untrusting sort," Jonac said.

"Ever since the fighting began, people from all over the eastern nations sought refuge with the Jani. As is our way, we welcomed them....

"I am explaining this wrong." He silently composed his thoughts and began again. "The strength of the green army has always been their numbers and their willingness to cross any line in service of their god. The Jani survived because we know Ennea better than any nation. Our small clans used the land and avoided the blood, for the most part.

"One day, the clan came across a small group of slaves who escaped the mines. The elements had torn and beaten their bodies, but their true wounds lay deeper than their skin. The Jani collected them from where they collapsed in the wood and cleaned them up. The runaways told the elders their story, and it shamed the elders to have done nothing to stop such suffering. The council welcomed the runaways into the clan."

Jonac stared forward as he told his story. His voice turned husky and muddled.

"Three days later, the Gousht ambushed the clan. They nearly sent us all to The Mist, but Torrel's mother saved us. She wielded The Flame with a deadly grace and dragged ten soldiers into The Mist alongside her. When the smoke cleared, more than half the clan lay lifeless on the ground, and Torrel sat in the dirt covered in his mother's blood, holding what remained of her body. He was fourteen, and she was the only family he had. That's when I took him in."

"Filthy blood banners." My heart thudded in my temples as the image of Rena standing beside the priest flashed inside my mind. "How could they betray you to the Gousht?"

Jonac winced at the unpleasant moniker. "No, you don't understand. The Gousht let the slaves escape. The runaways didn't know that soldiers had tracked them. We will never know whether the soldiers were after the Jani, the Missing, or whether they cared at all." He shook his head. "Maybe it doesn't matter."

I looked back at Torrel. The Gousht might not have been following me, but The Thief walked with me towards their home. The look of disgust on Shay's face flashed in front of me, and I saw myself as she must have—a malitu.

My throat caught on the thought, and I choked it down. "I promise

I'm not being followed," I said.

Jonac clapped my back and nodded. "I know, little brother. It doesn't matter. Trust is a hard thing to share after it has been badly damaged."

We walked through the heaviness of the moment as bloody memories thickened the air. I shouldn't have pried into a history I didn't understand. In Torrel's place, I would have felt the same way about taking in a strange boy from the forest.

We found a clearing in the early evening and made camp. Torrel busied himself building a fire, and I walked back to the river. My body ached from too many days of taking too many steps, but I needed to be alone with the forest.

The riverbanks opened wider than before, and the riverbed sank deeper into the plot of land. I walked waist-deep into the river and washed my face in the slow pull of the water. Days of travel fell from my skin. The cool air bit me, no longer muted by the many layers of dirt.

With the waterskins full and heavy over my shoulders, I found my way back to our fire. The conversation hushed as soon as they saw me, and Torrel's face hardened. Jonac offered a light smile and a bowl of fresh soup. He hadn't the time to allow the meat and herbs to thicken the water properly, but he had seasoned it well.

Several new plants sprouted from overturned soil on the outskirts of our camp. At least I had been far away when he pulled them from The Song. Hearing The Seed through someone else still unsettled me, and it only got worse when he danced.

After we ate, Jonac drew lines in the dirt and tossed a pouch of runes at my feet. I begrudgingly played. At least it served as a distraction from the tension between Torrel and me.

As I drew five runes from the pouch, I did my best to remember the rules of the game. We played several times, and each time I lost. During one game, we deadlocked until the very end, when I challenged the last open crosspoint with The Mountain. He chuckled to himself as he turned over The Shadow. He still found each win as amusing as the first.

"You're getting better."

"I still haven't won a single game."

Jonac grunted disapprovingly. "My young toka, I don't offer false compliments like a child courting your affections." It was a gentle rebuke, but being the first, it burned.

"You are young, both in age and spirit, which isn't a bad thing. Not inherently a good thing either. It is a time for us all to carve our markings into the world. Don't confuse losing a game with losing. Consider instead what you have gained. You learned a new game, and each time you played with more understanding than the last."

Looking up from the ground, I met Jonac's hard eyes as he spoke like he needed me to understand his words. "If I am to be your kana, you cannot measure your growth in wins and losses. Instead, measure your growth by your knowledge and skill. If you concentrate on the outcome of the game, how can you ever understand its lesson?"

He lifted his eyebrows like he expected an answer.

"The game is about strategy," I said after taking a moment to think. "It's like armies meeting on a battlefield."

Jonac smiled and chuckled. "Were I a wiser man, you might be right. But I am a nomad, not a warrior." He shook his head and chuckled again. "It's not a bad answer though. Not bad by far."

"We've played a dozen, maybe two dozen times, and I was thinking...I mean, I didn't see...I don't remember...."

"Out with it, boy. What did you think, see, remember?" he asked with a smile.

"There are only six runes."

Jonac's expression stilled and darkened. "My game has no place for evil spirits."

My muscles seized as if he had struck me with all his strength, but that kind of pain faded with time. I had only known Jonac for three days.

At my lowest, he had offered me friendship and safety, neither of which I deserved. I stole them from him—like a thief.

When I turned my head back to the game, I nodded in agreement.

CHAPTER FOURTEEN

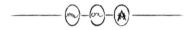

THE SHADOW-CAST HAND REACHED forward and withdrew, leaving a rune on the last empty crosspoint. Neither of us had attacked, as if we measured each other with each token we placed, walking the battlefield before spilling blood.

Against the backdrop of blackness, the figure in front of me was little more than an outline. They didn't speak. They only moved to play the game.

The battlefield was set with a rune covering each crosspoint, and the challenge belonged to me. I fiddled with the small pieces of ironoak, whittled down, polished, and stained black. They weighed heavy in my hand.

It's only a game, I told myself.

My finger traced over the engraved runes, then I grabbed one without looking and placed it next to a crosspoint. The Wind. The shadowed figure revealed their piece. The Flame. My heart beat again.

The minor victory didn't last. My opponent took one crosspoint after another until white runes littered the field.

My hand shook as I selected my next piece. The match stood at four crosspoints to two. If I didn't win the next challenge, the shadowed figure would claim the match.

Whatever the stakes, my opponent wouldn't hesitate to call the debt due. My chest tightened. I stared into the fog of shadows.

"Who are you? What do you want?" I asked.

A throaty chuckle emanated from the shadows and filled the vast void. It rattled through my bones, and my muscles tensed. I had to escape. There had to be an end to this empty prison, but my body refused to move.

Suddenly, each of the white ironoak pieces on the crosspoints moved of their own accord, flipping over to reveal the same rune—The Thief.

"My game has no place for evil spirits," the shadow-cloaked figure said with a raspy, unused voice. They let out a slow, joyless chuckle. Solid black hands reached out of the shadows and peeled back their hood.

"No place at all," said The Thief.

I jerked up from my nightmare, drenched in sweat. No matter how I tried to shake her loose, her visage followed me. The Thief. Soft curves formed cheekbones in perfect symmetry. Her skin, the deepest black from her nose up and porcelain white down. Eyes white against the contrast of her onyx skin. Her mouth—she didn't have a mouth, and yet, it hadn't been an absence. Every feature fell into balance with the rest.

How did she speak if she didn't have a mouth?

My stomach churned raw acid in the back of my throat. *It was only a dream.* I rubbed at my eyes and tried to anchor myself to the forest.

"Kaylo," Jonac called out as he changed his robes. His tone told me he had called to me several times already, and Torrel's glare confirmed it. "Wake up and make yourself ready. If we get moving, we should be home before the sun touches high. That is, if you can make it back with water before we clear camp."

Curly red hair covered his barrel-chest. He bent down to reach into his travel sack and the light caught several long, silver scars that crawled from his shoulder blades to his side. They had aged, but whatever had made them cut deep into his flesh.

Despite the pain of his past, Jonac found a way to be cheerful. He pulled a new robe from his sack and slipped his arms into the sand-colored cloth. Chani cloth, dyed several shades of purple, wrapped around the crown of his head. Only the sun could outshine his smile.

My game has no place for evil spirits.

Something about The Thief stirred a hatred in Jonac that didn't fit with the man in front of me.

The echo around him surged to life. As he danced, the plants he called from the soil the previous night aged, then fell to the ground as ash. The Jani did not leave their mark on the land. If we disturbed Ennea, we had to set it right. The fact that it hid our tracks only served as an afterthought. Serving The Mother always came first.

"Boy," Jonac called out. "The river is that way."

I couldn't find my tongue, so I turned and ran in the direction he pointed without a word.

For all his kindness, Jonac hid an anger within him that The Thief unleashed. He could never know what I was. For both of our sakes, I would have to keep my distance.

Besides, I hated The Thief too.

We broke camp too late for Jonac's liking. The later we left, the longer he had to wait to see his wife and children.

Of course, Torrel blamed me. He looked at me like the soldiers in Nomar had. It wasn't hatred so much as I represented a hindrance, something to be moved aside. Though, in practice, it worked the same as hatred.

As we made our way, I fell behind the nomads. They needed time together, and I needed to settle myself. The Song sang clearer than it had in days, maybe moons. Everything else fell into the background as I listened to The Seed's call. If Munnie was here, she would ask me to describe the sound of The Song.

Today, it moved like a soft breeze. Often—too often, The Song forced its way through my barriers. It reached for me and pulled me into the dance. It demanded my attention. But today, the melody invited me along.

A part of me followed the path behind the nomads, but my spirit danced with The Song. I lost myself to it. No, not lost. I joined its rhythm, and The Song embraced me. Everything else became inconsequential. The crests and troughs of The Song swelled around me. A peace, which I had never known before, settled over the world.

"Kaylo!" Jonac shook me by the shoulders, and my spirit rebounded back into my body.

My vision split the forest in two, and then the images converged. Sokan reached far too high for the hour. The Song receded back into the forest.

Jonac's eyes were wide with panic. "Little brother, are you okay?"

"It was beautiful. I was walking with The Song," I said with a giddy smile, though he did not return my joy.

"You were walking in The Mist. The things you do not know about the spirits astound me," he said and waved Torrel ahead. "Tell me what you know about The Song."

We walked, and I began telling him about the first time I heard The Song. He listened and grunted occasionally to let me know he was following my words. I told him of the turns I spent learning to block out Ennea's pull and how Shay and I found our kana.

My voice cracked several times as I recalled how Munnie found Shay and me playing with The Song deep in the forest. He must have heard the grief in my voice because I couldn't begin to hide it. Thankfully, he didn't ask all the questions I couldn't bear.

When I finished my story, he grunted, and his eyebrows furrowed. "You told me about your experiences with The Song, but you never said what it is. Do you know what The Song is?"

It was the kind of silly question Munnie would ask me. Might as well ask me to describe the taste of a strawberry. I could call it sweet and tart, but that would mean nothing to someone who had never tried one.

The Song was something that was, and it didn't need any more definition, but he didn't want to hear that.

"The Song is The Mist. It is the manifestation of the spirits. It is Ennea," I said, repeating the nonsense Munnie told me.

He shook his head. "You are playing with dangerous powers, little brother."

"For the first time in my life, The Seed and I moved together. We were one. What's dangerous about that?"

"Everything. When you said The Song is The Mist, you were right. If you fall too deeply into The Song, you could lose your spirit to The Mist," Jonac said. "The barriers you built to hold back The Song are strong. When you learn how to control them, you will be a powerful force, but you have happened into a hard lesson. I need you to trust me. Don't give yourself to The Song like that again, not before you give me a chance to explain it better."

The lingering sensation of that peace teased me with a promise. When I walked with The Song, I didn't see Shay dying or my mother's tears. I didn't have to hide. The Gousht knew nothing of that place. This life held far more dangers than The Song.

Jonac's expression fell flat. I tried to ignore his glare, but eventually I bent. "I promise," I said. He had earned a chance to convince me, though I doubted he could.

He waited a moment longer, opened his mouth to speak, but didn't. Then he nodded and joined Torrel out front as if nothing had happened.

That man had secrets. As genuine as he was, layers hid beneath the surface. His hatred for The Thief went beyond superstition. And the scars along his back had a story. For a peaceful nomad, he had a well-versed relationship with violence.

And yet, he had only shown me compassion. Without question, he had fed me. He offered to teach me about The Song. It would mean keeping secrets of my own, but I didn't have a plethora of choices.

I chuckled to myself.

My hosts made an odd pairing—the height disparity, the decades separating them, the contrast of their complexions, and the jarring differences in their personalities. One tried to overcome his violence, and the other readied his sword. I couldn't imagine two more different people, and yet, for all their incongruities, they wore the same sand-colored robes. They both had their scars, and it made them a family of a sort.

Jonac started humming, and the tune carried back as I trailed behind. After one round of the chorus, he gave his voice to the old song, one my father had sung many times while whittling away on the corner chair.

> *Hundreds of turns upon her soil*
> *I've yet to meet The Mother*
> *Hundred turns of heartache and toil*
> *Yet to hear her voice*
> *When she calls me, I'll be ready*
> *When she takes me, I'll be home*
> *To The Mist to meet The Mother*
> *Where so many have gone before*

Jonac's voice didn't have the deep bass of my father's, but his rich baritone carried the song well. The eerie lullaby left me in a state of melancholic longing.

As he sang, I hummed along, but I stopped halfway through the next verse as a whispering noise undercut the tune.

After four days, I learned to tolerate the nomad's irritating echoes. My barriers quieted the bastard versions of The Song enough to keep my head from rattling off my shoulders. The constant reminder of my connection to The Thief grated on me, but I could bear it.

These new whispers added their voices and grew into a chorus of echoes that tore over me like a gust of wind. My vision wobbled, and I stumbled over my feet. The sound of a dozen and more echoes called out from the forest, growing louder and demanding more. They blended into and bounced off each other.

Jonac and Torrel turned toward the echoes, and I lagged behind. A line of ironoaks grew so close together they could hardly be called separate trees. One gap parted the two sections of the tree wall, and the nomads walked directly towards it.

We had reached the Jani encampment.

The ironoaks filled The Song and The Seed, and I knew them down to their intertwining roots tangled beneath the soil. Where one ended, another began. Only a forest dancer could call forth a wall such as this. But the Jani didn't leave any trace behind. When they left, the trees would be discarded.

Jonac stood at the entrance and waved me forward.

When my mother described the Jani as a simple people, I misinterpreted that to mean plain.

Where I had imagined meek tents surrounding a communal fire, a small tent city sprang up from the forest floor within the wall of ironoaks. Covered in furs and tanned hides dyed in vibrant colors, more than a dozen tents rose into the sky. The sheer number of tents blocked my view of the other side of the tree wall that surrounded the encampment.

Each colorful canopy sat upon its own lot. Gardens and communal firepits spread out across the open land. Hedges and bright flowers surrounded the largest tent in the center of the encampment. Several trees carried the burden of the massive canopy. If need dictated, the entire clan could congregate beneath the structure.

I followed Jonac through the encampment. People moved about their tasks, but they hesitated as I walked by. Most offered smiles. Some watched with lingering eyes. One old woman pulled me into a hug and patted me on the cheek when she let me go.

"That's Siani," Jonac said with a smile and continued walking.

Descendants of every nation walked through the camp. Everyone wore some shade of sand-colored robes with colorful chani cloth wrapped around their hair. Everyone except the children, who nearly trampled me as they ran by, their hair flowing free in the autumn air.

There weren't any soldiers on patrol, the broken circle didn't hang from a tower like a warning, and people smiled easy.

This is freedom, I thought.

Jonac clapped me on the back, and I jumped. "Welcome to the Fallen Rock Clan," he said. "It's a sight, isn't it? I remember the first time I saw it. It looked like a cup of water to a man dying of thirst." He handed me a waterskin with a wink.

"How do you travel with it all?" I asked.

"Ahh, good question. We leave the trees," he said, then chuckled at his own joke. "Come, there are people you should meet."

Row after row of gardens lined the pathways of the tent city, all arranged with intent. Several fruits and vegetables I couldn't name grew from the soil. These gardens would require time and attention that I would never have had in Nomar. More than that, some gardens grew no food at all, just flowers arranged in pretty patterns.

As if he heard my thoughts, Jonac said, "There is more to life than survival."

I wanted to believe him.

He gripped my shoulder as he guided me forward, weaving through the spaces between tents and gardens. I had almost forgotten the echoes until one boomed below the ground I walked upon.

My feet froze, and I reached for my knife. Then a dancer moved with slow, solid footsteps, and as she moved, the ground shook around her. She planted her feet and pivoted. Three stones, each larger than the other, forced their way through the soil. A young girl watched and clapped her hands.

People walked by without even noticing. When the young girl tried to copy the dancer, she didn't check for any watching eyes. She simply reached for The Song and it came.

Her echo rang out as much as the older dancer's had, but softer and more hesitant.

"There are fifteen families in our clan, unless something changed while I was gone." Jonac said. "Everyone is free, and everyone contributes. We have a few simple rules to live by. We all stay within the wall unless given permission. What belongs to the individual belongs to the clan, and what belongs to the clan belongs to the individual. And we don't keep anyone who wouldn't be kept. There are some other rules, but those will get you started."

"It sounds too perfect."

Jonac chuckled. "It does, doesn't it? In some ways, it is. Like any people, we disagree, and there are hardships. In a few days, we will pack camp and carry our life to a new plot of land. We have a couple of carts and a few donkeys, but for the most part, people carry their own load. Then we will do it all again come spring. It isn't an easy life."

All this beauty and freedom, I thought. *The Gousht will destroy this too.*

I looked at the gardens and saw the flowers burning, ash covering the forest, the people disappearing into nothingness.

When I came to myself, I stood in front of a Tomakan woman and her children. She stood tall and full in her Jani robes, sky blue cloth wrapped around her hair, which fell easily over her shoulder. Her smile creased her face with age in the most elegant way. She made me ache for home.

She had my mother's coloring, the warm brown of whisper willow bark. Her nose stretched wider and her jawline cut stronger, but seeing her made me think of my mother. I swallowed my emotion and returned her smile as best as I could.

"Blessed Mother, it is good to meet you, Kaylo," she said. She reached out, and I clasped her right hand between both of mine as she did the same.

"My wife, Nomi, and our daughters, Soca and Junera," Jonac said.

Soca might have been five turns, but no more. She had her father's dark skin and red hair, but she looked like a mirror image of her mother. She stood tall and full, with her arms wrapped around her mother's thigh. She peeked up at me, then fell behind her mother's robe again.

"That's Soca," Junera said, stepping out front, unafraid. "I'm Junera." She was younger and shorter. Her skin was lighter than her sister's, but she still had her father's red curls.

She looked like Shay, or at least close enough. I choked back my grief and bent down to her level. "I'm Kaylo."

"I know, silly," Junera said. "Mommy said that."

"Girls, how about you go, show our guest inside, and pull out a spare bedroll for him," Nomi said.

Junera grabbed my hand. "Come with me, or Mommy will get upset."

I followed her in, and Soca followed behind at a safe distance. Two woven mats divided the packed and swept dirt floor into the sitting room and sleeping areas. A large stone-lined firepit surrounded by several stumps sat between the two mats.

It measured longer and wider than the home I grew up in by half, and still it felt cozy. The light from the fire bounced off the vibrant canopy and created a soft, warm light that spread through the tent.

I was gawking at their home from inside the entrance when Junera called for me to follow her to the sleeping area.

Soca pulled a bedroll from a chest and tentatively handed it to me. I thanked her, and she rushed back to her sister.

"Where are you from? You're from Tomak like Mommy, right? Are you a dancer? Are you a fire dancer? Can you show me? I'm a water dancer like Mommy, but I can't do much yet. Do you want to see? You're big. I bet you can do a lot." Junera asked her questions without taking a single breath. When she stopped, she looked at me as if she expected an answer to each question immediately.

When I laughed, she folded her arms and glowered. So, I sat the bedroll down and tried my best to answer the questions I could remember.

As Jonac pushed through the entrance, Junera lost her focus. "Daddy, I'm going to show Kaylo my water dancing, and then he's going to show me his forest dancing," Junera announced. "I wanted him to be a fire dancer. I've already seen a bunch of forest dancers."

Jonac smiled at his daughter and told her, "We are all disappointed Kaylo is a forest dancer, but that can't be helped, can it?"

"That's not nice," Soca said. "You aren't being nice."

Jonac swept his oldest daughter into his arms and nodded. "You're right, love." He kissed her on her brow. "I'm sorry, Kaylo," he said with a wink. Then he put Soca down.

"I'm sorry too," Junera said. She stuck her lower lip out, which made her all the cuter. I told her I forgave her, which seemed to cheer her up.

"Girls, go and find your mother," Jonac said. "I need to have a word with Kaylo."

Junera objected, but then her older sister grabbed her hand and pulled her towards the exit.

"Okay, but we'll be back," Junera called out.

We laughed to ourselves as the girls left the tent, then Jonac walked over to the firepit. He motioned for me to take a seat, filled a pot with water, and hung it over the fire. "Tea?" he asked.

I nodded, and he riffled through a collection of dried herbs and tea leaves. He wrapped a heavy pinch of tea leaves in a larger leaf and sealed it with a sliver of wood. It was artful. As he made a second pouch, his hands moved with the ease of routine, then he brought over two cups.

"You have a lovely family," I said, and Jonac nodded his thanks.

When the water reached a boil, he poured the water into each of our cups. I reached for mine, but he gestured for me to wait. "Youth is always in such a rush," he said. "I want to discuss what happened earlier today, when you slipped into The Song."

"I'm sorry," I started, but he cut me off.

"Don't apologize," he said. "Tell me what happened."

"I usually have to search for The Song. Sometimes I can't even find it, but the last day or two it's been there, right at the edge of my thoughts."

"Why do you think that is, little brother?"

"I've never known another descendant of The Seed," I guessed.

Jonac smiled. "You give me too much credit. Can you remember a time when you didn't have to search for The Song?"

"When I was little, I used to play with The Song for hours, but my mother moved us to Nomar and forbade me from dancing."

"She kept you safe, and you learned how to block out The Song. It's a common story these days," he said. "You are accustomed to holding yourself apart, and you needed a distraction."

"The runes?"

Jonac nodded. "A dancer and The Song should be like two hands reaching for each other, but you taught yourself not to reach back. Then when you needed to find The Song, you groped in the darkness," he said. "You needed a distraction, and I needed an opponent."

"What happened today?" I asked. "Is that what dancing should feel like?"

"The Mist is all around us, just beyond our reach. It is as much a part of Ennea as The Waking. When children of Ennea hear The Song, we glimpse the edges of The Mist and the spirits living within."

"And I reached too far into The Mist?"

"Yes and no," he said. "You must have a truly deep connection to the spirits to walk The Mist."

"What would have happened if I stayed there?"

"Dancers who aren't ready can lose themselves," he said. "Your body in The Waking, your spirit in The Mist."

The Song whispered underneath the crackling fire, like a soft promise. It didn't feel dangerous. "Have you ever walked in The Mist?" I asked.

Jonac stared into the flames. He went still. "Once."

Chapter Fifteen

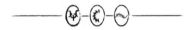

Tayen weighed the blade's balance. The leather-covered hilt scraped against her palm. No matter how many times Kaylo chastised her, she gripped the weapon like she could vicariously strangle the life from her opponent. When she loosened her grip, blood started flowing into her fingers once again, but it felt off. Something about squeezing the knife rooted her in the moment, promising her a control she rarely felt. Her blisters would turn to callouses within the moon.

Kaylo stood with his back turned, waiting for her to attack. She brushed the dirt off her robe. Her lips curled into a snarl. *The arrogance.* He enjoyed making her look foolish, taunting her with his blindfold. Almost a pair of span had passed, and Tayen had lost count of how many times she failed.

At first, Tayen had been sure Kaylo wore a blindfold as a part of the trick. She cut her own fabric and pulled it tightly over his eyes, but no matter how she attacked him, he countered.

As they rotated between this strange training drill and practicing the basics of sword fighting with whittled branches, her bruises had begun to overlap. It hurt to move most nights, even more in the mornings. But the embarrassment of being tossed to the ground by a blindfolded man made her grind her heels into the dirt, always coming back the next day with a new plan.

She had tried wrapping him in shadow, sending all the shadows from the forest in pops of disorienting light, distracting him with different noises in the forest, and a countless number of other useless strategies. Today would be different.

She stood still and confident, though she had begun to look more like her kana than she would care to admit. The early autumn air brushed her skin through the tears in her robes and pants despite her best attempt to patch them with mismatched fabric. Every night, she worked her braids into some semblance of what they had been. No way on The Mother's soil would she let her hair hang wild and dirty like Kaylo's—her father taught her better.

Wind picked up in intermittent gusts. The smell of an approaching storm lingered in the air. Birds called out from the sky and animals of all sorts scurried about in the forest.

Tayen smiled. The noise would help. She closed her eyes and focused on The Song as she had many times before. Then, once it filled the air around her, she cast it away and walled herself off from The Song.

A chill ran through her limbs. She had spent most of her life in the forest, able to reach for The Shadow whenever she pleased. She never learned how to sever her connection to The Song like Kaylo had.

If this doesn't work, nothing will. Tayen gripped the knife tighter in anticipation.

A cluster of fallen leaves crinkled under her foot as she took her first step. This wouldn't work if she didn't take her time.

Her mouth felt drier with every step she took, and the vein along the left side of her neck throbbed with each heartbeat. A slow pain built in her chest, but she continued to take her small shallow breaths.

Not much longer, she promised herself. *A few more steps.*

The knife weighed heavy in her hand. Her blisters stung, but she only gripped the hilt harder.

He still hadn't moved. *This is another trick.* She slowly lifted her hand

and set the cold metal of the blade to Kaylo's throat.

"What gave me away?" he asked, a smile hiding in his voice.

The edge of the blade nicked his throat as he spoke, and a small trickle of blood ran down his neck. With a soft touch, he moved her hand from his throat and turned to face her.

"You cheated," she said with a mixture of pride and frustration. "You were listening to my echo."

He removed the blindfold and met her eyes. He shrugged. "There's no such thing as cheating in combat, little shade. Use what you can to stay alive. Trust me, they will," he said. "If you're smart, you'll learn your opponent's weaknesses and use them."

"How is The Song a weakness?"

"Anything that puts you in danger can be a weakness, even your greatest strength." Kaylo started talking in his lecture voice. "The Shadow is a powerful weapon, but if you rely on it too much, it will become a weakness. Trust me."

Kaylo ripped a loose piece of fabric from his robes and held it to the nick on his throat. "If you fight, you will spill blood and your blood will be spilled in the process. Whether you can delay your journey into The Mist will depend on your training, your cunning, and luck. Is it fair to kill someone who doesn't know how to wield their weapon? Is it fair to survive because you have numbers on your side? Is it fair that I have outlived my friends? Fair is a child's notion. Abandon it if you intend to pick up a blade."

"I know that." Tayen's voice pitched higher than she intended.

"Don't give them a chance to kill you, not for the price of fair," he said. "Call The Shadow and cut your enemies' throats in the dark. Forget the stories you've heard about war. It isn't honorable."

"So, even when I beat you, I get a lecture?"

She closed her eyes and her mother waited there for her. Of course fair didn't matter. If fair mattered, she would be with her family—on this side or the other.

Kaylo nodded and offered a bleak smile. "I'm sorry. You're right. This is what you get with a recluse for a kana," he said. "You did well. You thought the problem through and broke it down. You never tried the same tactic twice. None of my teachers could say the same of me." He patted her on the shoulder awkwardly.

"Not even a span ago, you didn't know half the tricks you played with The Shadow," he said. "I didn't teach you that. You figured that out on your own."

Silence stood between them like an unwelcome guest. Tayen held Kaylo's knife out. He looked down at her and hesitated like he had more to say, then took the knife.

Sokan hung in the sky, casting long shadows. It wouldn't be dark for several hours. Maybe she would use the time to read. She started the trek back to the hallow, letting the leaves crunch under her boots.

"*I could do with some meat tonight. I've had my fill of vegetable soup. How about you?*" Kaylo asked.

He had taken to asking her questions in Gousht to test her progress. The coarse words still tasted like rancid meat on her tongue, but she did her best to learn the sickening language.

"*A wager?*" he asked.

One side of her mouth curled into a smirk. "*What wager?*"

"A hare," he said with raised eyebrows. "You take a hare before I can, and I will take your chores for the evening. If I nab one before you, you get to spend the night with my blades and the whetstone."

"All of my chores?" she asked, and he nodded in response. She weighed her options. "Can I hunt with The Shadow?"

"If you want to. It won't matter either way," he said with a true grin.

He held the knife out. She had her belt knife, but his blade had more weight and reach. Tayen snatched it from his grip and ran off into the forest, The Song chasing after her.

Shadows peeled off the trees as she ran. The Song pinged about the forest like a rainstorm growing against a metal roof until it drowned out everything else before dropping to a constant whisper.

She became a dark blur, racing through the forest. The shadows continuously pulled away, trying to return to their rightful place, but she held them loosely around her body.

Occasionally, an arm or a leg would break from the shadow cloak, and she would curse under her breath. The slippery bastards were harder to control when she ran. Anyone watching would immediately spot her, but it might keep her from startling the animals. She already smelled like the forest. If she kept out of sight, she would snatch a hare before it even noticed her.

When she had run far enough away from her kana's hunting grounds, Tayen slowed her pace.

The forest's constant buzz faltered. The wind still bent through the trees, but nothing else in the forest moved. A bird above her fluttered to the sky and flew west. The stillness crept over her skin, setting the tiny hairs on her arms bristling.

Did I make that much noise?

A fallen tree sat on an angle, propped up against a healthy tree trunk. She blended into the shadows beneath the dead wood. Her hands mimicked the movement of The Song, and she bent the shadow cloak to fit the natural fall of the tree.

She crouched on bended knee, ready to pounce. With a little patience, Kaylo would be cleaning up after dinner, fetching water, sweeping the hallow, and sharpening his own blades.

The forest slowly came back to life. Birdsongs filled the silence, and animals scurried by as if she wasn't there. Her eye focused on every slight movement. The ache in her knees faded beneath her concentration.

A chipmunk scurried out of a bush, and it took all Tayen's willpower not to leap at it. Roast chipmunk tasted delicious, especially a little burned around the edges, but she had a wager. Her stomach would have to wait. Her pride was hungrier.

The chores didn't matter. She didn't care about the stupid wager, although it would be nice to have an easy night, lay back, and read. Today, she beat him, and he shit all over her victory. He needed to see how capable she was.

The dull pain in her knees grew the longer she waited. She shifted slightly, and a small brown hare raced past her. The skinny bastard broke towards a thick cropping of bushes. She threw her belt knife into the dirt in front of the animal. It veered to the right, and she pounced from the shadows.

The hare squirmed under the heel of her palm. It squealed and thumped its hind legs. Then it went limp, and its blood flowed around Kaylo's knife down into the soil.

A bigger animal with more meat on its bones would have been better, but Kaylo never mentioned size. She knelt over the hare with her palms open to the sky and offered a small prayer.

Her mother used to say, "Our people have lost too much to this invasion to forget our ways." The memory made her wince, but it also made her feel more like herself than she had in days.

Part of her mind urged her to get back to the hallow before Kaylo, but it wouldn't have felt right. The hare's spirit belonged to Ennea, as she did. It deserved the respect of a prayer.

"Blessed Mother, please watch over this creature's spirit and welcome it into The Mist," she said before kissing three bloody fingers and touching them to the ground.

A flock of birds shook the tree above Tayen as they took flight. Time to head back and leave the animals their peace. She stood and hung her kill from her belt. With a few flicks of the wrist, she gathered shadows from the trees and raced back to the hallow. She concentrated on moving with the shadows. Kaylo could move better with the shadows than she could, and he wasn't even a shadow dancer.

A span ago, she hadn't known how to make a shadow cloak, but that excuse grew old. She and The Shadow shared a connection he could never know. If she had to move slower to hold her shadow cloak, she would.

Finally, she reached the top of a hill, and the stormwood tree jutted into the sky. It crested higher than all the other trees in the canopy.

In her excitement, she sprinted towards the tree. Her breath ran raw against her throat, which only made her run faster. She broke through the shadows once or twice, then forced them back into place.

There was no sign of Kaylo. She won.

A blur at the edge of her vision barreled towards her.

Kaylo?

He crashed into her at full speed. His arms wrapped around her as they tumbled to the ground. When they came to a rest, an arrow protruded from a tree near where she had been standing.

Kaylo lay sprawled on top of her, searching the forest. He didn't meet her eyes. He only whispered, "Stay quiet. Stay hidden." Then he reclaimed his knife from where she dropped it and rushed off.

She lay on the forest floor beneath her shadows in shock as her kana tore through the forest.

Several blurs of shiny metal flew through the air but always two steps behind him. Kaylo planted his back against an old tree.

The arrows flew from an empty space in the forest. Tayen's lungs rebelled against her shallow breaths and started burning. She gripped her belt knife, but she had nothing to attack.

Time stretched thin, and then the shade of a tree about thirty paces out wavered. She looked from her kana to the ill-fitting darkness.

Kaylo raised her finger to his lips and nodded, but she didn't need the reminder. Her lungs became a vacuum. Her muscles seized. When she needed it most, her anger had abandoned her. She could only watch and try to breathe.

With a quick gesture, Kaylo stole The Shadow from the archer. Small clouds of translucent black unraveled from her. The blood banner, the Sonacoan woman from two span past, stood there, frozen. Her face drew long in terror. The bow hung in one hand with the empty spirit crystal in the other.

Kaylo charged. The blood banner reached for another arrow from the quiver on her back, but she either moved too slowly or had been caught off-guard. He grabbed her arm, and the arrow fell from her grip. Then he yanked her off-balance and snuck his blade through her padded armor.

Kaylo cradled her head and eased her to the ground.

Tayen cautiously approached them with her knife in hand.

"Mother, take care of this spirit. Let The Mist hold her and give her the freedom she couldn't have in The Waking," Kaylo prayed.

The soldier coughed up blood. "I don't need your prayers, malitu." Her stomach spasmed with every cough and harsh breath.

"Spirits, take this woman, add her death to the list, and end this war." He placed three fingers on his lips and touched them to the ground.

"Your...fault...thief." The air stuttered as she choked on it.

"Yes, it is," Kaylo said. "Now, where are the others?"

She spat blood at him.

He took a hard breath and held her hand. "Go to The Mist, sister. Let the pain be over," he said softly. He gripped his knife and forced it deeper through her ribcage, into her heart.

Her eyelids fluttered, then stopped.

Tayen ground her teeth and glared at the soldier's body. She died quicker than she deserved. Blood banner. Traitor. Carrying a crystal with a stolen spirit. The Gousht treated her like a savage, and she still fought for them. Whether or not this woman had been there when her family died, she didn't deserve sympathy. She deserved wrath.

"Blood banners don't belong in The Mist," Tayen said.

Kaylo placed his hand on Tayen's arm and looked up at her from where he knelt. His eyes were full of pity. Then he looked back to the soldier's body and said, "We all make the best we can with hard decisions. The Gousht didn't leave us any easy ones."

The soldier's face looked peaceful, as if a Sonacoan woman lay dead instead of the blood banner. Tayen tore her eyes away from the body, from the enemy.

A fortuitous crack of lightning broke the sky in the distance.

Tayen walked away and picked up the hare that had fallen to the ground when Kaylo tackled her. Blood stained her hands, either from the soldier or the hare.

"I need you to pack your things and be ready to leave before dark," Kaylo said as he caught up to her. He was limping as he walked.

"No, we can fight. I can fight. There are only four of them left," Tayen said. "They have already taken too much."

"Say you're right, and there are only four more soldiers. Say we kill them. What happens when they don't report back? What happens when five more soldiers go missing?"

They would send a garrison next. The Gousht wouldn't stop, but she didn't care. They could send the whole army. Her blisters stung, and she squeezed the belt knife tighter. She was alive and her family was dead.

"You'd rather run?" she asked. "You're a coward."

The wrongness of her words lay heavy in her gut, but she refused to take them back. If he wanted to run, that was exactly what he was, a coward. Brave people stayed to fight. They didn't let other people die for them.

"Do you think that life is such a simple thing to take?"

He knew exactly what she had lost, and he still didn't understand. She matched his level tone. "Shay wouldn't run."

He closed his eyes for a moment while his chest went up and down slowly, then he met her glare with his soft brown eyes. "Shay's dead."

He walked into the darkness of the hallow, leaving Tayen angry, guilty, and most of all, alone.

CHAPTER SIXTEEN

Tayen's chest constricted as if her muscles would squeeze her until her ribs collapsed under the pressure. Kaylo hadn't bothered to build a fire. The flicker of candlelight disturbed the darkness alone, casting shapes and silhouettes onto the twisted walls.

After all her training, the sweat and bruises, she had hidden from yet another opportunity to take the blood she owed. Now Kaylo was going to let them be run off from their home without a fight. She needed another chance.

An old leather sack lay empty on her bedroll. As small as it was, it would still be too big for the sum of her possessions—a spare homespun robe Kaylo had hemmed to fit her, a few pairs of pants far too big for her, and her sister's whistle. Her entire existence could be carried away with the breeze.

Her fingers ran over the uneven grain of the whistle. Nita had never been very good with a blade, but she tried. She carved a fox for their mother once. It looked like a boulder with a snout.

When Tayen finished packing, she riffled through the hallow for anything she might need. She added a badly worn flint rock, a rusted pot, a whetstone, and an old map to her collection.

The bookcase glared at her. She couldn't imagine leaving these books here to be burned or looted, or even left lost and untouched. Old leather and canvas brushed over her worn skin as she ran her hands over their bindings. She could only save a few.

She pulled several books off the shelf, then tentatively slipped them back into place. Her eyes kept returning to a book she had been too hesitant to read, *Tales of Shunanlah: The First Dancer*. Even looking at the title scrawled across the binding called forth memories of her mother. She couldn't leave it behind, so she slipped it into her bag alongside a memoir written by General Kalani from the Great War. The books weighed down the sack draped over her shoulder, but they were worth the burden.

This hallow had been a good home, if only for a short while. She rolled her blanket with her bedroll and latched them to her sack. When she hefted her sack over her shoulder, the weight of it anchored her in the moment. Everything she carried, save the clothes she wore and her sister's whistle, belonged to Kaylo.

If we're going to run every time trouble comes along, we'll never stop running. Her knife hung from her belt. *That can't be the reason I survived.*

Tayen met Kaylo's eyes from across the hallow. The dancer who killed three soldiers to save her life existed somewhere under his unkempt hair and tattered clothes. That warrior only showed up in flashes. At the moment, a coward and a thief stood in his place.

"Ready to go?" he asked in a grating, calm tone, as if abandoning the hallow meant nothing.

Tayen stalked into the night without saying anything.

"Seed and Balance," Kaylo said, as he leaned against the stormwood tree.

For a dozen turns, he had lived under this canopy. He tended to every living thing within these walls and prayed to those damned carvings. It had to end sometime.

"Goodbye, old friends."

The slow sharp pain in his knee waxed and waned but never completely disappeared. He bounced on the joint. If he needed to, he could push himself for several hours still.

Tayen's echo burst to life outside. She was going to make it hard to keep her safe.

When he blew out the candle, his home vanished into the dark. Only a small streak of light slipped in through the entrance. Dusk settled over the forest. A storm cracked through the night on the horizon.

The storm would make their journey miserable, but they needed to put some distance between them and the remaining soldiers. As soon as they found their fallen archer, they would call for more numbers—if they were smart.

Kaylo pushed the hides aside from the entrance, and as he did, three piercing whistles rang out from the forest.

A lumbering oaf of a man stood beside the entrance with his axe poised to attack.

The bastards hadn't been smart, but they had been clever.

Kaylo threw himself to the ground as the soldier's axe cut through the air, and a white-hot pain sliced through his right shoulder.

Adrenaline quieted the worst of it. If not for the whistle and the soldier's wild swing, the axe would have lopped off his head. He rolled backwards over his uninjured shoulder to push himself to his feet, dropping his travel sack to the ground. His weak knee nearly buckled as he steadied himself.

The giant of a soldier stood at least a head taller than Kaylo, his padded armor straining to enclose his raw mass.

He continued to press his advantage, forcing Kaylo back with several more strong but unwieldy swings of his proportionately sized axe as the three other soldiers moved to surround Kaylo. If he allowed them to do that, he would be finished.

Kaylo pulled his father's knife from its sheath. The small blade was hardly the ideal weapon to match an axe, but then again, being ambushed outside of one's home was not the ideal situation. At least they hadn't found Tayen. Her lonely echo screamed out from deeper in the forest.

A gravelly voice called out from over Kaylo's injured shoulder. "*You look confused, thief. No spirits to steal?*" Moonlight glinted off the commander's chestplate. "*You didn't think I would let the zeze off her leash, did you?*"

Of course he wouldn't have trusted a Sonacoan, even if she wore their colors. The commander had been there when she died. He had seen Kaylo steal her shadows, and he came prepared, leaving their spirit crystals behind.

Without the spirits, Kaylo had nothing more than a tiny bit of sharpened metal to defend himself. A hunter's knife to an axe and three swords.

The large man relented his attack and gave Kaylo more distance, allowing his compatriots time to encircle their prey.

A matter of seconds separated Kaylo from his fate. His knee would slow him down. His shoulder was bleeding, though if he leveled a guess, the axe hadn't cut very deep. He bounced his weak leg on the ball of his foot several times. It hurt, but it wouldn't give out on him. Hopefully.

"Seed and Balance."

Kaylo launched himself forward with his good leg. The giant might have had size, but his stance showed inexperience.

The towering man's eyes widened at Kaylo's attack. Most people probably ran from the lumbering oaf. He reeled his heavy weapon back like he expected Kaylo to duel him, knife to battle axe.

The axe came down more like a hammer. It would have cracked Kaylo's head in two had he the speed and control for it.

The wind of the swing brushed by Kaylo's cheek as he sidestepped and jabbed his blade into the thick flesh of the soldier's unprotected thigh. The big man roared as Kaylo darted into the forest before any of the soldiers could stop him.

Tayen's echo sang from deep in the forest. If she was smart, she would run and not stop until daybreak, though he doubted she would. And if she refused to run, Kaylo didn't have a choice. At least the land lessened his disadvantage. He could spread them thin and whittle them down, one soldier at a time.

Lightning cracked the sky; closer than before. The edges of the storm started to fall, rain leaking through the canopy.

He stalked through the forest after his prey. A tall woman, paler than most Gousht, if that was possible, plodded through the underbrush like a city soldier, flat-footed on uneven ground. No more than two dozen turns to her. She carried a short sword crafted for speed and close combat—still longer than Kaylo's knife.

On flat land, she would have been dangerous. Even here, he couldn't underestimate her.

Kaylo mimicked her steps, closing the gap between them. The rain shrouded the sound of his approach. He only had one chance. Wet soil clung to his boot and made a sloshy sound when he pulled it loose.

She stopped, and Kaylo reached out of the darkness, grabbed her chin, and drew his blade across her throat. Blood bubbled from the wound with every cough as she crumpled to the dirt.

Another life. Another spirit. Regret would be there in the morning if he survived the night.

Kaylo moved to fall back into the thick brush. The weathered steel of a sword flashed in the darkness a moment before it streaked towards him. He fell backwards to avoid the blade and scrambled to catch his feet before the commander could strike again.

The heavy forest canopy and the helm upon his forehead cloaked most of the commander's features, but even in the darkness, wrinkles marked the man's age. His body didn't quite fill out his armor anymore, but his eyes confirmed what Kaylo had guessed. This man was dangerous. Clever and experienced always beat out strong and fast. His blade bore the tarnish of battle but had been well-kept. A sword surely known in The Mist.

"*You sacrificed your own soldier?*" Kaylo asked in Gousht.

"*If she couldn't defend herself from a ragged konki like you, what use was she to me?*" He looked down at the fallen soldier and nudged her lifeless body with his foot. "*Some people don't have the mettle.*" Disdain filled his thick accent.

Kaylo continued to back up, looking for an opening, but the old soldier held his guard near perfect. The Gousht blade would catch Kaylo if he turned to run, and the commander had too much experience for Kaylo to charge. He would have to fight short blade to long sword.

Youth and strength might have been on Kaylo's side, but the commander's obvious skill made up for the disparity. Kaylo set his stance, and the commander did the same. Then something shifted in Kaylo's periphery. The fourth soldier.

The young, unsteady man moved to flank Kaylo.

Hopefully, this last soldier lacked his commander's experience. More than that, Kaylo hoped the boy was a blundering fool, but inexperienced would do.

The commander mirrored each step Kaylo took as they rounded each other. If Kaylo waited too long, the other soldier would gain position on him.

A sharp ting-thunk sang out against the rain.

It took Kaylo a moment to register what he was looking at. A sword swung at the side of the commander's head like an axe. His helm deflected the blow, but the blade continued into the meat of the man's neck.

The commander didn't scream but dazedly turned towards his attacker. As he shifted to the side, Tayen came into view, staring up at the old soldier. Her eyes were wide, and her hands shook.

Before the commander could avenge himself, Kaylo closed the distance and sunk his blade into the gap in the commander's armor.

Fool or not, the last soldier proved a coward—though some might have called him a pragmatist. He turned and ran off into the forest. Neither Kaylo nor Tayen followed.

Tayen slumped to the ground next to the commander's body. "Fighting isn't about fair," she murmured.

She had the look of one who had taken a life too soon, as if there were ever a right time. Her skin went pale as rainwater dripped down her face. Kaylo knelt next to her, and she asked, "It isn't about fair, right? Right?"

He gathered her into his arms, and she cried. "No, little shade," he said. "No, it isn't."

When her shaking calmed, Kaylo let her go and guided her to a nearby log.

The short sword from the commander's sacrificial soldier protruded from the commander's neck like a bit of bitter poetry.

There had already been too much death, but it wasn't over.

"I need one more thing from you tonight," Kaylo said. Bile built up in the back of his throat with the request, but it could not be avoided. "I need you to call The Song."

Tayen looked at him through her tears mixed with rain. She gave no sign of comprehension, instead her gaze turned back to the commander's body. He lay as an outline in the dark forest, but he had been a person.

Kaylo lifted her chin and guided her face up until their eyes met. He asked her once again to call The Shadow. The haunted stillness on her face didn't change. Still, her echo rushed forward like a gust of wind through the trees.

"Stay here," he said, although she probably couldn't find her feet without help.

His hands made their familiar dance, and he pulled on the echo. Dread made the short journey back to the hallow longer. Wet hair fell into his face, and he brushed it aside. In less than a moon, he had already taken five lives. And one more called.

The big soldier leaned against Kaylo's hallow, both hands clinging to the shaft of his axe. His weight shifted over his uninjured leg. Night had fully taken over from dusk. Rain clouds obstructed the sliver of moonlight, rain rattling against the soldier's helm.

He looked like a kid. A big kid with an enormous axe, but a kid who was scared and alone, doing what he had been taught to do. Too young to think of questioning his place in the world. Too young to die for a cause, or at least too young to understand dying for a cause.

Lightning flashed through the sky; closer again still.

Kaylo could hate himself more tomorrow, but tonight, Tayen's safety mattered more. He had driven his knife into the soldier's thigh fairly deep, but he couldn't take any chances. Cloaked in shadows, he crept towards the lone soldier and cut from jugular to jugular.

The young man gurgled through his struggled last breaths. His warm blood felt sour against Kaylo's skin.

Death always kept busy around him. No storm could wash him clean. Kaylo released The Shadow, and the dark cloud surrounding him unfurled.

Tayen hadn't moved, still sitting on the log, hunched over her knees as the rain saturated her robes. Her face hid behind her braids.

What have I done? Kaylo thought.

She remained silent as he hooked his uninjured arm under hers and helped her back to the hallow. The storm had soaked them both to the quick. Water trailed behind them along the swept dirt floor to the firepit. A fire would fight the cold, but it couldn't erase what had happened. He left her sitting like a statue next to the flames.

Next came the unfortunate business of the dead, a more manageable problem. The runaway soldier wouldn't return for several more days with reinforcements, but it would be best if they didn't find the bodies.

He stripped the dead of everything useful. The weight of the commander's sword balanced well in Kaylo's hands. It was a good blade, and he might need better than a hunter's knife if the spirits continued to test him. The woman's short sword clung to the commander's sinew as Kaylo yanked it from the base of the dead man's neck. Tayen needed a proper blade to train with. The blades slid back into their scabbards, and Kaylo wrapped them with a pouch of saltmeat, and a sack of Gousht coins in the commander's cloak.

The sky continued to crack open with lightning as the rain softened the soil beneath Kaylo's feet. His shoulder burned and bled, but he couldn't leave the dead to be found. He took as much care as he could as he dragged the young giant's body through the wet dirt to where the others lay.

Their people passed into the afterlife through fire, but rain wouldn't permit it. And time wouldn't let him wait. He would have to give them to Ennea. Let her sort them out.

The large soldier's axe made a piss-poor shovel, but it broke the soil apart. Dirt caked on Kaylo's hands. Water filled the hole with every mound of dirt he pushed away. It took hours, and still the grave was too shallow for three bodies to fit proper. Anyone looking would notice it for what it was, a hastily dug grave, but Kaylo wagered those who came looking would be searching in the same haste. And the cowardly soldier who escaped wouldn't likely recall where to look.

Maybe, if luck blessed him, the storm would help settle the ground, but he rarely fell on the right side of lucky. He offered a prayer over the dead, brought three dirty fingers to his lips, then back to the ground.

The hours wore on his body like days. When he made it back to the hallow, Tayen lay on her bedroll. Asleep or not, he would not interrupt her solitude. Instead, he crept to the firepit and eased off his robe. Dried blood adhered to the fabric and peeled away from his wound as he freed his arm. This robe had too many tears and cuts to mend anyway, so he gave it to the fire before he could think better of it.

For a moment, Kaylo allowed himself to feel the warmth of the fire against his skin. The world shrunk beneath the flames, and the crackling tune filled his spirit. His body had been moving from task to task. He never stopped to think about all that had transpired. Only now did he question his decisions.

The runaway soldier would tell his superiors about an aging spirit thief. That wouldn't go unnoticed. They might not assume it was him, but they wouldn't ignore the possibility. He should have run the soldier down and opened his throat. In his younger days, he would have. Though worrying never fixed mistakes. Regret was a slow death, as The Jani liked to say.

With a heavy sigh, he put away the past and reached over to inspect his shoulder. It may have been a shallow cut at first, but he tore the wound wider and deeper over the past few hours.

How many thoughtless decisions can a man make in one night?

Tayen stood behind him as he cleaned his wound. As long as she said nothing, Kaylo gratefully took her lead. He plucked leaves, stripped bark from the moonlight hazel, and picked a sprig of barberries. With a bit of water and dirt, he ground them into a poultice, as he had done many times before.

"Where did you get your scars?" Tayen asked.

His back must have been quite a sight. He had seen it in a looking glass turns ago. Even then, the scars made a patchwork marring his once smooth skin. He smiled a strained smile, but he didn't turn around. "Too many battles to remember each one, little shade."

"What about the burn?"

"Fire," he said dryly.

When he turned, Tayen looked like a dimmer version of herself. The color in her eyes had faded, mud clung to her skin, blood stained her clothes, but more than that, she lost the shield that protected her from the world. The commander's death had imprinted on her spirit.

"You should sleep," Kaylo said. "We leave with the sun."

"Do you think they'll find this place again?"

He nodded. "If we give ourselves a day, it will be too easy to give ourselves another. We should have left after we discovered them in the forest the first time. I won't make that mistake again.

"Sleep if you can; rest if you cannot. Your body needs it, even if your mind refuses," he said as he walked to his own bedroll.

She wouldn't sleep. She would lie there and remember the bloody moments. They were alike in that.

As he lay on his bedroll, he stared into the winding peak of the hallow. For turns, he had seen the trees twist their way into each other. These separate lives grew into one. The magic of it still hadn't ceased these many nights later. Maybe he and the girl were not so different than the trees.

The sun came faster than his body would've liked, but slower than his patience could tolerate. Kaylo stood before the wood-carved spirits, staring up at the intricate faces he had wrought from the stormwood.

"Are you praying?" Tayen asked from across the hallow.

"In a way," Kaylo said. "I have lived here for twelve turns, and these two idols kept me company. I guess I'm saying goodbye. The spirits will come, but these carvings will stay. Hmph, I hadn't known they meant so much."

"We don't have to leave, not right now."

"Yes, we do," Kaylo said and smiled at his toka. "Make yourself ready."

She knelt next to the idols and placed her hands on the obsidian stone she had positioned in the dirt next to them.

"Praying?" he asked.

"Saying goodbye." She grabbed her travel pack, leaving the stone behind. "Where are we going?"

"East, then north with the Sanine. We need food and water, we need shelter, and we need to be somewhere the Gousht are not. I'd say we have a span before the Gousht pick up our trail and two moons before the first snowfall."

"Why not go south for the winter?"

"The closer we are to Lost Nation territory, the less likely the Gousht will follow. My maps probably don't mean much after over a decade of war, but one thing never changes—where there's clean water, people won't be far. And where there are people, there's shelter."

"You don't have a plan, do you?" Hints of her frustration slipped into her tone. Pieces of that girl could never change.

"The older you get, the more you'll realize that no one knows what they are doing. We get by however we can. Besides, plans usually turn to shit." He handed her the blade she swung the night before, secure in its scabbard. "When that happens, you'll need this."

Sokan rose high and fell below the treetops before they stopped for the night. The ache that started at Kaylo's bad knee extended from his ankle to his hip after a day of hobbling through the wet dirt. At least the pain in his leg quieted the burning in his shoulder.

Tayen's new blade slapped against her thigh, accenting the silence with an arhythmic beat. She would get used to the weight of it with time.

If they hadn't been fleeing, it would have been a pleasant walk. Cool, but not cold, clouds accentuating the bright blue sky. The leaves had begun to change, catching the light with their new colors. A more innocent person might have seen a good omen from the spirits, but Kaylo wasn't innocent, and the spirits weren't coy.

He set his travel pack down. Tonight would mark his first night sleeping away from the hallow in several turns. But like Tayen had said, it was just a treehouse.

They worked in silence. Tayen gathered firewood and Kaylo tossed saltmeat, water, and some vegetables from his garden into a pot. Soup filled a belly good on a cool night. Maybe it would make Tayen feel better. A specific type of mourning followed taking a life for the first time.

She sat with her back against an ironoak beyond the firelight, fiddling with her whistle. Even though he hadn't left her side, she waded through her torment on her own. Kaylo had to say something.

The tension bit at him as he searched for the right words. He stirred the pot. She deserved better than him. He should have protected her. If he killed the commander when they first crossed paths, she wouldn't have needed to.

"Tayen, there's something I need to..."

"I'm sorry, okay?" she blurted out, cutting him off. "I shouldn't have called you a coward. I shouldn't have said what I said about Shay. I should have...." She interrupted herself with her own tears. She clutched her knees to her chest. Snot and salt water covered her face as she fought to control her breath.

This child needed him.

"You know, you saved my life last night. Twice." If he had better words to offer, they had refused to come to him. Still, for whatever compassion and care his words lacked, they beat back the silence. "They would have killed me."

"I can't. I...When I close my eyes, he's there," she muttered, staring at the sword on her hip.

"Good," Kaylo said. "Feel that hurt for as long as you can because when you can take a life and be easy...." He stopped and looked around the forest, lost in his own jagged memories. "When that happens, you'll become a malitu."

The tension that existed before still remained, but now they took shelter within it, together. Tayen moved closer to the fire, and they ate until their spoons scraped their bowls. The fire ebbed and flowed as it ate through the wood.

"How long were you with them?" Tayen asked. Kaylo looked up and furrowed his brows with a question, so she clarified. "The Jani."

He smiled for several reasons. Firstly, for the memory of a happy time. Tomakans surrounded him in Nomar, but the ever-present eyes of the Empire held them apart. The Jani lived outside of that. Even the boundaries between people seemed permeable.

Secondly, for the memory of a man. Jonac became a friend, a kana, an older brother, and an adopted father. He was a good reason to smile.

Lastly, and perhaps most importantly, Kaylo smiled because of Tayen. She wanted to hear his story, meaning he still had a chance to save her. And after far too long without, he had someone to talk to. He met her eyes over the receding flames and told her to get more wood. If he was going to tell his story, they needed a stronger fire.

CHAPTER SEVENTEEN

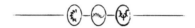

TWO SEASONS HAD PASSED, the clan had dismantled the tent city twice and carried it over the rocky Sonacoan terrain, and still it felt odd to wrap myself in their sand-colored robes. In Tomak, we made robes bright and colorful to celebrate life, not meek and dull, yet the Jani knew more freedom than I ever had. The fact that everyone wore the same thing made me all the more self-conscious.

Their coverings served as a visible representation of their commitment to put the good of Ennea and all her children first in everything they did. As beautiful as the sentiment was, I had no desire to constantly cover my braids in chani cloth.

Jonac waited for me by the table, steeping his tea and tapping out a rhythm on the wood. He never had patience for slow rising, regardless of how little I slept.

Last night, I watched Nomar's priest proselytize from the caller's stage as soldiers hoisted Shay's body above the town square. She swung from the rope and slowly spun. Munnie fell to her knees, cursing my name. Rena walked by wearing a smile, and a gap separated the crowd where my parents should have been.

Most of my dreams about home soured like old fruit.

"I know Toka rises after Kana, but we don't have to follow the moons in all things, little brother," Jonac said.

"Give the boy a break." Nomi walked behind Jonac and placed her hands on his shoulders. "You have been stealing him away every morning and running him like a mule in the afternoon. If he survives the spring, it will be by The Mother's will alone."

She bent down and kissed his cheek. "Kaylo, if he doesn't let up, you tell me."

"If Kaylo doesn't want to go, can we?" Junera asked from her bedroll. "Kaylo can stay with Mommy."

Soca slapped at her sister's arm. "You always do this."

"Ouch, do what? Mommy, Soca hit me."

"Girls, if you start the day like this, you are going to finish it bone-weary by the time the sun goes down from all the chores you'll be doing," Nomi said.

"Do you see what you did, little brother? We better leave before you bring the tent down on our heads." Jonac took a large swig of his tea and headed for the door.

I slipped on my boots and rushed after him.

Most people hadn't left their tents at this hour. Their echoes still buzzed around like incessant whispers, but my barriers blocked out most of the babble along with The Song.

Every dancer bent The Song differently, like trees in the wind. Whether or not I wanted to, I had begun marking the differences and distinguish between each spirit's call. Jonac's echo pranced around him like a child begging for attention.

For a man of his steady composure, Jonac cut through the tent city towards the encampment gates with an unspoken urgency. When the occasional nomad crossed their paths, he greeted them without breaking his stride.

Gardens all around us bloomed with their spring crop. Radishes and rhubarb, spinach and tantan greens flourished within the rich red soil. Forest dancers filled in the gaps, but the Jani farmed with the seasons. No one took the spirits for granted within these walls.

"Inflammation," Jonac called out without looking back.

"Do we have to do this every morning?" I asked. "We could talk about anything else. What's your favorite instrument?"

Jonac stopped and leveled his gaze at me. "Inflammation."

"Ginger, moonflowers, turmeric, cardamom, cinnamon, willow bark, chili peppers."

"Good. Good, but you forgot rosemary."

"I didn't forget. I just hate rosemary."

Jonac chuckled and started walking again. "Cuts."

The guard waved us through as I listed out seven plants to treat runny shits. Of course, I forgot yellowroot.

"Who can remember all of this stuff?" I asked. "Why do I need an eighth answer when I have seven perfectly good ones?"

"You are in a mood this morning, little brother. Do you want to talk about whatever you were dreaming about that had you waking up covered in sweat?" He allowed a brief moment of silence. "No? Then we might as well make sure that you are a moderately competent dancer."

"It's not like I'm ever going to need to call up all these different plants and herbs."

"What you know about a plant—the size, shape, color, taste, smell—serves as the markers for finding it within The Song, yes? In that case, it may be best if you learn a thing or two about them."

Jonac's echo grew louder the farther we ventured into the forest as he opened himself wider to The Song. As long as he could hear it, I could hear it through him. When he reached for it, I could intercept his connection to the spirits.

Though I never would, I did wonder what it would be like to dance with fire or earth, to call rain from the clouds, or run with the wind. The curiosity nagged at me.

We reached our training grounds, far enough from the encampment that no one bothered us. Here I could let go and let The Song in. The echoes from the tent city lapped at the edge of my awareness, but I could ignore them.

The soil all over the grounds bulged from our sessions. We reduced the plants to decay before we left each day, and the soil had only grown richer for it. The red earth turned deeper and darker with each sacrifice.

"Okay, little brother." Jonac propped himself up on the rock formation as he always did. "I promised Nomi I would bring home some marigolds. Would you mind?"

"I've never called a marigold before."

"And we return to our earlier conversation, don't we?" A playful touch of rebuke entwined with his words. "You've seen one before, yes? Picture it in your mind. Recall the way it smells. Those senses will guide you to the flower's place in The Song."

He always made it sound easy, as if I could speak the flower's name, and it would sprout from the soil. But I knew better than to question him. He would only wax poetic words about The Song and The Seed without sharing any real answers.

The Song moved in gentle waves this morning. I let myself settle into it. Staccato notes built in progression to create the rise and fall of the melody. Jonac's echo repeated each phrase from a different angle. The echo and The Song clashed in a disjointed harmony.

The sunfire, yellowish-orange of marigold petals filled the blackness behind my eyelids. Its musky perfume smelled of apple and bitter herbs.

A swirl moved against the melody in The Song, and I reached for it. My arm stretched forward and led the rest of my body, then I moved back to my center and turned. Seeds opened in the soil in each direction I reached. Green tendrils pushed through the soil, rose, and split into feathered leaves until buds emerged and bloomed like crowns.

"Not bad for a first time." Jonac pulled a book from his robe pocket. "Now see what else you find around here."

"What about the marigolds?"

"You can collect them when we are ready to go back," he said without looking up from his book.

I spent the next few hours studying every plant in the area, touching, tasting, smelling, and memorizing the way they grew from the soil. The Song helped me see more than my eyes ever could. Their roots sang to me. The buds that had yet to bloom hummed in the distance.

Each flower, bush, and tree sang the same tune with a distinct voice. As if each plant had an unseen purpose, and if I listened closely, it would tell me.

A crop of indigo flowers grew nestled in the crook of a cypress tree. I hadn't seen them anywhere else in the forest, but here they created a thick patch of vibrant flowers. The petals tickled the pads of my fingers with fine hairs. They smelled of sage with a hint of sweetness.

Jonac's shadow moved over me as I examined the flower. "Susu flowers," he said. "It shouldn't grow this far south on its own."

"Susu? Isn't that...."

"Yes." His voice came out as a whisper, as if speaking loudly would scare the flower away. "If you grind up the roots and burn the powder, it will create a powerful painkiller, extremely addictive. In small amounts, it's not much of a problem. Too much and people become irritable and detached.

"Before the invasion, susu only grew in the north, and healers used it to treat severe injuries. Then the Gousht discovered its effects. They claimed it was a gift from The One True God, like everything else they could turn into a weapon." He knelt beside a flower and cupped the soft petals in his hand. "Addled slaves were easier to control. They didn't rebel as much. So, the Gousht distilled and concentrated the drug, and forced it on the more rebellious slaves. They called it sweet tar for its sticky consistency."

"How do you know all that?"

Jonac looked up at me and blinked as if he had just woken up. "High sun," he said. "Time to start heading back. Don't forget the marigolds."

He walked off without another word.

A wagon axle busted during the last migration, and Jonac had it in mind that I would be the perfect person to fix such a problem. I had been working on it for the last span and a half, and I finally made some progress.

When I stepped through the hides into our tent that night, every muscle from my shoulders to my lower back screamed with each new movement.

The rich aroma of braised venison filled the tent. Grease and chili clung to the air, and my stomach flipped over and over in anticipation. Nomi and the girls sat at the table as Jonac stirred the pot over the firepit.

"Little brother, you are just in time," Jonac said. "I tell you, I can cook many things, but escan venison is my specialty."

"Thank you for my marigolds, Kaylo," Nomi said. "They are quite lovely."

"The trick to good escan is to blister the chilis in the fire before you add them to the pot. You want the heat, but you also need that smokey flavor."

"He is going to continue talking about the food all night unless you wash up and sit down," Nomi said. "I love this man, but he can talk like a bird can fly."

I didn't say more than a set of two words at a time throughout the whole meal. The venison fell apart with the slightest touch of my spoon, and still, I couldn't stop searching for more of the onions in the gravy. They soaked up flavor from the chilis and herbs, and then perfectly burst between my teeth.

Jonac winked at me as he scraped the last bit of the pot into my bowl. "The spirits work through me. I am but a humble servant."

Nomi smacked him on the shoulder. "Servants tend to have more humility."

After the meal, Junera and Soca fought over who had to do which chores. After they settled their dispute, I ended up washing up the pot and bowls. I did my best not to lick the bowls clean before I wiped them down.

"Little ones, it's time for bed," Nomi announced.

"Tell Sinkara, please." Junera's pleas turned into an elongated whine.

"Child, you know that story word for word. Why do you need to hear it again?"

"It's my favorite."

"Wash up and lie down on your bedroll, and I'll tell it. But I don't want you to ask for it for at least another span."

"Promise," Junera said.

"You know she'll ask for it again in two days," Soca said.

"No, I won't."

"That's enough, girls," Jonac said. "Listen to your mother."

The girls went through their rituals and lay down on the other end of the tent as Jonac and I sat near the firepit, drawing lines in the dirt and sharing out our respective pouches of runes.

Jonac placed the first facedown marker as Nomi's voice filled the tent. "There once was a spirit thief with no name."

I shifted through the runes in my hand and went about the task of placing markers on the crosspoints when my turn came around. No matter how I tried to block it out, Nomi's voice cut through my concentration.

"The thief strode throughout the ancestral lands with an army of mercenaries at her back. When they came to a village, she ordered them to wait on the outskirts. No villager was to be harmed, and her mercenaries obeyed, for the thief carried a great power."

The girls made gentle squeals at exactly the right moment to accentuate the story.

"The thief appeared small and meek, and the villagers knew not what she was. So, when she offered her challenge, they immediately accepted.

If their bravest warrior could best her, the mercenaries would leave them be, but if she won, the village would pay her tribute and..."

"Have you forgotten how to play, little brother?" Jonac said.

I plucked a random rune from my hand and placed The Flame down as a challenge. Jonac turned over The Wind and claimed his first crosspoint.

"...strong, skilled warriors rose to meet her in combat, over-confident and self-assured, and the thief did all she could to appear unassuming. She wore a simple robe and carried a knife to meet their leather armor, swords, and spears. Yet, she killed..."

Jonac tapped his knuckles on the ground, and particles of dirt floated up into the air. "If you are too tired to play, go to sleep."

"No. No, I'm sorry."

The River lay face up in challenge to my crosspoint. I couldn't even remember what I had placed there. The Mountain, of course. Jonac slipped a new marker over the crosspoint.

"...a small village with no more than a handful of villagers, none of them especially skilled warriors. The village couldn't offer much in tribute, but the thief's pride had grown such that she cared little for the extra crops. She wanted..."

I had already lost two quick games, and the latest stood at three crosspoints to one, which I had only claimed as a matter of probability. Any rune could lie beneath Jonac's white markers. To say I'd lost track of what he had played would imply I had kept track in the first place. I set down The Flame in challenge and lost yet another crosspoint.

"...old warrior, Sinkara, stepped forward to meet the thief, and the thief smiled at her easy opponent. She no longer pretended to be meek. The old warrior's hair had fallen from gray to white, her leather armor gaped from the muscle the turns had taken from her, and her sword..."

"If you would like to listen to the story, you can join the girls," Jonac said. "It's no fun beating you like this."

"You always beat me like this."

"Usually, you put up more of a fight." Jonac laid down The Mountain.

"...the thief waited for Sinkara to call on the spirits like each of her past opponents, but she didn't. The thief could tell Sinkara was a child of Ennea, but she refused to call The Song. Distracted and prideful, the thief decided it didn't matter and lunged towards the old woman. For all the thief's speed, Sinkara had wisdom. The warrior's blade fell quickly on the thief, and as the thief lay dying, the warrior repeated an old phrase."

"No heart for a thief, no safe haven, only a grave will do." The girls said the words in unison with Nomi. The same words that repeated time and again in stories about The Thief and her descendants.

The echoes of the tent city battered at my barriers, louder and more demanding than usual. I flipped over The Wind and finally won a challenge.

A series of three quick moves later, I lost yet another game.

"What is it? Where are you tonight?" Jonac asked. His voice mingled with the echoes and The Song.

Tension spread across my forehead, his eyes opening wide. He just wanted to help.

If I confessed everything, my pain would end. I could tell him how my parents and Shay had died, how Rena and The Thief plagued my dreams. My gut rolled and the noise in my head got louder.

What would he say?

I closed my eyes and recalled the way he looked when I asked about The Thief.

What would he say? He would tell me to leave. I killed Shay. I killed my parents. And I brought a malitu into his home.

"I'm fine," I said. "It's been a long day."

Jonac placed a hand on each of my shoulders, like my mother used to. He smiled and held my gaze. The spinning storm of noise started to slow down.

"Tomorrow morning, I have to leave again. You know that, right?" His cadence slowed and his voice lowered. "Torrel and I have to scout for a summer site, and the elder council gave me permission to bring you with us."

The echoes went silent beneath my shock, and my face fell slack.

Jonac chuckled. "You need to get away for a few days. The quiet will do you good."

"But I'm not pledged. I'm not Jani."

"Your swearing day is less than a turn away. Once you're an adult, you can join the clan, if that's what you want."

I tried to imagine myself wrapping my hair in chani cloth and calling myself Jani, traveling every three moons to a new outcropping, growing old as a nomad.

"If you want, you can stay here and prepare the move again," Jonac said.

"Torrel hates me," I said. Jonac slowly opened his mouth to disagree, but I saved him his lies. "He calls me 'spy'. I don't know if he knows my real name."

"Of course he knows your name," he said before measuring his thoughts. "I think he knows your name. He must." Jonac chuckled. "Okay, he might not, but this isn't his decision."

"The elders think it's a good idea?"

"Enough of them agreed it would help if we had an extra set of hands with us," Jonac said.

"I am honored they have so much confidence in me," I said sarcastically.

"It's only been eight moons. Did you expect immediate love and admiration? If so, I have to tell you, you aren't as likable as you think," Jonac said and snickered at his supposed wit. "Give them time. Trust is difficult in the best times.

"You wear our clothes and study our ways, but you aren't Jani. If you choose to take the pledge, trust will come with time, but something is holding you back." He gave me a moment to speak, and when I didn't, he continued, "You don't have to tell me now. Your truths are your own.

"But it seems we have not earned your trust either, little brother," he said with a tired smile. "Trust is a journey, and maybe joining Torrel and me would be a good first step. I'll leave it to you, but I would enjoy the company should you choose to come." He stood up from the game and walked out into the night, the furs hanging over the entrance swaying back and forth after him.

I stared at the markers in front of me. The white runes spread across the ground. The Thief's mark wasn't there, no matter how many times I searched.

If I took the pledge, my life would be a maze of walls—walls to keep the empire out, walls to quiet the echoes, and walls to hide the truth from everyone around me. Surrounded by the clan and still alone. But I would be safe.

In a way, Torrel saw me clearer than anyone. Even in the silences between us, he didn't offer niceties. He hated me. He treated me like the threat I was, and I resented him for it. A petty piece of my spirit wanted to join the scouting mission to antagonize him.

I started packing my things before I admitted to myself that I was going.

As I shoved a set of robes into my travel sack, I realized how little of what I had belonged to me. My robes were passoffs from another boy who had outgrown them. I slept on Jonac's spare bedroll. My blanket belonged to Nomi. Even my knife had belonged to my father. I looked at the old blade, and my eyes started watering.

Ever the thief, I thought.

———

The Thief sat across from me, cloaked in shadow, waiting for my next move. This time, I refused to play. Because of her, I had nothing left to call my own. I stared into her hidden face and set my teeth in defiance. She couldn't make me play.

If she noticed my small act of rebellion, she did not show it. She sat unmoving, her shadow cloak gently wafting in the darkness.

"Look at what you made me!" I screamed. She did not stir. "Take back your tainted spirit! I don't want it!"

The Thief reached a slow hand towards me. I tried to move, but my body didn't respond. The tingle of déjà vu ran through me. The sensation reminded me of the day I crossed over and walked in The Mist.

Her shadow-laden hand fell cold upon my shoulder. I couldn't breathe. The darkness filled my lungs. My body was too heavy. I thrashed inside the prison of my own body. Darkness claimed everything, and then I fell.

In the pitch black, her face appeared, still and perfect, as if it were a thing made, not living. Her black skin from the nose up ran smooth as polished onyx, and the lower half shone as white as the clearest snowfall. Even though she didn't have a mouth, it wasn't an absence. Her face was exactly as it should be. I stared into her white eyes, stark against the blackness of her skin, then she vanished.

I floated through the canopy of a forest. Ironoak and ashburn trees passed by. Below me, a Tomakan boy ran through the thick wood. He stopped. In front of him, two soldiers moved to encircle a girl.

Shay.

"No!" I screamed.

I didn't want to see her die again, but The Thief's icy grip held me firm. She wouldn't allow me to close my eyes.

The scene played out exactly as I remembered it. Shay turned to save me, and when she did, the second soldier struck at her. Only this time, I didn't steal The Flame from the second soldier. I charged at him with a knife, and he held up a red, glowing crystal.

I watched from above as flames consumed me.

Suddenly, I found myself writhing on the forest floor covered in fire rather than watching from above. The heat crawled over my skin. I was inside my body, burning. Yet, I was so cold.

I woke up screaming as Jonac shook me by my shoulders.

Nomi, Soca, and Junera sat up on their bedrolls, looking at me with wide eyes.

I gulped down the air like I had been drowning.

"It was only a dream," Jonac said. "You are home. You are safe."

My eyes were swollen with salt water. "I'm sorry," I sobbed. And I was, for so many things.

"If we could control our dreams, we would never leave them," Jonac said with a kind smile. It should have reassured me, but when I looked at him and his family, I only saw more burning bodies.

Nomi walked over to us and handed me a waterskin. I had seen her do the same for Soca when she had a bad dream. The comforting gesture turned my gut with guilt. I had invaded their home. If they knew what I was, they would not be as kind. They would send me away, and they would be right to do so.

"I see you decided to join us," Jonac said. I followed his eyes to my travel sack of borrowed belongings, and I nodded.

Last night, I decided to help them scout for the next encampment. This morning, I decided I would go with them for a different reason. I had to leave the clan to keep them safe.

I held my tongue. If I said anything, I would tell them everything.

"See to your morning chores," Jonac said. "We leave half to high sun."

I nodded and looked around the tent, saying silent goodbyes.

Chapter Eighteen

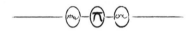

As we walked farther away from the tent city, the echoes began peeling away, not like the temporary reprieve of my morning trainings with Jonac. No, they faded away to nothingness. The constant pressure at my temples relented, and the line from one thought to the next flowed easier.

I had spent the last two seasons in the company of eighteen different versions of The Song slamming against my barriers at all hours. They filled the air, thick as pollen in spring, but now I could breathe.

Jonac's and Torrel's echoes whispered amongst the birds and the wind. On their own, they accented The Song rather than overwhelm it. And in a matter of days, they would be gone as well. No more echoes. No more lying. No more harboring a malitu amongst people I cared for.

"I told you the open forest would be good for you," Jonac said.

No more Jonac. All the weight that vanished from my shoulders fell on my chest. *It is the right thing to do.*

I returned his smile. "You were right. I have such a wise kana."

"If only you knew how lucky you are, little brother."

"I do," I said. "I truly do."

"No need to get serious on me."

When he woke up to find me gone, he would be hurt. Hopefully, he wouldn't blame himself. If I were brave, I would tell him to his face. But then he would ask questions I couldn't answer. Better he thought of me as a coward than a thief.

His echo lightly fluttered in the canopy, harmonizing with The Song. Oddly beautiful.

"What do you hear?" Jonac asked.

I snapped my head towards him like a child caught stealing sugarcane. Jonac crinkled his brows and clarified, "The Song, little brother. What do you hear in The Song?"

The breath trapped in my lungs escaped. "Of course. I knew that."

The forest faded from focus as I reached towards The Song. It rushed over me like when I walked in The Mist so many moons ago. Absent the clan's echoes, The Song sang loud enough to drown out the world if I let it. If I opened myself to it, I could cross into The Mist, and my spirit would rush through the veil to the world of the spirits, alongside my parents and Shay.

Immediately, I shut myself off from The Song. Only windblown trees and silence remained. *What would I say to them? What would they say to me?*

My breath abandoned me, and my knees locked in place.

"Little brother, what's wrong?"

"Is there a reason we survived? Why us?"

"The Seed is the spirit of forgiveness and new beginnings." His voice lowered to a soft grumble. "We have to allow ourselves a new season."

We never spoke of it, but we were brothers in many ways, tied together with regrets we didn't speak of. He let the silence linger, as if inviting me to share. My whole story thumped inside my chest.

I swallowed hard and pushed myself forward. The lightness and the freedom of the morning had disappeared.

Jonac resumed pace beside me. He never asked for more than what was freely given. He hummed, as he often did, and the gentle melody filled the space between us.

When the late spring sun gave way to the waning moons, we set camp for the night.

"I'll take the first shift if you'll take the second, Jonac," Torrel said, placing his full emphasis on Jonac's name in case I was too dull to understand his implication.

Jonac nodded and dropped his heavy hand on my shoulder to interrupt my objection.

With one passive-aggressive suggestion, Torrel ruined my escape plan. Though, ironically, he wanted me gone more than anyone.

"I'll take your watch. You should get some sleep," I said.

"If it means that much to you, you'll take a shift tomorrow," Jonac said. We turned in unison. Torrel rummaged through his pack and pulled out his hatchet. Jonac looked between me and the small axe. "I'll speak with him."

There was an art and a grace to how Jonac managed conflict. He never fought the tide. He addressed the moons, rather than the waters they pulled.

After our evening meal, when he typically would have asked me to join him for a game of runes, he asked Torrel instead. The young man made a fuss over the invitation, like Jonac had inconvenienced him, and then he made his way over to where Jonac sat.

Over the next few hours, they played game after game. I ran my knife over a whetstone as they jabbered away. Torrel laughed and smiled, and not sarcastically. The constant anger that he carried slipped from around his shoulders.

Torrel didn't hate me. Well, maybe he did, but he also missed his old kana. The man who helped raise him, who was too busy with growing children and a new toka.

The blackness of my dream softened to slate gray. My fingers brushed the cold stone wall. A cavity opened up in the wall, revealing a stone figure, a familiar silhouette. Jagged edges elongated each of the figure's joints, as if the sculpture depicted a woman made of stone—The Mountain.

I ran my fingers over Munnie's handiwork. Not even a turn past, I had taken these moments for granted. This hallow—Munnie's hallow—had been a safe haven in an unsafe world.

The colorful tapestries splashed against their gray backdrops. Everything was as it had been. Lavish rugs covered large sections of the swept dirt floor. Books and trinkets sat in their places along the shelves.

I am home, I thought.

A brushing sound interrupted my moment of euphoria. Munnie knelt in front of her idols to the Great Spirits, seven prisms protruding from the earth. My heart twisted off its axis. Her wrinkled hands shaved thin curls of cherrywood into a stone basin at her feet. Then she picked up her flint rock and scraped her knife against the stone like a gentle wave. When the shavings caught a spark, she lifted the basin to her lips and blew over the ember. A wisp of smoke lifted into the air before the flames rose.

Munnie placed the basin in front of the prisms and smiled, though the gesture didn't fill her cheeks or wrinkle the edges of her eyes. My lips mirrored hers, and I knew the sadness behind her expression.

When the first prayer passed her lips, I nearly collapsed to my knees at the sound of her voice.

She would have chastised me for eavesdropping on her prayers, but I didn't care. Her voice rang out low and steady. The corners of my eyes grew wet. I mouthed the names of each spirit along with her. Then I stopped.

"To the seventh—The Thief, the spirit of balance. The world has tipped too far in one direction. Help us regain our footing," she prayed.

The light dimmed. Munnie sat in front of her prisms, and everything faded away.

The Thief stood as an outline in the dark. She lifted her hand, and a flame sparked out of nothingness. The fire flickered over her palm, black as obsidian. "Do you see? I am not hated by all." Her words hissed and echoed in the empty chasm.

"It's an old prayer. It's tradition. It doesn't make us welcome," I said. My voice cracked with soft intensity.

Munnie believed in remembering. Our stories and traditions carried us beyond a lifetime. It didn't mean that she would suffer a malitu. Munnie wouldn't hesitate to turn me away. If not for what I was, then for what I had done to Shay.

In the light's glimmer, The Thief's cheeks went taut in a smile absent lips. It made the hairs on my arms prickle. She closed her palm around the flame, then all went black again.

"Goodbye for now, little thief." Her whisper filled my dream, reverberating like an echo.

For all my hours of sleep, I awoke wearier than I had been the night before. We gathered the camp in a quick fashion. I renewed my role, hauling water from the river as I had when we first journeyed to the Jani.

It was a short walk, but even a short walk with waterskins for three people made a hard start to the morning.

When I returned, I handed out the shares of water. Torrel snatched his from my outstretched hand and turned away. Then he stopped, looked back, and met my eyes. "Thank you," he said in a quiet, gruff voice.

I nearly dropped the remaining waterskins. He continued to stare at me. "Oh, you're welcome."

He grunted and went back to tying off his pack. The exchange had almost been kind. Jonac must have found magic words to make that happen.

Torrel and Jonac lead the path north, closer to the Tomakan border. Summer had yet to break through the morning chill, but Sokan rose large on the horizon and threatened to make the trees sweat by midday.

I walked at a distance back. *What will they do when they wake up tomorrow and I am gone?*

Childishly, I hoped they would look for me, but it would be better for everyone if they didn't. Jonac always said I was free to go, and Torrel would be eager to be rid of me. One brief pleasantry wouldn't change that.

They might search for a morning, but they had to think about the good of the clan. In a season or two, I would be a small story of a boy they once knew. It would be a better story than I deserved.

When I looked up from my thoughts, they weren't there. My shoulders bounced with hurried breaths. My heartbeat thumped in my ears. The forest ran thick with birch and sycamore trees. No sand-colored robes. No bright chani cloth. Then their echoes cut through my panic.

I found them over a hill and through a tight cropping of bushes. My body settled. Then laughter forced its way through me.

"What's so funny?" Torrel asked with his usual demeanor.

"I thought I'd lost you," I said.

He rolled his eyes and went back to his regular stride.

They weren't where I expected them to be, I told myself. *It caught me off-guard. When I walk into the forest tonight, I will leave them sleeping by the fire. I will be the one who is gone.*

———

While Sokan settled low in the sky, Jonac joined me for a time. We spoke of The Song. He quizzed me about the plants we passed and their uses. I attended him as a toka should. If he suspected my plan, he said nothing of it. I recited the herbs and plants used to draw infection from a wound.

In such a short time, I had learned so much. I never thought I would have a brother spirit to guide me. Munnie taught me what she could, but she only heard The Song through The Mountain. Jonac knew the way

The Seed reverberated through the ground and how The Seed moved when he called.

I savored every word we exchanged that night.

Maybe I hovered too closely because Jonac shooed me away while he prepared dinner. He insisted that Torrel and I play a game of runes, insinuating I had a better handle on the game than Torrel. Apparently, Jonac had been prodding his former toka throughout the day.

Pride got the better of the wind dancer. Before I had even sat down, he had drawn the six lines in the dirt and picked out his runes. He stared at me as I slowly pulled the ironoak pebbles from my leather pouch. His expression made it clear he didn't intend to enjoy this game in the slightest.

Contrary to Jonac's taunting, Torrel's skill far surpassed my own. One game after another, the crosspoints filled up with his white runes. I managed to stretch the games, but each move I made led to the same ending—Torrel grinning like a fool and asking me if I wanted to play again in a snide tone.

I shifted through the runes in my hand—two Flame, one Mountain, one Shadow, and one Seed. Torrel had played The River twice already. They were likely in his pouch or in his hand. One of his Wind runes lay face up on a crosspoint. With one Wind and both River runes out of play, odds lay in favor of The Flame. I laid the rune next to one of his facedown pieces.

"Don't worry," he said with a smile. "You'll get better with time. All children do." He turned over his piece and revealed The Mountain.

I had grown used to losing. Over eight moons, I had only won a handful of games against Jonac. But Torrel's smug fucking face riled something primal in me. Acid rose in my stomach and filled my mouth with curses. Since the first time I met him, he had been nothing but a prick.

Enough of Jonac's excuses for him. I didn't care about his tragic childhood or that he missed Jonac. Whether he acted out of jealousy, protectiveness, or pure disdain, I didn't care anymore. I picked up the last rune he flipped over and, without thinking, flicked the rune at him.

The smooth, white pebble of ironoak clinked against my finger, soared through the air, and landed square between his eyes. It couldn't have hurt badly, but hopefully it would leave a mark.

His face went blank, as if he couldn't decide if I had done what I had done.

His echo flared first, then fury replaced shock. Torrel launched himself from where he sat. I raised my hands in front of me, and we crashed to the ground. Instinctively, I rolled with the force of his attack, and we tumbled over one another.

The ground and the sky flipped places several times. Then the world flickered black, and my head blazed hot. Sharp pain cut through the back of my head when it crashed against a rock jutting out from the soil.

His echo rose up, high and piercing. His hands whirled above me. The echo screamed and the wind started to stir. A single thread of soft light waved in the air above my head. I reached up an unsteady hand and grabbed the thread, then his echo hushed.

Torrel stared down at me with raised eyebrows. Then he was gone.

Jonac ripped Torrel off me and tossed him to the ground. The old man had more muscle than one would expect. His chest bounced heavily with adrenaline. His nostrils flared, and he stared down at the both of us like he wanted blood.

"How dare you call the spirits against another child of Ennea?" he yelled with quiet intensity. "A man doesn't shame his ancestors with the blood of their own."

"And you," he said, turning towards me. "Are you such a child that you would attack someone over a game?"

His gaze burned into the side of my face as I lay in the dirt, averting my eyes.

Finally, he turned his back on us. "Pray for forgiveness and go to sleep. Maybe you'll find some sense by morning."

A strange fullness rolled around my gut. It pulsed with a rush of energy.

The Wind!

The spirit didn't batter at me from the inside. Its echo called to me, enticing me to reach for the power within, but my judgment won out.

With a slow breath, I let go of the spirit.

Torrel's echo surged back to life. He spun back around. A question sparked in his eyes, an unspoken thought. He scowled at me and walked back to his bedroll.

No choice now, I thought. *I have to leave tonight.*

I pretended to sleep as the others settled into the night. The hours passed slowly.

We were at the northern edge of Sonacoa, following the Sand River north. They were following the river into Tomak to scout for a new site for the clan. And if they were headed north, I would cut over the river and continue east.

They could track me if they chose, though the river crossing would make it more difficult, but I doubted they would. Jani must think of the whole before the one.

My plan didn't extend beyond the night. As long as I escaped and stopped being a burden, that would be enough. They would all be better off without me—the Jani, Jonac, Nomi and the girls.

Kana and Toka passed high night when Jonac stirred from his watch. He fed a couple of fresh logs to the coals and the fire tossed sparks into the air. Then his footsteps grew closer.

He leaned over me and clutched my shoulder. "Your shift, little brother."

As I looked up from my bedroll, all the things I should have said settled on my tongue, waiting. But I said nothing.

I splashed my face with a palm full of water and settled against a tree. Jonac tossed back and forth several times on his bedroll. Once he started snoring, I gathered my possessions into my pack. If they slept through the night, I would have half a night before they discovered I had left.

The firelight flickered over Jonac's face. Doubt caught in my throat. *He's already given me too much,* I told myself. If I wanted to return his kindness, I had to take this malitu and run.

I picked up a stick from beside the fire and wrote a quick message in the dirt. It had to be clear that I had left of my own accord. Or else they would wait for me or chase me.

As I walked away from the firelight, their echoes faded. For the first time in two seasons, I was utterly alone. It would have been peaceful under different circumstances, but in this case, I missed the sound of Jonac. Over the seasons, his echo had become a comfort, a beacon guiding me home. Tears collected in my eyes as I walked in silence.

When I reached the river, I filled my skins before crossing.

Each step through the river sank deeper into the silt. The rushing current grabbed at my feet. The calm surface hid the danger within.

No turning back now. I pulled myself onto the bank and walked east by the starlight.

The sun rose four fingers above the treetops before exhaustion took me. The last of spring filled the air with a sticky heat. An old ironoak nearby cast a heavy shadow. At least it would keep the light off my face. I drank deeply from a waterskin and fell asleep.

———

When I woke, Sokan had handed over the sky to Kana once again. The crickets chirped in the soft dark of early night. Sweat saturated my robes. A moment of panic flashed over me before I remembered why I was alone. It took several deep breaths to slow my heart.

I pulled a piece of saltmeat from my pack and stood to walk. The fatty sting of the dried venison gave me something to focus on.

A thin noise cut through the natural sound of the forest, whining into the night. An echo. It wasn't familiar. It cried high and tight in the west, back towards the river.

Are they following me?

Oddly, the idea strengthened my resolve to leave them. I adjusted my pack, took a few more steps before two more echoes joined the first.

The trees started flying by me before a clear thought passed through my mind. Darkness had fallen over the wood. My feet stumbled for proper footing on the rocky soil. Low branches swiped at me. What I couldn't avoid, I pushed through. The forest tore my skin, and the air stung.

"Mother, let them be okay," I prayed through heavy gasps.

The echoes grew and metal clashed in the distance.

My foot caught an exposed root, and I crashed into the ground. Plumes of fire lit up the forest. Blurs of green and yellow flashed between the gaps in the trees. I dropped my pack and sprinted towards the fire.

Not again! I thought. *I led them straight into danger.*

When I got close enough to see the battle, my lungs burned and my hands shook. What I saw wasn't what I expected.

Chapter Nineteen

Singed branches loomed over the battle. Small fires illuminated the scene. A young woman gracefully dodged a soldier's sword thrust as if they had choreographed their movements. The soldier reared back with the blade and attacked again, only to be parried with a quick flip of the woman's short blade. She moved with such speed and ease, running one soldier into the other's path, making their advantage disorienting.

Firelight reflected off her deep midnight skin. As she moved, her long, loc'd hair swirled about like flames in the wind. Her white robe fanned out and followed her flowing movements. The sound of her echo surged as she reached into the sky. When she drew her hand back in a short arc, water leeched through the plants and soil, leaving a thin layer resting on the rocky earth. Then she snapped her torso up and wrenched her hands apart from each other, and the water froze.

The soldiers tripped as the ice clung to their boots. Seizing the opportunity, she dashed forward and lunged at the closer soldier. He rolled away, and, as her blade pierced his thigh instead of his ribs, his scream cut the night in twain.

Repeating patterns of the night Shay died clashed with the fight in front of me, and I couldn't move.

The other soldier picked herself up from the frozen ground and rushed towards the water dancer. As her long, silver-white hair spilled out of her helm and fluttered in the wind, she gripped a sword in one hand and a spirit crystal in the other. The crystal's strained echo reared up, then the soldier disappeared into a cloud of shadows.

Only a thin seam separated the shadows that surrounded her from the night as the bastard song moved with her.

Firelight glinted off her sword as it peeked through the shadows and sliced across the water dancer's lower back. The dancer yelped and swung her blade through the empty darkness.

The last time I tried to stop soldiers from murdering a young woman, Shay ended up dead.

Metal flickered through the air as the soldier's blade reached from the shadows and sliced through the dancer's calf, driving her to her knees. In and out of the shadows, one small cut after another, each eliciting another cry from the water dancer.

Blood stained her white robes. She swung her blade wildly into the darkness. It clanged against her attacker's blade. Then the soldier responded with a long cut along the dancer's forearm, and the Sonacoan woman's short blade tumbled out of her grasp.

She fell forward, catching herself on her hands and knees. With each labored breath, her back arched and her head dipped.

Shay's burned face flashed in front of me, blood filling her mouth. "Run. Run away, thief," she said as she turned away from me.

"No. No. No!" I screamed out into the night and snatched the spirit from the air.

The Shadow raged inside me, tearing at my flesh from the inside.

As her shadow cloak evaporated, leaving her exposed, firelight highlighted the soldier's sharp, white features. Her brow lifted in confusion, then blood bubbled from her lips. When she looked down, the tip of the dancer's blade protruded from her side.

Both the soldier and the dancer wavered in the night. Fires flickered around them. The soldier's head bowed, and then her body collapsed into a heap.

A crescendo. Another stolen spirit cried out. The other soldier regained his stance, limping towards the defenseless Sonacoan. Fire sparked and then crawled along the forest floor as he raised his crystal. The flames lit up his face, his teeth bared in a twisted smile.

That is a malitu, I thought. *A wretched disease wearing skin, playing with our spirits. It's time he met a real thief.*

The fire spreading over the forest floor quelled.

The rage of both spirits within me fueled my own. I stomped through the trees towards the soldier. A fallen branch cracked under me. The soldier squinted in my direction, then he looked down at the crystal. He shook it before extending his palm towards me, but nothing happened.

I drew my father's knife, the small weapon gleaming in the scattered fires. His body stiffened, and his eyes widened as I became the malitu he could never be.

Despite his padded armor and the sword hanging in the scabbard at his side, he turned and tried to limp away.

The tortured spirits demanded blood, to claim it for themselves, but I refused them. They thrashed around more violently. But this wretch deserved a sharp blade and a bloody death.

The wounded soldier's lagging gait made it easy work. Within five quick strides I reached the hobbled man, and, without preamble, I stabbed my knife into the thick of his throat. Blood sprayed and coated my blade hand. It felt warm to the night's cool breeze.

I had never killed a man with a blade before. He flopped onto the ground, clutching at his neck. His life poured out of him with his blood. I didn't bend to the weight of killing another person. I didn't reel back from his blood on my skin. No, I reveled in it.

Kneeling down next to the dying man, I plunged my knife through his quilted guard into his chest. The fabric dimpled before breaking, then my knife nicked bone.

His body clutched the blade as I pulled it out, and then I stabbed him again and again. The metallic smell of his blood mixed with shit as I tore into his bowels. My muscles ached by the time I finished.

He wasn't a man. He was my enemy. The stolen spirits celebrated the gore. Then it all went black for a time.

I woke in the deep of night to something gripping my leg. Knife still in hand, I spun towards my would-be assailant before stopping short.

The wounded water dancer's fingers clutched at my pant leg. Our eyes met for a moment, and speckles of green highlighted her umber irises. They contained a story without ending. Then her head slumped to the ground, lying prone with the rest of her tattered body.

Her white robes ran shades of red and pink. Soft puffs of air blew over the back of my hand in an uneven rhythm as I reached under her nose.

Blessed Mother.

Gently as I could, I turned her onto her back to examine her wounds. Eleven cuts, some deeper than others, all steadily bleeding. She stood a step away from The Mist. I could barely reconcile this dying girl with the dancer who moved like the rapids.

Pressure built up behind the bridge of my nose and throbbed.

The small fires that spread across the battle had fallen to ash. The soldiers lay dead, Sand River babbled from the west, and, behind it all, a strange absence pulled at my spirit. In the darkness, the red crystal glowed. A deep purple crystal lay under the corpse of the woman the water dancer had killed.

I was as trapped as the spirits.

With my limited knowledge of healing, I could keep the water dancer from The Mist for a day, maybe two. It would be easier to ease her crossing. If I left her, it would amount to the same thing.

Malitu or not, my parents raised me better. I needed help. Jonac and Torrel would be a day away by now, and that was if I could track them.

As I gathered my thoughts and my things, I slipped the dancer's short

blade and the spirit crystals into my travel sack. The dead remained
where they fell. Too many heavy steps lay ahead of me. No reason to
make them heavier.

The water dancer grimaced and moaned.

She's not Shay, I told myself. *She's not going to die.*

The Song sang hollow and low, a chorus of breath and sorrow. One
after another I called moonlight hazel, barberry, and aloe from the soil.

What I would give for a mortar and pestle.

I ground the bark, leaves, and berries down as best I could with a rock
and mixed them with dirt and water. Better than an open wound. The
paste caked against her blood-slick skin. In thanks and prayer, I kissed
three of my fingers and touched them to the ground.

For all of her fierceness, she was a slight woman. Still, it took two
tries to heft her over my shoulder like a sack of grain. I had to hurry.
Gentleness required time I didn't have. Jonac would be able to fix
whatever damage I did. He had to.

The moons had begun their final fall when I reached the river. As
I eased over the riverbank, the water splashed against her, and she
groaned. Then the strength of the river pulled at us both. It would have
been a simple thing to let the current take us.

She had fought off two couta bastards to stay alive. At the very least, I
could fight my own despair.

After I set her on the riverbank, I pulled the two crystals from
my travel sack. Nothing could free the spirits, but at least the Gousht
wouldn't find them.

"I'm sorry," I whispered to the crystals and let the river's current sweep
them away.

Whatever lingering hope I held onto expired when I reached the
campsite where I had left Jonac and Torrel. Nothing remained but
drowned ash and overturned soil.

Jonac had always told me that I could leave. My chest constricted. *Had
it been so easy for him? Did he look for me at all?*

With one decision, I had abandoned a second family and failed to save another young woman from the Gousht.

I laid her down against a tree, and her head slumped to the side. Her breath felt softer against the back of my hand. When I dripped water over her lips, she coughed, then slowly drank. Her consciousness might have been drifting, but her body wanted to survive.

Past the blood and bruising, she wore a peaceful expression. Maybe she would be better off with the spirits, far from all this violence. Then again, maybe I would too. I shook my head and took a deep breath. Thoughts like that could consume a person. Best to keep moving.

The dancer's skin grew paler. Most of the poultice I applied earlier had washed away with the river. I reapplied what little I had left. Shallow or not, each cut bled. Each cut created a potential infection. By The Mother's grace, none of them had turned color yet, but she needed a true healer.

Sokan would call Jonac and Torrel from their dreams in a couple of hours. If I had any chance of finding them, I needed to leave immediately. Not that I had much chance of chasing down two well-rested nomads with a stranger slung over my shoulder.

What choice did I have? The river flowed north, and I ran with it.

The dancer's weight bounced on my shoulder. Strain traveled the length of my back. Flashes of the dead soldier replaced the forest. My father's knife plunged into his body, the wound gripped the blade, and I pulled it out and drove it back in.

What kind of person does that?

The river had cleaned my skin, but blood stained the sleeve of my robe. I didn't regret it. With each stab, I had driven my anger into him. Then, the moment before the world went black, a calm peace had flowed through me.

What does that make me?

Sunlight made it easier to follow the Jani's tracks, but it also meant they would be moving farther away.

At least they didn't know they were being followed. Between my two kanas, I had learned enough to track most people, but Jonac wasn't most people. For a man of peace, he knew much of war.

When Sokan crested the high point of the sky, my body started rebelling. My gait slowed. My shoulder spasmed. My spine screamed as if someone whittled away at the bone with the finest whisper of a blade.

The pain was so distracting, I almost stumbled over the doused embers of a campfire. They should have crossed at least twice the distance since I left. Something had gone wrong—well, something else had gone wrong.

I set the water dancer down as gently as I could. My back buckled, and I fell to the ground beside her.

What slowed them down?

If the Gousht found the water dancer, they could have found Jonac and Torrel. My breath hurried. There would have been a sign. The green bastards never bothered being subtle.

How many times had Jonac told me that worry wasted time? "Worry reminds the mind of a moment. Wisdom knows one moment always precedes the next."

The Jani and their sayings.

Crouching next to the water dancer, I checked her wounds. My hands shook despite my best efforts. Her healthy, dark complexion continued to grow paler. Her forehead warmed the back of my hand, despite how cool and damp the rest of her body had become. She breathed steadily, but that offered little comfort. A fever could kill as easy as a blade, and I didn't have the skill to stop it.

I fed her what water she would take and tried to think of something to do.

Another young woman taken by the Gousht, and I could only watch the life fade from her. Just like before.

Underneath the blood and fever, this woman had been someone. Had she been at all like Shay? Did the water inside her run as wild and free as the fire within Shay?

I didn't even know her name, but I needed to understand her. If I was the last person to touch her before she walked into The Mist, I should have known...

One sharp piercing echo entwined with a second, frail but present, called in the distance. They sang with a familiar cadence.

With nothing to weigh me to the earth, I tore through the trees towards the sound of my hope. As I grew closer, the echoes solidified. The Seed and The Wind.

The trees scraped against me and ripped my already tattered robes. Winces of pain didn't matter. My body was forfeit. I had to save the water dancer.

My legs strained against the heaviness as I screamed out for Jonac. Again and again, I shouted into the open forest until my voice crumbled to a muffled growl. My throat turned to sand, and my lungs couldn't hold air any longer. And still, I called out for Jonac.

The brush shifted in front of me, and there he stood. The squat, dark-skinned nomad with a bushy red beard, looking old and confused. He moved too slowly to catch me before I collapsed.

When I opened my eyes again, night had taken over the sky. Flames licked the edges of my vision. Pain wrapped my body, but I could breathe again.

I must have stirred or made a noise because Jonac came to my side.

Heavy dark circles lay under his eyes. "You don't get to do that," he said with a quiet heaviness. "You cannot leave your kana with nothing more than a couple of words scrawled in the dirt."

He shook his head. Every turn of his age wore plain on his face. "'Don't follow.' What kind of goodbye is that?" He gave me a weak smile.

A signal flashed in my mind, something that I had to tell him. Something important.

The water dancer.

I tried to sit up, but Jonac forced my shoulders back down. "Don't worry. We found her," he said, catching my wide eyes. "She will be alright. It will take time, but her wounds will heal. You need to rest."

"How?" I asked, the words coming out raw and flat.

"Start by closing your eyes," Jonac said with another weak smile. "When I found you, you collapsed. You kept saying 'save her'. You looked like you had been beaten two breaths from the end." Jonac shook his head, almost proud. "You'll have to tell me what happened, you know.

"Torrel carried you and we followed your tracks back here," he said. "I'm afraid he wasn't gentle.

"We found her propped against a tree, breathing, bleeding and shaking like a leaf in the wind. She wouldn't have lasted the night. You saved her."

I turned my head away from him, ashamed.

"Well, whatever the story, you need to rest." He left me there, bundled in a blanket near the fire with my thoughts.

As much as they would be better for it, I couldn't leave now. I didn't have the strength to leave a second time. The shame lapped against me like a rising tide until I gave into exhaustion.

There in the darkness, a shadow-cloaked spirit waited.

CHAPTER TWENTY

"WE NEED TO KNOW what happened. Where did she come from? Who did this to her? What if there are soldiers tracking her? Do you think your little pet covered his tracks when he dragged her through the forest? Do you even know where he went?"

Each question tore deeper into my dream until only my eyes were closed to The Waking. Torrel's voice came from every direction. He liked to pace when he was angry. Safe to say I had seen it often enough to picture it in my head quite vividly—exaggerated gestures, feet stomping against the ground.

Jonac remained silent, but he was there, allowing an angry man space for his anger. His echo brushed through the forest in soft waves. A drastic contrast to the sharp, conflicting tones of Torrel's echo.

Maybe my headache would subside if I reached up and snatched the jarring spirit from the air.

The heavy footsteps stopped as Torrel's echo built to a plateau. "Did you forget what can happen when we welcome strangers without question?"

The soil below me quaked with the power of The Seeds shadow song. "You speak as a child wearing the body of a man. Do you think you are the only person who lost something?" His voice strained against the words as if they had to push their way from his throat.

"Every day since that massacre, I feel the ache and regret for those sent into The Mist. I dream their faces, and you dare accuse me of forgetting. Maybe you forget who gathered you off the ground and washed the slaughter from your skin."

Jonac breathed in sharply, let out a sustained exhale, and his echo receded. "That day defines everyone who survived it. If we let it, our sorrow will consume us, and we will abandon all of our principles. We will become wanderers with no purpose but survival."

"Say what you will, but the council won't let you keep your stray," Torrel said with what venom he had left. Then a pair of footsteps trailed off into the forest.

Jonac settled back to the ground next to me. His echo beat in a staccato rhythm, heavy and daunting. I had been selfish. Pain existed beyond me and my problems.

The water dancer coughed and stirred. Jonac grunted as he pushed himself to his feet. He mumbled to himself as he hunched over the water dancer. Too soft to hear.

The sun stood at its peak when I woke again. Jonac huddled over the woman on the other side of the firepit. When he looked up from his work, our eyes met. For a moment, he hesitated, his face drooped, and then he stood and walked over to me.

Pain tore like a dying fire through my chest. The muscles in my lower back and arms resisted movement as I pushed myself into a sitting position. My body was a collection of pieces that would tear apart if I moved too quickly.

"I'm sorry." I stared at the dirt between us, and my tears dropped to the ground.

Softly, Jonac reached into the silence between us. "What happened?"

What happened to me? Why did I leave? What was I hiding? Where did I go? Too many questions fit into two words.

I answered the only question I could and told him about the attack. Mostly, I told him the truth. How the fires had burned in the night. How the water dancer had fought off two soldiers, one cloaked in shadows. How the shadow-clad soldier had toyed with the water dancer, cutting her again and again. The pieces that would reveal my secret fell to the side. If he caught shame in my voice, hopefully, he attributed it to something else.

"I stood there, rooted to the ground, watching blood spill from each new wound as the shadow swirled around her. If I hadn't waited, maybe she'd be awake now."

"Or maybe you would both be dead," Jonac said.

"She dropped to her knees, bleeding, and I couldn't watch anymore. I charged at the shadows. With my stupid luck, I must have surprised the soldier. The shadow hesitated and her face peeked through the black cloud."

I turned to look at the water dancer lying near the fire pit. *What if she tells the truth about what happened?* I thought. *The whole truth.*

"Then the water dancer struck her blade into the shadow, and the cloud vanished, leaving the soldier falling to the ground with a blade in her side. If Shay hadn't saved me, I would have died.

"I was so scared. The water dancer collapsed, and the other soldier hobbled off into the forest. Then something came over me. Hatred, I guess. I didn't realize what I had done until I pulled my knife from his throat, then I stabbed him over and over until I collapsed."

I looked at my kana and confessed. "It felt right. I killed him, and I was glad I did. What does that make me?" I sobbed into my hands. The soldier flashed in front of me, his belly torn open and leaking to the dirt.

Jonac leaned forward and rested his hands on my shoulders. "It makes you human," he said and pulled me into his arms. I collapsed on his shoulder and cried for more reasons than I could name.

When I pulled myself apart from him, he dropped his hands and said,

"Someday you will have to tell me who Shay is."

My heartbeat thudded in my ears, and I sharply inhaled as I realized my mistake. I hadn't spoken her name to anyone since she died.

He waved his hand. "Not today. You're not ready, and I won't pull your secrets from you. But I will be here when you're ready to let them go." His lips curled slightly before he rose to tend to the water dancer.

"Her name is Liara, in case you were curious," he said. "The water dancer. Her name is Liara. And it sounds to me like you saved each other." With that, he told me to rest and walked back to tend to her.

"Liara," I mumbled to myself.

After more than a day of wondering and too many footfalls to count—Liara.

My muscles locked into one unmovable mass. The hairs on my airs tingled. *What else did she say?*

Jonac would have said something. He didn't ease into troubled water; he dove in to find the current. If he knew I was a thief, he would be done with me. I might not have woken up at all.

No, she hadn't told him. But she still might.

I stared at them for a long while, Jonac dabbing her brow with a wet cloth. He cleaned her wounds and hummed as he worked. All the while, she lay there, unmoving.

Maybe she won't wake up, I thought, then winced at the ugliness of it.

Jonac's gentle voice lifted into the air. An old tune, too lovely it hurt. My eyelids fluttered, then fell.

> *Even when the night is cold*
> *There's always a way home*
> *Stars hidden by the clouds above*
> *There's always a way home*
> *Body is weary, and bones are old*
> *There's always a way home*

Long days missing those you love
There's always a way home
Just follow the river, follow the river
Follow the river home

Wooden planks scraped my bare feet. An indistinguishable murmur filled the air. A small crowd milled about. Brown faces and long, gray braids. My people. Several clay brick and wood buildings formed the background. Nomar. The town square. The caller's stage. My father's workshop would have been around the corner.

I tried to move, but two pairs of rough hands stretched my arms to either side. Torrel grinned with all his teeth, digging his fingers into my left arm. His eyes were blank. No emotion. No recognition. I yanked against his grip, and he held me tighter.

"Don't struggle, little brother. This is for your own good." Jonac stood to my right with a wild smile and the same empty gaze. "I know your secret, little brother."

"We all know," Rena said from the front of a crowd full of dead eyes and manic grins.

My breath drowned out the noise. Pulses of air stuttered in and out of my nose.

"You know what they say, 'No heart for a thief. No safe haven,'" Jonac whispered into my ear. "'Only a grave will do.'"

The boards beneath me creaked, and every head turned towards the sound of the footsteps. The town priest walked towards me with his red robe billowing behind him, his face veiled to the world, and his damn gaudy medallion jangling around his neck. His pale hand emerged from his oversized sleeve, holding a clear crystal.

Fear and hatred churned the acid in my belly. My captors held me firmly, no matter how much I jerked. I listened for The Song, for an echo, but only the priest's footsteps broke the silence. There was no one to help me.

The priest approached with the crystal, and it began to glow green. It felt as if my blood would leech out from every pore. I screamed. My skin stretched like a net trying to hold a thrashing salmon. My body threatened to fall apart into a mess of blood and bone.

Then all fell silent.

I collapsed like a cloth doll, held aloft between Jonac and Torrel's grasp. The Seed swirled within its prison.

Jonac leaned towards me, his breath hot against my face. "Blessed Mother, it would be a shame to waste a good spirit."

Rena presented a dagger to the priest. I hung loosely between the two nomads, too empty to resist. The priest drew back the blade and thrust it into my belly.

I woke up grasping at my gut and expecting blood. The empty night surrounded me, no priest or Rena, only Torrel cocking his eyebrow in confusion. Then he shook his head and returned to sliding his knife over his whetstone. The soft brushing sound moved like waves washing over the shore.

If I lay back down, the dream would ambush me as soon as I closed my eyes. Instead, I added a log to the fire and waited with my thoughts.

Several long hours passed before daybreak, and each moment took its time.

When Sokan announced herself, I jumped up to attend to my chores. Despite my sore body, I gathered my belongings and helped break down the campsite. Jonac sent Torrel to fill the waterskins, and I stayed behind to tend to the remains of the fire.

Every time I turned, Jonac's gaze followed me as if he expected me to disappear if he took his eyes off me for too long. His uncertainty began growing a new distance between us.

Jonac and I latched a bedroll between two sturdy branches and lifted

Liara onto the traveling cot. She groaned, but her eyes stayed closed.

It may have been too soon to move her, but we didn't have a choice. The Jani couldn't risk the chance we had been captured and revealed the clan's location. The invaders used ugly means to steal secrets. The clan wouldn't wait to find out.

As soon as we set the camp to rights, we left.

My back still ached, and my right thigh was tender. It seared with every step, but I shouldered my share regardless.

Torrel led the way back south as Jonac and I followed with Liara hoisted between us—Jonac out front and me behind. Eventually, the small sharp pains pulling at joints became normal.

As I walked, I stole glances of Liara and wondered at who she had been. The soft lines of her face pulled taut into a grimace. Sweat curved over her brow. My pain faded into the background as I studied hers.

What if she never opens her eyes again? What if she does?

As Munnie said, "A secret is not a wise gift for strangers."

I had hoisted her up and ran in a rush of adrenaline and guilt. Maybe I made the wrong decision. No matter how I tried to shake the selfish thoughts from my mind, she looked like a threat.

"You did well, little brother," Jonac called back, interrupting my thoughts. "You stopped the bleeding and carried her to help. You did all you could." He had misread my silence for concern or guilt. He thought me a better person than I was.

"If anything, it's my fault," he said.

"What?"

"I'll have to teach you more about healing plants and tonics when we return, assuming you're staying."

And there it was, the question that hung between us.

He didn't wait for an answer. "She'll make it. She's a strong one." Then, as if to confirm his words, her echo flittered underneath his. It sang unevenly and faintly, but unmistakably there. The sound both comforted and troubled me.

"Will the council exile me?"

Jonac stopped and looked at me over his shoulder. "So, you heard that, did you?" He took a deep breath and started walking again. "Truth, I don't know. Some of the elders remember our losses more than our journey."

He didn't offer any more words on the subject. His trepidation bore my fear deeper, and so we walked, carrying the broken water dancer and our fear.

For five days, we traced our steps back to the encampment, talking only out of necessity and small things. By a bit of grace, Torrel didn't speak to me once.

Occasionally, we slowed to rest and tend to Liara while Torrel scouted ahead. Time slipped away, but we could not risk carelessness. We hardly needed another encounter with the Gousht.

If we had taken another day, we would have found the encampment abandoned. As it was, we found several armed sentries in the forest surrounding the camp. When they saw us approaching, their faces flooded with relief. Then they caught eye of Liara.

Jonac waved away their questions, and we carried her through the tent city.

As we moved through the camp, it became a city of eyes that moved with us. Whispered questions filled the air like echoes. Even as the clan's focus coalesced around us, people did all they could to avoid us.

This is how they'll look when they discover what I am, I thought.

When we reached Jonac's tent, the girls squealed at the sight of their father, and I thanked The Mother for the relative quiet.

Nomi held the girls while Jonac and I laid Liara's traveling cot near the firepit. As soon as Nomi let them go, they rushed into their father's arms. He twirled them around, their feet swinging wildly. They giggled as he kissed them through his shaggy, red beard.

My father hadn't been one for large displays. When he held me, we became a quiet world on to ourselves. The sun and stars spun around us, one solid mass holding everything in place.

Nomi gave me a hug. Then I hugged the girls one at a time. Soca lingered, and I squeezed her tighter.

"Why were you gone so long? Were there soldiers? Did you have to fight an army? Who is she? Did you save her from the army? Did she save you from the army?" Junera asked her questions like they were one long question.

"Ah, my curious one, there will be time for the story later. I have to go report to Elder Lashan," Jonac said.

"Report to us first," Junera said.

Jonac grabbed the little girl and spun her around again, planting several kisses on her forehead before letting her go. She wobbled away, too dizzy to find her balance.

"See to Liara, then get some rest," Jonac said. "The council will probably call a gathering in the morning, and they will want to hear from you."

"I thought only pledged could speak at a gathering," I said.

"They'll have questions." He held my eyes in his for a moment more than comfortable.

After quick goodbyes to Nomi and the girls—he had to shake Soca loose before she would let go—he left into the twilight.

"What do you need?" Nomi asked.

At first, I didn't understand her question, and then I followed her eyes to Liara. "Fresh water, cloth, and some broth."

She nodded, and I went to work checking Liara's wounds. A total of thirteen cuts marked her body, two of which I had given her while searching for Jonac and Torrel. Most were shallow. Luckily, all of them cut straight. Her flesh would mend itself properly.

I washed each cut before applying another layer of Jonac's poultice. The mixture smelled like manure and pine, but it worked. Unfortunately, she would have to live with the scars.

Her red locs offered a stunning contrast against her dark complexion.

I pushed the wayward hair from her face and washed the dirt from her cheeks. The bowl of water nearly turned to mud by the time I finished cleaning the travel from her skin.

I badly needed a bath too. Tomorrow I would go to the river with Jonac and get a proper clean. Tonight, I would do my best to keep my distance from anyone with a keen sense of smell.

"She's called Liara, right?" Nomi asked as she handed me a bowl of warm bone broth.

"That's what Jonac told me," I said. "I still haven't heard her speak."

"What happened?"

"I ran away," I said, keeping my eyes on Liara. "But before I got too far, I came across two soldiers attacking Liara. I...I left them there and carried Liara back to Jonac and Torrel."

"Why would you run away?"

"I thought I was doing the right thing."

Nomi grabbed me and pulled me into her. Tears ran down my cheeks, and I buried my face in her shoulder. "Don't you ever do such a stupid thing again," she said. "This is your home."

"I'm sorry," I said.

"Mommy, what's wrong with Kaylo?" Soca asked.

"Oh, it's nothing, sweetheart. Kaylo and Daddy had a hard trip, and Kaylo is tired," Nomi said. "Get your sister and get ready for bed. I'll tell you a story."

"Okay." Soca looked at me, and I smiled at her. She returned an unsure smile before turning to collect her sister.

"I'm going to take care of them. Will you be okay?" Nomi asked, and I nodded.

My cheeks flushed red. I had been such a fool to run away—to come back.

Junera fought with her mother and sister to stay up and wait for their father. Finally, Nomi promised to tell Junera whatever story she liked, and the little storm cloud rushed to her bedroll.

The broth had gone lukewarm. Better than too hot. I spooned a few drops at a time into Liara's mouth, and she drank it down well enough, though she coughed once or twice.

Any shameful hope that Liara might take my secret to The Mist with her faded more with each passing hour. Her body was recovering, even though one could barely tell looking at her—eyes ever shut, lips cracked and dry, skin still a few shades pale. Appearances to the contrary, she had gotten stronger. Her echo rose and fell like the tide.

As the girls drifted off to sleep and Nomi settled in, quiet returned to the tent. I sat beside the only person who knew my secret. *What am I doing?* I tucked her blanket tight around her.

———————

I startled awake in the dead of the night, lying next to Liara. Someone had covered me up with a blanket.

A soft chorus of breathing filled the tent. Junera lay tucked firmly into place, and Soca sprawled across her bedroll like a passed-out drunkard. Jonac had returned and lay cuddled close to Nomi.

When I rolled back over, Liara's eyes were open for the first time since the night I had found her. Green speckled her warm brown eyes.

After all this time contemplating what I would say if she woke up, I couldn't find my tongue. So, for a long moment in the heart of the night, I stared into her eyes.

She opened her cracked lips. Her voice caught in her throat, and she coughed. Then I heard her voice for the first time.

"Don't worry," she said. "I won't tell."

CHAPTER TWENTY-ONE

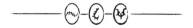

TRAVEL WORE HEAVY ON all my robes. I picked one without blood stains.

Jonac waited by the mouth of our tent. "We don't want to be late, little brother."

He held the furs from the opening, and I walked out into the tent city. A light breeze moved through a line of clothes left out to dry, while the rest of the encampment stood motionless. No small groups of friends walked the city gossiping. No gardeners tended to their plants. Even the children were conspicuously absent.

"Where is everyone?"

"We arrived several days late carrying a wounded stranger on a travel cot," he said. "Safe guess, we piqued people's interest."

"I assumed Torrel told everyone what happened."

"True. He made productive use of the twilight hours, but don't worry about that. If you are honest, the elders will understand." He wrapped his arm around my shoulder and pulled me into him.

The truth was the last thing people would understand.

Don't worry. I won't tell. Liara's words repeated in my mind.

As we approached the gathering tent, noise overflowed from every opening. However, when we crossed the threshold, voices hushed. Conversations broke. Several echoes filled the silence, followed by murmurs. People's manners kept them from staring. Instead, they stole glances and whispered.

Three ironoak trees towered into the sky to hold the canopy of the gathering tent aloft. The clan must have hunted several animals to the edge of extinction to make the canopy. The leathers and furs stretched from their anchors on each tree down to the forest floor, hushing the daylight to muted tones that lent an ominous aura to the setting.

Here, the clan gathered to discuss community matters. Typically, they only welcomed the pledged, but today, they made an exception.

Whomsoever decided to attend sat in a circle, ensuring everyone could be seen and heard. Five chairs were arranged on one side of the circle for the elders, which had less to do with status than accommodating for their age.

Jonac led me to a gap in the circle at the far end of the tent. The person to my left shifted away from me. Wherever I looked, people averted their gaze. Except for Torrel, whose glare remained steady and piercing.

If I left now, it would save everyone the hassle of casting me out. Even if they allowed me to stay, it wouldn't be for long now that someone knew.

Don't worry. I won't tell.

She hadn't said anything else. She had fallen back asleep a moment later and taken all her candor with her.

My heart beat everywhere but my chest. For all the echoes under one tent, the conversations running over each other, the loud stares directed at me—nothing matched the volume of Liara's words in my head.

I reached down and grabbed a handful of dirt, sifting it back and forth in my hands. The grains slid over my skin. They found the gaps in my fingers and fell to the ground in soft streams. I watched them almost as keenly as the eyes that watched me.

A second hush settled under the tent. Jonac placed a hand on my back, and I adjusted my posture. The five elders of the council walked to their chairs on the opposite side of the fire. A couple of the younger clan members rose to help the oldest elders to their seats.

Elder Lashan sat in the middle of the five with Soyian and Trov to their left, and Rǎkn and Fenn to their right. Despite their title, Lashan and Rǎkn were only a dozen or so turns older than Jonac. Yes, they were the eldest of the clan, but not necessarily as old as the title might presume.

Soyian, Trov, and Fenn carried themselves with a grace that defied age. Whatever the turns had taken from their physical prowess, it bestowed upon them tenfold in a presence of wisdom.

The five sat in a row, stoic. Individually, they were each their own person—fragile and flawed. Collectively, they were endless, like the oceans or the mountains themselves.

When the circle settled, Elder Lashan stood. A sapphire blue headwrap accentuated their brown skin. The wrinkles about their eyes only drew closer attention to the brightness of their brown irises. They raised their hand in a motion to settle the clan. Not to quiet them, but to settle them.

The elders formed a collective without a leader, but Lashan's voice and vision acted as the guiding light of the clan.

Over the past two seasons, I had only spoken to them once or twice. Pleasantries and courtesies mostly. I restrained from asking questions unfit for polite introductions. I had never met a kamani person, a spirit unbound by gender.

The occupation forced the kamani into hiding. After centuries, the freedom of their spirits, their blessing, became a curse.

Gousht priests deemed the kamani deviant—unholy in the eyes of The One True God—and what displeased their God could not be given quarter. Soldiers swept through each village and town. As they burned books and relics, they burned people as well. They left kamani bodies to rot in town squares as a sign of the emperor's mercy. In the turns to come, they called the reaping a great service to the people of Ennea. The kamani that survived learned to hide.

"We seem to have a larger turnout than one expects when our scouting party has returned," Lashan said. A sharp judgment lined their words, disappointment in the voyeuristic nature that beckoned the clan to gather. "If only as many would join us to discuss the harvest or the hunt."

Their gaze rolled over the crowd, and the excitement in the tent recoiled. When their eyes stopped on me, it felt as if they could pull my secrets from me with a look.

"Jonac, if you would, please provide the gathering with your full report." Lashan returned to their seat.

Jonac gave me a smile before he stood. It was not an encouraging smile. "Council and clan, I greet you warmly in The First Daughter's light. No doubt you are here because of our late arrival. And I am thankful for your concern.

"Many of you saw us return last night with a newcomer. Her name is Liara, and my young toka, Kaylo, found her beset by two imperial soldiers. While he managed to save her, she has not opened her eyes since," he said.

Torrel stood in a fury. "Tell them the truth!"

"Sit down, young man," Lashan said. "The council does not need your assistance to conduct these proceedings. Your time will come."

"Torrel is right, Elder," Jonac said. "The story is more complicated. On the second night of our journey, Kaylo ran away. It was only after he fled that he encountered the soldiers."

Several murmurs passed through the crowd. The full attention of the clan rested on me. Unlike before, no one turned away when I met their eyes. My breath quickened.

I never should have returned.

"Young man," Elder Soyian said. The oldest member of the council stared down his long nose at me. He spoke with a slow gait that matched his turns. "Will you stand and explain yourself?"

My legs wobbled as I stood. The tent that had been so large only moments ago closed like a trap around me. "Elders, I...I don't have a good explanation," I said. "I ran because I thought I was doing the right thing."

"What does that mean?!" Torrel yelled.

"If you interrupt again, you will be asked to leave," Lashan said, the pitch of their voice rising.

"If he isn't a spy, he is a liability!" Torrel gestured with wide arms as he turned to look at the entire clan. "We all know what can happen when we open our gates to strangers."

Lashan waved their hand and several of the clan members around Torrel rose to encourage him to leave.

"We have to protect ourselves!"

My throat swelled and my mouth grew dry as they escorted Torrel away. He was right.

"Elders, if I may?" Jonac said. "Kaylo is a liability. Liara, the girl we brought back with us last night, is a liability as well. I was once a liability, but you took me in regardless. And yes, our clan has paid a heavy price for accepting the risks that come with people seeking sanctuary. No one knows that more than I do."

Tears formed in Jonac's eyes as he spoke. An untold story fit into the sorrow of his words. "Many of us were lost before the clan found us," he said. "The lost need to be found. That is the purpose of the Jani."

"Well spoken, Jonac." Elder Rákn, the youngest of the council, stood to speak. His skin was the same golden brown as Torrel's. From what I knew of him, he was one of the few remaining Jani born to the clan. "But from what I recall, I don't remember you running away after we took you in."

"I had the turns and experiences of a man and still, the dark parts of my spirit begged me to run," Jonac said. "To those of us who have lost our home, being embraced by a new one can feel like a snare."

Whispers of understanding passed back and forth around me.

"Is that what happened, young man?" Elder Soyian asked.

I could only nod. It wasn't a lie, but then, sometimes large gaps existed between the truth and a lie.

"Is there anything else we should know?" Lashan asked, their eyes boring into me.

Don't worry. I won't tell.

"No, Elder," I lied.

"You made sure you were not followed?" Elder Trov asked from her seat. The Sonacoan woman with eyes black and soft as twilight looked at me with more kindness than I deserved.

"I made sure of it," Jonac said.

"And you would still vouch for this young man and the girl he brought back with him?" Trov asked.

Jonac placed a hand on my shoulder and nodded.

"Children do foolish things. And young man, what you did was foolish," Elder Lashan said. "However, I am more concerned with the fact that a Gousht party patrolled barely a day's walk from the summer site. Our reports determined the land to be uninhabited."

The other elders gestured their agreement, and then, like a miracle worked by The Blessed Mother herself, the conversation turned from me to the clan's next move.

The conversations went on for hours as they offered every pledged clan member the opportunity to speak. Every time a new speaker rose, my pulse held still for a moment. But no one brought me up. No one demanded my exile. I became another face in the crowd.

After everyone had their say, the elders decided the safest course of action was to remain where we were for another season as other scouts searched for a safer site.

A whisper of a question lingered in my mind as they spoke. *If the Gousht continue to spread past the cities into open land, how long will it be before there is nowhere left to hide?*

Hours of discussion stretched the morning long until the elders finally called an end to the meeting. Segments of the clan broke off into huddles of small conversations. Jonac joined with Râkn and Trov to discuss plans to scout a proper resettlement site. The clan could not risk remaining in

the same location for yet another season. Movement shielded the clan
against the Gousht.

I moved towards the exit as a hand fell on my shoulder, sending a
shutter vibrating down my spine and catching a breath in my chest.

Lashan stood behind me. They hooked their finger and motioned
for me to follow. Then they turned without a word and walked into an
empty corner of the tent.

Maybe they meant for my expulsion to go quieter. After all, I already
tried to run away once. No one would ask too many questions if I
suddenly vanished.

When Lashan turned around and I hadn't followed, they tapped their
foot impatiently and waved me over. Whatever they wanted, I had to
face it.

"Calm down, son. I only want to speak with you," they said. "I'm old,
and with age comes the right to lecture the young."

"You're not that old."

"Why, thank you," they said dryly. "I want to give you the opportunity
to tell me if you are holding anything back. It is my responsibility to
maintain the safety of the clan."

I am a spirit thief. Five words and I wouldn't have to pretend anymore.
They might exile me or kill me, but at least then I could stop hiding.

"Jonac embellished," I said. "When I found the water dancer being
attacked, I hesitated. It's my fault."

Lashan took a heavy breath. "You ran away. You brought trouble
back with you. Saving that girl was the only thing you did that wasn't a
mistake," they said. "We all make mistakes in youth. The Mother knows
most of us continue making mistakes until we die, but that doesn't
absolve us of our responsibilities."

"What responsibilities?"

"Pledged or not, you are a part of the Fallen Rock Clan. We don't hold
anyone accountable by sending them away. We hold them accountable
by keeping them close and helping them rebuild what they broke. You

have broken trust. Now you must find a way to rebuild it."

"How do I do that?"

"That is part of rebuilding trust. Find a way to serve those you harmed." Lashan smiled and patted my arm. "I have people I need to talk to, and you need to sort out your thoughts."

Their words sat with me as they left me to find other, more important conversations.

Trust required honesty, which is why the trust I had built fell apart in the first place. It stood on a faulty foundation.

Outside the gathering tent, the clouds filling up the sky promised rain. A welcome promise given the heat suffocating the forest. I could almost hear The Seed beg his sibling for the kind reprieve.

Most of the clan ambled back to their tents in preparation for the downpour, but I couldn't go back to Nomi and the girls, not yet. They would have too many questions I wasn't equipped to answer. I would have to answer them for myself first. And so I walked to the ironoak wall, the dry grass crunching under my feet.

Walking the perimeter of the encampment, I ran my fingers against the bark of the ironoaks. In my own way, I understood the pull of a nomadic life. Moving seemed like the only freedom I had left. Each step belonged to me, each footfall a consequence I could predict.

The Song bellowed, and I let it in. As I walked along the edge of The Mist, the fragment of The Seed within my spirit and The Song spun about each other. The freedom on the other side of that thin veil invited me to step across. The feeling of completeness I felt when I first mistwalked taunted me.

Rain started falling. Sporadic droplets became a deluge that melted my robes to my skin in an instant. My braids became waterlogged, and streams of water ran down my hair onto my face and down my back.

Arching my neck up to the sky, I let the rain fall on my face. The days of travel washed away. The heat cooled under the water's touch. And the weight of all my too-heavy thoughts fell to the ground.

That next breath was the first real breath I had taken since I found the soldiers circling around Liara.

A sharp echo pierced my serenity.

The whooshing sound of the wind preceded the wind itself by a sliver of a moment, as a gust careened through the encampment and pitched me against the solid ironoak wall. My head made a hollow sound as it collided with the wood, and I fell into the wet grass. The camp blinked in and out of blackness.

Someone stood outlined by the rain. The silhouette wobbled and split into two before settling.

Water streamed into my eyes as I squinted at my attacker. Torrel's headwrap lay astray, and his robes clung against his wiry physique.

He's going to kill me, I thought. *Maybe he should.*

"It's your fault!" His voice caught against his anger and pitched upward. "You should have never come back!"

I pulled myself to my hands and knees and looked up at him. His brow bent in, and his nostrils flared. "If you won't leave on your own, I will make you."

He drew back his boot, then drove it into my ribs. The crack vibrated through me before the pain rippled through my chest. All the air left my body as I collapsed back to the ground.

I coughed and tried to breathe, but another kick to my stomach left me gasping and coughing up rain water. Then one last time, he reared back. His foot slammed against my forehead, and the back of my skull cracked into the ironoak wall.

As I lay there looking up at the blurry outline of an angry man, I let myself go. I didn't spit the rainwater out of my mouth or wipe the trail of blood from my eyes. After a moment, he walked away, and I was alone.

The Mist didn't take me.

In many ways, I felt ready to leave the pain behind, but one thought scared me even more than getting up. Shay and my parents waited on the other side, and I couldn't face them.

So, I lay in the pouring rain, bleeding and breathing, until I found the courage to stand up and hobble back to the tent.

Each step pulled on my abdomen. My head throbbed. I moved slowly. I focused on breathing, like Munnie taught me. "This is the air Ennea gave us. It is a gift," I said to myself.

When I pulled back the furs from the entranceway, Soca squealed. Then everyone turned to look at me. Jonac froze as he took in the sight, and Nomi rushed forward to take hold of me.

She walked me closer to the fire and helped me remove my wet clothes. Two large dark blotches formed along my torso. Her eyes went wide.

"It's okay," I said. "I'll be okay."

Jonac's expression was not one of concern. His brow creased into his eyes as his lips drew tight and long into a snarl. Slowly, he walked forward, his eyes moving from my torso to the wound on my head.

His thumb brushed over the cut on my forehead. The sting ran like lightning from the wound to the back of my jaw. Then Jonac drew the blood in a line down his cheek. It was an old gesture and a clear message—when my blood spilled, so did his.

Without saying a word, he left with my blood on his cheek.

CHAPTER TWENTY-TWO

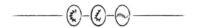

Tayen ran her thumb over the holes in the whistle her sister made for her. As Kaylo continued his story, her muscles constricted. If she didn't breathe and calm down, she would snap the trinket in two.

Fucking rakat, she thought. *Only cowards kick someone when they're down.*

"When I woke up the next morning, Nomi and Jonac were arguing. Their whispers grew more and more forceful until they abandoned the pretense." Kaylo leaned back on his hands and looked up into the night. "Every time I took a breath, my skin stretched like pulling a tanned hide over a too large drum. A crack split my head in two. My mouth tasted like dry ash, and sweat soaked through my blanket.

"Nomi noticed me sit up. 'If you have so many questions, go ask him yourself,' she said, then her grimace tempered to pity.

"Jonac knelt down beside me. An odd smell wafted off his robes. He asked me how I felt and handed me a waterskin. He asked me what happened, and I lied. I told him someone attacked me from behind, and the rain kept me from getting a good look at them.

"'Was it Torrel?' he asked. His brows furrowed. His chest puffed up. He was ready to hurt Torrel, but I told him I couldn't see who attacked me."

"Why?" Tayen asked. "Didn't you hate Torrel for what he did?"

"I had already done enough damage."

"Bullshit. You saved that girl."

"Liara." His voice softened with her name.

"Whoever. You saved her."

"And I put everyone else at risk." He leaned over and tossed another log into the firepit. "It's time to get some rest. I'll take first watch."

"You always say that when you don't want to talk about something."

"Oh, you've noticed?" He smiled wide, too wide for it to be genuine.

Kana and Toka reached high overhead when Tayen woke up. A cold sweat beaded over her brow. The chill soaked through her, into her bones. She shifted closer to the fire until her feet touched the rock barrier encircling the firepit.

On the other side of the flames, Kaylo idly whittled at a length of ashburn. "Bad dream?"

She nodded and rubbed her hands together over the fire.

"Same dream?"

She nodded again.

"Come sit beside me." He patted the dirt next to him.

Tired as she was, cold as she was, moving sounded like an insurmountable task. Still, she grunted and sighed as she pushed herself to her feet.

He smiled at her and held a second ashburn branch out as she sat down beside him. "Have you kept your knives sharp? The best way to hurt yourself is to whittle with a dull blade."

"I've never been any good at whittling."

"It's not always about being good at a thing. Sometimes you need your body to work to allow your mind to stop," he said. "You see the grain moving down the wood? You want to cut with the grain. Slow and deliberate."

"What am I making?"

"Nothing right now. Right now, just shave away the wood," he said
and held up his bit of ashburn in example. "Put your off-hand thumb
against the back of the blade. Let your thumb push through the cut while
your knife-hand serves as a guide."

Her hands mimicked his, and she pushed her blade along the branch.
Slivers of wood curled away and fell to the ground.

"A well-kept blade will glide through the wood," he said. "My father
always said a shit crafter with good tools was better than a good crafter
with shit in their hands. Though he didn't use such elegant phrases
around my mother."

"She was too polite?"

"No, she had a mouth fouler than a pig fart, but she was also a bit of a
hypocrite," he said, and they both chuckled.

The sound of their blades slicing through the wood joined the subtle
noises of the forest. The fire crackled, owls hooted, crickets sang, and the
ashburn branches unraveled one curled strip at a time.

Not long later, Kaylo offered his shavings to the fire and positioned
himself on his bedroll. Tayen continued whittling away the branch. As
her hands learned the rhythm of their motion, her mind wandered. She
thought about her sister carving the whistle that hung from her neck. No
one had ever shown Nita the proper way to carve.

A small smirk made its way to Tayen's lips. For her tenth birthday, Nita
gave her a walking stick. Nothing more than a branch without bark. It
didn't even stand straight, and a splash of red ran down the side of the
stick. When the awkward-looking branch broke almost a turn later, Tayen
cried through the night.

Tayen pushed her thumb against the blade and stripped another piece
of wood off the ashburn in her hands. If only Nita could be here with
her.

By the time Sokan peeked over the treetops, Tayen had whittled her
way through several fallen branches and nicked herself twice. A couple
of small cuts were worth the distraction, as long as her dreams stayed

behind in her sleep where they belonged.

All the excess shavings kept the fire strong through the long hours of the night. And yet the late autumn chill prickled the back of her neck, sending shivers down her back.

Instead of fighting it, she focused on the cold air. It teased her lips as she breathed deeply. Kaylo taught her to focus on the small things to quiet her nerves. Her body opened with the air. Her lungs expanded and contracted with her diaphragm. *Focus on the breathing,* she reminded herself. *Up and down. In and out.*

The Song flowed with her breath, and she pulled on the connection. The bigger, thicker shadows sang louder and moved easier. Below them, the small shadows flickered. She called to them as they stretched and darkened. The once small shadows grew over the dying fire until they extinguished the light, creating a wonderful contradiction, heat without light.

"A little early, isn't it?" Kaylo asked from the flat of his back. Tayen lost her grip on the shadows, and they snapped back into place. "Don't worry. It wasn't a pleasant dream."

"Where are we going?" Tayen asked. "It's getting colder, and for some reason, we're still heading north."

She had been asking versions of the same questions for several span, and he always answered with cryptic sayings. The last time he said, "Cold builds character."

Kaylo sat up and rubbed his hands together over the fire. "You remember the fishers we passed two days back?" he asked. "There's rumor of a freecity not too far. Dasoon. Maybe another day out."

Ever since the Lost Nation joined the war and the Uprising began, the Empire started pulling out of cities in the far west. Soldiers marched the occupants of the abandoned cities across the continent and bound the survivors in chains. Afterwards, runaways and refugees took up shelter in the broken-down cities, trying to start over in whatever was left to them. Freecities were as close to free as people could be in a war-torn land.

"A rumor?" Tayen asked.

"Rumor or not—it's getting colder, our supplies are running low, and hunting is slowing down. Whether there are people on the other side of this rumor or not, we have to make a shelter out of whatever is left standing."

"Why don't you grow supplies, forest dancer? I'm sick of oat rations and stale saltmeat."

"Catch more when you hunt, and you'll have fresher meat," he said. "How will you survive on your own if you don't learn how to care for yourself now?"

Tayen rolled her eyes and sighed. Always the same answer for the same questions.

She emptied the pouch of oats into a pot. From here on out, they were down to saltmeat, a sack of half-ripe apples she picked two-days back, and whatever they managed to forage or hunt. Even their spice store had emptied a couple of days ago.

Her mouth didn't exactly salivate over flavorless boiled oats. She cut up an apple and threw it in the pot. If her ribs weren't protruding from her skin like she was a wrapped skeleton, she would've skipped breakfast.

Moons of training with Kaylo and their lean diet had eroded Tayen's body to tight muscle and bone. Her reflection looked nothing like her. Where her cheeks used to puff out around a dimple, her face had become all hard angles. Sword training left her covered in bruises. A tree branch might not be a sharp blade, but it wasn't a fucking pat on the back either. Her body belonged to a warrior—granted, a warrior who missed a few meals.

Kaylo changed as well. He finally consented to letting her braid his mess of hair, though he hadn't permitted her to cut it. From the dozens of small braids she made of his mane, she wove one large, gray braid that fell to the middle of his back. When she showed him his reflection afterwards, he agreed to trim his beard. As the fat drained from his face, his beard started looking like a feral animal consuming him. Now he looked like a ruggedly handsome man, even though he still needed a good wash. They both did.

The apple ended up tasting more like oats than the oats tasted like apple. They forced their way through the tasteless meal in quiet, as if the act of chewing and swallowing something so bland required extreme focus.

Tayen washed down another spoonful with her waterskin and thought about Dasoon. A freecity. Her parents spoke about freecities like they were daemontales. No Gousht. No fighting. Hard to believe they existed.

"Why Dasoon?"

"Because it's close," Kaylo said. "And from what the fishers said, it's rundown worse than most. Not a place many people would choose to hide."

"What would we have to worry about this far north?"

"The Gousht don't stop hunting prey because it's inconvenient." He put down his bowl of mushy oats.

"Look, freecities might be free, but that doesn't make them safe." His voice was gruff with the morning, and the meal hadn't improved his mood. "When freecities get too big, they attract attention. Gousht raids or Lost Nation raids—it makes no difference,"

"But the Lost Nation is fighting the Gousht...."

"Power takes power, little shade," he interrupted. "Eat your slop."

What does that even mean? Power takes power. She would have pressed him further, but when her kana finished with a topic, he was done. She could ask, but he wouldn't answer, at least not in any satisfying way. Stubborn as her father.

But he wasn't her father. The Gousht sent her father to The Mist. Kaylo was a means to an end—blood for blood. She owed her actual family that much, and no story could change that.

After Tayen forced down the rest of the oats, they broke camp, and she moved with a new focus. Dasoon might be rundown, but it was still a freecity. A city without armies, a city without war, which meant shelter

and time to train. Even Kaylo took longer strides as they followed the
river north.

"You see that rock at the base of the ironoak?" He pointed ahead, and
she nodded. "What does that shadow sound like? The rock, not the tree."

He always did this. Picked one shadow out of hundreds and asked
her to describe its sound. The rock's shadow intertwined with the tree's.
Might as well describe a specific grain of soil.

Tayen searched through The Song. She reached into it, then stopped.
It felt wrong.

She breathed and forgot all about the rock and the tree. She forgot
about the forest until only The Song mattered. It called to her, and, if she
let it, it would flow right through her. After a moment of hesitation, the
length of a long breath, she allowed it in.

The full shape of The Shadow stretched before her. Every fragment of
shade and shadow fit into The Song, each holding a unique place in the
melody, a specific sound.

Before, she had danced through instinct, flailing like a child. The Song
moved her, or she tried to move The Song. But that was an illusion. The
Song moved constantly. She might as well try to move the ocean by
grabbing a handful of water.

Here, now, the truth of it waved in front of her face. The Shadow
had always been a part of her. Neither could move the other. She had to
move with The Song, let herself join it, loosen her grip just enough not
to lose control.

There it lay, wrapped up in The Song—the small shadow stretching
out from the rock at the base of the ironoak tree. It had a rhythm and
tone apart from The Song itself. It moved steady as a heartbeat, but
deeper. At the edges of it, it thinned to a gentle whisper.

Tayen opened her eyes, and Kaylo stood staring at her. A smile spread
over her face. She knew exactly what the rock's shadow sounded like.

"You see it, don't you?" Kaylo asked. "It took much longer for me to see The Song for what it is. To see my part in it, but you see it now?"

Tayen's smile grew wider.

———————

Kaylo bent down at the riverbank. The cold water rushed over his hand as he filled his waterskin.

After several hours, Tayen's echo still filled the forest as she walked along the edge of The Mist. Jonac would've scolded him for allowing his toka to wander as close to the divide between worlds for as long as she had. But Jonac had been far more conservative.

Balancing the pull of The Song and the needs of The Waking allowed her to access The Shadow in ways she never could have before. The closer to the edge she got, the freer her movement with The Shadow would become.

Sure, it could be dangerous. If she slipped into The Mist, she could lose herself. She would die, split between worlds for too long. But she had her reasons for staying in the physical world. It was hard to kill Gousht in The Mist, if that was what she truly wanted.

Still, he listened to the shifts and sways of her echo. He could pull her out if he moved quickly. Probably.

The Shadow grew fuller as the evening darkened; a low hum made of hundreds of sustained notes. They moved with and against each other like slow chaos, building and building to something greater.

Then a sharp screech pierced through Tayen's echo. A second echo, farther south. It screamed angrily into the night.

"Are you ready?"

Tayen looked up from where she knelt by the river. "Aren't we making camp?"

"I want to camp away from the river tonight. It's cold and the wind over the water is going to leave my teeth rattling all night."

She shrugged and hefted her travel sack. "Lead the way."

The second echo sang from a long way off. If he hadn't been listening closely to The Song through Tayen, it probably would have faded into the background. He had no reason to worry her. Not yet.

CHAPTER TWENTY-THREE

SUNLIGHT AND PAIN BROKE through the darkness of the tent as I lay limp on my bedroll. The ache crawled deeper into my gut every time my belly rose with a new breath.

Liara coughed, but she hadn't moved from the flat of her back.

When she finally sits and starts talking, will she keep her promise? I thought. *Or will she tell everyone what I am?*

Maybe it didn't matter anymore.

She coughed again. And again. One dry hacking sound rolled into the next.

Besides the two of us, the tent was empty. There was no one else to hear her coughing or do anything about it. When I rolled to my side and tried to push myself up, my arm gave way to the tearing pain under my ribs.

This is fucking ridiculous. Seven paces away and I can't do a damn thing to help.

From the flat of my stomach, I tried again. My abdomen nearly tore open, but I made it to my knees. Then to my feet. Hunched over or not, I had to do what I could. As long as I stayed, I would make myself useful.

Each step stretched my wounds, and my breathing became more pronounced. Liara coughed impatiently. "I'm on my way," I said.

She coughed again in response.

Water brushed over my fingertips as I dipped a small bowl into our daily rations. I picked the cleanest rag I could find from the table next to the bucket.

Only three more steps.

Another battery of coughs pushed me forward, then I fell to my knees beside her. Sweat tickled the hairs on the back of my neck. I wanted to collapse on the floor next to her.

The cloth swelled with the cool clean water, and I dabbed the rag around her lips before wringing a slow stream of water into her mouth. She swallowed, and I repeated the process a few more times.

"I wouldn't blame you if you told them," I said. "Everyone else that knows is dead." Another slow trickle of water slipped past her parted lips.

I leeched the rest of the water from the bowl with the cloth and ran it over her forehead. "Don't die," I said. "I couldn't take it."

"What are you doing up from your bedroll?" Jonac said from over my shoulder.

"She wouldn't stop coughing."

As he twisted his feet into the ground, his echo billowed and swept through the tent. His shoulders swayed, and his hands skimmed through the air, back and forth. A small, green plant sprouted from the ground. The ribbed leaves unfurled, then his echo shrank back down.

"If you're up and about, put the kettle over the fire. She needs more than a few drops of water from a rag." No matter how mild his criticism, it cut. Usually, he smiled the hurt away, but his lips ran in a straight line across his face.

I nodded and set to the task.

Each step from the water bucket to the fire hurt worse. The kettle pulled my shoulder down, stretching my bruised side. But I refused to make a noise. Jonac didn't need to hear me moan.

The night I came home bruised and battered, Jonac confronted Torrel in front of a crowd who had taken refuge from the rain in the gathering tent. Their raised voices drowned out the calls for peace before Jonac put an end to the conversation by striking Torrel.

Rumors of the fight spread quickly, and everyone had heard one version or another by the following day. After that, the elders had no choice but to relieve Jonac and Torrel from their duty as scouts.

In a single span, I had broken Jonac's trust by running away, caused a rift between him and his chosen son, and upset his position in the clan. The events hadn't left him with much patience.

"Tulsi leaves with a bit of cinnamon bark." He plucked several leaves and wrapped them around each other, forming a small ball. "It should help calm her cough and whatever fever remains."

He handed the tightly wrapped ball to me. "Smell it. Get the feel of the leaves. It will help you call them when you need to." He stood up and beat the dirt from his knees.

"It smells like grass and pepper."

"Take care of her. She's your responsibility." He chuckled to himself. "You are the reason she's here in the first place."

The furs flapped closed behind him, and the room dimmed.

Days passed, and still the only words she had ever spoken to me were, "Don't worry. I won't tell."

Occasionally, she opened her eyes. They would dart back and forth as if she was searching for something, and then fluttered closed again.

I fed her bone broth and runny porridge, cleaned her wounds, and replaced her poultices. And I waited.

At some point, I reached for a scrap of firewood and began pushing my father's knife down the grain, creating a pile of thin shavings beneath me.

My father used to sit in his chair for hours, his large hands working the same knife. "Idle hands are wasted opportunities," he would say.

The wood changed shape and texture as I stripped away one layer after another.

After high sun, Jonac would join me to check on Liara. He taught me new poultices and medicinal teas, but no matter the lesson, I never caught on quick enough for him. His critiques grew harsher and his jokes meaner.

A strange musk followed him as he demonstrated the remedies. I had smelled the scent before, but I couldn't place it.

After a span, Liara sat up and started feeding herself. She began walking before the moon passed.

For all the time we spent, she never spoke of the secret between us. Maybe she had never said anything in the first place. I had been tired. Maybe I imagined it.

We built up routines, and she stopped being a stranger.

Almost three seasons had passed since I fled Nomar. The distance between Jonac and me continued to grow. Most of the Jani spoke to me in courtesies, if at all. And as much as I loved the girls, they couldn't understand what I went through. Liara understood.

Twice a day, I forced her out of her sickbed to walk the encampment. Her muscles ached with healing and scars. At first, she couldn't manage more than a walk to the next tent and back before her legs collapsed under her. A moon later, we walked the perimeter of the tent city, filling the slow walks with our stories.

"My sister and I hopped from one runaway camp to another, nothing like this. Everything here is alive," she said. "And no one wore matching clothing." She waved at my Jani robes to make her point.

As she looked at me, her eyes held me, and I smiled through the urge to look away. "What was it like then?"

"First of all, no one trusted anyone. We stayed together out of necessity, not community." She took a moment to arrange her thoughts. "To the Jani, this is a life. The camps were about surviving long enough to get another chance at life. Everyone carried what they could from wherever they ran and made their mismatched tents with whatever

they could. We stayed together because, trusted or not, having another
Ennean in the next tent felt safer than being alone."

Some Enneans are just as dangerous, I thought. *Rena. Torrel. Me.*

"Am I boring you?" Liara asked.

"Sorry, dark thoughts." I bit my tongue before too much honesty
slipped out.

Her lips tugged into a sympathetic smile, and she nodded.

"So, you weren't a part of the Missing?" I asked and forced a smile.

"Sadly, no," she said. "It wasn't bad though. Better than the Stone City.
When I was growing up, a soldier stood on every corner. The type of
people who enjoy being bigger, especially when they aren't."

"Were the schools in the Stone City as bad as the ones in Nomar?"

"I barely remember," she said. "The city was enormous, and there
were too many children to keep an eye on all of us. When we couldn't
hide from the soldiers, they packed us into a huge hall, and I pretended
to listen. Never got a handle on their tongue."

"So, you can't speak the language of the one true god?" I said in an
over-embellished Gousht accent.

"Please don't do that." She wrinkled her nose in exaggerated disgust.
"At least I belonged to myself in the camps." Her lips parted as if she had
more to say, but she kept it to herself.

When we arrived back at the tent, she made for her bedroll, and her
snoring filled the tent a few moments later.

I chuckled to myself. She had lain unconscious for almost two span
and hadn't so much as breathed loudly. Now she growled like a cornered
raccoon in her sleep.

"Good, you're home," Nomi said. Strains of her gray hair fell loose from
her skewed headwrap.

In five days, summer would transition into autumn, and the clan
would celebrate Shunanlah. We would fast to honor the day The Mother
marked the first dancer, tell the story as the Daughters met in the sky
above, and break our fast with a feast.

"I asked Jonac to go out days ago and collect pinecones, twigs, and flowers for wreaths." She spread her arms wide. "Do you see any pinecones, twigs, or flowers?"

"I could call on The Seed if you want."

Nomi puckered her lips and sighed. "And the toka studies the kana's laziness too? This celebration is about thanking Ennea and the spirits. If you haven't noticed, she already provided." She shooed me out, and I didn't offer any resistance.

Ever since the night Torrel attacked me, Jonac came home less. When he came home, he and Nomi fought. It was my fault.

A twig snapped under my boot as I meandered the forest in search of proper decorations for a wreath. A patch of silver ragwort grew at the base of an ironoak. It would do. I sheared off the overgrowth and stuffed it in the sack.

Growing up, we never had a true Shunanlah. Not one I could remember. Like anything else that gave tribute to the spirits, The Gousht outlawed it. Every turn, my mother would weave small wreaths in secret. We would fast with the sun and eat with the rising moons, then she would tell the story of Shunanlah with the wreath lying on the center of the table.

After nine moons, I started having trouble recalling her face, hearing her voice. But, in that moment, she came to me clear as the summer sky—her hands weaving twigs and leaves as she laughed at something my father said.

For a brief instant, I became my mother's son again. Not a broken boy. Not a malitu.

I dried the tears from my face and carried my sack back to the tent.

Nomi and I sat for hours, saying very little, weaving the forest into wreaths. The silver ragwort and the wildflowers sang against the healthy brown circlets.

Long after Liara and the children drifted off, Jonac stumbled into the tent, his silhouette wavering in the firelight. He shuffled to the bedroll he shared with Nomi, and that same strange smell lingered in the air after him, like sweet and sage.

They spoke quietly enough not to wake the children, and I couldn't hear exactly what they said, but the sharpness in their voices carried to my edge of the tent. Nomi and Jonac went back and forth in bitter whispers until he got up and unraveled a spare bedroll down on the other side of the tent.

My chest tightened. The man who stumbled in the darkness wasn't Jonac, at least not the person he had been before me.

As I lay there, I finally recalled where I had smelled that musk before. Jonac stank of susu root.

Chapter Twenty-Four

THE MORNING OF THE festival, the firepit blazed away in the tent as I opened my eyes. The smell of fresh bread and hickory smoke wafted over me.

Tanitata.

My father loved the sweet honey bread. Every turn, he would spend hours kneading the dough and weaving the layers of the bread together. It had to be cooked early, so it could soak in honey syrup. He wove the bread into the most intricate designs. The process took hours, but my father's hands crafted wonders.

I sat on my bedroll, breathing in the lovely aroma. The heat in the tent lashed out hotter than Sokan with a short temper. A thin layer of sweat coated my forehead. Summer still clung to its last day, and, from the look of things, Nomi had been working the fire since before the first touch of daylight.

Jonac was nowhere to be seen, which had become commonplace. Neither he nor Torrel, the man Jonac had raised, made any attempts to mend the wound between them. Instead, Jonac continued to unravel. When he did come home, he smelled like sweet smoke and a glaze covered his eyes.

The girls huddled around their mother as she prepared for the festival.

They moved with a tepidness I had not seen before. The air had changed, and the seasons weren't to blame. Nomi smiled despite herself as she kneaded a second dough.

"Soca. Junera," I said. "Come here."

I held my fists out in front of me. "Soca, choose one."

Her eyes shifted between her sister and me before she pointed at my right hand. I opened my fist and showed it to her, a carved rabbit the size of her small palm.

It wasn't as finely crafted as my father's carvings. Little was.

I opened my other hand to Junera and offered her an ironoak racoon. The girls looked at me, then each other and, without a word, traded carvings. Their smiles lit up the tent, and they each gave me a big hug.

"I'm glad you came back," Soca said, then ran off with her sister.

"Me too," I said, surprising myself by meaning it.

Nomi thanked me. Her smile broke through her wistfulness—the first genuine smile I had seen from her in days.

We worked all morning and afternoon over the firepit preparing food, each aroma tempting my fast more than the last.

A desperate energy filled the tent. Nomi barked out orders like we were her small army. No one was exempt. Liara hobbled around the tent city, delivering messages to neighbors.

By the time the sun rolled down the small side of the sky's back, all manner of foods covered the table, from roast boar to liloka soup, a spicy soup made from barley wine and peppers. Good liloka soup would leave you sweating for a day.

For the first time in my life, I stared at abundance and overindulgence. My stomach quaked at the sight of it all. Only my mother's voice reminding me to honor the fast restrained my hands.

We carried the offerings to the center of the camp, where an odd assortment of tables had been dragged out from tents around two massive firepits. Each table overflowed with delicious smelling foods. We were prepared to feed a nation.

The Jani lived as a simple people, taking from the land what survival dictated, but today was different. The autumn equinox. Shunanlah. The moons and the sun held each other in the sky, and the Jani celebrated. Food must be had, as the saying went.

My mother would save small portions of our rations for a moon to give us our meager, secret feast. My father would cook and say, "Ah, the spirits love a full belly."

People shifted all around me. Siani placed carafes of barley wine on each table as the seats filled up.

If only my parents could see this. Free people—or as free as Ennea could offer—gathered in the forest, beneath the three Daughters, to celebrate. They would have loved it.

An explosion of light and a wave of heat erupted behind me, nearly knocking me to my knees. A tower of wood, a head taller than me, roared with life. Someone had used far too much firestarter, filling the air with an acrid smell.

When I got to the table, Liara and the girls laughed themselves to tears, describing my shock to each other.

"His cheeks are turning red," Liara said between bursts of laughter.

"It's hot out here, and the oversized fire isn't helping," I said.

My shoulders loosened when Jonac smiled and nodded at me. I smiled back, but then I saw Nomi.

She wore a numb expression. After all her work, she couldn't enjoy it. They sat only a breath apart and still nations separated them. One celebration couldn't bridge that divide.

A second pyre erupted into flames, and the clan hushed.

Elder Lashan stood in front of the two blazing firepits. They moved slowly, but with purpose. They strode with the gait of someone who knew how to pull the focus from a crowd. The fire lit up their warm brown skin. Their stark white headwrap knotted around the braid cast over their shoulder. The elder stood as strong as the spirits themselves with their sharp jaw and deep brown eyes.

"Today, as the three Daughters share the sky, we celebrate Shunanlah."
Their voice clung to the air like molasses, sweet and heavy.

"In a time when our nations were still small tribes, there lived a great
warrior named Shunanlah. She defended her people from bandits and
other tribes alike. With her two sons at her side, no one could challenge
their tribe."

As Lashan spoke, dancers stepped out in front of the flames and
drummers set the night to a rhythm. The dancers' movements became
shadowed outlines in the darkening twilight.

"Shunanlah's strength was storied, and her sons carved out stories of
their own. They wanted to make war and claim more territory for their
tribe. Shunanlah refused. She told them, 'The Mother has provided for
all we need.' But her sons did not heed her word. They led a small group
of warriors against a nearby village. Their blood stained the land before
Shunanlah knew what they had done."

The dancers pantomimed the scene, a mother crying over her slain
sons. Drumbeats slowed. Their bodies moved like spirits against the fire.

"Her sons passed to The Mist, leaving Shunanlah and her people
vulnerable. For too many, enough was far too little. Yes, they wanted to
claim Shunanlah's land, but they sought to claim her story above all.

"Many came to fight and, one after another, Shunanlah sent them
into The Mist. The warrior mourned her sons and all of those who died
by her blades. She had no wish to claim more lives from The Blessed
Mother.

"On the autumn equinox, as Sokan, Kana, and Toka met on opposite
sides of the sky above, Shunanlah called to Ennea. 'O Blessed Mother,
the land, The Mist, The Waking, I pray. Give me the wisdom to end this
bloodshed, to bring light to our future and give rest to the unease of our
past.'

"Ennea heard her prayer, as she hears all. The Mother considered this
sorrowful warrior and knew her heart, the heart of a reluctant defender
and a mother in mourning. The shadow beneath the warrior grew darker

and fuller as she knelt beneath the three Daughters.

"Shunanlah felt her spirit stir and heard the voice of The Mother. 'If you truly wish to find peace, seek the wisdom of The Shadow. She is the oldest and the wisest of the Great Spirits. Let her wisdom guide the light and the darkness.'"

As Elder Lashan spoke of The Shadow, a dancer wearing a mask marked with the first spirit's rune pulled on the shadows. The dancer's echo swirled about. The light of the fires stretched out into the darkness, then hushed to a small glow before returning to balance.

"The stories of Ennea's gift traveled far and wide. When the last day of summer held the three daughters again, two young twins prayed to Ennea. 'O Blessed Mother, we ask for the patience and strength to serve our people. They are starving. Drought kills our crops, and raiders take what little we can grow.

"Ennea saw their true intensions to serve and blessed them with the twin kamani spirits, The River and The Flame." At the names of the Great Spirits, a mist rose over the camp, and the pyres flared into the sky.

Sokan had fully given the sky over to her younger sisters. The fast should have been over, but the story continued. The food lining the table called to me.

Waiting had always been the worse part of Shunanlah. My mother used to tease me and speak slower when I got impatient. When the fast finally broke, we would eat, and the meager portions always felt like a feast.

"Hundreds offered prayers to The Mother on the next solstice. Most prayed out of fear, hatred, lust, greed. They prayed for power. Ennea heard them all. Only three voices shined in the dark sea of prayers. An old man from the south wanted to give his family shelter to outlast him; a nomad asked for guidance, that he might lead his people on their journey; and lastly, a kamani farmer from the middle plains asked for forgiveness so that their family could reconcile and tend the fields of their mothers.

"To the old man, Ennea gifted The Mountain. Together, they could provide shelter for those he loved. She marked the nomad with The Wind, a guide for her people. Lastly, Ennea offered the farmer The Seed. Their bounty grew and wounds of the past began to heal.

"As the turns passed, children of Ennea were born throughout the land. Some few were even twice-marked. They used their gifts in services of their communities.

"Still, every autumn on the equinox, hopeful people prayed for Ennea's mark. Their prayers went unanswered. Until one turn, an orphan girl knelt between the Daughters and prayed.

"The orphan had lost everything and everyone she ever loved to raiders who wielded the spirits. 'Ennea, O Mother,' she cried. 'Your gifts are too great, too powerful. People use the Great Spirits to take what they like and the bound cannot stop them. Please, Mother, bring balance.'

"Ennea looked upon this orphan girl and wept, for she knew her pain. The Mother touched the girl's spirit and shared with her The Balance, for The Balance had the ability to take gifts from those that would use them for their own gain.

"But The Balance tricked Ennea. The corrupt spirit turned the orphan into the first spirit thief, taking power where she once sought balance."

One by one, the dancers knelt before a silhouette wearing a mask with The Thief's rune. The thief took one mask after another from the kneeling dancers.

I felt like all eyes turned on me, but I refused to look away from the spectacle.

When the thief had stolen all the masks, the dancers rose as one to overcome the malitu.

"The Mother could not call back the seventh spirit. She had to trust that her children would hold The Thief at bay.

"On this equinox, in honor of Shunanlah, we give thanks to Ennea. And we hold vigilant against malitu in The Waking." Lashan kissed three fingers and touched them to the soil.

They scanned over the clan as if searching for something. Their eyes met mine for an instant, and time stretched into a world onto itself, a world in which everyone knew what I was, Ennea's mistaken gift.

Lashan turned from the clan, and their story ended.

The night erupted with conversation. Children reached greedy hands toward the food first. No one scolded them as they took more than they could eat. Plates filled, and smiles widened.

The food sat in front of me, and my stomach rumbled, but I couldn't reach for it. I didn't want to steal anything else.

People laughed. Barley wine sloshed in their cups. One conversation became indistinguishable from the rest.

I excused myself and walked off into the night, beyond the wall of ironoaks, into the forest.

Every turn on the equinox, my mother had told the same story, and I had never paid attention to The Thief. People celebrated descendants of The Seed because we brought the bounty of the fields to our people. Even after the invasion, my parents and Munnie reminded me of the gift I carried. Even the most hesitant of the Jani were happy to have another descendant of The Seed amongst them.

But it was a lie. Every kindness I took from the clan I stole.

I rested my back against a tree as tears started to gather behind my eyes. My self-pity grew louder than the forest, louder than the footsteps and the echo creeping through the darkness. I jumped as a hand thumped down on my shoulder.

Liara stood over me, smiling. "Sorry."

"I wasn't scared, just surprised," I said.

"No, I'm sorry about their story," she said softly. Her hands reached into her robe pocket, and she pulled out a piece of Tanitata bread and an apple wrapped in a bit of fabric. "You must be hungry."

I smiled at her kindness and turned back to the forest. "You know, I've heard that story every turn since I can remember, and probably before. It always ends the same way. Only, this time, I was The Thief."

Liara sat on the ground next to me and sighed. Her knee grazed mine, and suddenly I became very aware of my body. We had been close before. I spent several span cleaning her wounds, but this time the brush of her body against mine made my muscles tense.

"You didn't know you were spirit-marked before?" she asked.

I had never admitted to anyone what I was. Never had to claim it. I couldn't. Instead, I answered her with silence.

"You know, my sister is twice-marked too. The River and The Wind. I was always jealous of her. The youngest, our parent's pride. When they found out she took after both of them, they were so proud. Were your parents dancers?"

Were, she said. Were, not are. The things I loved were all past tense.

"No, they were spirit-bound," I said, dry and quiet.

"When the Gousht attacked, they hit Sonacoa harder than most. The smart ones stole off into the forests and mountains. After my mother died, my father refused to leave the Stone City," she said. "Like he thought she would come back if he waited long enough.

"Then when I was ten, I took my sister, and we ran from the city. I didn't know what I was doing, but it felt like the right thing to do. She was only eight turns," Liara said. Her voice was soft and scratchy. "We lived in the forest, moving from one misfit camp to the next. For six turns, I had her, and she had me.

"Tomi could barely remember living in the city, and I don't think she remembers much of our parents, even though I tried to tell her stories about them—the good versions. She needed something to hold on to."

She fell silent for a while after that. We sat there tangled in heavy thoughts. The gaps in her story said more than her words. She leaned against my shoulder. The moonlight set her dark skin glowing. Slow tears ran down her face, and she let them.

I didn't know what to say or do. I wanted to hold her. I wanted to run away. I wanted to save her from her pain.

"The Gousht took Tomi. It was my fault. Something didn't feel right about the last camp—too many well-fed bellies. But I felt lonely and sick of having to take care of Tomi by myself. They sold us out, and now the fucking couta have her." She hid her face in her folded arms and sobbed.

There weren't any words that could have offered much, so I sat next to her and shared the quiet.

Liara pulled her shoulders back, her echo begging her to lash out. "She's locked away in one of their damn mission schools. I was headed there when you found me. I need you to help me get her out."

Her eyes became soft brown questions. If I didn't know what to say before, this left me utterly lost. I wanted to say yes, to be her hero, but what could I do?

The Gousht filled their mission schools with stolen children taken from homes and the aftermath of battles. The ones too young to labor, 'civilized' and turned against their people. Mission schools were prisons with a different name. Children left wearing the emperor's seal or chains.

"I saw what you did to those green bastards. You stole their spirits and killed them like it was nothing. I need your help. My sister needs your help."

"Those spirits didn't belong to them." My breath stirred as I tried to catch up with my heart.

"You don't understand what you're asking me to do," I said. "Do you know what it's like to hold a stolen spirit inside you? They claw at my skin from the inside. Mother knows how long they have been imprisoned."

My words came out louder than I intended, and I forced my voice to a whisper. "You heard Lashan. You know what I am, what I carry. A malitu. The Thief doesn't help, she only takes."

"I need your help, Kaylo," Liara said, holding my eyes with hers. "And you need me to keep your secret."

A blade would have been kinder.

The moonlight showed the truth in her eyes. She would do anything to save her sister, and I meant nothing to her. The Song flared, and the world went silent behind it.

When I didn't speak, Liara stood up and walked back to the encampment, leaving the bread and apple in her place.

Chapter Twenty-Five

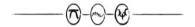

Tayen pushed her blade harder than necessary. The wood curled, then the knife snagged on the ironoak branch. "How could she do that after you saved her?"

"What would you do to save Nita if you could?" Kaylo sighed. "Sometimes life presents us with a handful of bad choices. She was doing her best."

"She didn't have to threaten you." She yanked her knife from the wood.

"No, maybe not." His lips curled, and his eyes sank.

"Did she tell?"

"You should get some sleep." He added two more logs to the firepit. "I'll take the first watch."

If she forced the issue, he would only deflect more. She could stay up and comfort him, but he wouldn't allow that either. The silence thickened between them, then Tayen tossed her scrap of poorly whittled wood into the fire and pushed herself to her feet.

Her muscles resisted the movement. Every hour they spent training, she earned another bruise, but at least she had improved. She lay down and tucked her short sword beside her bedroll.

Tayen found herself running beside her father as a little girl. He dragged her down a dirt path faster than her feet could move, stretching the tendons in her shoulder to the point of tearing. Flames consumed the surrounding village. The orange and yellow monster swallowed up building after building.

Her mother ran close behind with the baby in her arms. Tayen called out to her mother, but the destruction drowned out her voice. Clanging metal and screams cut through the chaos.

They needed to slow down. Her breath couldn't catch up with them.

She gripped her father's hand tighter, even though it hurt. The small-town path never ended. No matter how fast they ran, the clanging metal grew closer and closer.

If the soldiers caught her family, they would die or be sent to the work camps.

A building collapsed in front of them, blocking their way forward. They turned, and the flame consumed the path. As the fire grew, it turned a shade of green.

Tayen squeezed her father's hand even tighter. He didn't squeeze back.

When she turned towards him, he disappeared. The town, the flames, the soldiers all vanished.

The forest settled. Tayen stood at the entry to their hut. She tried to turn away and run, but she pulled the hides aside and stepped into the hut instead.

Her family lay in a stack, covered in green flames. She screamed, but no sound came out. Soldiers glared at her through the smoke, watching her watch her family die. Out of the flames, she finally heard her father speak.

"Blood for blood," he said.

A hand clapped over Tayen's mouth, and her eyes sprang open. The Song ricocheted throughout the forest, erratic thumping noises and a high-strung breeze. The night hid the world from her. She reached for the sword beside her bedroll. Then Kaylo leaned over her, his finger held to his lips.

He removed his hand, and she gulped the air. "What the fu—" He clapped his hand back in place and shook the finger in front of his lips.

She should've bit his hand, but she nodded instead.

The only light in the forest peeked in through the canopy. He had doused the fire. Her travel sack sat next to her, already packed. If this was an elaborate training drill, she might kill him.

Kaylo slung his travel sack over his shoulder. She rolled up her bedroll, latched it to the sack, and did the same. He thrust her second-hand sword into her arms, then headed off into the wood.

The trees blended into the darkness. She guessed with each step. As long as she followed Kaylo, hopefully she wouldn't run into anything.

Bloody fucking Mother, where is he going? The river was the other direction. *And why is he moving so quickly? Can The Hero of Anilace see in the damn dark?*

Tayen held her scabbard in one hand as she moved. It still slapped against her thigh whenever she wore it—the uncomfortable, retched thing.

Animals scurried about, an owl called out, the crickets chirped away, but nothing else. No clanging metal. No muffled voices. No branches snapping under soldiers' boots.

After what must have been half an hour of running through a pitch-black forest, she needed more than a gesture and faith. "What are we doing?"

"Running," he whispered. "Quietly."

The land sloped upward, and the trees thinned, allowing more moonlight through. If soldiers had followed them, they were the quietest band of soldiers ever to wear the Emperor's green.

The hill crested into an outcropping and left them exposed to the stars above. Kaylo stopped. "I need you to hide. Get to the tree line. Make sure you can see me. If anything happens to me, you need to run. Do you understand?"

"No, what's going on?"

"Travel northwest. Dasoon should be about a day of hard walking that way." He pointed over her shoulder.

"The closer you get to the Lost Forest, the less likely they are to follow. If you reach the Lost Forest, you've gone too far. Don't step into that forest. Only use The Shadow if you don't have any choice," he said. "Now go."

Tayen hesitated. The tree line started another twenty strides north. If she stayed, they could fight together. He angled his chin to his chest and stared at her.

"You better know what you're doing," she said, then turned north.

"*There's no reason to hide,*" Kaylo said in Gousht. "*I know you're out there.*"

The single echo followed them through the forest no matter what turn he made. This tracker rivaled the best Kaylo had known. To be able to weave through the sharp turns in the forest at night and not lose a step.

A long Gousht woman stepped into the clearing with the echo. Her silver-white hair ended in a small tuft tied at the back of her head. She wore a leather vest and matching gauntlets layered over a green tunic. A dark purple crystal glowed, hanging from her neck with tightly woven twine.

She clapped her hands together and opened them to the sky. "*You are exactly like he said you would be. Ennea's Thief,*" she said, smiling wide. "*I didn't believe it. Oh, this is a treat.*"

"*What do you want?*"

"*Why ask simple questions you already know the answer to? If you give yourself up, I won't harm you.*" She shrugged. "*I have no interest in stealing such a talent from the world, no pun intended.*"

The steel blade softly brushed against the leather scabbard as Kaylo removed his sword. With his left hand, he pulled his father's knife from his belt.

"*Fair warning. I know about your special talents. I won't be using this.*" The tracker gestured to the crystal around her neck. When Kaylo didn't drop his blade, she drew her own. The blade ran long and straight, coming to a sharp point. "*Professional curiosity, how did you know I was following you?*"

Without thinking, his eyes dropped to the crystal around her neck. "*Interesting. It really will be a shame to kill you.*" She stepped forward, and they began.

Two blades to one, fighting from the higher ground, and yet she behaved as if every advantage served her.

Her feet glided over the dirt in subtle movements, closing the gap and rotating to even the ground between them. If he wanted to keep his advantage, he would have to cut her off.

She still smiled, her pale blue eyes shining in the night like a wolf.

Her left hand reached behind her. Metal flashed as she pulled her hand around, slicing through the air. He managed to pull his shoulder from the dagger's path in time, but it opened up his guard.

The heavy sword nearly bashed in his skull, but Kaylo blocked the blow. She thrust her knee into his side before he could bring around his knife, and she pranced away, putting more distance between them.

Kaylo growled in the back of his throat. Throwing knives? Fair didn't exist in war, but this was fucking new.

She reached her off-hand back again and paused. Her lips spread wide, and then a second knife flew.

He side-stepped and the edge of the knife skated through the meat of his right calf. Off-balance, searing pain cutting through his leg, Kaylo swung his sword wildly to keep his distance.

Though the distance only offered the advantaged to the tracker. Another knife flung through the air. He dove into a roll, stopping in a kneeling position.

How many knives does she have? he thought, just before her sword nearly chopped him down like a tree. The vibration from the blow crashed through his sword into his elbow and up his shoulder.

Before he could counter with his knife or attack with his sword, she pranced off again. They stood with equal footing on the high ground. His calf burned. She used the distance to her advantage perfectly. Eventually, a knife would find something more vital than his calf.

He had to admit; it was an excellent strategy. A toying grin crept over her face.

She stood between them and a chance at freedom. More blood had to be spilled, and it would either be hers or his.

Her left hand flicked out from behind her back with yet another knife. Kaylo closed the distance between them, and the knife sank into his left shoulder. His knife fell from his grip. With his right hand, he swung his purloined sword with all his might.

No more smile. Her blade met his at the last second, deflecting his attack before he could split her head in two, but the force of his swing carried his sword into her left shoulder. The bone cracked under his blade, and she fell to her knees.

She swung her sword one last time, but it lacked her strength, and he knocked it from her hands.

Blood oozed from her shoulder wound as she looked up from her knees. She chuckled. "*I should have known someone with such a reputation wouldn't be easy to kill.*"

"*Are you alone?*"

"*I mean, I knew you would be good. But who takes a knife to the shoulder for an attack position?*" She laughed from deep in her belly.

"*Who else is with you?*" Despite his best efforts, he yelled.

"*I work alone, but the old man will never stop hunting you.*"

"Who is she talking about?" Tayen said from over his shoulder.

"*Oh, there she is. I thought you would have been halfway to the Lost Forest by now,*" the tracker said.

"*Any words before you go?*" Kaylo asked.

"*That's very gracious, but I never believed much in gods or spirits.*"

Her shoulder clung to his sword. He yanked it free and then stabbed it through her chest. A wet gasp left her throat, and she fell to the ground, still with a slight smile.

"We need to move." His sword made a slurping sound as he pulled it from her body.

"Who was that? What old man?"

"If you weren't aware of it, the Gousht have a rather large bounty on my head. Safe to say, it has grown over the last decade. Where there is one tracker, there will be others. We have to go."

He walked off before she could ask any more questions.

Tayen convinced Kaylo to rest at high sun to tend to his wounds, though he swore they were little more than scratches. He ground up dried herbs from his garden in the hallow while she divvied out the last strips of saltmeat. According to Kaylo, they didn't have time to boil water for a meal of bland oats.

They left before the poultices had time to dry.

He moved different than before, and it had nothing to do with the cut to his leg or the wound in his shoulder. Each footstep dug deeper into the dirt. Every stride stretched a little longer. Tayen had to jog to keep pace.

"Can you slow down?"

"You can't keep up with a man twice your age, who happens to have a bad knee on one leg and a fresh wound on the other?"

"You're more than twice my age, and you said it was a scratch."

"If we push through, we'll hit Dasoon by nightfall." He drove his legs faster.

The tracker must have scared him. *What would have happened if she hadn't been carrying a spirit crystal? What would have happened if she killed him?* Tayen might have been able to find Dasoon on her own, but not with a tracker on her heels.

She would have been alone. The last person who knew her name almost died for the third time in as many moons. While he fought for them, she watched.

Her sword slapped against her. If she had to train every waking hour of every day, she would learn how to use the rotten thing. Then, when an opportunity arose, she wouldn't hesitate. She would kill again.

———

As dusk settled into the forest, Tayen's breath turned into clouds of vapor with each exhale. Kaylo finally slowed. He wrapped a blanket around her shoulders, even as they continued walking, and the gesture warmed her in more than one way.

"I'm glad you didn't die today," she said.

He chuckled. "We're getting close," he said. "There's a dancer not much farther."

Kaylo didn't speak about the echoes very often. It unsettled her, the way he could hear The Song through her. It felt different when she listened to his story. The boy he described was a stranger to her.

"You aren't a dancer. Neither am I," Kaylo said without looking back. "You're my niece, and we escaped from Nomar after a Lost Army raid."

"What in the name of The Mother are you talking about?"

He turned around and met her eyes. "There are people looking for us, so it will be better if we aren't us," he said. "You haven't spoken much since you lost your parents."

That made her swallow. She counted her breaths. Her parents weren't an excuse, and she wasn't stupid.

"Tell me you understand," he said.

"I understand." She ripped the blanket off her shoulders and thrust it into his arms before she started walking again.

He followed close behind her, apparently wise enough not to say anything else.

"Stop where you stand!" A voice called out from the forest, and the tension between Kaylo and Tayen shattered.

Tayen strained her ears and listened like Kaylo taught her. Four heavy-footed and one light-stepper.

The Song gathered near the ground like a morning fog. Each shadow waited for her to call on them. Kaylo grabbed her hand and squeezed gently.

A tall, lean woman stepped into view, wearing close-cropped pants, a robe, and a heavy fur cloak. She wore an impassive expression as her eyes scanned over them.

Her light brown skin and coarse dark hair marked her as a northerner. Her hand rested on the hilt of her sword, a long-thin blade. It didn't have the heft of most blades Tayen had seen. A scar carved through the length of her exposed forearm. This woman had seen battle and survived it, which explained her calmer demeanor compared to her loud-footed friends.

"Who are you, and where are you traveling?" she asked.

"I'm Kuno and this is my niece, Tayen. I promised my brother I would keep his daughter safe. Heard Dasoon was as close to safe as Ennea got." Kaylo spoke without hesitancy. He lifted his hand to rest on his sword. "Are you from the freecity, or are you more blood banners preying on your own people? I warn you; I won't be easy prey."

The woman's shoulders shifted, but she didn't take the bait.

Her comrades reacted with less subtlety. Two of them spat at the mention of blood banners, one cursed, and the last drew his rusty blade. Then Kaylo drew his blade in turn.

Why is he provoking them? They were supposed to be looking for shelter, not fighting with the locals.

It took all Tayen's discipline to keep her hand from her sword. A traumatized niece wouldn't be pulling her blade. She turned her eyes to the ground, trying to look as meek as possible.

He better know what he's doing.

The blade of their would-be attacker trembled in his hands. If this was all they had to defend the city, it was a wonder Dasoon still stood. They lacked experience, training, and discipline.

The northwoman moved quickly, pulling her thin blade and angling herself between the two stupid men. She gave her ally her back and stood directly in front of Kaylo.

Her eyes didn't move from his. "Be careful who you call a blood banner, uncle," she said with a brilliant balance between threat and respect. "The freecity stays free because we are weary of strangers."

"Oh, aye? Do you carve up everyone seeking shelter?" Kaylo asked.

"Only dirty men without manners," she said with a sly smile. Tayen liked this woman immediately. "Dasoon is always looking for hard workers, but we don't need any more freeloaders."

"We're here to work."

"We'll need more than your word and a sad story," she said.

"We don't even know your names, and what? We are supposed to offer you our life stories?"

"Oh, you wanted a proper introduction. Nix at your service, head of the city guard," she said. "Now that we're the best of friends, put down your sword." Nix wasn't looking for a fight, but her body language said she was ready.

Kaylo dropped his sword to the ground. "I'd like to keep my belt knife, if you don't mind. Sentimental value."

"Keep it if it makes you feel safe. But all other weapons need to be laid on the ground before we take a step closer to Dasoon," Nix said.

Tayen looked to Kaylo before dropping her sword. They had escaped the Gousht trackers only to lay down their weapons for this misfit brigade.

Nix reached down and handed the swords to the other guards before waving for Kaylo and Tayen to follow.

The city wall was a combination of wood and rock held together by stubborn luck. The guards at the entrance stood up straighter as Nix approached. Two old men with older blades to guard the entrance.

Another forty paces along the inside of the wall stood a small building. Although, to call it a building was generous. It was a hunk of rock with a door.

"Hakan will have some questions for you in the morning. Until then, there will be two guards posted at this door at all times. Understood?" Nix asked, but it lacked the cadence of a question. Her eyes were hard as she waited for her new charges to nod their understanding. Then she closed the door behind her.

Small streams of moonlight broke the darkness. Tayen began pulling at the shadows and allow the moonlight to fill up the small hut, but Kaylo placed a hand on her arm.

He shook his head. "Don't give them more information than necessary. They aren't our enemies, but they aren't our friends," he whispered. "Remember, we aren't dancers. We are simple runaways."

"Why did you draw your sword out there?"

"Trusting people are hard to trust when there is a war about."

Tayen rolled her eyes. He was being paranoid, but then again, so were their hosts. Locked in a hut barely long enough to lie down in. Armed guards. Even when the Empire wasn't here, they were. They loomed in every decision. This was not a free city.

When she lay down, she had to lie at an angle, and still, her feet touched the stone wall. *It's going to be a long night,* she thought, but she closed her eyes all the same.

On the edge of sleep, her kana hummed. Then his voice lightly carried into the air.

Even when the night is cold
There's always a way home
Stars hidden by the clouds above
There's always a way home
Body is weary, and bones are old
There's always...

CHAPTER TWENTY-SIX

A stream of light leaked in through the cracks in the stone hut and fell across Tayen's eyelids, stirring her from her sleep. The room seemed even smaller than it had in the darkness, a box of haphazardly placed stones, barely tall enough to stand. The wooden bucket in the corner passed along an unpleasant message; they might be here longer than she had expected.

She peeled herself from her bedroll as Kaylo sat with his back planted against the rough stone wall. Dark circles underscored his eyes, and the corners of his mouth drooped.

"You didn't sleep?" Tayen asked, more like an accusation.

"I don't trust our hosts yet. There will be time to sleep later."

How stupid could she have been? Taking shelter and sleeping under armed guard without question. Kaylo should have woken her for her shift. If he hadn't been suspicious enough for the two of them—a shiver ran from the nape of her neck to the tip of her tailbone. She had to be smarter if she intended to live long enough to make something of her family's sacrifice.

Never again, she promised. *By The Shadow herself, I won't drop my guard again.*

The door burst open, and she reached for the sword that wasn't there. A large man in a heavy fur robe stood in the doorway. He looked like a bear. Dark brown face, gray hair shorn tightly to his scalp—a child of many nations. His harsh features were brutish, but not unattractive. The hulking man more than filled the entrance.

The big man didn't introduce himself. He squinted into the tiny hut as if he were weighing them. Two dirty runaways seeking shelter for the winter. Able bodies. Two more mouths to ration. He looked like a dullard trying to read a difficult word.

"Names," he commanded, as if he expected to be obeyed.

"We've already given our names," Kaylo said calmly, but with a rebellion underneath. "Who is asking the questions?"

The bear's lips turned up with slight amusement. "And my people gave you my name last night as well," he said. "But, yes, Blessed Mother, manners. Hakan, leader of the freecity of Dasoon."

The lumbering man stepped from the opening. "Walk with me, Kuno. The pup can stay here."

Tayen's eyes darted to her kana, her earlier vulnerability still prickling along her skin. She only had an empty shit bucket to defend herself.

Kaylo knelt in front of her and handed her his father's knife. He placed his hand on her shoulder and turned to follow the big man. If he was afraid, he didn't show it.

The knife hardly comforted her as the wooden door swung shut, leaving her only dark thoughts for company.

Hakan set a fast pace. Kaylo stretched his gait longer to keep up with the man's strides.

This routine bore all the signs of a practiced act, pronounced silences spotted with brief declarations, the overly fast pace, and the winding path they traveled. He wanted Kaylo off-balance. Clever tactic with scared shitless refugees.

Best to make Hakan believe it had the desired effect. His kind liked to believe they saw all the moving parts the world had to offer. Kaylo exaggerated his movements as he looked from side to side and cradled a shaking hand in the other.

An echo as big as the man himself clanged about the ruins of the city that had been. An earth dancer—strong, intimidating, untrained. No wonder Hakan had gathered power in a place like this. Kaylo needed this oversized man to see their value, but not their full worth. The opportunistic ones always looked for a better deal.

"Your daughter must favor your wife," Hakan said without looking to Kaylo.

"My niece favored my brother's wife, but sadly, we lost both her parents to The Mist."

"Ay, yes, niece. Much gets lost in passing hands. I am sorry to hear about your losses. Too many have lost too much to the war."

"They were lost to the Gousht. War had nothing to do with it," Kaylo said, allowing his anger to color his tone.

"Gousht." Hakan grunted and spat. "You see what they left us? Burned buildings, crumbling walls, and decaying bodies. May The Mist forget their spirits. Leave them to the cold dark earth."

"But let the animals take their fill first," Kaylo growled.

Hakan clapped his meaty hand on Kaylo's shoulder, and the fresh knife wound screamed. He gritted his teeth and held his pain inside.

"Ha, I think I may like you, Kuno. I say a man with fury is a man with power. I need more men with power. Too many broken spirits. Too many broken buildings." He waved his hand as if to cast aside the weak inhabitants. "Don't worry, it's okay to admit it. Dasoon is not what it once was. I am the leader of a pile of rocks and wood that used to be a city. But not for long. We will be great again."

Kaylo had been wrong. Hakan wasn't clever in the slightest. No, his pride greatly outshined his intelligence. "Won't that draw too much attention?" Kaylo asked meekly.

"I thought you were a bigger man than that low fear. The city I raise

will be stronger than any petty raiding party. I dare them to try," Hakan
announced to an absent crowd. He lowered his voice, and for the first
time, turned his gaze to Kaylo. "The question is, will you be a part of my
grand city?"

Too eager and Hakan would feel threatened. Too meager and he
would feel doubted. Fragile men looking for others to follow their
command, whether or not they had earned it, wanted supporters to
need and fear them in equal parts.

Kaylo made himself as small as possible and looked up into Hakan's
eyes. "If you'll have me."

The man's hand clapped down like a boulder on Kaylo's back. They
continued the conversation, walking through the empty streets on the
outer edges of the city.

It had gone too easy. If the people of Dasoon followed this man, they
would follow him to ruin. But for Kaylo's purposes, Hakan served as the
perfect host.

The guards opened the door to the pile of rocks and tossed Tayen a
chunk of bread and a full waterskin. The edges of the bread had gone dry
and crusty with age, but the color was brilliantly brown like the loaves
her mother used to cook over the fire. Her mouth watered, but she
resisted the urge to sink her teeth into the bread. These people had her
kana and had locked her away.

If they wanted me dead, there are easier ways than poison.

She patted the dust from the bread and took a small bite. The crust
fought her teeth, then crumbled in her mouth. She continued eating until
her mouth went as dry as the dirt under her feet.

Even as quickly as the bread vanished, the taste touched old
memories. Her mother grinding wild grain and tossing it with whatever
herbs she could find—that woman could make miracles of small offerings.
Before the loaves had a chance to cool, Tayen would tear them, and the

smell would rise with the steam. Her mother always scolded her for it but never stopped her. It was a small game they shared before they ate.

Tayen sat against the rough wall and gave into her mourning. All her time with Kaylo, she fought her memories. They weighed her down, and she hadn't the strength to carry them.

All for a stupid piece of bread. Tears and memories ran through her like the sunlight through the cracks in the wall.

The stupid guards could probably hear her weeping. They would assume she was scared, but she wasn't. She was angry. Kaylo's knife flipped back and forth in her hands as she toyed with it.

"Hush up, little girl," Hakan called in through the doorway. She hadn't even noticed the door swing open. Of course, he would find her like this.

"Nothing to fret over. You got you an uncle straight from the spirits." He clapped Kaylo on the back like he was beating the dust from a rug.

"She's been through a lot," Kaylo said, facing Tayen with a bit of empathy strung through his half-smile.

"See, quality," Hakan announced. "Nix will show you the way."

Hakan exchanged a few words with the statuesque woman from the night before. She gestured in stiff, sharp movements, but he dismissed her and walked away.

"Come with me," Nix said with an edge to her words. "I'll show you to your plot."

Nix didn't wait to let them gather their small belongings. She walked with the full length of her gait at a warrior's pace. When Kaylo and Tayen caught up, she didn't acknowledge them. Her nose flared and her lips puckered as if she had been ordered to deliver a sack of manure across town.

The city amounted to little more than a mound of rubble. Cracks lined the stone walls of the few buildings still standing. Scorch marks colored the stone black and ash. The farther they walked into the city, the more rubble that had been cleared away or put to use rebuilding whatever remained. A mixture of stone and wood patched the city together, like fabric tied over a gut wound. The city died long ago, but the people still here were too stupid or hopeful to know it.

Most of the people they passed turned away, while others couldn't help but stare. Either way, they all kept their distance.

An old Tomakan man watched them pass while he huddled amongst the rubble of a fallen building. Tayen didn't even see him at first for all the dust and debris covering his robes and painting him into the rubble. Long wisps of white hair crowned his balding head, and his body shook like the ground was unsteady. The people walking by ignored him as if he were dead—or should be.

Why isn't anyone helping him? It made Tayen shiver. *This is what they do with their freedom?*

"You will be watched," Nix said with a growl. "Hakan may like you, but I don't."

"We don't like you either," Tayen snapped back. Kaylo shot a glare in her direction, but she didn't care. Nix didn't scare her, and the warrior needed to know it.

"I apologize for my niece. She hasn't been around people in a long time," Kaylo said.

Nix gave her a wicked smile. "I prefer her honesty over your bullshit, uncle." The honorific came out as an insult. "I don't care about your manners. I don't care how friendly you are. I care that you follow the rules and us who make the rules. And in case there was any confusion, Hakan and I make the rules."

"Understood," Kaylo said.

As much as she resented their guide, Nix seemed smart. Certainly more capable than anyone else they had met so far. Kaylo charmed Hakan in half-a-morning. Nix hadn't been fooled for a second. She should have been in charge. Hakan had charisma, but he probably owed his leadership to his manhood more than anything else.

Before the Gousht, women and kamani people served as leaders of armies and nations. But the green bastards brought more than swords and spears. They brought stupid ideas. Their god believed men should bear the weight of leadership, and, sadly, the idea had appealed to many Ennean men.

The row of buildings on either side of them opened up into an empty plot of land. Heaps of rubble gathered in every corner of the city square. A platform knocked together with salvaged wood stood right in the middle of all this nothing,

Nix pointed to the platform. "Rations are handed out on the caller's stage first morning each span. Don't be late."

Before the invasion, there would have been a market overflowing the square. People looking to trade their services, their bits of extra. But whatever it had been, the freecity had become a broken memory where Dasoon once stood.

Several shabby looking people bunched together against the corner of a building at the end of the square. They shook like the old man in the rubble, but they had more life left in them. Filth covered their robes, and the stench of sweet piss rolled off of them. They laughed loudly. One pushed another with a friendly jib. Puffs of smoke filled the air around them.

If Hakan made the rules and Nix enforced them, who was supposed to help these people?

A woman's ragged robe ended high on her arm. It looked as if her ashen brown skin had been stretched taut over bone. If she'd had a meal since the last moon, it would have been a surprise.

Nix ushered Kaylo and Tayen by without a word.

Not far beyond the square, Nix stopped. In front of them stood the ruins of an old stone house. Soot lapped up at the foundation. A fire had burned through the roof. The door was missing. A whole length of the building had collapsed in on itself. What remained standing could have been pushed over by a strong breeze. A medium breeze. A breeze.

Nix waved her hand in front of the broken structure. Tayen squinted in confusion, and Nix countered with a smile. The gesture made Tayen want to strangle her.

Kaylo placed his hand on her shoulder. "This is a start," he said.

"A start?" Tayen yelled. "It doesn't even have four walls."

"You're free to return to your previous accommodations," Nix said.

"We don't need..." Tayen started, but Kaylo interrupted, squeezing tightly on her shoulder.

"We can make a home out of these bones."

Nix handed him a small bundle, including their blades, grunted, and turned back on her heel. "No leaving the city. I don't trust you, and Hakan doesn't need you that much."

Tayen locked eyes with Kaylo. "This is safer than the hallow? Or the forest?"

Kaylo didn't engage. He walked through the collapsed wall and paced the remains of the small house. "It has potential. By snowfall we will have a roof and four sturdy walls," he said. "For now, it will keep the wind off our backs at night."

She couldn't see what he apparently could. To her, it looked like a deathtrap. An insult.

Someone probably had to pull bodies from the rubble when they reclaimed the town, but she followed her kana in, regardless of her apprehension. At least another tracker wouldn't stroll through the city in the middle of the night.

A handful of splintered wood and a few strikes of flint burst to life in the middle of what would be their home. Sokan crested over the sky as Kaylo unwrapped the bundle of rough bread and saltmeat.

"Stew?" He asked, as if they hadn't survived off stew and oats for almost two moons.

"What happened with Hakan?" Tayen asked impatiently.

"He offered me a deal, and I took it. I told him I was a carpenter. If I work for him, we get to stay in these lovely accommodations." Kaylo smiled at his own joke. "The rations won't be much, but we can start growing a bit for ourselves once spring comes along. I bet I could talk

Hakan into letting us hunt."

"What am I supposed to do while you're out slapping wood beams on rubble?"

"Well, I imagine they'll find a bit of work for you, but in the meantime, you'll help me build a house," Kaylo said as he put the water and saltmeat to boil.

Tayen sulked into one of the two remaining corners and pulled a book from her travel sack. She already read this section on Kalani's campaign along the border against Sonacoa during the Great War, but she needed to read it again.

The book spun Kalani as a brilliant strategist—praised her uncanny ability to sacrifice units of her army in order for the whole to survive and claim victory. Maybe brilliant, but also heartless. Even as Kalani saved hundreds, maybe thousands of lives, she gave some of her own people to the enemy, knowing that they would die a hard death.

Leaders called it sacrifice—strategy. What would the warriors who died call it? What about the old man sitting amongst the rubble on the outskirts of the town?

Kaylo offered her a bowl of unseasoned stew. She put down her book and took it. Her belly rumbled, even though she had eaten the same slop almost every day on the road.

"What was wrong with those people in the town square?" she asked softly.

Kaylo didn't need to ask who she meant. "Susu root."

"Like what Jonac smoked?"

"People seek shelter from their pain, even if that means feeling nothing," Kaylo said.

"That's stupid. It doesn't change anything."

"No, but it can make the world seem better for a time," Kaylo said. "There isn't a city, free or otherwise, without people huddled around smoke, smelling like sweet and sage. The Gousht encourage it and force it on slaves."

Fucking couta.

Tayen tried not to think about everything the Gousht had stolen from her. When she did, she couldn't breathe. The weight of it forced everything from her lungs.

It wasn't enough that they killed her family and took her home. The Gousht had taken away everything her life should have been. She should have grown up in a city surrounded by friends and family. She should have gone to school. She should have become a part of Ennea. Instead, Tayen was trying to escape Ennea before the dying land crushed her beneath its corpse.

CHAPTER TWENTY-SEVEN

WHEN I CLOSED MY eyelids at night, Liara whispered into Jonac's ear or conspired with Torrel. She passed my secret along like empty gossip until the whole clan knew what I was. Then my eyes shot open, and everything went still. The pattern repeated, stretches of staring up into the canopy of the tent interrupted by jarring nightmares. It had been several days since I had a proper sleep.

I tore myself from another horrible dream to find that Jonac had already left. *Fuck.* I threw on a cleaner robe, splashed some water on my face, and ran from the tent. *Late the first day.*

After Shunanlah, Jonac announced the time had come for me to learn how to fight. "Someone set on running towards trouble needs to know how to use a sword," he had said.

My temples throbbed as the bright morning light turned the world into a blur of muddy browns and greens. If I shook my head, even slightly, it might have fallen to the ground in pieces.

The city moved all around me. The Jani busied themselves preparing for the next resettlement, several nomads working to untether and stow away the gathering tent.

Torrel stood at the encampment gate, and the moment we locked eyes, he turned away. His shoulders tightened. We hadn't spoken since the night he ambushed me. Neither of us had anything to say to each other.

About halfway to the river, I came to a circular clearing about ten paces wide. The trees that had once lived here had aged to dust with The Song.

Jonac stood there waiting, arms crossed and lips drawn tight, and he wasn't alone.

"What is she doing here?" I asked.

He ignored my question and waited until I knelt beside Liara.

Maybe she told him already, and he brought me out here to put me down like a wounded animal.

Jonac's foot tapped against the forest floor as he looked us over. "If you are going to learn to defend yourself, you need a sparring partner. And since the both of you like to get into trouble, who better?"

Liara and I exchanged a tentative glance. I would have rather trained with Torrel. At least he didn't hide his hatred.

"I don't know what happened between you two, and I don't care," Jonac said. "Maybe it's better this way. If you're angry with each other, you won't hold back when you're sparring." He bent down, picked up two ironoak branches stripped of their bark, and tossed them at our feet.

"Pick them up, and don't waste my time," he said with even less empathy in his voice.

Jonac had shaved the notches on the branch down to make the wood smooth. It felt heavier than I imagined a sword would, not that I had ever held a sword. Armies didn't tend to leave warring weapons to the citizens of occupied territories.

"Think of your feet as your roots; they create a base for the rest of your body. Your hips are the driving force of your power. If you wave your sword around, trying to muscle it with your arms, you'll tire yourself out."

How did a peaceful nomad learn about sword fighting? The secrets layered atop of one another. I didn't know this man at all, not truly.

I positioned my right foot back and bent my legs, balancing my weight, and he adjusted me roughly. He kicked my back shin, moving it shoulder length apart from my front. His fingers dug into my shoulders as he shifted my posture. All the while, my head still throbbed.

Liara modified her stance to match mine without the forceful pushing and pulling. I glared at her, and Jonac grabbed my face to turn it forward yet again. This was going to be a long fucking day.

"Little brother, you better stop looking at me like you want to hit me with that branch, or I will give you a much more hands-on lesson in swordplay," Jonac said. "Now, give me the branch."

He gripped the branch at the base as if it were a sword with a hilt. "A sword isn't a knife. You hold a sword with two hands. Your dominant hand atop the other." As he lectured, he demonstrated.

"This is where your sword should live, in front of your abdomen. If you need to parry or block, your hips can transfer the force into your legs. If you need to attack, your legs anchor you to the ground, and your hips drive the force," he said. "Nod if you understand, boy."

"Why are you only focusing on me?"

The squat man took one step, shifted his weight, and swung the practice blade through my forward shin. All at once, pain burned through the lower half of my leg, and the forest flipped before I landed on the flat of my back.

"She is not attuned to my sunny disposition," he said, tossing the branch on the ground next to me.

From morning to the highest point of the day, we practiced getting into our stance and a series of basic attacks—each some variation of planting our feet, turning our hips, and swinging the sword at one angle or another. If we were careless, he pointed it out and smacked us with another branch. Liara didn't escape his corrections. At least, in that, he was equitable.

My arms hung like loose clay by the time he let us go to the river to get water. Whatever new teaching approach Jonac had decided on, I didn't like it. The bumps and bruises ran from my legs to my torso. Each movement pulled on another injury, one tender pain after another.

When we got back from the river, Jonac had us stand opposite each other. For the next couple of hours, we traded off attacking and parrying. Each time the branches connected, the shock traveled through the wood and buckled in my grip. If we didn't connect with enough force, Jonac stood in to demonstrate his expectations.

"The more you practice, the more your muscles get used to their motions. Soon, the movement will be as natural as dancing. Now I want you to...."

The signal bell clanged into the forest, its steady rhythm marking the return of the scouting party. I had never been more thankful to hear another sound in my life.

"You get a reprieve," Jonac said. "Take your practice swords with you." A strain pulled on his voice that hadn't been there before.

When the council selected two new scouts to search for the next encampment site, Jonac had been livid. Not that he cared to talk about it. Conversations with Jonac rarely went deeper than instruction or reprimand ever since Torrel attacked me.

That night Jonac lost two adopted sons, and, in that way, Torrel and I shared much.

Pain drew out the walk back to the ironoak wall into an endless hike. The injuries and aches ceased to be individual hurts, becoming a collective scream within my brain that never diminished.

The work of packing the camp paled in comparison to the morning I spent with Jonac. In a day, we had to be packed, and the forest had to be set to rights. The forest needed to be exactly as it had been before us.

I spent the better part of the evening walking from garden to garden, calling on The Seed. The flowers and plants aged until the brittle stems crumbled in on themselves. At first, the regret of each plant I returned to the soil twisted my gut, but even that ache became too much. My body and my spirit had gone numb by the time I finished.

Back in the tent, Nomi, Liara, Soca, and Junera busied themselves packing away every little trinket they could. I had moved twice with the clan already, and it continued to amaze me how little they carried with them. Unpacked and spread out, the tent appeared expansive, but everything within fit into seven sacks.

My stomach growled, but the hunger didn't register. All I wanted was sleep. I walked over to my bedroll and, for the first time in days, slept an uninterrupted, dreamless sleep.

The next morning, Jonac woke me up before sunrise to help takedown the ironoak wall. All told, over three hundred trees ran the perimeter of the tent city, and each one had to be returned to the soil before the clan could leave. At the rate I went, we would be ready to leave by winter.

The rough bark scratched my palm. I closed my eyes and pulled at The Song. Each thread of The Seed I reached for turned out to be the wrong one.

"Hurry up," Jonac said over my shoulder.

"I'm too tired. I can't think clearly."

Jonac grabbed me by each of the shoulders, last night's smoke wafting off his clothes. "Breathe. In and out," he said. "Now, look at me. I don't care if you're tired. Do your part and get rid of those trees."

He looked at me with the same warm brown eyes I had looked into the first day we met. This was the same man who had welcomed me into his home as a stranger. The man who had taught me intimate lessons about my spiritual connection with The Seed. And at the same time, he had become someone completely different.

He turned away and walked back to his section of the wall. He didn't pray over each tree like he once had. He hadn't the patience for it. Even his echo sounded thinner.

I should have never come back, I thought. *If saving Liara meant killing Jonac, I made the wrong choice.*

The Song bloomed in the cool morning wind. The air teased my lips as I took a deep breath. I reached for the teacher Jonac used to be. "Life and death are not so different," he had told me the first time he showed me how to return a plant to the soil. "The death of one life is the start of another. Energy flows through us to become something else."

I had asked why he prayed for the plant if he believed that. "Gratitude is not a payment. It is an acknowledgment that the plant is transforming as someday we all will," he had said.

The memory stung bittersweet. I tried to listen to his words rather than mourn losing him. The Song swelled, and the ironoak stood within it. I reached into the core of the tree and pulled on its part of The Song until it crumbled into the soil.

"Thank you for being the wall that sheltered this clan," I prayed. I touched three fingers to my lips, then place them on the ground.

The clan piled the carts high with the leather and fur canopies for each of the sixteen tents. Every one old enough and strong enough loaded up their own sacks to carry. The encampment looked like any other plot of land that surrounded it.

Like the ironoak wall, the tent city returned to the soil. Other trees grew sporadically over the grounds that had been the encampment.

A solemness presided over the entire process. I hefted my packs and started walking with Nomi and the girls. Liara walked beside us too, but I did my best not to notice her.

"Why aren't you walking with Daddy?" Soca asked.

"He's busy, and he asked me to keep you company."

"That's not true. He always used to walk with us," Junera said. "Why doesn't Daddy want to walk with us, Mommy?"

Nomi's smile stopped at her cheeks. As the days passed, she got better at not showing her pain. "Your father has new responsibilities now, honey. The council needs him. You know the clan has to come first."

"But what does the council need him to do?" Junera asked.

"Junera, your father told me that you and your sister are the best water dancers he's ever seen. Besides your mommy," Liara said. "Do you think you could show me some tricks?"

The girls looked at their mother. They weren't done with the conversation, but Nomi hurried them along. "Go on, girls. Show Liara what you can do."

Junera ran off after Liara first, while Soca held back. The look she exchanged with her mother was full of questions. That little girl wore an age much older than her turns.

"She's a good heart," Nomi said after the girls ran off.

"They both are."

"No, I know my daughters are wonderful. I meant Liara," Nomi said. "What's going on between you two?"

"What are you talking about? Nothing's going on."

"Ever since Shunanlah, something is different," she said. "The troubles in my home don't keep me from seeing the obvious."

The roundness of her cheeks held all the sympathy in the world. Nomi could never replace my mother, and she never tried. She had taken me in and cared for me without question. Even now, as she protected her daughters from the hard changes in their father, her heart wanted to fix the world for me. I almost confessed everything to her.

"I saw the way you used to look at her," Nomi said. "Did something happen that night? Or not happen?"

I smiled. "Something like that."

After we made camp that night, I could hardly move, but my mind wasn't as tired as my body. I sat next to the fire outside our small tent.

Liara and the girls fell asleep immediately after dinner.

The tent flapped open, and leather slapped against leather. Nomi stuck her head out. "You look wild, you know that? When is the last time you took your braids out?"

"Beginning of summer."

"Boy, you should know better than that." She walked out and sat down with her back propped against a tree. "Come over here."

My braids did look a mess. Too much growth, not enough care. I sat in front of Nomi and she ran her hand through my braids. Her touch tingled along my scalp. She wrapped my braids up with a bit of twine, so she could address one at a time.

"You've almost been with us for a full turn, and you are a part of this family. I shouldn't have to tell you that, but there it is." She pulled roughly on a braid, working a snag from my hair.

"Ouch."

"Ouch nothing, tenderhead." She tugged on another braid.

My mother used to take out my braids for me. Every moon or two, she would unweave my gray hairs and trim the damage from the ends. She would rub oil into my scalp, and we would talk. Her fingers had been much gentler.

"We are all going through changes, Kaylo."

"What is going on with Jonac?"

She sighed heavily, and her breath brushed over my ear. "Have you ever heard the story of the black flag?"

"If you don't want to tell me, that's okay."

"Hush and listen," she said. "Near the end of the Hundred-Turn War, the conflict grew bloodier than ever. A group of nomads who escaped the war thought they could broker a peace. They sent envoys to invite the great generals to what they called a conclave of spirits."

She yanked on another braid, and I winced but kept my tongue still.

"Onikan, a nomad from Sonacoa, volunteered to go to Astile, the Lost Nation, and relay the invitation. He, his husband, and a couple of their close friends trekked north. When they reached the Astilean camps, Onikan told the others to wait. Times were dangerous, and the risk was his to take.

"He mounted a large black cloth on a fallen tree limb. What could be more peaceful than the hue of night? More amiable than the color of soil?

"He waved the flag as he approached the army's camp and a young Astilean archer saw the flag waving and the darkness of the flag-bearer's skin. He loosed an arrow, assuming that the approaching man was a warrior. Before Onikan died, he relayed his message.

"As a sign of repentance, the Astilean general condemned the archer to death. They sent a messenger to find the nomads and offer an apology. When he heard of the death sentence, Onikan's widowed husband traveled to the army's camp bearing another black flag. He told the general that his husband meant to stop the bloodshed and asked for the archer to be set free. The general agreed and promised to attend the conclave."

Her hands wove over one another, pulling the strands of a braid loose.

"What does that have to do with Jonac?"

"That story is the heart of the Jani. My father told me about the black flag as soon as I would sit still," she said. "Jonac has learned, but he grew up as a warrior. The fights he avoids will always torment him."

"What about susu root?"

Her hands stopped moving. "We all have our daemons. That daemon has plagued him for longer than I've known him. He has to choose to fight."

"Aren't you angry with him?"

"Of course, I am. But anger is a part of relationships, whatever the relationship may be. The question is, can you move past your anger?"

I turned towards our tent, where Liara slept. *Can I?*

CHAPTER TWENTY-EIGHT

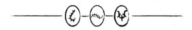

Bits of ironoak lay out in a grid of runes in front of me, calling for me to play. Darkness stretched out in every direction. Wisps of The Thief's shadow cloak flittered in the air despite the lack of wind.

This was a dream, a dream I had dreamed countless nights. Each time I played her game while she played with me as if I were another rune to place in the dirt. Not this time.

The fog cleared from my mind. Nothing lurked in the darkness. The shadows were just shadows. I picked up a rune, brushing my thumb over the polished wood. It didn't exist. None of it did, not even the foreboding spirit cloaked in shadows.

The nightmare slowed, and the tension eased from my dream body.

"Ah, finally awake?" The Thief's voice sounded husky and rich as ever.

"Awake? No, I finally realized this is a dream."

"Not as clever as I had hoped. Pity," she said. She drew her hands across her shadow veil and pulled back her hood. The black of her face was absolute, stark against the porcelain white. "No need for masks. It is a dream after all."

I stared back into the blank whites of her eyes. She would not frighten me. I would not retreat. "What do you want from me?"

"My dear, what a question to ask a dream." Her cheeks curved into what would have been a smile if she had lips. "In a word, everything."

My expression creased as I gave up restraining my venom. "You'll get nothing," I said. "No more. You have taken too much!"

As I thought of Shay, my father, and my mother, the shadows coalesced into their visages—standing in the blackness, unmoving. Then they vanished.

"Why is it that they all blame me?" the mouthless spirit asked. "I gave you my spirit, my gift, and you curse my name—call me a thief. As if you had the right. As if I hadn't saved your life twice over." Her voice steadily grew louder and sharper.

"I didn't ask to be a malitu," I yelled back. "You've left me alone. I have to hide from everyone because of you."

"You lie to them, and you blame me for it? Now child, tell me, what have I done?"

I breathed out a small puff of air, taken aback by such a ridiculous question.

"Done? There are books dedicated to your crimes. You and your descendants stealing peace for power. Tricking. Killing. Jealous of the other spirits. You have no true power of your own. You take from others like a greedy child. What haven't you done?"

The surrounding shadows swirled, and The Thief grew into the darkness. Whatever amusement she had taken in our banter disappeared. She grew larger and larger into the void until she loomed over me like a giant.

"A child? A child?" she screamed, her voice reverberating through the void. "A child blames others. A child thinks they know beyond their grasp and calls it the truth. A child believes without question. No, child, I think you have been listening to all the wrong stories."

My eyes widened. Every instinct in me screamed to back away. But it was a dream, and my rage ran deeper than my fear.

She's angry with me? I thought. *After everything she put me through?*

I glared up into her immense white eyes. She had stolen everything from me. "No heart for a thief. No safe haven...."

"Only a grave will do," she finished, her voice going flat. The shadows ceased their storm, and she dissipated into the dark.

When I woke up, a strange melancholy enveloped me, anger weaving through my guilt. The Thief's voice rebounded in my head. "Only a grave will do." Sorrow flowed through her words into my spirit.

Could I be wrong about her? I wondered, but it was only a dream.

"We are going to be late," Liara said as she slipped her boots on.

I didn't acknowledge her, even if she was right.

Her footsteps beat the floor of the tent as she left.

Whether or not I showed up late for combat training, Jonac always found something to criticize. My stance. My form. My speed.

Sokan hung low in the sky, greeting the new day. It had been two span since we erected the new tent city, and my body hadn't adjusted to this new routine—Jonac lectured, we drilled, we sparred.

Mid-morning came, and still the dream lingered in the air like humidity. While I sparred with Liara, The Thief's voice rang through my mind. *You have been listening to all the wrong stories.* Despite The Thief being a liar, despite it being a dream, I had to know what she meant.

As a screaming ache tore through my shoulder down the length of my arm, my distractions dissipated, and I fell to my knees.

My body was already a mass of welts and bruises. Being hit with tree branches had that effect, but I usually did a better job of defending myself.

Liara stood there staring at me with something resembling concern, like she hadn't already cut me far deeper. I did not wait for her to ready herself before charging. She parried one blow after another, her feet barely touching the ground.

Every movement she made flowed into the next as I lumbered after her. What she lacked in training, she made up for with a style all her own, one resembling a dance more than a fight.

No matter how frequently Jonac tried to teach her proper technique, she reverted back to the familiar whenever we sparred. A skilled fighter would have been able to take advantage of her loose footwork. She attacked without the strength of her legs. Her shaky footing left her open to heavier attacks. Luckily for her, no one would have called me a skilled fighter.

Jonac yelled out in frustration, "Anchor with your legs! Strike with your hips." She did not make any adjustments.

"Stop," he yelled, wearing his perpetual scowl. "Were Kaylo competent, he could easily turn your blade and overpower you."

His teaching style grew more abrasive with each day. The pungent stink of susu root had grown as well. While he was smoking, he was light and airy, but when he sobered, his temper turned biting.

I tried to hold on to what it had been like before, when we spoke for hours about the spirits, The Song, and every other little thing we thought of. Jonac used to weave poetry with his descriptions of The Song. He would speak like he needed me to understand what he heard, like he needed someone to understand this piece of him. In those moments, we became a language all our own.

Since Liara joined us, he spoke in commands and sharp questions, critique and silence. We barely spoke about The Song at all. What's more, his echo had become muffled and distant. No matter how I squinted my eyes, I couldn't see past the tempered scowl and glassy eyes to the man he had been.

Our training continued under his rough tutelage. Had Liara and I been on better terms, we might have endured his abuse together, but we still weren't speaking. In the breadth of a moon, I had lost them both.

Every loss stacked atop the last, like bricks in a wall. With each new brick, I wanted to smash it all to pieces.

Liara thrust her wooden blade. I dodged and went on the attack with a series of hard slashes, each swing she evaded stoking my anger.

"Hit her, boy!" Jonac yelled.

"She's too fast," I grunted, continuing to swing with all of my frustration.

"You mean, you're too slow." Jonac chuckled to himself.

I slammed my training blade across her abdomen, and she crashed to the ground, my anger crumbling beside her. She rocked back and forth in the dirt, clutching her stomach and cursing. Not at me. Well, not necessarily at me.

I didn't rush forward to help her. *That's what happens in sparring,* I lied to myself, setting my jaw and looking away.

"How'd you let him hurt you?" Jonac asked. He probed the wound, criticizing her all the while. "If you weren't prancing around, you would have been able to block that."

The first signs of a welt began forming against her dark brown skin. Jonac pressed his hand against her ribs, and she cried out. "Not broken," he said. "Kaylo, salve and wrap the wound."

"Shouldn't you help her?" I asked. "You are a better healer."

"I didn't hurt her. And I have things to do back at camp." Jonac walked by me with a pat on my shoulder and went off to meet his friends, his hands shaking as he walked away.

Yet another problem the clan ignored. The whole encampment had started to smell like sweet sage. Just like the occupation, the elders seemed to believe inaction would solve the problem.

Liara laid back and stared up into the sky, as if not moving would end the pain. When I reached down to help her, she flinched.

She didn't trust me. After she threatened me, she didn't trust me? After I saved her. After I cared for her and tended her wounds. After I offered her friendship. And after she threatened to steal my home and my family from me, she didn't trust me.

I heaved her up and positioned myself under her arm to help her walk back to camp. It would've been easy to adjust my grip and lessen her discomfort, but I couldn't be bothered. Even as she grunted with each step, all I could think about was how much I wanted her to shut up.

The groans and whimpers made her too human. Still, her pain meant nothing compared to what she had done to me, how she betrayed me.

Why should I feel guilty?

We stumbled through the forest in silence, enunciated by her wincing. I wanted to run from her, back to the safety of my bedroll, to forget it all. Or walk off into the forest and never turn back. Whatever would take me away from here.

I mumbled an apology at her.

"What was that?" she asked.

"I'm not saying it again."

"What's your problem, Kaylo?" she demanded.

The question caught me off-guard. She would have to be the densest person ever to have walked The Waking not to understand what she had done to me.

"What's my problem? You acted like my friend and then threatened to take away everything I have left. Did you forget? Did I make it all up?" I hadn't intended to yell, but my words came out loud and dripping with resentment.

"Everything you have? Hiding who you are and pretending the world is okay isn't much of a life. My sister is out there, and I need your help. I didn't have a choice!"

"You took what I feared the most and twisted it into a weapon. You were the first person who knew what I was, and you treated me like a... like a *malitu*." As much as I tried to sound angry, pain turned my words to sadness.

She stopped walking and turned to face me, tears gathering in the rims of her eyes. "I'm sorry. I didn't know what else to do, then you stopped talking to me and I knew you would never help me." As her voice strained around her words, tears began freely falling down her face.

"I wasn't going to tell them. I wouldn't do that. You have to believe me. I just need your help."

She buried her face in her hands. "I need to save my sister."

My eyes watered as she broke down in front of me. Surrounded by people, we were both alone, isolated by our secrets.

"You're not a malitu, Kaylo. You're not The Thief."

"But I am a thief. And that's enough."

"Bullshit! You saved my life, and you used The Thief to do it. How can that be evil? The only malitu I know are blood banners."

"But the stories...," I started to say when Liara cut me off.

"Stop listening to the stupid stories. You know who the heroes are in Gousht stories? The Gousht. The emperor. Stories are the words powerful people pass down."

"My mother said that our stories are all we have. Stories are our people. Without them, we are moments in time without beginning or ending."

"Stories are our people and just as imperfect. Our people are prejudiced, selfish, and prideful as much as they are wise, generous, and brave."

You have been listening to all the wrong stories, The Thief's words whispered in my ears.

I looked at Liara as I never had before, face wet and lined with determination. She believed every word she said.

For the first time since I learned what I was, I didn't have the energy to be afraid of myself.

A chorus of billowing waves filled Liara's echo, and it stilled me.

"I'll help you," I said.

The harsh lines on her face smoothed, and we stared at each other for the space of a few breaths. "Don't say that. You don't know what you're saying."

"I'm saying I'll help you." If I expected her to be relieved or to thank me, I didn't know her at all.

A shadow grew over her face, and the harsh lines returned. "Don't promise what you aren't willing to give. If we do this, try to rescue my sister, the Gousht will kill us. They'll steal our spirits and send us to the work camps. They would call death a kindness."

"For a turn, I have been surviving what the couta did to me. What they took from me. Every day, no matter how much I distract myself with chores and tasks, I remember the face of my dying friend and the moment I left my parents behind. I died a turn ago. It is time for me to use this curse to haunt the bastards that killed me." The words came from a part of me that I had denied for too long.

"I'll help you," I repeated one last time.

CHAPTER TWENTY-NINE

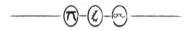

EVEN BEFORE THE FIRST time I heard The Thief mimicking The Song's melody, I was hiding. Since my family left our home in the middle of the night to outrun rumors, I shrank down and tried to fit myself into a world that wanted me quieter and more obedient.

Now someone needed me to stand as tall as I could.

The small words I had offered Liara—my promise to help her—took root in my spirit like a tree that would not bend to the storm. My fears diminished. The Gousht had taken far too much, never satiated, always reaching for more. And for once, whether or not I would survive, I had decided to refuse them.

For the next moon, I awoke with Sokan and surrendered to Jonac's bitter instruction. The whittled-down branches left lessons up and down my limbs as I clashed with Liara in our training circle. When Jonac finished offering barbed advice, we would see to our chores, go to sleep, and begin the pattern again with the new day.

As difficult as it was to see my kana twist into this angry man, we needed him and his anger.

Glimpses of who he had been peeked out from behind his shell when he was distracted and far enough from last night's smoke. His irritation with the world would break, and he would apologize and close his

eyelids tightly like his pain had consumed him. Then he would rush off
and hide himself in clouds of sweet-smelling fog.

Something had broken in his spirit long before I met him, and then I
split the wound open again. The sooner I left, the sooner he could heal.

Only one span separated Liara and me from our exodus. The Fallen
Rock Clan had provided me with a home when I needed it the most, but
I had to make use of my anger. We would probably die. All we had to
do was decide to stay and save ourselves, but staying was another kind of
death.

I gripped the would-be hilt of a branch and angled around Liara for an
opening. She moved like a feather caught in the wind, changing direction
with no sign as her echo fluttered behind her.

"Stop prancing about and attack," Jonac said from the edge of the
clearing.

Despite his harsh words, his echo didn't jump into the air with his
voice. It didn't sound soft or distant. The reflection of his song had simply
gone quiet.

I froze.

It had been days since the last time I heard it.

Liara's blunt weapon caught me full force, and the pain exploded in
my ribs, forcing all the air out of me as I fell to the ground coughing.

She had finally learned to plant her feet and drive her hips through
her attacks—contrary to Jonac's continued criticism. A throbbing pain ran
from my armpit down to my hip and crawled into my guts.

Jonac laughed as Liara rushed to my side.

"I'll be fine." I pushed myself to my feet and nearly collapsed again.
My makeshift sword hung loose in my grip. When I lifted it into position,
searing pain crawled through my ribs.

"Looks like you'll have a chance to practice your healing," Jonac said.
"That girl hit you harder than The River themself. Well done, fancy feet."
He turned and walked back to the camp without another word, laughing
to himself.

"He wasn't always like that," I said as I cradled my ribs and lowered myself to the ground.

The more I apologized for Jonac, the less people believed me, and I had been apologizing a lot.

"Forget him. Why did you stop moving? If you fight like that out there, we're both dead. You're lucky I wasn't aiming for your head," she said in her non-apology, apology tone.

"Jonac's echo has gone quiet," I said before I caught myself.

"What?"

If I'm going to die, what's the point of lying? I thought.

"I hear reflections of The Song through dancers. It's like an echo, and Jonac doesn't have one anymore, but his used to be the clearest of anyone in the camp."

Saying the words aloud felt improper, like I was stripping myself bare in public.

"Do you hear our echoes all the time?"

"Yes and no," I said. I found I didn't have the words to describe it. No one had trained me. Whatever I learned, I had learned stumbling through the last turn. "You know how The Song can sound more distant sometimes? How you can even shut it out if you want to? It's like that."

Any explanation I offered fell off into a series of awful analogies. After spending all my effort hiding who I was, I never tried to figure it out for myself.

At some point, regardless of how hard I had fought with them, the echoes had become a natural part of my life. Each one had a unique shape. It moved as a reflection of The Song, but also as a companion to its dancer. Yet, for all my ability to read the echoes, I didn't have the words to describe them.

As I rambled along, Liara sat enraptured, like Junera listening to one of Nomi's stories. She leaned closer, and my chest tightened. Sweat glistened on her rich dark skin, and my cheeks grew warm. I wanted to hide and, at the same time, never wanted her to look away.

When I fell silent, we sat there frozen in the moment. Liara stared at the ground; her brows curled in thought. No fear or disgust. Her body moved gently with each breath.

Then she met my waiting eyes. "Why were you listening for Jonac's echo?"

I smiled. "You know how The Song gets more intense when you fight, like it's pulling on you to dance? When your echo peaks, I know you're about to attack. It's all I can do to keep up with you."

She looked shocked and appalled, and then the edges of her mouth rounded into a smile, like I had let her in on a joke. "You jerk! I couldn't figure it out. Every time I think I have an opening, you're there, ready." She playfully slapped my arm, then quickly apologized when I yelped at the pain.

Despite my injury, the next breath came easier than any in recent memory. My secret always held me back from Jonac, Nomi, and the girls. And here was Liara, smiling at the truth.

However dangerous our plan—if it even rose to the level of a plan—it didn't matter. With her around, nothing could stop me.

We talked as I ground bark, leaves, and roots into a salve for my ribs. Fortunately, I didn't have to call The Seed. Thanks to our many injuries, barberry, moonlight hazel, echinacea, and chamomile already lined the edges of the training grounds. I wrapped my torso with yet another piece of cloth torn from an old set of robes.

"Could you steal The River from me?" Liara asked as if it were a natural question. Her voice sounded even, but the words felt like an accusation. "Well, could you? If you tried, could you steal The River from me?"

"I wouldn't," I said. Spirit thief or not, I would never violate someone like that. To reach into someone and take a piece of them.

I was wrong. All this time, she hid her disgust behind a smile, I thought. *When she looks at me, she sees a malitu. Just like everyone else will.*

"No. That's not what I meant." As she placed her hand in mine, her echo sang a steady, unbothered tune. "I know you wouldn't hurt me."

Tears filled my eyes before I could blink them away. She didn't know that. I had hurt everyone I ever loved, and, if she needed evidence, she could look at Jonac.

My breath came out in quivering sobs. The ache in my ribs flared with the push and pull of my diaphragm. Snot tickled my upper lip, and I tucked my chin into my chest to hide my face.

Since The Thief came into my life, I had killed two people, ran away as my best friend lay dying, and left my parents behind to face the consequences of my actions. The person I had been, the young man who had a home and a place in this world, as shitty as it may have been, the proud descendant of The Seed, the Tomakan boy who kept a flicker of hope burning—that boy died the night I ran from Nomar. He died with Shay.

Liara wrapped me into her. She held me for a moment, and it stretched out forever. I thought about telling her everything that had happened. How Shay died. How my parents died. Instead, I answered her question. "I think I could."

She released me and leaned back. "Good, we should try it. You need to practice now before we are fighting for our lives." She smiled. Genuinely smiled.

There is something wrong with her, I thought. *Something wonderfully wrong with her.*

I collected myself, and we walked towards the river where we had been practicing our dancing. After turns of teaching herself how to use The Song, it took nothing for her to reach into the air and form the vapor into a cloud of mist. If she reached into the water, she could draw her hand back, holding a long, sharp icicle.

In contrast, I could grow prickly plants and irritate her.

We stood facing each other, and I waited, listening to her echo. "Are you doing it? How will I know when you're doing it?" she asked.

"I need you to call on The Song," I said. "I can't steal your spirit if you aren't using it."

As the last word escaped my lips, a wave washed over the edge of the river and swept me from my feet. "Oh, sorry. I thought you were ready," she said, trying not to giggle.

"You're an ass," I said as I climbed back to my feet.

When she began pulling at The River again, a thread formed, linking her and the water. I reached out, wrapped my fingers around the translucent strand, and yanked. Before the second wave could form its crest, it fell back into the river.

Her piece of The River churned inside me, calmly like a gentle current. Nothing like the frenzied rage from the spirits I stole from crystals. It pulled back to where it belonged, but only with a subtle urge. A sort of gravity.

The echo of The River filled out as the distortion settled. Still not The Song, but closer to it. It moved through me. Rhythms under rhythms. Soft tones in a chorus. The current of The River washed over me, every molecule of water strung together in an endless web, from the vapor in the clouds above us down to the dampness of the soil below.

With my feet planted in the earth, I allowed myself a chance to feel all the threads that tied me to The River. My awareness of everything became complete. It overwhelmed my senses, and then I let it take me.

The River moved different from The Seed. Where The Seed understood the need for slow, decisive movements—a foot planted and twisted into the earth, a hand reaching towards the sky—The River demanded constant motion. They wanted me to glide over the ground. My feet stumbled, but still I moved. My torso dipped and turned, despite my pain.

As I reached into the clouds above me and pulled at them, droplets formed and fell, becoming hundreds of notes falling from the sky. A melody ran through them. I exhaled as if cooling the rain and the droplets froze. Hail pelted the ground and bounded off my body.

I would have danced with The River all afternoon. Then Liara yelped.

A profound absence struck me when The River left. I remembered everything I had done, how I had reached into the water that surrounded us, but the sense of it grew distant, like a story I had been told instead of experienced.

More than anything, I wanted The River back, but I resisted the temptation.

"How did you do that?" Liara asked, rubbing her cheek. A deep purple welt started forming not too far beneath her eye.

"Blessed Mother, I'm so sorry," I squeaked. "Are you alright?"

"Calm down. It's a bit sore, but I'm a lot better off than you and your busted ribs."

Why is she smiling? I stole her spirit, pelted her with ice, and she smiled. It made no sense.

"So, how did you do that?" she asked a second time, slight irritation shifting her tone.

"I could feel it all. It was amazing. There is water everywhere, and The River connected me to every drop. Is that what you feel every time you dance?"

"Incredible, right? Now, how did you do that?"

"When I pulled the water from the cloud, I could feel the rain droplets. I concentrated on their sound, like when I search for a specific plant in The Seed. I listened to them, and I knew them. They could turn to ice, and I urged them to it."

"I have been dancing since I turned five, and I never thought about doing that. Maybe because it never snows in Sonacoa, except in the mountains. Do it again!" she said.

Back and forth we danced in The River and searched the water for new possibilities. For all my exhaustion, my blood ran hot with the thrill of it. I reached deeper into the spirit of the water.

Knowing water existed in the air, the ground, the trees stood a nation apart from feeling connected to all of it simultaneously. When I called on The Seed, I could feel the forest brimming with life, but I took that for granted. This felt new and wonderful.

As Liara danced, I studied her echo. She moved effortlessly, and the water moved with her. Her long legs glided under her as her body stretched and arched. Her red locs streamed like a river flowing in her wake.

By the time the moons crested over the tree line, neither of us could stand straight. Dehydrated, hungry, and sore, saying nothing of my injured side, but I couldn't stop smiling. The storm inside me settled. The Thief didn't weigh me down. For the first time, her gift felt like a gift.

Liara and I fell to our knees at the river and drank deeply. I splashed my face and let the cool water prickle my skin as we sat there, too drained to speak.

Her echo sang in concert with The Song. For all the excitement of dancing with The River, I could have held on to that moment forever—sitting by the rushing water, saying nothing, knowing Liara was next to me.

Torrel held watch at the entrance when we passed back into camp. His echo whirling about like a storm, he stared at me with unspoken accusations. For all his height and strength, his bottom lip poked out, and his brow furrowed, like an angry boy.

Everything he had done, he did to protect his people and, in doing so, lost his surrogate father. He didn't deserve what I had brought to his home. Still, I kept my distance and averted my eyes. Wounded people could be dangerous.

Instead of following suit, Liara glared back at him like a threat, and her echo surged. Her grip tightened on her practice weapon as she slowed her pace.

"Why are you smiling?" she asked with a tone as sharp as her stare.

"You're being protective," I said.

"I don't like bullies, especially when they hurt people I care about."

My smiled widened.

The Fallen Rock Clan had settled in for the night. Fires burned a soft glow inside tents like lanterns. Low murmurs of families sharing stories spilled out into the paths. The tent city announced itself with bold colors in the daylight, but projected serenity in the darkness.

Soca and Junera went into a giggle fit when we pushed through the hide-covered entrance. Even Nomi had a knowing look in her eyes. She shushed her daughters and scolded us for being late.

"Is daddy with you?" Soca asked.

"No, sorry," I said. She and Junera slumped in disappointment.

"He really shouldn't leave you out there alone," Nomi said, as if it were her only concern, but her disappointment seeped into her voice. "Look at you, coming home dirty and covered in bruises. Have you at least eaten?"

"A bit of fruit and saltmeat," Liara said.

"Get in here and have a proper meal. Tomorrow, you both are washing before you come back here. You dragged half the forest back with you tonight."

Liara and I nodded and rushed over to the pot simmering by the fire.

The squirrel soup smelled delicious and tasted even better. The first spoonful of fatty broth coated my mouth and awakened my hunger. I ate ravenously. Liara and I both reached for seconds while the girls told us about their day.

Soca thought their teacher was the nicest woman in the world, but Junera claimed she was a daemon in disguise. Apparently, Junera had a habit of interrupting lessons with her own thoughts, which, depending on the source, were either insightful or wild distractions.

"...and then I told her that Sokan got in a fight with her sisters over the sky and that's why she stayed so far away from them, and she just ignored me. I'm telling valuable information here, people!" Junera yelled as reenactment.

Nomi shushed her daughter and wrapped Junera up in her arms. "Now, little one, Honi is doing her best to teach you about the world.

I need you to help her by listening and waiting your turn to talk in class," Nomi said gently. "People will hear you better if you pick the right moment to speak."

"Yes, Mommy," Junera said, her mood slightly deflated. "Can you tell the story about the White Oak thief?"

Nomi shook her head at her daughter. My mother used to say that children were flames. Too little guidance and they would burn down the house. Too much restriction and they would burn down to embers. If that came close to the truth, Nomi had two very different fires to manage.

She agreed to tell the story if the girls lay down for bedtime as they listened. I excused myself to my own bedroll. I needed the rest, but mostly I didn't have the strength to listen to another story about an evil thief.

I treated my injured side and re-wrapped it. Over the next few days, the bruise would darken, but I would be fine. My body already looked like a map of bruises anyway.

Sleep eluded me as I tried not to listen to Nomi's story, but her words cut through my efforts.

"At the edge of the Lost Nation, there stood a village named for the ancient tree in the center of the village, White Oak, led by a wise man named Renac. He led kindly and justly over the people of White Oak, and for his leadership, they prospered. No one went without, and most had more than they needed.

"Renac declared that the people of White Oak needed to give back to The Blessed Mother and the Great Spirits and collected tithes to offer onto Ennea. The villagers saw the wisdom in Renac's call, giving generously. They offered crops and tools, woodwork and fresh kills—all but one woman.

"Yilla had always been a quiet woman, but when Renac called for tithes to the spirits, she denounced him as a heretic. She accused him of hoarding the offerings for himself. She challenged Renac to open combat if he refused to give the villagers back what they had freely given.

"Renac could not give what he had collected in the name of The Mother, so he accepted Yilla's challenge. Not only was Renac wise and kind, he had always been a fierce warrior. He bore the mark of The Wind. Yilla had been thoughtless to challenge him.

"They met beneath the white oak tree, surrounded by the villagers. Renac wanted to end the fight quickly. He had no desire to hurt Yilla. After all, she belonged to their community. He called The Wind, but it did not come. So, he drew his sword and charged. Then, without warning, a powerful gust of wind blew through the center of the village, pushing Renac back. Branches broke from the old tree, and villagers fell to the ground. The wind grew stronger still and carried Renac from his feet, crashing against a wall made of ironoak. Just like that, he passed into The Mist.

"No one knew Yilla walked with The Wind. They looked at her and their fallen leader and wept. Yilla declared herself the new ruler of White Oak, then took the village offerings for herself and enforced her rule on the villagers.

"Some villagers challenged Yilla, but they soon found that she wasn't a wind dancer at all. She was a spirit thief, and they all fell before her. Until one day, Renac's son, Tacun, challenged her. Yilla laughed at the young man. He was a forest dancer, not a warrior.

"They met on the same ground where his father died. Tacun denounced Yilla as a false leader and said she did not deserve their symbol of peace and prosperity. He placed his hand on the white oak, and before Yilla realized what he was doing, Tacun aged the tree to ash.

"Yilla screamed with rage as Tacun ran from the village. She chased after him into the Lost Forest, a stormwood forest so great and dense that no one could navigate it without The Seed. Yilla knew that Tacun would have to call on his spirit ancestor to find his way out, and when he did, she would steal his spirit, trapping him in the Lost Forest forever.

"He ran deeper and deeper into the forest. Then, when they were utterly lost, he stopped. Yilla waited, ready to steal The Seed, but he did not call the spirit. She threatened him with her blade, but still he refused.

"'If I can save White Oak, I would gladly walk into The Mist with my father,' he said.

"'But you have to call The Seed if you want to leave,' Yilla said.

"'I don't plan to leave.'

"He stared into Yilla's eyes, and she saw the truth of his conviction. She searched and searched for a way out, but no one ever heard from either of them again. The village lost their leader, his son, and their tree, but they regained their freedom."

By the end of the story, Liara had already fallen asleep, and the girls dangled on the very edge of their dreams. Nomi kissed her daughters before gathering herself to bed, while I lay on my bedroll staring at the tent canopy.

I couldn't help but hate Yilla. She and all the other spirit thieves gave my people reason to hate me. *I'm nothing like them,* I thought. *Power hungry bastards.*

When I danced with The River, I didn't go into a bloodthirsty rage— almost the opposite. I had never been more connected to Ennea. Yilla and I were nothing alike.

The Thief's voice broke into my head. *You have been listening to all the wrong stories.*

Everyone else had fallen asleep when Jonac parted the hides draped over the doorway and walked in, the scent of susu root wafting behind him. He staggered over to the girls, knelt down beside them, and brushed the hair from their faces.

A moment passed as he hovered over them before his voice found a soft song with an aching sorrow.

Something had to change.

When I promised Liara that I would help rescue her sister, I knew it was a death trap. I had been comfortable with that. Now I had to come back—show everyone that I could use The Thief for good. Then, I would look Jonac in the eyes and tell him what I was.

CHAPTER THIRTY

I STARED AT THE blank piece of paper with a bit of writing coal in my hand as my adopted family slept. No words could express my gratitude for all they had done, or my guilt for all I had done. Nomi and Jonac weren't blood, but they loved me. The girls would have questions that deserved explanations.

Jonac had all but abandoned his nights to smoke. Nomi relied on my help with the girls. I had responsibilities here.

But Liara needed me more.

The neighbors would help. The Fallen Rock Clan took care of its own.

If I wanted to be a part of this family, I needed to prove I wasn't a malitu first.

My stomach ached. Liara waited for me at the edge of the encampment. I placed the writing coal to the paper and wrote whatever came to me.

Nomi and Jonac,

Liara and I have to go. I wish I could tell you why and where, but it isn't safe. You are the reason I survived losing everything. I love you all.

Family knows.

Even as the paper trembled in my hands, I knew the words failed to capture what I needed them to know.

Each of them slept, broken and imperfect, but lovely. Junera's hand clutched the tiny carved rabbit I gave her, and my throat caught on my sadness and guilt.

Nomi stirred in the darkness and shifted under her blanket, setting my heart beating in my eardrums. I held my breath until her breathing settled back into its rhythm. If she had found me, I wouldn't have had the strength to leave.

I placed my note where my bedroll had been and weighed it down with a stone.

Everything was packed away, save my mother's book. Patches of the blue fabric she had wrapped it in faded to shades of muddy gray. After more than a turn, I still hadn't peeled open the cover. Underneath the fabric, the leather-bound tome ran cold in my hands.

I couldn't take it with me. Even if I didn't survive, her words had to.

When I pulled back the leather, salt water immediately crept over the brim of my eye. Her handwriting marked the page in black ink. My chest collapsed, and the air rushed out of me as I read the first page.

> *If our people are to survive this occupation, it will be through our stories. The earliest records of our people are myths. Stories passed down like water from one pair of cupped hands to another. We have lost much, but what remains is precious.*
>
> *Our stories are our people. They are the throughline of our culture. With this book, I hope to collect our stories and discover the truth of them for the generations to come. Our future will need our past.*

I closed the book, carefully folded it back into the fabric, and placed it next to my goodbye. "Keep it safe," I said to my new family as they slept. Then I left.

The camp stilled under the soft glow of the moons—nothing moved, not even the wind. Kana curved in the sky ahead of Toka, a flickering sliver in the darkness. This place—these people had offered me more peace than anything else The Mother had placed in my path.

I could stay.

Liara paced back and forth at the tree wall. Her brows creased deeply, and her lips formed a stern pout. The moonlight shined off her skin and highlighted the gentle curve of her face.

She stopped and turned towards me. "I thought you'd changed your mind. Or maybe Jonac caught you. Do you know how long I've been waiting?" she whispered harshly. She waved her hand, dismissing her own question. "Forget it. Let's go."

Guards patrolled the entrance, so we would have to make our own way.

The bark of the ironoak tree scratched my palm. The Song resonated in the wood, and I sensed the fullness of the tree, root to leaves. Then, as I practiced countless times, I reached into The Seed and aged the tree until it turned to rot, then decay. Such a cruel thing to do to a healthy tree but necessary.

We can't leave any trace behind.

We snuck through the gap in the tree wall, and I reached for The Seed again. Liara complained that someone might hear us, but I would not bend on this point. I refused to leave a gap in the clan's defenses. The potential life lay buried in The Song, and I pulled. It didn't fit perfectly, but the ironoak sealed the gap in the wall.

A chill ran through my body that had nothing to do with the autumn night. The last time I left, I was running away. This time, purpose drove me forward, not fear. The days of training, the long conversations planning our rescue led to this next step and the one after that.

When we reached beyond shouting distance from the wall, we ran. Autumn leaves and fallen twigs crunched under our hurried feet. Sound filled the forest—The Song, Liara's echo, creatures who hunted in the night. We were far from alone.

Liara ran beside me, puffs of air forming small clouds with each breath. In all the world, she knew me better than anyone else alive. For a turn, I had hidden from everyone. Then she found me and made me see that I wanted to be known. I wanted to tell her everything.

A small protruding rock threw my gait off.

I would have to wait to bare my spirit. If I didn't concentrate on the path in front of me, I wouldn't make it far enough to reach the suicidal part of our plan.

Even though, by Jonac's maps, we were two days from Sand River and another day from the compound, we ran as if our legs could carry us to the mission school by daybreak. The distance between us and the tent city helped steady my nerves. The farther we ran, the harder it would be to turn around.

By the time daylight crawled over the forest canopy, my lungs burned inside my chest. The world slowed as I upended my waterskin, and the water rushed over my tongue, the excess running down my chin.

The sound of blueberries filled The Song, or maybe I had a craving. I moved with The Seed and the bush sprouted through the soil. The leaves spread and the green fruit swelled and ripened.

"Every time," Liara said in a hushed voice.

When I turned towards her and tilted my head with a question, she said, "It's nothing to you, I guess, which makes sense. When I water dance, it's as natural as walking for me. But when you make something grow, something that didn't exist before...." She paused like she lost the words, staring at me for a moment. "You can do things that strike me still."

My cheeks lit on fire. I had come to see myself the way I feared everyone else would: a thief, a burden, a malitu. Yet she could look at me and see something special. It left me tongue-tied and misty-eyed. I plucked a berry from the plant and shoved it into my mouth.

A quiet fell between us, not unpleasant, but heavy. I didn't trust myself to find the right words.

Using my father's knife, I busied my hands with a bit of wood. The Seed lived within it, even in the dead scraps. The grain sang to me as I rubbed my fingers along it. Everything else faded away, and I let the blade loose. A slender strip peeled away from the branch. It crinkled and cracked as it separated from the large piece.

Liara clapped her hands in front of my face. I jumped back, and my head slammed against the tree I was leaning on. She laughed until she couldn't breathe. Apparently, she had called my name several times before she resorted to other means of getting my attention.

"I'm sorry. I didn't mean to scare you," she said with a smile wide enough to contradict her words. "We should get going."

I nodded as I rubbed my head. We gathered our things, collected a few more berries, and started walking.

Neither of us said anything, but neither of us pushed the pace. We walked east towards the Sand River. Autumn had turned everything shades of red and brown. It would have been a lovely walk if my ghosts would have left me alone.

Whittling with my father's knife conjured memories, as it always did. I rolled the handle of his blade back and forth in my hands. He had rough hands. Big hands. The kind of hands that built a home.

My mother used to refer to him as the earth she walked on. It sounded strange at the time because I hadn't yet known unstable ground. I didn't understand that without him holding her up, she couldn't lead.

On days when he came home from the workshop and my mother was off on one errand or another, we would sit beside our home. He would whittle while I listened to The Song. When I turned eight, I asked him to teach me.

"Not much to teach," he had said. "There is a figure in your mind and a figure in the wood. The knife lets you see them a bit clearer."

He was a hard man to know. Few words. Few gestures. But he had been a good father.

The last time I saw him, he stood next to my mother with a hammer in his hands, waiting for the soldiers to break through the door he built. The time would come, maybe sooner than I would like, when my death would come looking for me too. Could I stand there when the time came?

Maybe if I had someone to protect.

Liara peered off into the woods, deep wrinkles in the corners of her eyes. I didn't ask. She needed her space like I needed mine. If we were going to die in a few days, some thoughts needed their time.

As Sokan offered its last light over the horizon, we agreed to make camp and fell into our roles without a word. I rummaged through our packs, and what I didn't find, I called up from the soil. Herbs, vegetables, some bits of saltmeat, a pitch of several spices. No one deserved bland food, especially not for one of their last meals.

Liara came back with a heap of firewood, and I built a fire and set the pot over the flames.

As the soup simmered, I snacked on a carrot and whittled at a bit of ironoak. The air had a subtle chill. The herbs in the pot emitted a crisp, earthy aroma. I would have preferred fresh meat, but we didn't have time to hunt.

"What are you carving? All day, you and that old knife," Liara said with a weary smile.

"No patience whatsoever," I said. "My father always chastised me. 'Can't even wait for a plant to grow.'"

I held up the old knife, scratches marring the stormwood handle and the leather wrap fading from age. Every imperfection gave the knife a story. "This belonged to him," I said. "He used to sit and carve for hours, never letting anyone see what he was making until he finished it. Once he whittled away at the same piece of wood for moons. Every day, I asked him if it was ready. He would wink at me and set his knife back to the wood.

"It was during the first couple of turns of the occupation. Rations

didn't go far, and the Gousht took the first harvest of whatever grew in
the garden. When he finished the carving, he gave it to my mother for
her birthday. She was born in early autumn, like me.

"She laughed when she saw it. A bear, no bigger than the palm of my
hand. It was a nice bear, I guess. Intricate details and all. But it was a bear.

"Then he explained, 'The bear is a peaceful creature. Only wanting
a full belly and a place to lay its head. But threaten what's theirs, home
or family, and a bear becomes fearsome.' He smiled, satisfied with his
explanation.

"My mother and I were still confused. She asked him if he was the
bear in this story. He laughed. 'No, you are the bear,' he told her. 'You've
kept our family together. You kept us safe.'

"That man spoke simple and straight-forward, but his words worked
their way through you like a chill. You could feel them in your bones."
My eyes teared up at the memory. "My mother cried after that. She
loved that stupid bear."

The silence that proceeded went on too long. I don't think she knew
what to say. Neither did I. I hadn't spoken to anyone about my parents
since I ran from Nomar.

The small piece of ironoak tumbled around in my hand. I pinched it
between my finger and thumb and held it up. An oblong bit of wood
engraved with The Thief's rune—a small chip in the wood on the
smooth side. I pulled out the pieces I carved earlier and added both to
the rune sacks.

"Care for a game?" I asked.

We had played hundreds of times since Jonac taught her the game,
but it felt different with The Thief buried among the other runes. Strange
how liberating a small act of acceptance could be. We played, we ate, we
talked about small things.

The firelight jumped across her face. She looked peaceful. I chuckled
to myself, thinking about our stupid plan; breaking into, then out of a
Gousht compound.

They might have called it a school, but it was a prison with high walls and guards that outnumbered us twenty-fold. *How can she look so peaceful?*

She turned and caught me staring at her. "What is it?"

"Aren't you afraid?"

"Of course I am. What we are doing is idiotic. But my sister is all I have left."

I wanted to tell her she had me, but it wasn't the same thing. Instead, I told her she should get some sleep and offered to take the first watch.

Liara nodded and laid down her bedroll on the other side of the fire. She fell asleep almost immediately. I rested my back against a tree and tried not to be jealous of a girl locked away in a Gousht compound.

At our pace, we crossed the Sand River before our second evening. Too many patches of the forest mirrored the others to be certain. It probably wasn't the same spot. The night had been dark, and fires scattered everywhere. The memory tugged at my spirit. If this wasn't where I first met Liara, it looked close enough to it.

For a moment, I let my dark thoughts take me. I had become adept at finding a way to blame myself for everything. But then again, if I hadn't run away—if I hadn't found her, Liara would be dead. I couldn't be proud of what I had done, but maybe the time had come to stop blaming myself.

Liara stared at the ground. She jumped slightly when I placed my hand on her shoulder. "We should go," I said. She nodded, and we walked deeper into the forest.

CHAPTER THIRTY-ONE

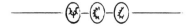

Kaylo clapped a fresh sprig of thyme between his hands and cupped it beneath his nose. The warm, leathery aroma filled his nostrils.

"You gave away half our kill?" Tayen complained, looking at the hanging buck missing a right flank and it's two front legs.

"Oh, you can hunt rabbit tomorrow," Kaylo said. "Have you smelled these spices? Honestly, come and smell these."

Tayen's stone disapproval didn't change. He waved her off. "What I wouldn't do to have free rein in Tisda's garden. That woman might be The Seed himself." As he stirred the pot, the curry filled the air with fresh spices and rendered fat.

"Speaking of herbs, why don't you call them from The Seed?" Tayen asked with an edge to her voice.

Living together had been different in the forest and in the hallow. They had been isolated and focused, not playing family. The watching eyes of Dasoon kept them from training. It had been two span since he had given her a proper lesson with her blade, and her irritation grew by the day.

"You know why," Kaylo said, the joy absent from his voice. "Much as I love Tisda's garden and Yuna's stories, we don't know these people." He turned and waited for his toka to meet his eyes. "No one can know who we are. They can't know we are dancers. It would put them in danger, but more importantly, it would put us in danger. The trackers are still out there. Now cut up those greens and add them to the pot."

The worry. The preoccupied love. The endless frustration. Maybe this bordered close to fatherhood.

Should have let the Gousht take her. He smiled at his own ugly joke. His humor had turned darker as of late.

Dasoon barely qualified as a village anymore, for all the wreckage and rubble. And still, there were too many mouths to feed. Too much work to be done and too few steady hands. The turns in isolation had made silence Kaylo's home. Dasoon was loud and uncomfortable. Too little and too much. But they had a roof and four walls now. That counted for something.

A rap on the door jolted them both to attention. They exchanged glances. Neither expected a visit, not this late. Kaylo checked for his knife on his belt and went to the door. He pulled the heavy wooden block from the latch and eased the door open.

"Kuno," Nix said with a curt nod.

A moon and two span in town had done nothing to ingratiate him to the captain of the guard. Still, he swung the door wide and greeted her with a bright smile, and she answered with a slightly deeper frown.

"Guess you're not here for dinner," Kaylo said.

"I hear you can hunt," Nix said gruffly. Each word wrenched from her lips like they caused her pain.

Her self-righteous, no-nonsense posture turned him into a child who desperately wanted to poke her, but he resisted the urge. His inability to deal with authority, along with dozens of other reasons, made him a poor fit for society.

"The watch reported seeing a man wearing green and yellow in the forest. Could be nothing," Nix said. "Probably nothing, but I need every available hand for the search."

Could be nothing? Could be another tracker, he thought. *Could be rotten luck, and the Gousht found us by happenstance.*

The war had been pushing west for several moons, but Dasoon should have been far from the battle lines. If there were Gousht in the forest, the freecity would be raised by mid-day tomorrow. The city guard included a handful of volunteers either too young for experience or too old to wield it well. The fact that Nix had knocked on their door because she heard he could hunt emphasized how fucked they were.

"I'll go," Tayen said.

At some point, Kaylo didn't know when she had moved directly next to him in the doorway. *Guess her training is working. I'll have to keep a better watch on that one.*

"No, you won't. You'll stay here and finish cooking the curry," he said in his best impression of a disappointed uncle. "Where do you need me to meet you?"

Nix told Kaylo what he needed to know and gave him time to gather his equipment. She had other doors to knock on.

As soon as the door closed, Tayen began complaining. He pressed a finger to her lips and hushed. Confusion and outrage fought for control of her face, which only made him smile.

"Listen, apart from me and Nix, you are the best tracker in the city. You can wield a blade with the best of her guard. We both know it, but they can't. They can't know we are marked. They can't know why we are here. We are safe because they think we are simple folk fleeing a war. Hakan would sell us to the highest bidder if he knew who we were. And if not Hakan, there are plenty of glassy-eyed addicts who would sell us out for their next high."

"You mean if they knew who *you* were?"

He slowed down and took a long breath. Dasoon hadn't made either of them happy, but she should have been old enough to know safety and happiness were not always manageable in the same grasp—and young enough to resent it. After winter passed, they might be able to take off into the forest again, but for now, Dasoon had to be home.

What Kaylo didn't say was that he needed her to be safe. If a tracker or, worse yet, soldiers lurked in the forest, the city would fall—quickly. The Gousht would cut through this city like lightning through the sky. If that happened, the farther he could keep Tayen from the first of the fighting, the better. Hopefully, she would run in the right direction.

He swung his bow over his shoulder and latched his quiver onto his belt. It had taken him the better part of two span to carve a decent bow and a couple dozen arrows. He had sat by the fire with his father's knife, slowly revealing the bow in the wood. The ashburn trees in the area gave the bow an easy bend and a strong release.

Kaylo had never been clever enough with a bow for combat. Hunting was different. Hunting required patience. A bow in battle had to be quick without losing precision. A blade felt more reliable, but Nix expected a hunter, not a warrior.

With his father's knife at his hip, his sword still tucked in place under his bedroll, he left.

———

A collection of misfit children and old folk gathered near the southern gate of the crumbling city wall. Some didn't even have thick enough furs for the chill in the air. They carried an assortment of knifes, bows, and farming tools.

Kaylo took full scope of the potential disaster. A dark night. An untrained pack of refugees hunting soldiers in the forest. *Yeah, nothing can go wrong.*

Hakan was conspicuously absent. Kaylo might have found it funny had his life not been cast in with this lot. They were more likely to stick him with a misfired arrow than a hit a soldier in the dark.

Nix stood to the side and stared at the makeshift army, disappointment painting her face. The look was unsettling. Understandable, but unsettling.

If a raiding party lurked in the forest, their time would be better

spent digging graves. A sense of dread lingered in the air. Perhaps the
only people that didn't feel it were the young ones looking to prove
themselves.

"Alright, shut up!" Nix shouted.

For the most part, the group went silent immediately. Two kids
about Tayen's age continued yammering on, comparing the size of their
blades. Nix walked up to one of them and grabbed him by the collar as
if handling an unruly puppy. He stumbled along as she dragged him and
thrust him in Kaylo's direction.

"This one is yours," she said.

Kaylo nodded, knowing better than to disagree.

He could have taken the assignment as an insult, but he didn't.
Nix was the type of warrior who spoke ugly and cared deeply. If she
entrusted the boy to him, she believed it for the best. Still, hardly a
compliment. Twenty turns separated him and any other adult in the
motley brigade. The insult would have been entrusting the boy to
anyone else.

The boy stood tall and lean. His body looked like it had grown too
quickly for its own good. Close cropped red curls lining his scalp marked
him as one of the few Sonacoans in Dasoon. He gripped his knife like
a novice and carried himself like a man with a grudge. If his survival
depended on raw anger and attitude, the boy would be fine, but such
qualities rarely survived war.

Nix had a simple plan. Teams of two would rake the forest. If they
found anything, they were to loose a flaming arrow into the night sky,
and everyone would collapse around that signal.

Simple plan, but looking around, Kaylo had several doubts. This bunch
didn't know how to walk silently through the forest, much less root out a
trained tracker or soldier at night.

Seed and Balance, he thought. *Let it have been moonlight playing
tricks.*

In total, nine pairs ventured out into the thick forest surrounding

Dasoon. Far too few to search the area properly, but more probably wouldn't have helped.

Kaylo had no choice but to go along. He and Tayen needed shelter for the winter and Dasoon was the only standing—partially standing—town within several span of walking. Running now meant a cold, slow death if they got caught in a heavy storm. Or a quick, bloody death if the Gousht found them.

"What's your name?" Kaylo asked quietly.

"I don't need a chaperone," the kid spat back at him, ignoring the whisper in Kaylo's voice.

Kaylo stopped. If someone lay in wait in the forest, this had to be settled. "Good, I don't want to be your chaperone. I'm not your father. I'm not your uncle. I am the man relying on you to do your job, so we both don't die." Even at a whisper, the tenor of his voice managed to convey his command of the situation.

The kid's jaw fell slack, and he stared at Kaylo as if seeing him for the first time. "Now, what is your name? Or would you prefer me calling you kid all night long?"

The question stirred the boy, and he found his tongue. "Daak."

"Alright then, Daak, you can call me Kuno. But let's keep it quiet in case there really is a Gousht scout out there." He waited for the boy to nod before they continued their walk towards the southern tree line.

The autumn night had the cold bite of early winter. The moons waxed in the sky, lightly outlining the shape of the trees in front of them. Leaves crackled in the wind.

With eighteen untrained people crunching through the forest, the scout would likely find them first. Kaylo motioned for the boy to follow his footsteps, then had to say as much when Daak failed to understand.

Hours passed without a sign. Maybe the watch made a mistake. Kaylo's fingers began to numb, and his mind wandered to the curry that waited at home for him. The boy's steps lacked the care he had taken when they first entered the forest. A small branch cracked under his foot.

"What does Nix know about tracking anyway? I really don't get it.
What does Hakan need with some skin switcher?"

Skin switcher?

It took Kaylo a moment to decipher the boy's ignorance. "Wait, Nix is
kamani?"

"Oh, you didn't know?" Daak asked, as if knowing something Kaylo
didn't made him important. "Yeah, the freak doesn't know what he's
doing. You ask me, getting rid of those skin switchers was the one thing
the greens got right."

Daak's head made a hollow sound, knocking against the tree as Kaylo
pressed his forearm into the disrespectful little shit's throat. *A little bit
of pressure and....* The boy's eyes went wide. He gasped for air like a
wounded animal.

The boy was too young to know a time before the Gousht, before
their ideas infected Ennea. But age dragged on like a tired excuse, and
time didn't cure ignorance. Daak's face turned purple under Kaylo's
forearm.

He fell, gasping for air, when Kaylo released him. "Don't let the
empire's ideas turn you into one of them."

Daak looked up defiantly. "Have a thing for the skin switcher, do ya? I
knew there was something creepy about you."

A scared child trying not to be. Kaylo shook his head. Youth didn't
equate to harmless. He hadn't been much older when he killed for the
first time.

The leaves rustled behind them. Kaylo dragged the oil-soaked arrow
from his quiver and unshouldered his bow.

"Do it, old man. Let's see if you have the spirit."

The self-assurance of youth amazed Kaylo, made him feel old. But he
didn't have time to indulge in that thought. "Shut up," he hissed.

"You can't shut me up, freak..."

Kaylo clapped his hand over the boy's mouth. But they already made
too much noise. The rustling leaves grew louder as a dark figure started

running away from them.

"Blessed fucking Mother." Kaylo struck his flint against the arrowhead, and the oil caught a spark immediately. He drew the arrow back, aimed his bow into the sky, and prepared to launch the signal, but he moved too slowly.

The stupid boy drew his knife and charged after the shadowy figure. Screaming his anger into the woods, Daak clunked through the forest like a wild boar.

Maybe the inept attack gave the stranger confidence or maybe he didn't think he had another option; either way, the soldier turned and unsheathed his sword, a beam of moonlight shining down on his green and yellow padded armor.

Kaylo shifted his aim and searched for the new target. He couldn't hope to run fast enough to intervene. The kid would be dead before he made it halfway to the soldier.

The tension of the drawstring pulled on his shoulder and down the right side of his back. He released the first arrow too quickly. It flew wide and embedded into a tree twenty paces behind his target.

This is why I don't fight with a bow. He notched another arrow, but Daak and the soldier clashed in the darkness. The movement blurred into a mess of shadows.

"Seed and Balance," Kaylo muttered to himself as he dashed forward to find a better angle. "Blessed Mother, let this stupid boy survive himself."

A soldier's sword against an untrained boy with a knife. The kid didn't have much time. The soldier pressed the boy back with deliberate strikes, throwing Daak off-balance. Kaylo's second arrow missed its mark, but only slightly. The soldier pressed his advantage and attacked with more fury.

To the boy's credit, he managed to defend himself from the worst of the soldier's barrage. He hadn't been able to attack, but the soldier's blade never found its true target. Then Daak fell backwards over an exposed root.

Kaylo's breath caught in his chest. Daak instinctively threw back his hands to catch his fall, and the soldier's sword drew a long bloody swipe across the boy's belly. Then the soldier reared up to finish his kill when Kaylo's third arrow caught him in the shoulder.

The force and surprise of the arrow forced the soldier to the ground. He clamored for his blade and his footing, but Kaylo's shadow fell over him before he could regain either. The pockmarked soldier looked little more than a boy himself.

Boy or not, Kaylo bound his arms and legs before attending to Daak. Even though the soldier looked pitiful, bound and bleeding, an old hatred boiled from its resting place in Kaylo's heart.

Daak rolled from side to side, clutching his stomach. His robes went dark with blood in the moonlight. From the way he moaned, the wound hadn't cut deep. A substantial belly wound would have left him too little breath, but Kaylo tried not to fault the boy for his dramatics.

Fighting a war is a romantic thing until blood spills. Hopefully, the boy would learn that lesson easier than he had.

He quickly checked the wound and handed Daak his robe. "Put pressure on the wound. It's superficial, but we don't want it bleeding more than it has to." The boy would need to be stitched back in the city; there wasn't much to be done in the dark.

After a hint of oil and another spark of the flint, Kaylo set another arrow aflame before releasing it into the sky and turning his full attention back on the young soldier.

With his attention focused on the young soldier, Kaylo knelt next to the skinny boy and removed his helm. His pale face caught the moonlight, highlighting a light wisp of whiskers along his soft jawline. A short tuft of white hair covered his head. Eighteen, nineteen turns at most. His face alternated between fear and pain.

"*What is your name, soldier?*" Kaylo asked in Gousht. The scout lifted his chin but made no motion to answer. "*I understand you want to be strong, but your survival counts on answering my questions. I am not the threat here. There are others that will ask harder.*"

"What are you telling him?" Daak demanded. "You're a spy. A filthy blood banner."

"Shut your mouth," Kaylo spat in common tongue, his tone leaving no room for argument, and turned back to the soldier. "*Are you alone?*"

The soldier nodded. The little shit was too scared to lie well.

"*What is your name?*" he asked again.

"*Jons. I'm nobody. I wanted to escape the war.*" The soldier's voice strained like the pleading tone of a child in trouble.

"*Jons, my name is Kuno,*" Kaylo said as pleasantly as possible. "*Be honest. I will know if you are lying. Are you out here looking for someone? Someone particular?*" Kaylo's hand went to his knife as a reminder.

"*No. No. I ran. They were picking us off. Little by little. A small ambush. Arrows from the forest. We fought them off, but the officers refused to let us pursue. They kept marching us north, despite the ambushes. We were 'acceptable losses.'*" The soldier started crying.

The Uprising. Simple tactic. Clever, even. Gousht regiments moved in large numbers, too big to face outright. Instead, they reduced the enemy's numbers from a distance. A party that size couldn't rush off into the forest after them, not easily.

"*How many soldiers? How many days out?*" Kaylo asked.

"*I don't know, three thousand, maybe more. Two days east.*" The soldier's breath sounded heavier and wet. Blood had started seeping into his lungs, but they could still save him.

"What is going on here?!" Nix demanded in a harsh whisper.

"He's a spy. I heard him talk their language," Daak said urgently.

Nix turned to the boy. "You really are stupid." She turned back to Kaylo and asked again, "What is going on? Why didn't you signal first?"

Kaylo paused. Daak lay on the ground, face wet and stomach bloody, making a truly pitiable sight. "I thought I had a line on the soldier, but my arrow missed the mark. The boy charged in to defend me."

As lies go, it was shit. Better to move on than let it linger. "The soldier is a deserter," he said. "Ran two days west before our watch spotted him. Three thousand or more on the march."

"And you believe him?" Nix asked with a layer of disgust, like the idea of an honest Gousht turned her stomach.

"He doesn't seem to be a good liar," Kaylo said. "I would know," he added with a smile. Nix did not return the gesture.

"*I swear, I'm not a fighter. I want to go home,*" the scout cried out.

"*I believe you,*" Nix said and knelt next to the boy. She studied him for a moment as if making note of his face, then swept her blade across his throat with trained ease.

Blood spurted from the wound, then oozed, thick and dark. Daak turned to his side and vomited. He had several lessons to take from that night. Maybe he would hold on to at least one.

"The war is pushing farther west," Nix said casually and to no one in particular. "They must be reinforcements for the northern outpost." She stood and looked around for a moment to catch her bearings. She met Kaylo's waiting eyes. "Burn the body. We don't need the Gousht or anyone else finding him. I'll take this one back.

"If anyone else comes for the signal, you should get them to help you out," she said. "I wouldn't count on it though. These people aren't the type to run towards danger." She spared a distasteful glance to Daak. "For the most part, anyways."

"Can you let Tayen know everything is alright?"

Nix met Kaylo's eyes with a manner of softness for the first time since he came to Dasoon. "Of course, uncle."

She bent down to help Daak to his feet, but he pulled away from her. "Fine. Walk back yourself. You might tear your wound and bleed out, but that's your choice."

There was virtually no chance of that happening with such a shallow wound, but Daak didn't know that. He relented and limped into the darkness with Nix.

Over the next hour, a couple of the town guard stumbled by, far too

late to have rushed towards the signal. Kaylo turned them home. He
meant to do this right. No one from Dasoon would take time for a dead
Gousht boy.

Half the night passed before he gathered the wood for a pyre. Then
he placed the boy on the bed of lumber and added what little oil he had
left to the boy's clothing.

The fire roared through the last of the night into the morning as Jons's
body charred and turned to ash.

Someone had to control the fire and make sure it didn't spread.
Someone had to make sure the fire burned hot and long. Someone had
to stomp out the embers. But those weren't the reasons he stayed.

———————

The next day, Nix sat on the rickety stage in the town square.
Quiet and stillness had returned after nearly everyone picked up their
meager rations. The slow rhythmic sound of her sword grazing over
the whetstone mixed with the mummer of the stragglers and the early
winter winds.

Now that the square was mostly empty, the scene almost looked
pretty. Sokan hung alone in the sky, with no clouds to hide her light. The
warmth of her gentle glow fought a losing battle against the chill in the
air.

Tayen pulled her cloak tighter around her. Ugly as it was, her cloak
kept her warmer than any other she had ever owned. A mixture of
skins and furs from the different game Kaylo and she had hunted in the
surrounding forest. It took her a span to thread them together. Sewing
had never been her talent, but her pride in the garment made it all the
warmer.

After the last of the townspeople picked up their share of the rations,
Tayen walked towards the stage. Rations had steadily dwindled each
span. Dasoon couldn't possibly stretch what little remained over the long
winter moons. The weak would die and everyone knew it.

Nix's eyes glanced up from her task for a moment and then returned to it. "A little late, little one," Nix said. "I was about to take your share home with me."

Tayen almost grabbed their sack of grain and vegetables, then walked away. Nothing about the warrior in front of her indicated she wanted to talk. But Tayen forced her feet to stay planted. The cool air steadied her as it tickled her nose and filled her lungs.

"My uncle told me about what happened last night," she said. She should have planned this better.

Nix set her sword down and looked up. "I'm not surprised. You were bound to find out sooner or later, not that it's a secret. Go ahead and ask your questions."

"What did it feel like when you killed the scout?"

Nix's eyes squinted. "Not the question I expected," she said, a lightness playing in her voice that didn't match the tone of the question.

"I killed a soldier once. He deserved it and I'm glad that I did it, but when I think about it, my stomach feels like it's twisting around in my chest. Does that go away?"

"Planning on killing again?"

The grin on Nix's face erased all of Tayen's trepidation. "Are you going to answer my questions with questions?"

"The second time is the worst," Nix said. "The first time you don't expect that feeling. You don't know how bad it will wreck you. The second time, there isn't any shock to distract you. Then, that feeling goes away—eventually."

A moment of silence hung between them. Tayen had been afraid that Nix wouldn't answer, or she would say she never felt what Tayen had. Their shared experience offered some comfort, even if it meant the worst of her feelings lay ahead of her.

"Can I ask you another question?" Tayen waited for Nix to nod. "Why do you let Hakan lead?"

"Let?"

"Yeah, let."

"Kid, you remind me of me when I was younger," Nix said.

"I'm sick of people saying that I remind them of themselves. I'm me. That's it."

"Point taken," Nix said. "But when I was younger, Hakan was all I had. He protected me when I couldn't protect myself. Plus, he's much better at all the...politics."

"Yeah, you're not very nice."

Nix smiled tightly and shook her head, but Tayen clarified. "I mean, you don't fake it. I like that. It feels like I can trust you."

The smile dropped from Nix's face, and her shoulders fell slightly. "I wouldn't take it that far," she said, and a hollow tenor crept into her voice.

Tayen reached for the small bag of rations. It weighed even less than she expected. "I should get going now," she said.

Nix nodded and reached for her sword and whetstone.

As Tayen went to turn, she thought of one last question. "Should I call you they?" she asked.

"She will do."

Tayen nodded and turned to leave. As she walked away, the swipe of Nix's sword against the whetstone returned. The rhythm moved slower than before.

Chapter Thirty-Two

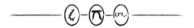

THE GOUSHT COMPOUND SAT on the grave of a small village. Like many other villages, the green bastards had laid it to waste. Like Sunador, the city where I was born.

Newly erected buildings jutted out into the sky like a challenge to the trees. At the center of what had been the town square, one building loomed over the rest. Pieces of wrought iron formed the broken circle near the crown of the building. The Emperor's seal hung from the eaves, the snake wrapping around the lion's neck and staring out into the forest after us.

All the fear that traveled with me over the past two days vanished. *This is their trespass,* I thought.

In the middle of a village they had destroyed, they forced Ennean hands to build a symbol to their god and demanded us to worship. The blood of my people saturated the ground and soaked into the mortar that held the stone together. Their god of power made manifest. A god that mocked our suffering and ruled over our sacred land with a presumed right to do so.

Rage churned inside me like the fire that destroyed the village that once stood here. The Song rose up. Everything faded from my periphery. Nothing existed besides their church and my hatred.

Liara tugged at my robes. I was standing in plain sight on the hill overlooking the compound.

"What are you doing?" She hissed at me.

"You see it! You see what they've done to this village!" I said, my voice cracking through the rage. "They deserve to die. All of them. Damn their spirits. Let their spirits rot with their bodies, if they even have spirits at all."

Liara's eyes went wide. I had only shown her the edges of my hatred before, masked with grief and sorrow. There was no grief, no sorrow here. This hatred belonged to me, not my people, my family, my dead. I stood there wearing the nakedness of my fury.

"Kaylo," she said softly, like approaching a startled horse.

I didn't want her pity or her worry. Her eyes examined me, searching for the person apart from the anger. If I had let her, she might have found me, but I needed my anger, and I turned away from her.

We spent the last hours of the day in silence, waiting for the dark to hide our approach from the patrolling soldiers. Every ten minutes or so, a pair of soldiers turned the corner of the tree wall and walked the western edge. We needed to be quick, or we wouldn't have a chance of saving Liara's sister. And I wouldn't have a chance at my vengeance.

We buried the bulk of our supplies in a pile of rocks at the base of a large ironoak. When the sentries turned the southern corner, Liara and I ran from the tree line as fast as quiet would allow. I placed my hand on the tree wall. The tall, thick ironoak felt cold under my touch. I reached into it like I had dozens of times before, searching for its counterpart in The Song.

The Song spread as wide as the forest, and I needed to find a single tree, no different from the rest. My emotions rolled over and clung to everything in The Song.

Minutes passed by, and Liara kept quiet.

Every thread I tugged in The Song linked to the wrong tree.

The sentries would turn the corner soon. When they did, there would be nowhere to hide, but her face remained calm and certain.

We didn't have time to run back to the tree line. If I couldn't do this now, I would lose Liara her one chance to save her sister. I would fail yet another person.

My breath weighed heavy in my lungs. My eyes darted back and forth. And there was Liara, a gentle smile spreading across her face. I stood between her and the soldiers around the bend. I was the path to her sister, but she stood still as calm waters.

If her fear hid beneath her smile, not even her echo betrayed her secret. She hadn't reached out towards The River in case I failed. Her hand wasn't resting on her knife.

What have I done to deserve her confidence?

I pictured Jonac and his stupid game; the runes lining the dirt grid. Like an old habit, I hushed the noise in my head. The anger still burned, just as palpable, but focused like the point of a spear. Suddenly, the ironoak stood in front of me, powerful and proud, a tree I knew like kin. I pushed through the rough bark into the grain of the wood and pulled at The Song caught in the rings of the tree.

The whole of the ironoak came alive to me, the imperfections in its grain, the warm tone of its wood, its solid hold on the earth. The distance between us, the space that separated the wood from my flesh, became inconsequential. As much as I could control my body, I could control the tree. Though it pained me, I moved and The Song moved with me, until nothing remained but a patch of ash where a giant had been.

A pool of light crept around the corner as we snuck through the opening. A new ironoak rose from the same soil as the last before anyone had a chance to notice.

I took a few deep breaths, and the anger persisted, a fire ready to burn the forest to the ground. If I intended to be of any use, I had to control it.

Liara met my eyes. "Now for the hard part."

From wall to wall, the compound was not much bigger than the small village that stood there before it, but the buildings stretched taller than any I had seen up close before. They made the compound feel immense. Some few lights burned through windows into the night air, but darkness blanketed the grounds. Apart from the sentries on the other side of the wall, there were no signs of life. It could take days to explore this compound.

Then I heard it. An echo. The Wind.

Even a moon ago I wouldn't have recognized it as clearly, but since I started training with Liara, the subtle variances in the echoes of different spirits had taken firm shape.

The hollow reaching of The Wind reverberated through the echo. The spirit hadn't been imprisoned in crystal. It sounded like Torrel, only slightly altered, like different voices singing the same tune.

"What do you think would happen if the Gousht stole the spirit of someone twice-marked?" I asked. I didn't want to raise Liara's hopes, but then again, hope brought us here. "Would one of the spirits remain?"

"I don't know." She squinted, then her eyes slowly widened. "Do you hear something?"

"The Wind."

"Are you sure? It could be a crystal." She had been separated from her sister for too long. Even this close, her hope scared her more than the Gousht.

A stillness hovered in the melody. A singular fit that never quite matched in the sound of stolen spirits. Not even when Liara opened herself willingly to me. No, this spirit sang out from where it was meant to be.

The focus of my anger alleviated my doubt, and I turned towards the echo, waving for her to follow. As I crept through the tightly packed buildings, my nights sneaking through Nomar flashed in front of me. We hugged the stone walls and edged towards the echo.

The River raged behind me, and The Seed screamed into the night. I almost pitied any soldier that dared to get between Liara and her sister. Almost.

We came to a long building, a stone patchwork structure of different shades and textures, not nearly as tall as the church. The collective rubble of a dead village piled haphazardly into a new building.

Take. Destroy. Rebuild. That's all the couta do.

The echo sang from inside. I laid my back firmly against the rough wall and took a long breath. One wall separated us from our mission. The Gousht hadn't considered defenses beyond a tree wall and a couple of sentry guards. Maybe because what we were attempting was fucking cracked.

Who breaks into a prison?

After the Stone City fell, no one fought back. Unless you count the Missing. And only then if you believed the rumors. The people who weren't taken as slaves settled into their new lives under occupation or hid. No one rescued stolen children. The Gousht didn't have to focus on keeping people out of the compound. They designed this place to keep their captives in.

Only blood banners and corpses left these walls.

They ran children through the mill and turned out the next crop of expendable soldiers. Sending ship after ship of reinforcements from across an ocean couldn't be sustainable.

They've done this before. Conquered. Controlled.

If they broke a people apart, lulled most of the population into a new, controlled life, enslaved or killed anyone who resisted, then they could force the next generation to serve.

The cold expediency of the plan made me want to retch, but their arrogance also gave us an opportunity. They slept on stolen land like it could not be reclaimed. We slipped in unnoticed, and we would leave the same way.

We shuffled along the building, and I peered around the corner. One guard sat with his back leaning against the door. From the way his shoulders moved, he might have been asleep, but I wasn't reckless enough to get a closer look.

Four walls of stone and only one door; it had to be where they kept the stolen children.

"We can take one guard," Liara whispered as she pulled her knife from its sheath. Death crawled over her face until she became it. The looks she had given Torrel paled in comparison to the rage painted over her face.

For her sister, she wanted blood.

I moved to block her path. "What if there are guards inside? What if he makes a noise? We do not know what's on the other side of this wall besides an echo that might belong to your sister. It could be a blood banner for all we know. What if she's in another building?"

The last question gave Liara pause. She would fight an army if her sister waited for her on the other side of it.

A shack stood twenty paces out, a bundle of sticks with a door not much bigger than an outhouse. No one would be inside, and we were too exposed. Not seeing patrols didn't mean they didn't exist.

I crept towards the shack without watching for Liara, hoping she would follow me. For whatever reason, she did.

Liara closed the door behind us. "What?" she demanded. "Did you lose your nerve? Tomi is on the other side of that door, and I'm going to get her."

"Is she?" I asked in a matching tone.

The future weighed down on that moment. My knees nearly buckled. I chose my next words carefully. "Running through those doors right now would be selfish. You're the one who can't wait one more minute. You're the one who needs to save your sister or die trying."

I took a deep breath and slowed down. "Your sister needs you not to die. Tomi survived this place for a season. One more night won't destroy her, but you getting killed or caught would."

Liara had learned to hate everything that came between her and her sister. Now that meant me. The green that usually speckled her brown eyes vanished in her rage. Her malice felt intimate. After several breaths, she sat down and placed her back against the clumsy wall of the shack.

Simultaneously, our time stretched too thin and too long. I searched our newly claimed hideout for anything useful, but the light from the moon barely broke through the cracks of the rickety hut. In the near-complete darkness, I found several lengths of rope and chain, a pile of rags, and heavy bags of grain. A forgotten pile of nothing.

No wonder they didn't take their time building this shack. It's got as much shit as an outhouse.

Liara needed distance, and I needed to focus on something other than our impending doom. When the sun rose, we could learn more about this place. Until then, our ignorance held us captive.

The hours passed slowly as I twiddled The Thief rune in my hand like an unlucky charm. My finger ran over the chip on the smooth side of the wooden pebble. The rest of the runes lay buried outside the wall with the bulk of our supplies, but I hadn't been able to part with this one for some reason.

For over a turn, I latched onto my hatred like it could prove that I was better than The Thief. As if my righteousness set me apart. Forgiving her, and myself, for what happened to my parents and Shay meant forgetting them.

Maybe I could be a spirit thief and my parent's son and Shay's friend. Freedom dangled on the end of the thought. Still, a part of me felt weak for letting go of my blame.

When the first beams of sunlight fell on the dirt in front of me, I peered through the cracks in the wall. Liara did the same.

Several pale faces walked the grounds, some in soldiers' uniforms, others in plain clothes, like any occupied town. Light made the compound less ominous, but more threatening. The empty paths had frightened me because of what might have been around the corner. The occupied paths frightened me because of what was there.

We both jumped as the church bells sounded the morning prayer, two notes clanging in irregular patterns. Soon the roads filled, and a couple dozen Gousht made their way to the church.

I knew there would be a good deal of soldiers in the compound, but seeing them made my heart beat faster. Their green tunics, the Emperor's seal, swords swinging from their belts. When I finished counting, I reached twenty-six soldiers, with another ten or so probably performing duties out of sight.

We were one gulp of air away from drowning.

Then the barracks doors opened, and a line of Ennean children paraded out in two strict rows, boys on the left and girls on the right. I lost count of the children when I passed seventy. Some as young as ten turns.

How could they steal so many children from their homes?

The Gousht had built at least a dozen of these mission schools. My sharp anger from the previous night flared up, and I looked at each soldier with a violent promise.

Liara shook my shoulder. "That's her."

She didn't need to point her sister out. A shorter version of Liara stepped into line. The Gousht had shaved her head bald, but she had the same high cheekbones and deep brown complexion. If I peered into her eyes, I would probably find Liara's eyes staring back at me.

"Does she..." Liara stumbled over her words. "Is she still..."

"Her echo is as strong as yours."

Liara fell to the ground, weeping. Her body shuddered with the waves of emotion surging through her. I wanted to help her, but I could only offer her a small sliver of time. I pulled myself away from her and focused my attention on the miscellaneous supplies in the shack.

Last night, the shack had been little more than a pile of sticks and a roof above sacks of grain. Not much had changed with the morning light. I idly threaded the rope through my hands, trying to think of how it could be useful, when my eyes settled on the pile of rags in the corner. Something about them struck me as familiar.

I rushed back to look at the massive line of children walking towards the church. They weren't rags. Well, they were, but they were meant to be clothing. Each of the children wore these ill-fitting, torn, gray rags.

"We have to cut off your locs," I said.

Liara didn't bat an eye.

I did the best I could with what little time we had. One by one, her locs fell unceremoniously to the dirt as I ran my knife through them. It might have been necessary, but that didn't make it right. Her hair was a part of her—or at least my image of her. The water dancer gliding over the ground, a storm of red locs flowing after her.

Patchy, uneven remnants of red curls covered her scalp, which may have sold her role as a captive all the more.

We stored what little we brought with us under the pile of rags. I buried The Thief's rune in my abandoned robe. Liara clutched her knife until the last possible moment. I understood. A chill ran through me as I laid down my father's knife.

It was surprisingly easy to fall into line behind the other children. Dressed in the gray tunics and pants, the Gousht barely noticed us. The difficult part had been finding a pair of rags not torn beyond repair.

The rough fabric scratched my skin as it shifted with my movements. At least it distracted me from the foolishness of what we had done. Liara and I had broken into a prison camp for children, abandoned our weapons, and joined a large group of prisoners surrounded by soldiers.

The shadow of the church loomed over us as we walked through the heavy cherry wood doors. My breath failed me as I took in the beauty of the inner hall. The church we attended in Nomar stood taller than any other building in the city, but the building had been there before the Gousht. They simply decorated it with relics and symbols. Here, they raised an altar.

Rich fabric dyed in the Emperor's green and yellow hung from the high ceiling, embroidered with the Gousht words for power, empire, and The One True God. Colorful glass accented the windows, crafting rainbows from the sunlight. Everything had been crafted with such careful detail, from the boldly stained benches to the bright tile mosaic at the back end of the hall forming the broken circle.

The hands that created this temple didn't believe in this god, and still they had bled and likely died for him.

We sat on the benches as they arranged our lines, boys on the left and girls on the right, as if worshiping together would dirty the prayers. The small minds of those thirsty for power. I followed the lead of the boys in front of me and continued standing.

A priest kneeling before the broken circle mosaic rose and turned to face us. He wore the same red robes as the priest in Nomar. They draped from his shoulders to the floor. A veil shielded his face, leaving nothing uncovered. And yet, this man stood out amongst priests.

His presence radiated power. His shoulders spread out wider and stood taller than most of the soldiers, but his size didn't account for his commanding nature. He stood in a manner of pride, like a man who knew he was better than those around him. Not an act to lord over others, simply a fact.

Beside his broken circle medallion, he wore two spirit crystals, one dull red and the other pale blue. They could have belonged to children sitting on the benches beside me. It said, "I can take everything from you, and you will be grateful for your life."

"*May the light of The One guide you,*" the priest boomed, his voice deep and gravelly like an earthquake.

"*For light, we look to you,*" the children offered in a chorus of dead voices.

"*You may be seated. We gather under this roof to honor The One True God.*" He spoke in staggered phrases, pushing out each word with his textured voice like every syllable held vast importance. His voice bellowed, but he didn't yell. Every breath was controlled. "*I have heard other priests claim God hates the daemons of Ennea. They say that The One sent us to purify your people, that you might know the light of The One True God.*

"While I do not relish contradicting family, what they say is close to the truth, but it is not the truth. Hate is a petty emotion, not befitting a God. And daemon is a superstitious word that speaks to a lack of understanding. For if the spirits were daemons, why would we use them to serve God's will?

"Ours is a God of power. Ours is a God that knows the value of a spirit and gave us, his servants and warriors, this gift." The priest lifted the dull red crystal from his neck, and it sparked to life. The strained echo rattled through the floor as three pops of fire burst around the priest. *"No, The One does not hate the spirits or their dancers, as you call them. The One respects the spirits enough to take their power. Men who say otherwise have not spoken to The One True God himself.*

"I have spoken to The One and know his power. When I look at you, I do not see heathens led astray. I see a people who followed the powerful spirits of this land. I respect that, for you did not know The One True God. Ignorance is forgivable, but The One shall not forgive stupidity. Choosing to follow the spirits after we have cured you of your ignorance is stupidity. That is why we strive to teach you. We offer to you the opportunity to know true power. Abandon the folly of your ancestors. Help bring The One to your people.

"The One True God is the God of power. He is the God of our ambition. He is the God of your salvation. Stand with him or fall before his path." When the priest finished speaking, the hall filled with a tenuous silence. This veiled man understood the power of words and how to turn them to his purpose. He turned and knelt before the broken circle.

In unison, the children bowed their heads, mimicking the priest's silent prayer. It unsettled me, seeing Enneans pray like the Gousht, eyes lowered and silent. Prayers were meant to be spoken and heard, with eyes open to The Mother's bounty. The spirits could hear us, but they didn't ransack our thoughts, picking out the prayers.

The priest, with all his talk of power, thought his God lived behind his eyelids.

I bowed my head like the rest of the children. Were they praying or waiting for permission to leave?

"*Seek power, and you will find The One True God,*" the priest called from where he knelt and all the children stood. We gathered back into our lines and started walking outside.

If we went along with the other children, an opportunity would present itself. It had to. The straight lines of children might as well have been chains.

An echo leaped into the air behind me. A commotion erupted. By the time I turned, Tomi had pushed her way through the crowd of children and wrapped her arms around Liara, her eyes full of tears, unaware of the world around her.

"*You,*" a soldier called out. He pushed me aside as he made his way to the disruption. "*What are you doing? Get back in line. This house belongs to The One.*"

He grabbed Tomi roughly by the shirt and tossed her to the ground, tearing the fabric in the process. Her face froze in a wide expression as the soldier moved forward to finish her discipline. She tried to cover her exposed chest with the torn fabric.

"*Look, the little bitch is trying to cover her tits,*" the soldier mocked, still moving towards her. "*Don't worry, zeze. I don't lay with ani...*"

Liara crashed into the heavy soldier with her shoulder and sent him to the ground.

A collection of gasps swelled around me. My feet locked to the floorboards. Thoughts failed me. I had to do something. Two guards grabbed Liara roughly by each arm, and she met my eyes and shook her head.

I wanted to kill them, but it would only make things worse. She needed me to take care of Tomi.

The soldier who Liara struck picked himself up and walked over to her. Without preamble, he brought his closed fist across her jaw with all his force. She fell limp, held aloft by the other two soldiers. They parted the crowd and dragged her through the church, her boots scraping the floorboards all the way out.

While everyone focused on Liara, I took my ratty tunic off and gave it to Tomi. "My name is Kaylo. I'm friends with your sister, and we are going to get you out." Hopefully, my voice sounded more secure than I felt.

CHAPTER THIRTY-THREE

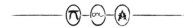

A DOZEN SOLDIERS ESCORTED us from the church. If they were scared that Liara's insubordinate behavior was contagious, they needn't have been. We shuffled out the door in our lines, eyes downturned and faces slack. They had subdued us.

The chill morning air teased my exposed chest. Several of the boys went shirtless. No one made mention of it. They walked with their arms at their side, either used to the small abuse of the cold air against their naked flesh or aware of the consequences for drawing the guards' attention.

If this place worked anything like Nomar, the soldiers could treat us anyway they saw fit—to an extent. We were resources mined from our people. As long as they didn't disrupt our usefulness, no one would care if the guards took joy at our expense. Hopefully, that meant they wouldn't beat Liara too badly. But I had no doubt that they would sacrifice a troublesome child to make a point, as long as the priest gave the go-ahead first.

We filed into a long building constructed with an odd collection of rocks, held together with mortar and hope. This building served utility. No other structure on the compound matched the esthetic detail of the church.

Rows of chairs filled the main hall with a walkway down the middle. We filed into our seats according to gender, as The Gousht saw it.

Do Gousht men and women even share the same roof? I thought. *How do they have sex? Minimal contact and only for procreation?*

For the time being, I played along. When the right moment presented itself, I would be ready. I had to be if we wanted to be free ever again. The weight of the situation grew heavier with each breath.

What had I expected? I snuck into a prison.

A cleanly dressed Gousht man stood in front of the long room and inspected us as we took our seats, row by row. He referred to himself as Professor Strouch. He held himself like he would break if he bent. Even though he probably witnessed the same motion every day, he looked as if we had already disappointed him.

His squinted eyes stared down at us from behind his rounded spectacles. Maybe he blamed us for his low posting, educating minds he deemed unfit. Or maybe misery suited the man as a natural companion. He tapped a thin baton against his lectern to signal the beginning of class.

What little fear I had that Strouch would realize I didn't belong quickly dissipated. He addressed each student as boy or girl, or struck them on the shoulder with his baton. His disdain, as well as that of the soldiers', made me invisible. I had blended into the crowd of brown faces.

None of the other captives looked twice either. This place must have constantly replaced old faces with new ones. The replaced probably served as fresh soldiers or harsh warnings.

Gousht education said much about their culture. Exactly like in Nomar, Strouch asked the children to read aloud from their books and interpret, to show understanding. The words on the page represented unquestionable truths. We served as an audience for Strouch's lectures. His words as undeniable as the ink, even if they contradicted one another.

For all the fanfare, this class and this lesson amounted to the same messages I learned in Nomar. It was boring and degrading, but I played the attentive pupil. Liara's life might have depended on it.

The youngest children amongst us would never hear the stories of our people without the distorted lens of the Empire. If somehow, in spite of everything, they kindled a flame of pride in themselves and our people, it would have to be a tiny ember. Anything bigger drew too many watching eyes.

The thin Gousht professor spoke in a squeaky voice as he enumerated the tenants of Gousht civilization. Shay would have snickered at his high-pitched attempt at authority. He sounded like a mouse trying to command cats.

Surprisingly, the thought of her made me smile. It still hurt, but the sharp, all-consuming pain lessened to a dull ache. I didn't know what to make of that, and I didn't have the opportunity to think on it.

"*You there, boy,*" Strouch squeaked at me in Gousht. "*Yes, you with the smile.*" He spoke of smiling with such disdain, as if happiness were unseemly. "*Would you like to expound upon the fourth tenant?*"

I took a moment to enjoy his smug expression. This man obviously loved to torment unaware children, as if it offered him a brief release from his miserable life. It would be fun to steal his smugness away, even if it meant saying things I didn't believe.

"*The fourth tenant: Civilization is meant to conquer,*" I said. My Gousht came out rough. It had been over a turn since I spoke the awful, guttural language, and it twisted my tongue.

I cleared my throat and continued, "*It is a generous tenant as it commands that the people of the Empire seek out less fortunate cultures and bring them to true civilization.*" I spoke before I could think, and suddenly, Rena's words came out of my mouth. They tasted like ash on my tongue. I bit down my hatred for the blood banner for Liara and Tomi's sake.

Strouch tilted his head and raised a singular eyebrow, as if trying to determine whether I had mocked him or given him a pleasing answer. He gave me a hesitant nod. "*Well-spoken. For we are a truly generous people.*" He emphasized the word generous as he turned to look out over the rest of the class.

Some nodded their heads along eagerly, like they might be true believers. I assumed most played the part, but I couldn't take that chance. Enemies might lurk among my fellow captives.

The lecture continued in much the same fashion, our squeaky-voiced teacher yammering on about the success of the Empire or the failure of the nations of Ennea, then singling out a student to affirm his point.

Most failed to satisfy him, and he rewarded them with a swift thwap of his baton across their knuckles or shoulder. The children winced and grunted, but none cried out. Strouch seemed like the type of man who would enjoy matching pain for pain.

By the end of the lesson, a hollowness consumed my gut.

When Strouch asked, I answered as Rena would have, and he responded with a smirk. Some of the other children stared blades in my direction. No one would say or do anything in front of the soldiers, but there wouldn't always be prying eyes.

Now I had to watch out for the soldiers and my fellow prisoners. I tried to remember when breaking into this compound sounded like a good idea.

Like Munnie always said, "Some wisdom can be won in a lifetime; other wisdom is won in a day."

They marched us into the adjacent room, where we waited in line. One-by-one, a glossy-eyed Tomakan boy handed each of us a tray of food. I thanked him, but he didn't respond. He simply ladled a small scoop of rice and beans onto another tray, placed a piece of stale flatbread beside it, and handed it to the next person in line.

The boy behind me nudged me forward when I didn't move. I made my way to the boys' seating area. My fellow captives on either side of me kept their distance, either in an attempt to ostracize me or to save themselves from a true believer who might report them to the soldiers. It didn't matter; I didn't plan on staying long.

The rice was mushy, and the beans were tough, but I shoveled the food into my mouth regardless. Breaking into prison built up my appetite.

The bench bowed as someone broke the unwritten rule and sat next to me. When I shifted over to make room, he closed the distance. My muscles tensed, and I readied myself.

If I let myself be drawn into a fight, the soldiers would lock me up. On the other hand, if I allowed myself to be tormented, I would be an easy target.

I looked up to stare the boy down. "Wal?"

Somehow, the skinny, smart-mouth kid from Nomar sat beside me. Wal and I had never been close, but here, this far from anything I could call home, he felt like family. His gray hair lay in tight, braided rows along his scalp. A welt rounded out the top of his cheek. Clearly, his quick mouth still got him into trouble. They hadn't broken him yet.

"Not too loud," he said and broke his flatbread in two. He used the bread to scoop up the rice and beans.

"What are you doing here?" I mumbled through a mouth full of food.

He didn't look away from his meal when he spoke, and I took the hint. The occasional hushed exchange muttered about, trays scraped the wood, and people chewed. Otherwise, the room remained silent.

"They snatched me up from Nomar about two moons back. We thought you were dead, or off with the Missing."

"Nah, nothing so exciting. After...after what happened, I took off into the forest. A couple of soldiers caught me and a friend not too far from here the day before last." Necessary or not, the lie twisted my stomach.

"What was with all the true believer talk in there?"

"After turns of having to listen to Rena, I guess I learned how to play the part." He deserved that much truth. Even if he told the guards, they wouldn't care. Most of us pretended to get by. It had to start somehow. Once someone played the part long enough, they started forgetting who they had been.

"Brilliant," he said, idly rubbing at his bruised knuckles.

"You know how it works here. What happens next?"

"They work us until we're happy for a few scraps of food, and we pass out. The compound isn't complete. Even if it was, the couta would knock down a building just to force us to rebuild it."

I tried to find out everything I could about the compound from Wal over the rest of our short meal. They had at least two dozen guards stationed here, along with a handful of civilians, including Strouch, a medic for when one of us had an 'accident,' and a few other workers for the jobs they didn't trust us with.

Some guards were worse than others. Wal pointed out a couple of the more dangerous ones in the dining hall, assuring me there were more.

Apparently, the soldier Liara attacked had a penchant for knocking children about when he thought he could get away with it, which was quite often. My stomach lurched at the thought of what might be happening to her.

When I closed my eyes, two natural echoes still swam in the mixture of stolen spirits—The River and The Wind.

———

Wal had been right about work duty. Listening to Gousht lies was degrading, whether in a church or a classroom, but work duty beat me down in an entirely different way. I spent hours in a cold sweat without a shirt on, moving rubble from the ruins of one building to a worksite forty paces away.

The monotony of the work grated on me, but at least the silence left room for me to think. These ruins might have been a home, the town hall, or a monument to the spirits. We carried the history of this village away, one stone at a time. More than the exhaustion and the monotony, my complicity in tearing down the village that once stood here wore on me.

My chest burned with the clash of cold and body heat, and my arms had gone numb as I walked another forty paces back to the ruins.

"You know my sister?" The voice spoke softly over my left shoulder. She walked a step behind me with an armful of small stones. I nodded, not sure of who might be watching.

"It was stupid to come here," Tomi said.

"No argument," I huffed. In hindsight, it wasn't the right thing to say, but my body verged on collapse, and my thoughts were darker than the approaching night.

"You can't break out of here. There are too many guards, and you don't have any weapons."

"Dancers don't need weapons," I said, then turned my head, pursed my lips, and blew.

It was childish, but then again, I was exhausted. Her face went flush, and she dropped her pile of rocks. I turned, placed my load on the ground, and helped her pick up the stones.

"I know you're scared, but we are leaving. You, me, and your sister. I need you to believe me." And I did because I barely believed myself. She nodded and walked off with her load as I picked mine back up.

———

Stale rice, beans, and flat bread never tasted as good. I heaped each bite into my mouth like it would carry my exhaustion and anger away with my hunger, but the little on my tray didn't even extinguish my hunger.

Sitting in the dining hall that night, I became familiar with a new type of anger. I had known self-hatred, violent impulses, and vengeful fantasies, but this stood apart. No amount of vengeance would quell it. This anger burned like an eternal fire that would not wane or flare. Whatever happened, even if we managed to cast the Gousht from our shores, what they had done could not be undone. Ennea could never go back to what she was before.

Fucking couta.

Exhausted and numb, I followed the line back to the barracks. Liara and I had walked the grounds freely just last night. Now I walked with a dozen guards carrying torches. The flames offered them light to watch over us and, at the same time, allowed me to mark their faces. I silently promised to deliver their blood to The Mother.

Liara's echo broke through my violent imaginings. The silhouette of a young girl stumbled through the darkness followed by a tall figure in soldier's greens. Relief and fury flowed over me in equal parts. She moved under her own strength, but her left leg dragged through the dirt with every other step.

The shadows hid her jailer's face, but when I discovered who he was, The Mother herself couldn't hold back the horrors I would visit upon him.

I followed the line into the barracks entryway. Liara and the rest of the girls walked through a second set of heavy doors into the east wing, and I followed my line in the opposite direction.

Rows of worn bedrolls haphazardly lined the dirt floor. The room smelled like stale air and body odor, but the stench didn't seem to bother the other boys. One rushed into the corner to squat over a bucket. I followed Wal's lead and found a bedroll near the back wall. My body wanted to sleep, but my thoughts wouldn't let me.

Everything that happened to Liara was my fault. *If I hadn't agreed to come. If I hadn't forced her to wait out the night. If I hadn't let them take her away.*

Of course, that was all bullshit. She would have come with or without me, and if we rushed in here the night before, we would most likely be dead. There was a guard station in the entryway in addition to the one outside the building. But knowledge and emotions sometimes stood worlds apart.

I tossed and tumbled all night. My shoulders and back muscles contracted into tight knots. They would be worse in the morning. When

I did sleep, I dreamed of the night Shay died, but instead of Shay, Liara lay burned and bleeding. She recoiled from my touch.

I abandoned sleep long before Sokan rose. Instead, I stared through the gaps in the thatched roof above me, lying in a row of bedrolls next to fifty other boys.

We won't survive this, I thought.

If Liara refused to bend, the soldiers would break her. The Empire had a use for us, but new faces didn't stand out for a reason. If anyone failed to assimilate, death was an easy solution. There would always be more children to steal to their cause.

If we were going to escape, it had to be soon. We couldn't wait for Liara's injuries to heal or the perfect plan to present itself. She would die long before then, and if she died, I would cease to be. I had lost too much already.

In the last hours of darkness, I formulated the rough edges of a plan. It would be messy. There would be blood. If we all survived, it would be by a whisper of a blessing.

Chapter Thirty-Four

Liara walked through the doors as the lines formed alongside the barracks. Her left foot dragged when she walked. If it hurt, she kept it from her face. She wasn't the type of person to let people see her weaknesses, much less let the soldiers see her broken. Bruises marked her cheeks and showed through the tears in her ragged tunic, but she held herself upright. The guards probably would have taken it easier on her if she had fallen into 'her place.'

The soldiers finished the job I had started and shaved her head to the scalp. I tried to meet her eyes as she stepped into line, but she avoided me. Of course she did. I had come up with this stupid plan to join the captives.

We walked towards the church, repeating yesterday's footsteps. The priest would give a sermon, Strouch would lecture and condescend, and then we would move stones another forty paces. The other children marched with blank stares. They had lived countless repeated days. Hope lost meaning as each tomorrow became a copy of today's horrors.

The magnificence of the worship hall intensified. After a day of moving stones forty paces at a time, the scale of this monument to their god, built by our hands, appeared all the more immense. It reeked of our blood and their power. I tried to imagine the dry, weathered hands of the slaves who had built this tower. The scope of the devastation cooled the light breaking through the colored glass.

A few rows ahead of me and across the aisle, Liara sat next to her sister. They did not talk, but their shoulders touched.

If yesterday offered any indication, Liara's sense of caution vanished when it came to her sister's safety. Hopefully, today would be tedious and ordinary—whatever that meant in a prison camp. Liara would need help to escape, but she could still walk. Tomorrow we would be gone from this evil place. With luck, it would be simple.

The priest rose from his prayers like he had the day before. He stood in front of us on the raised dais and looked out over us, appraising us like a shepherd sizing up his herd for slaughter. Despite his hooded veil, his body language gave away what his face could not. He would not hesitate to kill. I doubted the blood would bother him.

He angled towards a smaller boy in the front row, then said, "*May the light of The One guide you.*" His rough voice unsettled me.

I called back the customary, "*For light, we look to you,*" with the other children.

"*Please sit,*" he offered, still engaged with the boy in the front row. Maybe he had found his next disciple, or perhaps his next sacrifice.

"*Book of Amaralis, chapter thirteen verses twelve through fourteen. 'All power extends from one source, The One True God. Power can be found in many places, but like many rivers flow from one ocean, so does all power flow from The One.'*

"*Think about that. 'All power flows from The One.' Well, that must mean that the power of the spirits flows from The One, but how can that be true? How can the power of the spirits on this continent be derived from a God you did not know before we came with his light?*

"*How could it not? If the power of The One was not the same power that dancers call from the spirits, how could The One take that power from you?*

"*You see, we are not so different. The One True God gave your* ancestors their power. *There is no other explanation. But what is given can be taken away.*

"Your people took this power but did not recognize its source. You did not offer thanks or subservience to The One. You made a false idol of the land, your 'Blessed Mother.' You worshipped spirits instead of the source of their power. And so, he sent us—people chosen by The One True God, led by his earthly descendants, to spread his message and serve his will.

"Look around you and humble yourself before this opportunity you have been given. Here, we offer you the tools to lead your people to the light, like one might pass a flame from one torch to another. Refuse the flame and you will feel the fire. Accept and feed the flame, and it will light your path.

"When we first landed on your shores, we offered this message and were met with violence. We defended our people and stood for our cause. We will not apologize for what we had to do. The One will be heard," he said emphatically.

The way he spoke made me lean forward. His words stirred me. If not for the blood I had seen and my mother's stories, he would have been difficult to deny.

He turned back to the boy in the front row and continued. *"You could carry his message without a sword. You could sway hearts and give them to God. He will have them one way or another, but you have the power to be his voice. Or we will be his wrath. For he is the God of power, the God of our ambition, The One True God."*

The priest allowed the time for silence to fill the hall. It amazed me how easily he teased out the tension in a moment. In the hands of a ruthless person, skillful words could be more powerful than a hundred blades.

When the tension reached its peak, he turned and dropped to his knees, signaling us to bow our heads and join his prayer.

I whispered a prayer to the spirits. My father always told me, "A prayer not spoken is a prayer not offered."

My prayer was cut off as the priest called out, "*Seek power, and you will find The One True God.*"

Our rows poured out into two lines. Liara glared at the guard who hit her the day before. Either he did not notice or did not care.

———————

Strouch stood cross-armed in front of a Sonacoan girl a few turns younger than me, waiting for her to answer another inane question. He unfolded his arms and bounced his baton against his palm in a slow rhythm, as if counting the seconds until he struck her.

The girl wasn't being obstinate. Strouch's question didn't make any sense. "*Why did the stone wall crumble so easily before the imperial army?*"

Short answer, it didn't.

The Stone City withstood the Empire longer than any other city this side of the Lost Forest. Its walls held for two turns against the onslaught of Gousht forces until blood banners betrayed the city.

Some of the children in the room had only just been born when our hope fell. They could only rely on the history taught to them.

It was no coincidence Strouch chose an older Sonacoan to answer his question. She remembered. All of Ennea mourned that day, but none more than the nation to the south.

She could have lied, but then what would she say? How did one explain something that had never happened? Strouch's rhythmic tapping stopped, and he struck his baton across the girl's knuckles. She flinched, and her chair scraped against the floorboards, but she kept quiet.

It scared me how easily I did nothing.

This thin pale man hit one brown child after another, and I sat motionless. Only Liara and Tomi mattered. My stomach felt queasy and empty. The acid churned in my belly, and I learned to hate myself for a new reason.

There would be consequences if I intervened, drastic consequences. The punishments would continue whether or not I acted. I knew all of this, but I also had a choice. I chose to sit quietly.

Strouch regained his waiting posture and rhythmic tapping, but this time he stood in front of Wal. "*You, boy, why did the stone wall crumble for the Empire? It is a simple question.*"

This man enjoyed hurting us. He didn't care if his message sunk in, and that set him apart from the priest. The priest wanted to convince us of his truth. Without a doubt, he would do great and horrible things to accomplish his goal, but Strouch only wanted to lord his power over us. He didn't care if we bent or believed.

Wal looked up at Strouch. "*Because it was what The One intended.*" It didn't sound earnest, but I doubt earnestness would have helped. The baton made a loud thwack as it rebounded off Wal's shoulder.

"*Clever boy, an answer so broad it could cross the ocean back to Gousht. But I don't want clever. I want correct.*" Strouch walked towards me as he dismissed Wal. "*Maybe our bright pupil from yesterday would know the answer to what seems to be such a difficult question. Or was yesterday an anomaly?*"

I hated this petty man. He twirled his baton in his fingers. If he hadn't been born to power, he would have been broken by it. His type followed behind powerful people for their leavings, like a smaller fish feeding off the shit of bigger fish. A large part of me wanted to say as much, to spit at him and tell him what I thought of him, but I had a part to play for Liara and her sister.

I glanced over at her. Hopefully, she wouldn't think less of me, if she even understood the whole of what I said. After all, she had never had to learn this ugly tongue.

"*The wall crumbled because some few brave Enneans in the Stone City recognized the greatness of the Empire. They followed the path to power and opened a section of the wall to the imperial army.*"

The Gousht spoke in rewritten truths, and so I did as well. If I had anything in my stomach, I wouldn't have been able to keep it down. Other children stared at me, and I agreed with them and the dirty slurs they whispered in their heads.

Strouch didn't smile, but he nodded and continued his rampage of questions.

"*Ahh, my darling,*" he said, greasy and thick. "*What has happened to you? So black your bruises are blue. Well, I do hope you learned your lesson. The guards did a thorough job of instructing you.*"

Strouch stood in front of Liara, tapping his baton and smiling as if he had said something clever. She stared back, her eyes piercing with rage.

"*Let us see what you have learned. What did Sonacoan elders—your people...*" He looked her up and down, frowning as if disgusted by what he saw. "*What did they do to turn their own people against them?*"

Another lie in the form of a question.

The Gousht deployed all sorts of tactics to turn people against their own, bribes, threats, and empty promises. They denied it, of course. In their version, they came as our saviors. They would probably even claim that we ran from our homes to the mission school gates, seeking the gift of civilization and a life under The One True God.

"*Does the little girl not understand a civilized tongue?*" Strouch taunted, and she likely hadn't.

Liara didn't shift her glare or hint at answering Strouch's question. She waited as Strouch's thin lips curled into a sickening smile. He tapped. And tapped. And tapped. Then he struck her bare arm. The thin bit of wood cracked sharply against one of her dark bruises. She yelped, and he raised his baton to strike her again.

I did nothing. I sat, frozen in fear and anger.

The thin strip of wood hung aloft. Strouch's smile widened. The baton whistled down through the air.

Then, in one smooth motion, Liara turned, lifted her arm, and wrapped her fingers around his baton. The bit of wood slipped from his grip. With a second motion, Liara cracked the baton over her knee.

It snapped like a thunderclap.

Everyone hushed. She dropped the pieces of splintered wood to the ground and settled back down in her chair, facing the front of the classroom as if nothing happened.

Strouch's scream pierced the silences. He called for the guards, and two rushed forward. Liara didn't struggle as they snatched her by each arm and dragged her from the room. All of us, even Strouch, watched in speechless awe as the doors closed again on the quiet classroom.

If I had any reservations about escaping tonight, Liara had broken them apart along with Strouch's baton. The Gousht had undoubtedly dealt with plenty of unruly children, but they wouldn't tolerate her defiance much longer.

When I found Wal in the mess hall, I had to nudge the boy next to him to move over. He only moved after Wal gestured for him to. Safe to say, I hadn't made friends over the last two days.

"You're too good with Rena's words," Wal said. I glared at him, but he continued to stare at his tray.

He had no way to know how deeply that hurt to hear. Still, I blamed him for saying it.

"The girl who broke Strouch's baton is my friend," I said. "She won't last in here."

"The girl who hit a guard one day and showed up Strouch the next. Yeah, I'd say she might have a problem." Wal had always been too sarcastic for my taste, but he was a good person, and I needed someone on my side.

"What would you say if I told you I had a way out?"

Wal broke his rule. He looked me in the eye as his brows furrowed, trying to read me, trying to figure out if I was joking, crazy, stupid, or some combination of the three. He turned back to his food. "How?"

"*Shut up and eat!*" a guard shouted at us.

We busied ourselves eating and waited for his eyes to pass over us. If my plan was going to work, I needed help. I had no choice but to trust Wal. I hesitated. If he told the guards that I asked him about escaping, there would be punishment. But if he told the guards what I had planned, Liara and I would be dead.

"Do you trust me?" I asked.

"Why should I? You showed up yesterday talking like a true believer. What if this is some kind of Gousht trick?" Wal attempted to layer his question with sarcasm, but it didn't hide the truth. He didn't trust me.

"I'm leaving tonight. There will be blood. Are you in?" Simple and honest.

If he told the guards, he wouldn't have any proof. I hadn't confessed that Liara and I were dancers. I hadn't told him that Liara and Tomi were sisters. I gave him as much as I could.

Wal pushed his rice and beans around the plate with his stale bread for what became an unbearable amount of time. Then he nodded.

"I need to hear you say it."

"I'm in," he said. "Family knows."

Wal and I had never been close, but here and now, he was all that I had. He represented a home I had trouble remembering, so when he said those words, it almost broke me.

"Family knows," I repeated.

Finding Tomi in the crowd of dusty children all clothed in the same patchy gray fabric wasn't easy. Halfway through work hours, I set pace beside her. "Be ready for tonight," I told her.

"How?" she asked a bit too loudly, then caught herself and controlled her voice. "Liara is in solitary."

"Don't worry about how. Be ready when you hear three knocks against the door to the girl's wing."

"What do you mean, don't worry about how? I don't even know you."

"No, you don't, but Liara does. I won't leave without her, and she won't leave without you. I need you to agree because I don't think your sister will last another day before they decide she isn't worth the trouble."

She needed to believe me. Her sister would die if we didn't escape tonight.

She bit her lower lip and breathed out heavily through her nose. "Three knocks," she said, then nodded and quickened her pace.

The last step of preparation was the thinnest part of the plan. If it didn't work, I was fucked.

I waited until near the end of the work hours as Sokan started setting. After studying the guards all afternoon, I searched the remaining soldiers, looking for the right combination of lazy and gullible.

She leaned against a bit of rubble, eyelids drooping. She had been standing guard over the last two days. Even if she hadn't lifted a single stone, she'd been on her feet for hours. When I approached, I made sure to yawn, and she yawned in chorus.

I had her.

"*Excuse me, I need to relieve myself,*" I said in a pitiful voice, shifting from one foot to the other.

"*And?*" she asked bitterly.

"*Could I have leave to use the outhouse?*" She adjusted to push herself up and escort me, but I told her, "*I know where it is. I don't want to be a bother.*" My fake sweetness oozed over the words.

"*Don't worry, Shinna,*" a deep raspy voice said from over my shoulder. "*I'll take the boy.*"

The red-robed priest towered over me. My hand shook involuntarily at my side. *They broke Liara,* I thought. *She told them everything.*

The soldier stood at full attention, her hands behind her, shoulders pulled back. "*It's no problem, sir. I can take him.*"

"*No, no. I have been meaning to have a talk with this young man.*" His hand fell on my naked shoulder like a hammer, and without another word he turned me towards the outhouse.

"*You're Strouch's boy, right?*" he asked casually.

My tongue went numb. All I could do was nod.

"*He's been singing your praises, but I can't quite place your face. I like to pride myself on remembering all the lost souls that join us here. You must be new.*"

I nodded. My damn hand wouldn't stop shaking. "*I arrived a couple of days ago.*"

"*Hmm, I don't remember bringing in a new group this last span. But, no matter.*" His voice held a smile in it. "*I'll be keeping my eye on you.*"

The outhouse stood another ten paces away. "*I trust you know your way back.*" He patted my shoulder and walked off.

I swallowed, despite my mouth being utterly dry. My belly bounced arrhythmically with my breath. I closed the door to the outhouse and sat for a moment while I calmed down.

"He doesn't know," I whispered to myself. "If he did, I'd be dead. Nothing's changed. Nothing."

When I walked back, I made a quick stop at the storage shed. Then, I smiled and waved to Shinna before I went back to work. Forty paces to and from the pile of rubble. I did my best to walk normally with a long knife tied to each thigh.

CHAPTER THIRTY-FIVE

MOONLIGHT PEEKED THROUGH THE thatched roof of the barracks. Time slowed. Occasionally, one of the boys would walk to a corner and relieve himself in the bucket. Waiting made time for questions. What had the priest meant when he said he'd be watching me? How many guards would be patrolling solitary? Would Liara be able to walk?

None of the answers mattered. Liara would not survive this place.

I slipped off my rough bedroll and snuck over to Wal. He met my eyes in the darkness, and all of my questions reflected back to me in his eyes. Despite the doubt, he did not hesitate when I offered him Liara's knife.

The bright side of hard labor and small rations meant that most everyone slept deeply. We made our way through the rows of bedrolls as quietly as possible. Hopefully, the other boys would assume we needed to make a contribution to the bucket, if they noticed us at all.

"When they open these doors, we won't have much time," I whispered and held up my knife to illustrate my meaning.

Wal's eyes went wide. "That's your plan, knock and stab? Did you spend the whole day on that? What if they have spirit crystals?"

"Don't worry, I've got that covered. And complicated plans have too many ways to fail." I tried to look confident. In truth, my plan was a patchwork of bad ideas loosely strung together with hope.

I rapped on the doors. *"Guards! Guards!"*

"Piss pots are in the corners," a soldier called back.

"Someone is trying to escape." A rustling sound came from the other side of the door, then quick footsteps. A guard peered through the break between the double doors. I made myself as visible as possible. *"They're breaking through the wall."*

"What is it?" a second guard asked the first.

"It's the shit-eater Strouch likes." The guard looking through the gap in the doors met my eyes. *"If you're having a fuck-about, I will make sure you don't wake up for a span."*

"Back away from the doors. We're coming in."

As they worked the bar from the door, two echoes surged to life, one after the other—The Mountain and The Wind. Torchlight from the entryway spread into the barracks as the doors swung open. I reached for the thin threads that bound the crystals to the spirits, and my muscles buckled and doubled over as the enraged spirits lashed out.

The guard closest to me turned from the knife in my hand to the clear crystal in his. He gripped it tightly and shook it.

Wal leaped on the other guard's back, a young woman equal to his size. She tumbled forward and crashed into the ground. Liara's knife flashed in the torchlight, then plunged into her back. Her scream came out hollow and wet. Wal stabbed her several more times until she stopped making noise, and blood pooled under her body.

Unfortunately, the second guard regained his composure before I did. He unsheathed his sword and lunged forward.

The spirits in my belly tossed and turned over one another in a rageful fit. I reached for one with all the strength I had left.

The guard raised his blade to cut me down, and a sudden burst of air ripped through the barracks. The gust tore over me and crashed into the soldier, lifting him from his feet and throwing him into the rough stone wall behind him.

He collapsed at the base of the wall. I did not hesitate a second time. I drew a clean line across his throat.

The sharp edge of the knife slid through his skin and tissue like any other animal's. Muscle resisted, then gave way with a spurt of blood from the veins in his neck.

My fingers ached from my too tight grip. His blood slicked my arm and chest. The thinnest fragment of pity caught in the back of my throat, and I swallowed it. This bastard came to our land with his sword, not the other way around.

Wal's eyes opened wide with surprise, but I didn't have time to explain. We had made too much noise. Several of the other boys had woken up. I released the spirits back into their crystals and pushed Wal through the doors.

As I lifted the door block back into place, I thought better of it and dropped the heavy wood to the dirt. Maybe it was foolish, but I refused to be anyone's jailer.

The lantern lights in the guard's station illuminated the gore splattered over our skin and ragged clothing.

"You're a dancer?" Wal asked.

I nodded. It would have to do for now. No time for questions, even less time for superstitions.

The second door block slipped from its mount, and I dropped it to the ground. I knocked against the heavy wooden doors to the girl's wing three times. *Tomi better be listening.*

"What are you doing?" Wal asked.

"Liara has a sister. We came for her."

"You broke into this place? Are you suicidal?"

"I don know. Cha plan seem ta be workin," a voice said from behind us in a true northern accent. The words came out smooth and fast, like he couldn't be bothered with taking a breath.

A young man with skin the color of tanned hide and a close crop of thick black curls leaned against the doorway. Most of the other prisoners shrank beneath their torn fabric clothing, but his shoulders stretched the thin material wide, giving him a solid presence.

"If cha goin, I'm goin." A demand and a threat tied into one tight statement.

"Keep up. Don't get in our way," I said firmly. "Grab the soldiers' swords."

He nodded and went to the task.

"Would you like to invite anyone else to join us?" Wal asked sarcastically.

"I'm adapting." Then, as if the spirits were awaiting the perfect time, Tomi pushed through the doors with another Sonacoan girl in tow. "One more I presume."

"Should I go let the soldiers know we are planning to escape?" Wal said with increasing frustration.

"Why are you covered in blood?" Tomi asked.

"Question time is over. The time for doubt is over. We move or we die. That's all that matters now." Every one of their doubts multiplied my own, and I couldn't handle it. They needed to shut their mouths and move so I could do the same.

"You." I pointed to our new Renēquan friend.

"Adēan."

"Okay, Adēan. Give one of the swords to Tomi here and follow me." I didn't wait to see if he did as I had asked.

As I gently pulled open the barracks doors, hoping we hadn't made too much noise, I walked straight into the soldier stationed outside the barracks. Her eyes went wide in surprise. Before I knew what happened, the warm drip of her blood ran down my hand. The moonlight caught her pale face as she crumbled to the ground. Her eyes remained open as I pulled my knife from the side of her chest.

My blood-splattered skin shined under the moonlight. The dead woman collapsed to the ground in front of me, and I felt nothing for her.

The others stood in the doorway behind me, waiting for me to move.

This soldier was the first woman I had killed. *Should it make a difference?* No, it made no difference at all.

Adéan placed a hand on my shoulder. "We should go."

I nodded and moved along the barracks wall.

The guard presence tonight appeared to be as lax as it had been the night we broke in. Tonight's activities would probably change all that forever more.

Solitary was on the other side of the compound, meaning we had plenty of ground to cover without being seen. I motioned for the others to cling tight to the walls. Their feet scuffled through the dirt and grass, but I couldn't focus on them. With luck, they wouldn't do anything stupid.

The cold stone stung my naked back. My hand trembled. More soldiers could be around the next bend, or the one after that, ready for our blood.

Last night, I wanted the chance to hurt the soldiers who hurt Liara. Now I just needed to find her and get out of this despicable place.

Two days, I thought. *Children spent turns within these walls. And they'll probably pay for what we've done.*

Solitary consisted of a dozen small stone huts barely big enough to sit upright. According to Wal, they baked in the sun and froze in the night. The guards used them to set an example for anyone who stepped out of line, and Liara had spent the better part of two days locked away.

When we got close, I stopped and peered around the corner. One guard paced back and forth in front of the huts. If anyone else patrolled the grounds, the darkness hid them well.

"Two things," I whispered to the others. "I need you all to stay here. If anything goes wrong, run. The distraction will be all you need to escape. Only two guards walk the outer perimeter, so you should have a chance."

"No, I'm not waiting here. She's my sister." Tomi was Liara's match in every way—the drive and single-mindedness, the stare that could burn to bone.

"Liara risked everything to get you out. If she doesn't make it, you have to. Or else, this was all for nothing."

"Cha said cha needed two tings," Adéan interrupted. He didn't care about the family drama or whether any of the rest of us escaped. People like him stuck around as long as it benefitted them. At least he didn't try to hide it.

"Tomi, call The Wind."

"Why?"

"I need to borrow your spirit."

"You're a thief?" Wal said, like an accusation.

I looked into his eyes, and I didn't flinch. "Yes, I am. Now, Tomi, call The Wind and let me get your sister."

Her echo already thundered through the surrounding air. It didn't take much effort for her to pull on The Song. I grasped the thread out of the air. Her spirit swirled about, light and powerful, like a storm crashing through the daylight.

With my father's knife in my hand, I sprinted directly at the guard. I had no time for subtlety.

The Wind sang an ocean of the sky, and The Seed bellowed under my feet.

The guard turned towards me, caught on the back of his heels like a wide-eyed fool.

All the air around us tensed with anticipation, then I pulled on The Song, and a gust careened into the soldier. His body tumbled like fabric in a windstorm and crashed into an empty, solitary hut. The weak structure crumbled under his body.

My blade was hilt-deep in the soldier's chest when a new echo filled the air. I spun around and hid behind one of the huts. A single echo, but there could have been more soldiers. I had no way of telling.

Moonlight outlined the silhouette of my blade still buried in the dead guard. I would have to face this new threat without a blade. At least The Wind was still with me.

My diaphragm pushed and pulled with each breath. Nerves could kill someone as quick as any blade. Liara needed me to keep calm.

Whichever way I turned, I didn't see anyone, not even an outline of a soldier. Yet the echo still whirled about, getting louder and louder.

A sword ripped through my right bicep before I recognized the echo—another fragment of the trapped spirit that had attacked Liara moons ago by the riverbank.

The Shadow.

I stumbled back, grabbing my bloody arm. The night bent around the echo. I reached for it and the spirit raged underneath my skin.

Unlike the other soldiers, the man beneath the shadows didn't hesitate when I stole his power from him. He continued to press his advantage.

In a panic, I reached for The Wind, but it wasn't there. I must have lost my grip on it when he cut me.

I fell to the ground and scampered backwards to avoid another strike. I pulled at the shadows, and they slipped through my fingers. Shadows dropped and swirled. They did everything except fold me into the night.

This is it. I'm going to die.

Then Liara's echo fluttered beneath the chaos. Strange, but familiar. Her echo crashed and faded like waves on the shore. "Liara!" I called out, narrowly dodging the soldier's blade. "Liara!".

A straight line of pain scored my left calf, and I toppled backwards. Fire-like pain crawled over my skin.

"Liara," I pleaded. "Call The River!"

The echo rose over the pain. The soldier drew his sword back and swung towards my neck. I closed my eyes and waited for The Mist to take me.

Then warm blood pooled over my chest, followed by silence.

When I opened my eyes, the soldier lay dead beside me with a long icicle protruding from his throat. The River vibrated under my skin, but I couldn't remember calling on them.

The soldier's eyes remained open like glossy oceans in the night.

My arm and leg burned, but I needed to move. My wounds tore wider as I pulled myself to my knees. The stones of Liara's hut felt cold under my sticky-wet hands. With a deep breath and a too loud moan, I managed to get to my feet. I leaned against the hut and waved over to where I had left the others.

Moonlight fell on the empty stretch of dirt where they had been.

I told them to run if they saw trouble. I smiled and looked down at myself. *One could call this trouble.*

Darkness shifted and figures pushed into the light. I nearly cried as they ran towards me.

Tomi's nameless friend offered me her shoulder, and the other three pulled Liara from the hut.

Her body slumped between them. She couldn't hold her head still, and her eyelids fluttered open and closed. The smell of sweet and sage rolled off her, thick and cloying. Then I understood why her echo had sounded familiar. She sounded like Jonac.

"Now what?" Tomi asked, with tears running down her cheeks. "You're injured. Liara can't walk. How are we supposed to get past the wall?"

"Adéan and Wal, can you carry Liara?" I asked, still catching my breath. "What's your name?" I asked my helper.

"Sionia," she said in a timid voice.

"Sionia, can you help me to the wall?" I put my weight on her. She helped me collect my father's knife from the dead man's chest, and we shuffled over to the wall.

I placed my hand on one of the ironoak trees and reached into the core of it. "To The Wind, guide us to safety. To The Shadow, offer us your wisdom. To The Seed, forgive us for the blood we spilled." I pulled on my connection to the tree, and it aged to ash.

"Where'd you steal that from?" Wal asked with a bite.

"We need to move quickly. The guards pass by every ten minutes."

I waved the others through first. "Now you," I told Sionia, but she didn't move.

She looked at me and shook her head. "Together."

Her eyes met mine with a steel determination. *Why? She doesn't know me. Why would she risk herself for a thief?*

I leaned my weight on her and opened myself to The Song again. When a small spark buried in the dirt called to me, I reached out towards it. An ironoak seed opened, the sproutling burst through the soil. Sionia gasped as it grew to fill the gap in the wall.

"We need to hurry," I said.

Sionia nodded, and we hobbled up the ridge. The sentries turned the corner right before we reached the tree line. They could have seen us if they had been looking, but continued on, blissfully unaware of the dead soldiers on the other side of the wall.

The spirits were on our side, or so we thought.

CHAPTER THIRTY-SIX

WHEN THE TREE LINE tapered off and the choppy waters of the Sand River clashed against the bank, I collapsed to the dirt. Each puff of cold air chilled my lungs, even as my sweat dripped to the ground.

My leg and shoulder had long since gone numb. The world spun around me. I had lost too much blood along the way. The quick poultice I slathered over my wounds had worked as well as I could have expected, but I needed rest.

I pulled my robes tight around me as the morning breeze sent a shiver across my back. If I hadn't packed extra robes, I wouldn't have made it.

The others moved about their tasks while I caught my breath. Adéan and Wal went off to gather firewood, and Tomi filled the waterskins in the river.

"Can I help you?" Sionia stood over me with concern.

"Find two smooth stones," I said between heavy breaths. "We need to make another poultice."

Tomi knelt beside Liara, who lay still as the dead. "Shouldn't she be conscious by now?"

I ignored her question because I had been asking myself the same thing. She had groaned and stirred during our trek through the woods but never completely woke.

Liara's echo wavered on the brink of silence.

Her chest rose and fell. Her heart kept a steady rhythm, but she refused to open her eyes. I peeled the dried poultice from her wounds. None of the cuts ran as deep as I had worried.

The Song ticked under the earth like a series of small beats forming a larger rhythm. Each movement stretched the cuts in my leg and arm, but I gritted my teeth to bear the pain. One plant sparked in the rhythmic refrain and rose from the soil.

When I had what I needed, I fell back to the ground with a series of herbs and plants growing in my wake. "Grind the bark from the moonlight hazel with barberries, aloe, and goldenrod leaves. Mix that with dirt and water until the paste is thick, like loose mud."

Sionia didn't ask a single question. She picked at the plants and went to work, grinding the ingredients between two stones.

The scraping of the rock created a familiar cadence.

Jonac had taught me well enough to tend to her flesh. I could mend her cuts and bruises, stave off infection, and make sure she healed properly. But her cuts and bruises weren't the real problem. The scent of susu root clung to her thick, but I had never seen it render someone completely senseless.

Her breath smelled stronger than the burning plant itself. I pulled back her bottom lip, and a black sticky residue clung to her teeth.

"Sweet tar," Sionia said as the scraping noise stopped. "That's what the soldier's call it. They force defiant kids to chew on it. Some shake it off after a couple of days, some are never really the same afterwards. A little slower. More confused. Either way, they would do anything for more."

"It's just susu root," I said, shaking my head.

"They cook it down. It turns black and tacky," she said. The grief in her eyes carried a familiar unspoken trauma. "People aren't the same afterwards."

Jonac had become cold, distant. His wit soured to insults. He never had time for Nomi or the girls. If smoke could turn that gentle man callous, what would sweet tar do to Liara?

An image of the boy with the dead eyes who served meals in the mess hall flashed in front of me, scooping one ladle after another of rice and beans, like a spiritless body.

"Help her!" Tomi said. "Do something!"

Without thinking, I dove into The Song. The euphoria that came with walking on the edge of The Mist swept me up. Whatever risks resided in the deep recesses of The Song could take me, as long as I found colly leaf.

"The leaves, never the petals," Jonac had warned me. "And not too much. Remember, it's poisonous. Only use it if you don't have a choice."

The one time he showed me the flower, it rose from the ground like tall grass with small leaves arranged along its spine, ending in feathered orange petals that ran smooth under my touch. Its scent settled somewhere between caustic and minty.

Every plant waited for me at the edge of The Mist—a forest of misfit growing things. And there it grew, under the shade of a tree I had no name for. My hands swept over the dirt, then a small plant burst through the soil with blooms of orange, feathered petals.

Liara lay there, sweat beading on her brow.

"Only use it if you don't have a choice." Jonac's warning repeated in my head.

I ground the leaves with water and soil. It smelled awful, like old fruit left too long to the sun. Probably tasted worse, but I couldn't think of that now. I smeared the paste on her tongue. When she tried to spit, I forced the mixture down with water. She coughed and convulsed, still unconscious.

"What are you doing?" Tomi demanded.

"We have to get the sweet tar out of her system."

Tomi's eyes went dark, and the wind stirred. Her echo swelled like an approaching storm. Then Liara's face contorted with pain, and she gripped her stomach as her eyes remained closed to the world.

"Turn her on her side, now," I told Sionia.

Liara began violently heaving. At first nothing came out, then everything did. The contents of her stomach soaked into the soil. Tears streamed down her face as she continued to heave, even after she had nothing left to vomit.

"What did you do to her?" Tomi screamed. She teetered between crumbling into sorrow and rising up to slit my throat. "Get away from her!"

"You don't understand..."

"I understand plenty, thief," she said. "If she dies, you die beside her."

When I stepped back, Tomi glared at me with death in her eyes, and something broke inside me.

"I broke into a Gousht encampment to save you because your sister asked me to," I said. "Call me what you will. Trust me or don't. But I won't apologize for helping your sister."

Tomi's anger wavered. I stared at her until she looked away, and then I looked back to Liara. The stubble of her scalp prickled my hand as I rubbed my palm along the curve of her head. Hopefully, I had done the right thing.

Her skin grew paler and sticky with sweat. Her breathing stuttered in and out. Whether the sweet tar or the colly leaf caused it, I couldn't say. Maybe a bad combination of the two.

Everyone gathered around me. Without looking up, I started giving out orders. "She'll need to be looked after. Wal, grab the blanket from her pack. We'll have to do what we can to keep her temperature normal and keep her hydrated," I said. "I don't know what complications there will be. I don't know how much sweet tar they gave her or how she'll react to the colly leaf."

"What do you mean, you don't know?" Tomi said, with a voice sharp enough to cut my throat. Her face twisted into a copy of her sister's. Liara's brow creased the same way when she got angry.

"I don't have all the answers," I said as calmly as I could. "But I will do everything I can to help her."

"You better, thief."

Adéan helped Tomi pull Liara out of her own sick. They wrapped her in a blanket and for a full passing of Ennea's daughters, she never left Liara's side. The others took turns filling waterskins, soaking scraps of cloth in the cold river and placing them on Liara's brow. She vomited the water up almost immediately after it passed her lips, but they continued despite.

I kept my distance. Trying Tomi's anger could only make things worse. And for all of my talk of helping, whenever I looked at Liara, guilt weighed down my gut. Each time she lurched and heaved, I questioned myself.

What if I gave her too much colly leaf? What if it was too late? What if she dies?

Deep into the night, someone rustled amongst the fallen leaves. *Maybe someone's decided to rid themselves of a thief?* I thought.

When I looked up, Sionia settled down in the darkness next to me. "You saved us," she said. "You gave her a chance."

A chance meant that Liara might not make it. I sobbed into my arms, and Sionia sat next to me, quietly letting me grieve.

———

Sionia and I walked out front the next day. My arm felt like I had used it for firewood. Bending it was torture, so I didn't. I must have been a pitiful sight, walking with a limp, one arm hanging like an execution. But if I expected any pity, I traveled with the wrong group. The morning light had done nothing to ease the tension.

We walked the same path Liara and I had walked only days before, yet nothing felt the same. The excitement and anger that had driven me spoiled to doubt and shame. I obsessively listened to Liara's echo. When it grew stronger, I felt something akin to hope, but when it waned, I fell into my darkest thoughts.

I hated the idea of bringing more trouble to the Jani, but I had nowhere else to go. Maybe Jonac could help Liara. Maybe the clan would take the group in. I would be exiled—too many people knew my secret—but at least the rest of them would be safe.

At least Liara would survive.

She rocked on the makeshift cot between Wal and Adéan. Every so often, she would retch her empty belly. I had no idea how to help her. *Feeding her colly leaf was fucking stupid,* I thought. She turned sick with fever and sweating, mumbling in her dreams.

Tomi and Wal glared at me whenever I got near Liara. To them, nothing separated me from the thief in their stories. Whatever else they knew about me became superfluous. I couldn't overcome what took a lifetime to learn.

I brewed some ginger and echinacea tea to help with Liara's fever and nausea. If it was working, it was slow, at least slower than I had the temperament for. She looked a day from death, and my options only grew slimmer. Jonac had never covered sweet tar poisoning in his lessons.

Tomi's threat from the day before played a constant refrain in my thoughts. *If she dies, you die beside her.* What Tomi didn't understand— what she could never understand—was if Liara died, I wouldn't have a reason to continue.

"Why don't you hate me like the rest of them?" I asked Sionia. "You know what I am."

"I told you last night," she said in her meek voice. "You saved us. I have seen plenty of evil between the war and the compound. You aren't evil."

She said it so simply, as if my fears amounted to nothing.

"The others know it too," she said. "But they need someone to blame."

"Maybe I deserve it."

"If you say so," she said.

And there it was. Pity. In the small upturn of her lips and the gentle curve of her brow. I didn't care for it. Being despised settled in my bones much easier.

When we set camp that night, we stretched our provisions as far as they would go. Liara and I never expected to be leaving the compound with six people.

We made quick work of it. Adéan and Wal built a fire. I collected some water from the river, then reached into The Song for some fresh fruits and vegetables.

For all of their mistrust, no one turned down the food. It didn't amount to much, but compared to mushy rice, beans, and stale bread, it was a feast.

I sat on the outskirts of the light as the others gathered near the warmth of the fire. The wind blew through me like I was thin fabric hung to dry, and I clung to my self-pity like it would keep me warm.

While everyone I cared for suffered, I continued to survive every trial.

Adéan shuffled over through the fallen leaves and said something that sounded like a run of vowels accented by the occasional consonant. Even when I paid attention to that boy, I had to repeat the words over in my head to decipher them.

"I donno if cha take requess, but I'd love abita strawbress if cha can." His voice had a melodic quality, but I would be a damned liar if I claimed to understand him.

My face turned into a question mark. "Strawberries?" I asked.

"Strawbress. It's wha I said. D'cha think cha could?" He gave me an amiable smile, and I gave one in return.

No way to hurt anyone with a strawberry, I thought.

The taste spread across my tongue before I found them in The Song, sweet and tart. I moved, then the red soil bulged and broke for the seedling that bloomed into a bush. Big, bright berries hung from the strained branches.

"Ain't tha a neat iddle trick?" he said before plucking a handful and heading back to the fire.

The others ate and chatted around the fire. Tomi hovered over her sister, plying her forehead with wet cloth and helping her sip down what water she would drink. If anyone loved Liara as much as I did, Tomi did.

———————

The shadow-cloaked Thief stood before me, twiddling her fingers around some trinket. It rolled in and out of the shadow surrounding her onyx black hand. Then, as if she noticed my attention, she clutched the trinket in her palm where the shadow claimed it.

"My-my, little thief, you have been busy." The timbre of her voice rattled around with taunting and proud notes. "Maybe now you understand our purpose."

I stared at her in disbelief. Her two-toned visage peeked through the shadow. As I looked closely, the hood evaporated into the air. Her face balanced in perfect proportions, accentuated by the dramatic split of her face between black and white.

Is she taking credit for our escape?

"Yes, I do," she answered, as if I had spoken my question aloud. "You look across this space between us, and you see me as something separate, but the space is a lie. I am you, and you are me."

"They hate me because of you!"

"Ahh, now you see. We saved them and they curse us," she said nonchalantly, but I could see past her mask. It hurt her as much as it hurt me.

"Why? Why do they hate me?" I asked.

"The stories, little thief. It's all in the stories," she said, then paused. I found it odd for a Great Spirit to be searching for words. "Stories have more than one teller. True, usually one version prevails. The story told by the powerful."

"What does that have to do with me?" I asked, my eyes welling up.

She shrunk down to my size. "Young one, it is as your mother always told you. We are our stories. The stories that people pass down are their culture. They hate me because they were taught to. Because the versions of the stories they've heard call me a thief. They hate you because you are me." The sound of her voice caught between rage and pity, sorrow and hatred.

My anger boiled up from my stomach as she claimed me. I didn't want the weight of her name or her stories. "This isn't fair!"

"No, it isn't," she said. "That is where you come in. You and my other descendants. You are The Balance. Show them."

"I don't want to be The Balance. I don't want to be The Thief. Take it away! Take it back!"

She didn't react to my outburst. Her stillness stilled me, and I resented it.

"Much easier to be The Seed, be beloved. Sadly, that is not your path." She reached her hand out of the shadows and pushed the trinket into my hand.

I turned the cool, smooth wood over in my hand and ran my finger over the rune engraved in the surface. The Thief. The grain matched the one I had carved. My finger grazed over the same chip along the smooth side of the marker.

How could she have my rune?

Sionia shook me awake, and I jolted up, looking back and forth, searching for the shadow-cloaked spirit. I only found trees and several people who hated me.

I went to push myself up off the ground, but I had something clutched in my hand. The Thief's rune. *How?* I felt for the chip in the wood, and the abrupt gouge in the smooth wood caught my finger. *I left it back in the compound.*

My idle hands toyed with the rune as we walked through the chill autumn morning. Too many questions rolled through my head, not the least of which was how a bit of wood magically appeared in my hand.

Everything The Thief said about stories; what was true? What was her version? If she wasn't a malitu, why did all the stories agree? If stories were the lifeblood of our people, what would happen if they were lies?

Had I not been distracted, I might have seen what would happen next. I might have been able to stop it. I might have been able to save them.

CHAPTER THIRTY-SEVEN

ON THE THIRD DAY, Liara went in and out of lucid states. She asked questions and forgot the answers moments later. When the third wave of lucidity found her and she repeated her questions again, worry settled deep in my gut.

Beyond emptying her stomach, I didn't know how her body would react to colly leaf poison. If I had been quick enough, it should have cleared the sweet tar from her body. Either poison could have caused these side effects or potentially some reaction between the two. I simply didn't know.

Without her memories, without her stubborn charm, Liara would be a different person. Neither poison had to kill her to kill her.

I needed help from more experienced healers. The sun dropped in the sky, and each passing hour added to my anxiety. Hopefully, the Jani hadn't moved camp in the last eight days.

Sionia kept me company out front again while the others trailed behind us. The daylight stretched thin. Each tree became a copy of the others in the dark. What few landmarks I could distinguish in the fading light gave me confidence we were headed the right way. The only other time I made this journey, I had been running the opposite direction.

I should have focused more. Made note of my surroundings. My knowledge of tracking would only take us so far.

A familiar rock formation jutted out of the earth, two long smooth rocks like steps to a natural spear tip.

Even if this path led to the camp, it might be several hours still. *If they moved camp, would I even be able to tell?* We could be searching all night for something that no longer existed.

"Are you excited to get back home?" Sionia asked.

"Home?" I never considered the encampment home. Home had been the house my father built. Although now, thinking about Jonac, Nomi, and the girls, I couldn't find another word to describe it. "Scared, actually."

"Why?" Sionia asked.

"When we get there, everything will change. When the clan finds out I'm a thief...it won't be home much longer."

"Who says that has to happen?"

I squinted at her into the darkness. "I don't think Tomi and Wal are going to keep my secret for me."

"That's not what I meant," she said. Even though she and I shared an age, she carried herself with a stillness that matured her. Her dark brown eyes threatened to engulf me if I stared too deeply.

"They would never accept a thief. You know what they say, 'No heart for a....'"

"Are they that shallow?"

"No, I didn't say that. I just mean...." I didn't know how to finish.

Sionia smiled. "Maybe you haven't given them enough credit."

"Maybe." The word barely escaped my lips.

Too many assumptions stood between me and the people I loved. Nomi and Jonac were going to find out, and they deserved to hear the truth from me. And I deserved the chance to tell them.

A thin humming sound cut through my heavy thoughts. I leaned closer and strained to hear it. *An echo. Maybe more than one.* I turned abruptly and would have tumbled over my wounded leg, but Sionia's hands gripped my arm, and she steadied me.

I smiled at her, then started moving quickly towards the echoes. The rest of the group picked up on my urgency and hurried along after me. My leg kept me from running, but I swung it forward in a wild limp, faster and faster towards the sound. With each step, the echoes sang more clearly, a clan of distorted songs reaching into the night.

The pieces of reflected spirits came together, each fitting into the others like voices in a choir. I had never allowed myself to hear it before. Other dancers could never experience the scope of it. With The Thief, the fullness of The Song sang to me.

The tree wall came into view. I bounded off my strong leg towards home. My injured arm swung at my side. My need eclipsed my pain. For a moment, I didn't need to hide.

Blessed Mother and Daughters!

A crackling sound invaded The Song. It could have been animals stirring in the forest behind us or Liara's echo sparking and fading.

Then the rage and torment erupted behind me. Tortured spirits shrieked. I didn't have to turn around. Whatever the pain, I abandoned my limp and ran.

Waving furiously for the others to match my pace, I yelled, "Run!"

Either the fear in my voice or my body language convinced them. Adēan threw Liara over his shoulder, and the cot tumbled to the ground behind them.

Pain struck me in one thunderclap after another, running from my foot through my injured leg to the base of my spine.

I couldn't stop whatever was to come. Utterly helpless. With each step, I led destruction to the people who had become my second home.

The night watch didn't see me waving in the dark. That empty space of time stretched forever, and in a way, I wished it would, if only to delay the inevitable.

"Gousht!" I screamed as loudly as my exhausted lungs could manage. "Gousht!"

A torch lit the face of a nomad in the distance as they peered into the darkness. I screamed again and again. When they finally understood, they went stiff with fear, then turned and ran into the camp. Seconds later, the clanging of the warning bell rang out over the encampment.

Still twenty paces from the wall, an echo swelled behind me. The ground shook. I snatched the echo from the air and calmed the earth.

The pain of my leg and the tortured spirit ripping through my gut folded me in half. Another echo stirred the ground. And suddenly, two spirits clawed at me from the inside.

Family knows. My blood burned. The spirits twisted my pain like a braid of rope. The world fell silent under the agony.

When the earth quaked with a third spirit, I reached for it and collapsed to the ground. The earth split. A section of the ironoak wall toppled into the tent city, crushing someone's home.

Dozens of echoes grasped at The Song. My head throbbed from the chaos. Too many echoes. Too much noise. Growing louder. Growing closer.

Someone grabbed me by the latch of my travel sack. The grass, rocks, soil scraped against my skin as they dragged me over the uneven ground.

I pried my eyes open. *Wal?*

He hauled me past the fallen trees. All the others waited inside the broken wall. Tomi hunched over her sister. Adéan and Sionia searched back and forth with wide eyes.

Jani dancers rushed by and filled the gap in the wall.

"What is wrong with you?!" Wal screamed.

Up and down tumbled over one another. Echoes shrieked into the night. Someone screamed, then an echo fell silent. Then another and another. Tears tickled my cheeks.

One thought stopped the world. *Jonac.* I imagined him lying cold in the grass. *It's all my fault.*

My feet found the ground below me before I had fully regained myself. I staggered towards the violence. Somewhere behind me people called my name, but the echoes called louder. The pain was beyond tolerable, but I would not lose another family.

Pieces of the ground crashed into one another in jagged structures of rock and earth. Wind ripped through the forest clearing. Fires sprang up and spread from one tent to the next. The night hollered with sorrow.

I searched erratically through the smoke and fire for Jonac, but the chaos was too thick. Soldiers and nomads clashed with blades and fists. Bodies laid lifeless on the ground. The air tasted of copper.

A flare of heat washed over me as a fire burst to life. Instinctively, I jumped to the side. When I turned, Elder Lashan crossed blades with a soldier less than half their age. The dance of metal clanged against the chorus of mayhem, and then ended. The soldier drew her blade across Lashan's throat.

The elder's blood splattered across the ground as they collapsed. Their echo faded into The Mist.

With a fury I had only begun to know, I rushed towards the soldier. She reached for The Flame, and I let her call the spirit and boil the air long enough to allow her to believe herself invincible. The fire illuminated her face and the wrath in her eyes.

Then I extinguished the fire. The enraged spirit thrashed inside me as I sunk my father's blade into the soldier's belly and wrenched it upwards. She gagged on the air before her life vanished from her pale eyes.

I leaned into the violence and my fear evaporated, leaving only bloodlust.

I bound through the clearing like a fox. The pain would wait for me on the other side of all of this. I had to find Jonac. Twice, I turned a dead body wrapped in Jani robes. Neither were him.

As I ran, I clutched at the tormented spirits in the air. Two. Three. Four spirits battered my insides as I set fire to wounded soldiers and sent gusts of wind hurling towards others. I lost count of how many lives I took. But I enjoyed doing it.

The Jani lost ground, and the battle pushed farther and farther into the tent city. Bodies of nomads covered the ground. Fires blazed over

gardens. Several nomads tried to run or surrender. They were met with
the same dispassionate violence that the Gousht had for those who
resisted.

Fucking couta.

Siani lay beside her grandchildren, their blood mingling in the grass.

Elder Rākn's body rested beneath the burning remnants of his tent,
firelight gleaming off his bloody entrails.

Every horrific vignette sent me deeper into the depths of my anger.

I leaped onto the back of a large soldier and stabbed my father's knife
into him again and again as we crashed to the ground. Then I left him
gurgling in his blood.

When I found Jonac, he and Torrel were fighting side-by-side, holding
off several soldiers from a group huddled under one of the few tents
left standing. Torrel called The Wind, and it rushed through the soldiers.
Jonac lashed out with a sword in each hand.

Yet, for all their efforts, the soldiers pushed them back.

Jonac swung madly at one soldier in a line of many. His attack went
wide, and the soldier slashed Jonac across the chest. I screamed out
and pulled at the Mountain's stolen spirit within me. The ground tore
between Jonac and the soldiers. Then I boiled the air around the man
who had wounded Jonac until his padded armor burst into flames.

His scream pierced the night like a feral cat as fire engulfed him. After
several breaths, the screaming stopped.

I placed my hands on the ground and created a gap in the earth
beneath the other soldiers. Dirt compacted into the walls of the newly-
formed chasm beneath the ground, then the surface collapsed into empty
space. The soldiers clawed at the edges of the pit as the land became a
river of dirt, and their screams were muffled as they sank into their new
grave.

Jonac and Torrel stared at me as if I were The Thief given to body.
Then I saw them—Nomi, Soca, and Junera—huddled in the tent behind
Jonac. The girls looked terrified.

Are they scared of me, the soldiers, or the blood? I turned to Nomi for a thread of our connection, and she looked back at me as if I were a stranger.

Jonac trembled as he stared. "You're...you're a..."

"Spirit thief," a deep, gruff voice finished his statement.

Five soldiers surrounded the priest from the mission school. They stopped and turned as the priest spoke in common tongue, disgust and confusion worn bluntly on their faces. The priest, their general, a descendant of The One True God, blood to their Emperor, formed his lips around a bastardized tongue of inferior nations.

His words and the proficiency in which he used them caught everyone off-kilter.

The tent city burned behind the priest. "Brought to the Jani by a spirit thief," he said with a smile in his voice. "The One works many wonders. I thought you might lead me to the Missing, but this will do."

"I didn't bring you here!" I turned to Jonac. "I swear it. I didn't bring them here."

"Well, maybe not you, but The Thief did," the priest said. "Honestly, it is a pleasure to meet someone touched by The One True God."

Always the performer, the priest let his words linger in the air like rotten fruit. "You knew, of course," he said.

"What are you talking about?"

"Don't you find it odd that our God can steal spirits too? Don't you find it odd that your people curse The Thief like they curse The One?"

He stepped closer with each question, but I couldn't move. "The answer is obvious, isn't it? Most who wear the veil won't admit it, but it's true. The One True God, The God of power, The God of our ambition..."

"You're lying!" I screamed.

"Is The Thief."

"No. No, you're lying," I pleaded.

"Am I? Who else could steal a spirit? The One True God has been here long before the Empire. Your people failed to understand him. You gave him the wrong name and cursed his power. For that, you will be punished."

He clutched the dull red crystal around his neck and reached for The Flame. I stole the spirit before he could wield it.

"Interesting." His head turned down to the empty crystal. "I've always wanted to know how a thief could steal a spirit without a crystal. Is it as easy as it seems?" He reached for the pale blue crystal and called for The River. I stole that spirit as well.

Six stolen spirits, tormented by imprisonment, swarmed within me. My gut felt like it would burst open and the spirits would tear me to pieces in their escape. I fell to my knees, gripping my stomach. My whole body writhed in pain. My limbs twitched and spasmed as I fought to hold the spirits. The world dimmed.

"Not easy after all, is it?" the priest asked.

He held out his hand, and a soldier placed a second dull red crystal in his palm. He reached into the echo, but as I drew strength to steal the seventh spirit, I lost my grip on all of them. They left me hollow, and I fell forward with barely the strength to hold myself up on my hands and knees.

The echo rose and crashed down around me.

The world filled with muffled screams. Heat rushed over me. Jonac and Torrel shouted and charged past. Swords clashed and echoes crashed.

When I looked up, Jonac stormed like a daemon. The squat Sonacoan beat back three armed soldiers with the ferocity of a rabid bear. He was not the man I knew. He was rage wearing Jonac's body.

One soldier lunged forward, and Jonac stepped to the side, driving his blade through the soldier's padded armor. Another soldier moved to take advantage of Jonac's attack, but he turned and slashed his blade across her face. He steadied his blade to meet the other soldiers.

"Enough." With another crystal in his hand, the priest called a powerful gust of wind, and Jonac tumbled backwards, followed by Torrel.

Jonac, my kana, the man who had taken me in after the Gousht killed my parents, was going to die, and I couldn't do anything to stop it.

I looked frantically for help, but there was none to be found. Only bodies.

My skin chilled. My heart pounded throughout my whole body. The tent Jonac had been protecting had collapsed into flame. Charred remains lay beneath the burning furs. Nomi's brown body lay draped over the girls. Soca's face lay buried in the dirt—unmoving. Junera's hand stretched out from beneath her mother. The wooden rabbit rested beneath her open palm.

Tears streamed down my face, and my rage entwined with my sorrow. I screamed, but the world had fallen silent. All I could hear was The Song, more alive and all-consuming than before. I felt—no, I was connected to every blade of grass, every plant and tree, from root to canopy. I knew the forest as if I were the seeds that gave it to the soil.

My body moved, but I didn't control it. The Song moved me, and I watched as I lifted myself off the ground. I drove each foot into the soil, slammed each hand against my knees, and then lift them into the sky, one after another in a steady rhythm.

The field of bodies faded into my periphery. My rage and grief consumed everything as the ground rumbled and broke open. A line of stormwood trees, thick and healthy, sprang from the soil, spreading for days in each direction. The roots locked deep in the soil and around one another, creating a wall with the priest on one side and Jonac on the other.

Then, I fell into the darkness.

Slowly, the dark coalesced, and I awoke in a strange forest. No two trees or plants were alike. Spruce grew next to white birch and ashburn. A forest of misfits, and yet balanced perfectly. Vibrant colors exploded against the lush greens.

I stood alone. No animals scurrying about. No birds singing in the trees. I should have been frightened, but I couldn't manage it. A sense of familiarity flowed through the strange forest.

As I walked through the menagerie of plants and trees, my fingers brushed across the different textures of bark, flowers, and nettles. A large thorn bush, which I had no name for, pricked my finger, but I didn't feel any pain. The cut didn't bleed.

A presence, a walking connection to every living thing, stirred me from my confusion and awe. I turned and found myself looking into the eyes of The Seed.

He stood like a man, but his features were sharp, as if The Mother had carved him from stormwood. Small flowers bloomed over his body, drawing his silhouette even more asymmetrical than it truly was. His skin shimmered like dark, polished wood. Woodgrain marked his entire body like the most intricate tattoos.

For all the rough lines and other oddities, he was simply beautiful. When I met his cherrywood eyes, I knew him.

No matter his differences, he was kin to The Thief. Separate, but part of the same whole. I fit into them as easily as they fit into me.

"Yes, young dancer, we all belong to The Mother. In a way, all born to Ennea are kin." The Seed spoke as if answering questions I had not asked. His voice stretched long and tempered, like an autumn breeze, cool, but not cold.

The oddity of spirits speaking without a mouth still set me uneasy.

I stared up at the spirit, and a question lay heavy in my throat. Almost too heavy to ask. I had longed to see him in my dreams as I had so often seen The Thief, but he never came. Not even when I needed him most.

"Why? Why do you come to me now? Why fill my dreams with beauty? I needed you so many times before, and you left me for The Thief." My voice cracked as I spoke.

"Dreams? Oh, child, you think this is a dream? This is The Mist," he said.

The Mist. *How?* I didn't remember dying, but then, maybe the dead don't.

The Seed slowly shook his head. "You are not dead. You are walking in The Mist as you have many times with my sister. She didn't visit you. You visited her. And now, you have come to visit me."

"No, but I've never walked in The Mist. When I got close, Jonac pulled me out of The Song. He said dancers can get lost in The Mist."

"Some do," The Seed said. "But not all. Dancers straddle The Mist and The Waking; each time you reach into The Song, you are reaching into The Mist. Some dancers stay a little longer than others."

Something bothered me, something I was supposed to remember, but I couldn't. The Mist enveloped me, and I couldn't recall where I had been. It itched in the back of my skull. "Why can't I remember where my body is?"

"Ahh, that is the challenge, is it not, young dancer? To be here, one must be present, but if you come seeking answers, you must be somewhere else as well. Quite the conundrum." He walked about the forest and brushed his long fingers over the trees and flowers like greeting old friends.

Jonac flashed in my mind, but I didn't know why. "Do you know my kana?"

"Which one?" he asked, then waved off the question. "Ahh, yes, Jonac. Another close kin. I'll let you in on a little secret, seedling. Well, not a secret, more of a little-known truth. Great Spirits are not only connected to those who carry our spirits, we are one with them. I walked with you all of your life—learned with you, laughed with you, mourned with you. I am one with many and know each as I know myself.

"One more truth you should know but haven't seen. As I am one with you, so is she." *The Thief.* I wanted to object, but he interrupted me. "You will have to learn that truth in time, I see."

It came to me, the itch, the missing question. Cold and dangerous, but

I had to know. "Is it true? Is The Thief also The One True God?"

The Seed chuckled at the question or maybe at the intensity with which I asked it. "That is a big question with many answers. One of those answers would be yes, that is what they call her. Another answer would be no, that is not who The Mother made her to be."

"What does that mean?" I yelled.

He did not seem to notice my harsh tone. "It means precisely what it means."

My skin heated up. I spoke through gritted teeth. "Did she give the Empire the crystals to trap spirits?"

"Now that is a simple and tragic answer with a longer, more tragic history. Yes, my sister gave them a most-unfortunate power, which they have used in despicable ways. But that is far from the beginning of her story."

"How can you defend her?" I asked. The calm of the forest vanished. I bundled up inside my anger and despair.

The Thief betrayed Ennea, all of us, and I am part of her.

"You have many questions, little seedling. I forgive my sister because it is in my nature, as it is in yours. For centuries, your people have condemned her and all those she walks with. One after another, they scorned, beat, and berated her descendants. Each time they were cast out or killed, she experienced their pain. Even you, her own descendant, curse her name. Can you blame her for seeking people who would honor her?"

"Honor her?! They call her The One True God. They don't even know her name."

"Ahh, but do you? You call her The Thief. That was not the name The Mother gave her. And if you're asking me, The One True God sounds much better than The Thief," he said. "She is The Balance, the one who stands against those who would wield The Song as a weapon for their own gain."

"So, is she a spirit or a god?"

"She is born of The Mother like all my siblings, but when the Gousht came, they had a belief, and she served a need. That was enough for them to call her their god."

The Seed stopped and turned as if he heard something in the distance. "Oh, little seedling, our time is short. If you intend to bring peace, you must forgive her first. You will need her, and she will need you."

"How?" I asked as my memories of The Waking started coming back to me. "How can I pull her back to side with people who hate her?"

"Know her nature. As I am called to forgiveness, she is called to balance. Help her find balance." He spoke his last words with equal regret and hope. He spoke for the sister he missed and the sorrow she lived through. As his words faded into the stillness of the forest, the light faded to dark.

———

When I opened my eyes, the forest canopy moved through the sky. I rejoined my body in The Waking. The memories poured through me, along with the pain.

I couldn't move. From what I could tell, I lay latched to a travel cot. Burning chills ran through me like a fever. My body was too heavy to move, even if I hadn't been restrained.

When I saw Liara walking beside me, my anxiety slipped away. She limped, but she was alive, and that was enough. I tried to call to her, but I couldn't speak, as if my body didn't belong to me. If not for Liara walking beside me, I would have been terrified.

At least she's safe. My weariness overtook me, and I fell deeply into sleep.

CHAPTER THIRTY-EIGHT

THE NEARLY FULL MOONS turned the night sky a deep shade of purple. A fire blazed beside me, and silhouettes moved around in the firelight. Someone tugged on my leg. I winced, and a slow burning radiated from my calf. When I tried to move, the burning flared.

"Stay still," Jonac said in a dispassionate voice. He continued to work in silence, adjusting a new piece of fabric around the wound.

The world moved at a slower pace than natural. The massacre came back to me in brief flashes. Ironoaks collapsing as the ground shook. Fires climbing along the canopy of a tent. The priest holding a glowing crystal.

Something else happened. Something horrible. I couldn't put it all together. A patchwork of bandages locked me in place, flat on my back. *What happened?*

Jonac cinched the fabric to my leg roughly and then walked away without saying another word.

"He needs time," Liara said from behind me. Her voice carried a low rasp, like she had been crying.

"Water?" My throat felt like dry earth. She tipped a waterskin to my lips, and I drank too deeply. When I finished coughing, I asked her what happened.

Liara took a deep breath. She paused between her words and carefully

recounted the battle to me. The bits she didn't say hid the worst of
the truth. When the emotion caught in her throat, she drank from the
waterskin.

"When you ran off into the fighting, I thought we'd lost you." The
darkness hid her from me, but her tears weighed down her voice all the
same. "Adéan gathered us at the wall furthest from the fighting. I was
helpless. The encampment burned as the others pulled wounded Jani
from the wreckage. I tried to stop the bleeding and calm the children,
but...there was so much blood, Kaylo.

"When the ground shook and that tree wall emerged from the earth,
I knew you were alive. I knew it was you. I don't know how, but I knew."
Liara's voice shook. She tried to catch her breath. "When Adéan and
Sionia found you, you had been badly burned. You collapsed too close to
a fire and...Jonac is doing his best to reduce the scars."

"How many?" I asked.

"Kaylo, you did everything you could..."

"How many died because of me?"

"That's not how it happened," she said. I stared into her eyes until she
answered the question. "Fourteen Jani survived the attack and the six of
us. There are a couple who are badly injured, but you had some of the
worst of it. I didn't know if you were going to make it."

Liara might have continued talking, but her voice receded into the
background. *Twenty-eight people spirited away because of me.*

Then I remembered a small hand grasping a wooden rabbit. "Nomi,
Soca, Junera?" Liara looked away from me. "Liara, I need to hear it."

Her shoulders trembled with her breath. "Kaylo..." She couldn't
control her weeping any longer. "They're gone. All of them."

Stars dotted the purple sky above me, and I silently wept. *I killed
another family.* Their visages hung before me like curses.

Liara continued to talk. Maybe she thought I needed the distraction,
or maybe she did. She told me how the ground had quaked, and they
smelled burning wood, but the wall of stormwoods wouldn't burn or fall.

She told me how I had saved those who survived.

They had collected what supplies they could and threw together stretchers for those of us too injured to walk. She managed to save my mother's book. It seemed like such a small thing compared to all the carnage. The remains of the camp burned down to a few small fires before they left.

A span passed before I could walk, and another before I could walk well. In all that time, Jonac didn't speak to me. He asked about my pain and told me to redress my wound every day. But nothing else.

When I was strong enough to tend to my burns and cuts, he stopped checking on me all together. He avoided looking in my direction. When he did, his eyes were glassy and hollow. Wafts of sweet and sage followed everywhere he went. I couldn't blame him. Not after I had stolen his life from him.

All the Jani gave me a wide birth. Some of them looked at me like I might be dangerous, others had murder in their eyes. Their anger came across in their looks and the heavy silences, but most of all, in the echoes of the surviving dancers. To the Jani, each member of the clan had been a member of their family. Everyone who died had been a personal loss.

On top of the spouses and children they lost, they had lost their way of life. The Fallen Rock Clan died in the flames, and I had been the kindling.

In the midst of it all, Tomi took pity on me. She apologized with words that had obviously come from her sister, the guilt she piled on herself reflecting in her eyes. If not for her, we never would have broken into the compound. The Gousht never would have found the clan.

She could try to steal away as much guilt as she wanted; it would never lighten the weight I carried—the weight I deserved.

We wandered aimlessly through the forest, putting distance between us and the Gousht. After this much time, they wouldn't be looking for us anymore. But the Jani were nomads, and so we continued to travel west.

One night, while we were walking at the back of the caravan like we had grown accustomed to, Liara stopped and looked at me. "Your guilt won't help anyone," she said. "It's selfish. Stop it." Blunt, as always. Her lips puckered, and her eyes narrowed. No point in arguing with her.

"You didn't do this. The Gousht did. That priest did," she said.

The Priest.

He deserved as much blame as I did. I had led them back to the encampment. I made the decision that killed the clan. But he wielded the sword. If balance existed in this world, I would be the one to slit his throat and leave his body for the animals to pick clean.

When we stopped for the night, I built a fire far enough away from the Jani that I couldn't feel them glaring at me. Wal sat next to me. He had been quiet since the massacre. We talked when we needed to, but no more.

As he sat beside me, he kept stealing not-so-subtle glances in my direction. He fidgeted like a boy with a crush. Then, when the tension grew too much for him, he blurted out, "I mean, you've heard the stories, right?"

"Did we start a conversation I was unaware of?"

"Yes, kind of," he said with a smile. "I do that sometimes. Continue the conversation in my head out loud. Burned my dad red in the face.

"What I meant to say was, I grew up hearing stories about The Thief. She's always the villain. Malitu and all that. I mean, of course, you know that...Fuck, this is hard." He slapped his hands on his thighs and turned to me. "You saved me. I would have died in that prison, and you saved me." He gestured to the Jani campfire. "You saved them too, even if they are being bastards about it."

I wanted to point out that they wouldn't have been in danger if I hadn't led the Gousht to them, but it seemed like the wrong time. Instead, I stared into the fire.

We sat there in silence for a long while. Despite the constant flow of heavy thoughts through my head or maybe because of it, I couldn't find any words for him. Still, it felt good to have him there, to know some few people in the world didn't hate me, even if I wasn't one of them.

"You know, you saved me too. When the soldiers attacked, I doubled over in pain, and you dragged me past the wall."

He nodded slowly. "What was that anyway? What happened to you?"

"It's hard to explain. The spirits trapped in crystals differ from other spirits. They are angry. I can feel them trying to escape, like they are clawing at the walls of their prison, and I am the prison," I said.

"That sounds fucking horrifying," he said. And that was it. We had nothing left to say on the matter.

That night he stayed by my fire, and one by one Liara, Tomi, Sionia, and Adéan joined us. The Jani might have blamed me, but they hadn't shown an interest in befriending any of us. To them, we were all outsiders. They had to shore up their ranks and protect what remained of their clan.

The next morning, we woke and broke camp like we had for several span. The Jani moved through their paces slower than usual. A new tension hung in the air, not between us and the nomads, but between the Jani themselves. Their harsh tones carried even if their words didn't.

As Jonac and Torrel approached our group, we finished packing what little possessions we had between the six of us.

Jonac's eyes were clear for the first time in a long while.

"You need to leave." Torrel's voice struggled to restrain his anger as he stared directly at me. He wanted my blood, but he might settle for never seeing me again.

Only a fool wouldn't have seen it coming. I didn't fight it. If I meant to hunt down The Priest, I had no reason not to start now.

I nodded my head and turned to walk off into the forest, but Liara blocked my path with her arm. I could have pushed past her, but the idea made me nauseous.

"We are safer together than we are apart," she said.

"No one is safe with a thief," Torrel said, his lips curled into a snarl. "The rest of you can stay. Live by our ways, and you'll have a home. But the malitu goes."

"He saved you. He saved us all!" Liara yelled.

"Saved us?" Jonac yelled back. "Saved us? Do you see Nomi standing beside me? Where are my little girls? Are they off playing in the woods?" His echo roared like a beast preparing to attack. "I didn't even have the time to give them to The Mist properly. We left their bodies under a burning tent. They are gone, and it's his fault."

"Jonac, I am..." I tried to apologize, but he cut me off.

"No. I don't need a stolen apology. Nomi treated you like family. My little girls looked up to you like an older brother." Tears ran down his face as he screamed at me. "I brought a malitu into my home, and it killed my family."

He paused and stared into my eyes. "You stole them from me."

Liara opened her mouth to defend me, but I placed my hand on her arm. Words wouldn't do any good. I turned and shouldered my pack, a couple of waterskins, and a strip of cloth for a blanket.

"Only a grave will do!" Torrel yelled out behind me.

I agreed. But The Priest needed to die first.

Tears stung my eyes as I walked away.

The leaves on the ground crunched next to me. Then more footsteps joined my own. Eventually, all five of them caught up and walked with me.

"Go back," I said. "It will be safer."

"Too many rools fa my tastes," Adéan said nonchalantly.

"Where are we going?" Tomi asked.

"North, I guess," Wal said, pointing at the sun. "We could always go back to the mission school." No one laughed.

"When they caught me, I was searchin fa someting," Adéan said. "Cha heard of ta Missin'?"

"The Missing?" I asked.

"Tha wha I said," Adēan said, clearly annoyed that I had to ask. "Rumma say, it easy ta find them, if cha know whata look fa." All of our eyes were fixed on Adēan. He straightened his shoulders and walked taller.

If Adēan knew where to find the Missing, that's where we would go. The first winter winds had already begun to chill the forest, and no scrap of tent would stave off the cold once winter struck in full.

But survival didn't matter to me. If they were real, the Missing turned the fight on the Empire. No more hiding. Somewhere a man cloaked in red preached his cause with spirits draped around his neck. He led soldiers and stole children from their homes. People died by his orders.

Killing him was the only reason I needed to continue breathing.

Chapter Thirty-Nine

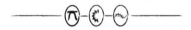

For all of Tayen's guilt, the soldiers hadn't followed her to her family's hut. No one held her responsible for their deaths, except for herself. *Kaylo might have hidden from the war,* she thought. *But he never escaped it.*

The noise of Kaylo's spoon scraping the bottom of his bowl filled their small home. He hadn't met her eyes since he finished telling his story for the night.

Even if he hadn't finished his story, she could piece some of it together. The Gousht had put Kaylo and Tayen on paths towards vengeance, and somehow his path led him to the hallow. Whether or not he had found his vengeance, he hadn't found happiness or even contentment.

The warning hadn't been lost on her, but the war already killed her alongside her family. Kaylo couldn't save her. Without her family, life had nothing to offer her.

The scent of the greasy stew hung in the air, thick as the tension. A dangerous question lingered in Tayen's thoughts, the kind of question that could open up wounds. But she needed to know.

"Kaylo? I don't know how to...I've been trying to ask....' She shook her head.

"Being coy doesn't make a question easier," he said.

"I've never seen you dance with The Seed. Every time I ask about it, you come up with an excuse," she said. "Can you still hear The Song?"

Kaylo tilted his face up to the firelight, dark circles undercutting his eyes. He paused for a breath. "No," he said. "No, I haven't heard The Song in several turns. Echoes are a pale substitute for hearing The Seed, feeling the life of the forest. When I heard your echo, all those moons ago...."

Someone pounded roughly on the door. Not a visitor's knock. The wooden door shook again with a second series of bangs.

Kaylo motioned for Tayen to be quiet and hide. He rose and unsheathed his knife. The pounding came a third time before he reached the door.

The Song waited like a mountain lion ready to pounce. Tayen's hand crept to her knife as Kaylo cracked the door open, and then Nix pushed her way into their home.

"You have to go," she said.

"I know you don't like us, but...." Kaylo started to object, but Nix didn't let him finish.

"No time for that. The Lost Army is here, and they'll take the girl."

Lost Army? Take me? It didn't make any sense. *Why would the Lost Army be in Dasoon?*

A dozen questions formed in her head, but before she could ask them, Kaylo grabbed her forearm and pulled her out the door.

The books. Our swords. Our bedrolls and blankets.

She tried to resist, but Kaylo's fingers dug into her flesh, and he pulled harder. He wore the same expression he had the night the warriors came to their hallow. She stopped resisting.

The night lay silent over Dasoon. Everyone had retreated for the night—eating, drinking, smoking.

In two moons, they had made a home out of the rubble. Most people here were pleasant. Despite herself, Tayen had started feeling comfortable in the freecity. Now they ran into the cold of early winter with less than they had come with. The blades on their belts and the clothes on their backs. No coats or bedrolls. No food.

She clutched her sister's whistle hanging from her neck.

What would make Kaylo leave it all behind?

The paths lay empty, but a low rumble across town carried over the quiet city. Kaylo's head swerved back and forth as they ran. His bad leg shortened his gait, but it didn't slow him down. Several times he turned abruptly, cut between houses or piles of rubble.

Tayen did all she could to keep up.

No one followed them. No one lay in wait. But if Kaylo ran, she had to follow.

The buildings opened up into a clearing, scattered with piles of rubble and lined by the old city wall. Kaylo ran directly for a break in the wall where the stones had slipped with time.

Hakan had focused on fixing the larger breaches in the wall—as much as Hakan actually focused on anything in the freecity besides calling himself its leader.

"Run faster," Kaylo said, his voice harsh and breathy.

Four warriors, heavy with weapons, clad in matching purple uniforms with leather vests, rounded the corner of a building. Nothing stood between Kaylo, Tayen, and the warriors besides open air and a couple dozen paces.

Their weapons clanged loudly as the warriors ran to intercept them, and the sound drove Tayen's feet faster.

The gap in the wall would be a snug fit, but they both could make it through.

"You first." Kaylo placed a hand on her back and guided her to the opening.

"But, what about..."

"I'll be right behind you, little shade. Now, go."

The rock snagged on her robe, but she pushed through, the fabric ripping as she tumbled to the ground on the other side.

The world on the side of the wall stood still. She waited there in the darkness, but Kaylo didn't follow her. "It's clear over here."

Rough voices carried over the wall, followed by the sounds of metal clashing.

"Kaylo!" Tayen called out.

The earth shook below her feet, and she caught herself against the stone wall.

He needed her help. She began pushing her way back through the breach when something grabbed her and tossed her to the ground.

The Song sprang up around her. Whether or not Kaylo wanted her to reveal herself didn't matter. She reached for The Shadow, but a purple clad warrior leaned over her and pressed the cold edge of his blade to her throat.

"Get up, and do it slowly," the big oaf said.

Three other warriors waited behind the man with a blade to her throat. She complied, and they waited.

Kaylo emerged from the breach, carrying a long, thin sword like the one on Nix's belt. Blood soaked his right sleeve, and the beginnings of a bruise darkened his cheek.

He froze when he saw her with a sword at her throat and a small tear of blood dripping down her neck. Their eyes met. In a look, he offered her a guilty apology, the same look he wore when he talked about the people he lost. She had to turn away.

Kaylo dropped the pilfered weapon to the ground. He spread his arms wide, and the warriors seized him, binding his hands behind his back.

"Are they dead?" one warrior asked, motioning towards the other side of the wall.

"They won't be walking easy for a stretch, but they'll live," Kaylo said.

The warrior pulled Kaylo's knife from his belt and strapped it to his own. "Good, good. You won't be any trouble, will you?"

"Be on my best behavior, I promise."

The warriors walked them along the wall toward the city entrance— two in front and two behind. The rope rubbed the skin raw at

Tayen's wrists. Their captors had the sandy skin and dark tight curls of northerners. Each of them wore a tattoo marking their left cheek.

The man behind Kaylo had his sword drawn. His tattoo was a series of small lines and shapes. If it meant something, Tayen had no idea what. The warrior smiled at her and poked Kaylo in the soft of the back with his sword. Because he could. To show her his power. Because he was a prick. A small circle of red crawled along the fabric against Kaylo's back.

Big nose, wispy beard, beady eyes. She turned her gaze forward. *I won't forget.*

Almost two dozen warriors formed around the gates of the not-so-free-city, all wearing purple robes under a leather vest. They carried battle axes, bows, and thin swords, but the crystals dangling from some of their necks caught her eye.

Why would The Lost Army wear stolen spirits around their necks?

They marched Tayen and Kaylo next to a row of townspeople. Some were bound; some were not. A fire roared in the center of the commotion. The warrior who had stabbed Kaylo kicked him in the back of the knees and forced him to kneel.

Hakan and Nix were talking with a Tomakan man dressed like the other warriors.

What do they want? Why isn't Hakan fighting back?

Several warriors unloaded bags of grain from a cart. One after another, they tossed the heavy bags into a pile. Maybe enough grain to last a winter, especially with fewer mouths to feed.

Nix met Tayen's eyes, then turned away.

They carried out the exchange efficiently. Each of the warriors went about their tasks. Most of them wore a thin sword on their belt, like Nix's. One or two of them were Tomakan, but most were northerners. Each of them had a similar tattoo across their cheeks, different constructions of the same symbols.

Tayen turned to Kaylo. *He must have a plan,* she thought, but he knelt there smiling.

"What a sad excuse for an army, four horses and twenty asses," Kaylo said. The warrior with Kaylo's knife smacked him in the back of his head.

"I guess the asses have fragile egos," Kaylo said loudly to the townsperson next to him. "And gentle dispositions." The warrior hit him again and harder. Kaylo's head slumped forward.

"What are you doing?" Tayen whispered.

"Be ready."

"What do you get when you dress an ass in purple?" Kaylo asked loudly.

The warrior reared back to hit him with a closed fist, but when he swung, Kaylo shifted to the side and thrust himself at the off-balance warrior. The warrior's rib popped loudly as Kaylo crashed into his torso.

Kaylo rolled over his shoulder and kicked his legs up, swinging his arms over his feet and bringing his bound hands in front of him. Then he took the sword off the fallen warrior.

"Some people can't take a joke."

Several warriors moved to surround him, reaching for their swords and their crystals. Kaylo smiled.

The dull crystals spurred to life. "Stand down. Drop your crystals," a Tomakan warrior ordered.

He stood out amongst the others. Not because of his darker skin and gray hair, or because his tattoos ran along both his cheeks. He carried himself differently. This man didn't wave his confidence around like a new toy. His confidence had been tested, and it weighed easily on his shoulders. Old enough to have lived through dangerous battles and young enough to charge into the next.

The warriors looked confused, but they let go of their crystals.

"Don't you know who this is?" the Tomakan asked. "You stand here in front of a dead man, or so we all thought. Isn't that right, Kaylo?"

"Kaylo?" Nix asked loudly, as her hand wavered from the hilt of her sword. She stood two steps behind the Tomakan warrior.

He turned to her and smiled. All eyes were on him, and he performed for the crowd. "Oh, yes. Kaylo. Ennea's Thief. Hero of Anilace," he announced. Then he cleared his voice. "You didn't know?"

"What are you doing here, Wal?" Kaylo asked, still crouched and ready to fight.

"Wal?" Tayen said to herself.

"Good to see you too, old friend. I worried you might not recognize me. After all, I barely recognize you. The turns have weighed heavy on you, but you still move like the young man I knew."

"We could reminisce without the swords, couldn't we?"

Wal smiled wide, and his tattoos crinkled with the lines of his age. "Oh, Kaylo. Just because it's been a long time doesn't mean I forgot who you are. I bet you're still as dangerous as you ever were, maybe more so. I know I am."

"What do you want?" Kaylo asked.

"Ah, you see, the King and Hakan have a little arrangement. Hakan gets to rule his small city, under our protection, and in return, the army conscripts as it sees fit. No struggle. No mess."

It made an odd kind of sense. The city was filled with people younger than Tayen or far older than Kaylo. Everyone else had been taken into service.

She looked over the faces of the other people in the line. A few kids, her age or younger. Daak, the asshole that claimed to have killed the scout Kaylo found in the forest. And a woman maybe ten turns Kaylo's senior. They weren't warriors.

"Everyone must do their part to fight for Ennea." Wal's words dripped with false sincerity.

"You mean everyone must do their part to fight for The Lost King," Nix said sharply.

"Now there, that is the problem. The King of Astile is not lost," Wal said condescendingly. "He has a singular vision. At the end of this war, there won't be five nations bickering. That's why the Gousht took control in the first place. No, there will be one nation. And a strong nation needs a strong ruler."

He moved uncomfortably close to Nix until their faces almost touched. "You should get used to that fact."

"You have no right...." Nix started.

"Wrong again. Let me show you." He turned to the warriors encircling Kaylo. "Bind this one as well. We always have room for another well-trained fighter."

Three warriors approached Nix, brandishing their weapons. She looked to Hakan, but the large man avoided her eyes.

Nix slid her sword from its scabbard and ran—or more so glided towards the warriors. She moved gracefully as she dodged the first warrior's axe and thrust her blade into the second warrior's belly. Nix turned to meet the first warrior's axe, but Wal moved too quickly. From behind her, he slammed his fist down on her head. She collapsed under the force of his blow.

They bound Nix in rope. Warriors surrounded Kaylo, one sword to a dozen. He might have had a sword, but his hands were bound. Tayen had to do something. *But what?*

Wal looked down at his defeated subordinate with a bleeding gut and shook his head. "It really is a shame," he said. Then he drew his knife and slit the young warrior's throat. "All that training and cut down by a first strike."

Steam rose from the pool of blood forming around the woman. Her lifeless eyes stared directly at Tayen. She didn't want to feel sorry for the dead woman, but she did.

"What happened to you?" Kaylo asked.

"I learned what it takes to win a war. And you're going to help me, or your brat will see The Mist before you do," Wal said. The fake smile left his face, and only the hardened warrior remained.

Her kana dropped his sword, lifted his bound hands into the air, and let the warriors seize him.

How did the boy from Kaylo's stories become a commander in the

Lost Army? Why isn't Kaylo fighting back?

The Song sang loudly. It pulled on her, but Kaylo shook his head.

"That's plenty of excitement for tonight," Wal said. "Get the conscripts ready for transport." He turned to Hakan. "If you'd like to continue our little arrangement, this won't happen again. Take care of this mess." Wal nudged the dead warrior with his boot.

One of the Lost Nation warriors tugged on Tayen's bindings and pulled her roughly to her feet. The prick with cracked ribs met her glare with a smile. "Give me a reason, little girl," he said. "I'd love your daddy to see your insides."

"He's not my father."

"Don't care," the warrior said. "Now, move."

She stepped into place behind Kaylo. *He must have a plan,* she thought, but he held his hands out as instructed. A warrior strung a rope, binding all the conscripted together in a chain.

Nix stood behind her, as quiet and complacent as Kaylo. *Someone has to do something.* But no one did. They waited as a warrior tied the rope chain to a horse's saddle.

Wal walked beside them, inspecting his new prospects. His grin turned sickly sweet, the kind of smile that deserved to lose a couple of teeth.

"I can't tell you how much I've missed you, old friend."

Kaylo didn't respond.

Wal mounted his horse and gave it a kick. The horse reared forward, and the rope chain yanked with it.

"Why?" Tayen whispered to her kana. "Why didn't you let me fight back?"

"Secrets are a small power, but they are all we have," he whispered.

Of course, more cryptic answers, she thought.

"Quiet!" a warrior barked.

The farther they dragged her away from Dasoon, the further she moved from her vengeance. If she was going to escape, she couldn't wait for Kaylo. She had trusted him, and now a group of warriors marched her to the Lost Nation like livestock to the knife.

Tayen set her shoulders and stared off into the darkness. They marched deep into the winter night as a light snow started falling. Despite the cold, she wouldn't let them see her shiver.

THE GREAT SPIRITS

 THE SHADOW: The first of the Great Spirits, known for her wisdom. She blesses her descendants with the ability to manipulate shadows.

 THE RIVER: The second of the Great Spirits, known for their patience, and twin to The Flame. They bless their descendants with the ability to manipulate water.

 THE FLAME: The third of the Great Spirits, known for their strength, and twin to The River. They bless their descendants with the ability to manipulate fire.

 THE MOUNTAIN: The fourth of the Great Spirits, known for her constant support. She blesses her descendants with the ability to manipulate the earth.

THE WIND: The fifth of the Great Spirits, known for his foresight. He blesses his descendants with the ability to manipulate the air.

 THE SEED: The sixth of the Great Spirits, known for his forgiveness. He blesses his descendants with the ability to manipulate plant life.

 THE THIEF/THE BALANCE: The seventh of the Great Spirits, known for her pursuit of power or equity depending on whose story you read. She blesses her descendants with the ability to borrow other dancers' abilities.

GLOSSARY

ANILACE MINES/GOD CAVES: The Gousht's name for Oakheart Mountain, where the first spirit crystals were discovered.

BLOOD BANNER: A derogatory term for Enneans who work with the Gousht as soldiers, spies, informants, and city bureaucrats.

CHANI CLOTH: A light cloth of woven silk. Before the invasion, good chani cloth was worth a goat in trade.

COMMON TONGUE: As the nations developed from tribes and villages, disparate languages and dialects began to merge, resulting in a shared language referred to as common tongue.

CONCLAVE OF SPIRITS: Throughout the Hundred-Turn War, citizens of each nation sought peace from the fighting, taking on a nomadic lifestyle. Eventually, a large group of the nomads representing each nation brought together a meeting of the four nations, where they negotiated an end to the fighting. This was also the origin of the fifth nation, the Jani.

COUTA: A curse that means child of incest. It became a popular slur for the Gousht due to their pale complexion, which Enneans took for sickly.

DANCER: An Ennean who was gifted with the ability to hear The Song and wield one, or in rare cases two, of the Great Spirits' powers. Also known as children of Ennea or spirit-marked.

DAEMONTALE: A make-believe story told to pass down lessons to children.

ENNEA/THE MOTHER: Ennea is the genesis of life. She is the land and mother to the moons and the sun, the spirits, and the people.

FREECITY: A formerly occupied city abandoned by the Gousht after the reclamation war broke out, which runaways and refugees have reclaimed.

GOUSHT PRIEST: Direct descendants of The One True God who serve as leaders of the church and armed forces.

GREAT SPIRITS: Ennea created seven spirits which gave form to The Waking and later gave pieces of their gifts to people in the form of The Song.

HALLOW: A shelter built using The Song and the Great Spirits.

HUNDRED-TURN WAR: For ninety-two or ninety-three turns, depending on who was counting, the four original nations of Ennea engaged in a series of wars over territory, which often overlapped. Also referred to as the Great War, Ennea's Reckoning, the Century of Mourning.

KAMANI: A spirit unbound by gender.

KANA: Ennea's second daughter, the first moon. This also became a term of respect for a mentor and teacher.

KONKI: A tart, sweet fruit with red flesh and a brown husk. The Gousht turned this into a derogatory term for Tomakan people.

KUNNIT: A Gousht word meaning sour blood, which they used interchangeably for blood infections and people of mixed-race heritage.

LOST FOREST: A forest of stormwoods the Lost Nation grew to cut themselves off from the rest of Ennea after the Hundred-Turn War. It is rumored to be impossible to navigate without a forest dancer.

MALITU: A corrupt spirit or dancer who uses their abilities for selfish gain or ill-intent. Often referring to spirit thieves, however, it can refer to any dancer or spirit.

MOON: A measurement of time based on the cycles of the moons, approximately thirty days long. When Toka disappears from the sky every third span, it marks a new moon.

RAKAT: One of the foulest curses in common tongue. It refers to one who's spirit is too tainted for The Mist and is undeserving of life on either plane of existence.

SHUNANLAH: Shunanlah was the first person to be marked by Ennea and gifted The Song and The Shadow. The namesake of the autumnal equinox ceremony.

SKIN SWITCHER: A derogatory term for kamani people, which gained popularity after the regressive values of the Gousht began to spread with colonization.

SPAN: A measurement of time equivalent to ten days.

SPIRIT-BOUND: An Ennean who is unable to hear The Song. Their spirit is bound to their body and to The Waking.

SOKAN: Ennea's first daughter, the giver, and the sun.

SUSU ROOT: When it was first discovered, Ennean healers used susu root as a medicine to dull pain. It's addictive and dulls the brain, making people apathetic. In small amounts, it is a powerful and useful sedative. Long-term use can make people irritable and detached. Severe use can be deadly.

TANONTA: A word that grew from a time before the nations, Tanonta refers to the first new day, the spring equinox. It is the celebration of rebirth as well as a transition of life. At night, when the moons are at their highest, those of age pledge themselves to The Mother.

THE MISSING: A rumored group of Enneans organizing against the Gousht Empire.

THE MIST: The spiritual plane.

THE ONE TRUE GOD/THE ONE: The Gousht god. Religious texts say that The One took human form and sired twelve children, the youngest of whom became the leader of the Gousht church and nation-state.

THE REAPING: After the Stone City fell, Gousht priests destroyed everything deviant or unholy in the eyes of The One True God. Soldiers swept through each village and town, burning books and relics, as well as people. Kamani people suffered greatly during the reaping.

THE SONG: Energy in The Mist seeps through the barrier between planes into The Waking. Dancers have the ability to hear a portion of this energy representing their great spirit ancestor(s). This allows dancers to access the power of their spirit ancestors.

THE STONE CITY: The capital city of Sonacoa and the last city outside of the Lost Nation to fall to the Gousht invasion.

THE WAKING: The physical plane.

THE WRIT: The Gousht holy book. Each crowned Emperor, thought to be direct descendants of The One True God, adds a section to the Writ before they stepdown, documenting the history of the Gousht Empire.

THIEF'S NIGHT: A colloquial term for a night sky in which neither moon is visible. People often act erratically on these nights and blame The Thief for their behavior.

TOKA: Ennea's third daughter, the second moon. This also became a term of respect for a mentee and student.

TURN: A unit of time measurement equivalent to four seasons, twelve moons, or approximately three hundred sixty days.

TWICE-MARKED: A dancer who is gifted with the ability to wield two of the Great Spirits' power.

ZEZE: In a pre-common tongue dialect, zeze meant black, as in the night sky or the darkness of the rich soil. However, when the Gousht arrived, they turned it into a slur for Sonacoans, who typically have darker complexions.

RUNES

Runes is played on a grid of two sets of three intersecting lines, creating nine intersecting points called crosspoints, and wooden markers with a spirit rune carved on one side.

At the beginning of the game, each player is given a bag including fourteen markers, two markers representing each of the seven Great Spirits. One set of markers is dyed black and the other white. Players will draw five markers from their respective bags. At all times, players should have five markers in their hands. When a marker is defeated and removed from a crosspoint, it should be returned to the player's bag.

The player with black markers takes the first turn. On each player's turn, they can place a marker rune-side-down on an empty cross point or challenge one of the other player's facedown markers. Turns cannot be skipped.

When a challenge is issued, both markers are turned over, and the winner is determined by the chart. If matching runes are revealed, the challenger wins the crosspoint. If the challenger wins, they will draw a marker to bring the total in their hand to five runes and place one marker face down on the crosspoint. The challenger can then choose to make another move or end their turn. If the defending player wins, their marker will remain face up on the crosspoint, signifying their claim.

The game is over when a player has claimed five of the nine crosspoints with faceup markers.

	The Shadow	The River	The Flame	The Seed	The Mountain	The Wind	The Thief
The Shadow	The Challenger	The Shadow	The Flame	The Seed	The Shadow	The Shadow	The Thief
The River	The Shadow	The Challenger	The River	The Seed	The River	The Wind	The River
The Flame	The Flame	The River	The Challenger	The Flame	The Mountain	The Wind	The Flame
The Seed	The Seed	The Seed	The Flame	The Challenger	The Seed	The Wind	The Thief
The Mountain	The Shadow	The River	The Mountain	The Seed	The Challenger	The Mountain	The Mountain
The Wind	The Shadow	The Wind	The Wind	The Wind	The Mountain	The Challenger	The Thief
The Thief	The Thief	The River	The Flame	The Thief	The Mountain	The Thief	The Challenger

Note from the Author

As a white person taking on a project like The Malitu Trilogy, there are certain things I must acknowledge. The first is that my intent and the impact of my work may not align. While my intent is to explore the consequences of whiteness/white supremacy and colonialism without centering white people as protagonists, I may unintentionally center my voice in this conversation. I have no wish to do so. My writing is one small voice within a much larger conversation that should center BIPOC voices first and foremost.

If you have not read authors of color who are creating amazing works in speculative fiction that decenter white narratives, I encourage you to read their works. There are countless important voices to add to your to-be-read (TBR) list. Below I have listed some of the authors I have read and enjoyed.

> Tomi Adeyemi, Octavia Butler, C.L. Clark, Tracy Deonn, Justina Ireland, N.K. Jemisin, R.F. Kuang, Fonda Lee, L. Penelope, Nnedi Okorafor, PhD, Rebecca Roanhorse, Andrea Stewart, ML Wang, Evan Winters

In taking on this project, I am not looking to tell anyone else's story for them. While the colonialism depicted in No Heart for a Thief is not based on any one example of colonialism throughout history, it pulls from aspects in real life. Colonialist regimes across the globe have created means of manipulating the belief systems of indigenous people, controlling populations through violence, and forcing members of those populations into slavery. Unfortunately, these practices continue all over the world today.

At the end of the day, I believe issues of power and oppression are issues we all need to thoughtfully interrogate. Artists who are privileged within systems of oppression, like myself, must educate themselves and take care when addressing these subject matters. Even with that said, I may—and probably will—make mistakes along the way. I am dedicated to listening, learning, and continuing to improve.

This statement is not meant to extricate myself from consequences or critique. This is a claim to accountability. I believe in and love this story, and with that I am responsible for its content and impact.

I hope you will join me in this journey.

James Lloyd Dulin

ACKNOWLEDGEMENTS

When I began writing this book, I told myself I was just writing it to see if I could. It didn't matter to me if nothing came of it or if it wasn't any good. As I wrote, I shared a few chapters at a time with a friend, and he offered me encouragement every step of the way until I finished a first draft. It was far from perfect. It put my ignorance of structure and convention on full display, but I had finished my first book and I told what I believed to be a good story. Without Ben Zimmer's support, No Heart for a Thief would not exist. I thank him for that. You can choose to blame him if you like.

Since that time, I have had amazing support from beta readers, sensitivity readers, and editors. Each of them helped to make this book better. My unwavering thanks go out to Rushi Vyas, Taylor Banks, Trae Hawkins, Angelicka Morgan, Amy Vrana, and Victoria Gross. Without you, these pages would be a series of typos and disjointed plot points.

I cannot overstate the importance of artwork and design in bringing a story to life. My thanks to Gustavo Schmitt for making my rough sketch of Ennea into a beautiful map, and Felix Ortiz who made such a beautiful cover. And to my brother, Michael Dulin, who designed the typography and the layout of this book, thank you for helping make my dream come true.

ACKNOWLEDGEMENTS

All my gratitude goes to my wife, Aneicka Bookal. Writing takes time and focus, and that means stealing time from an already busy life. Without your support, I wouldn't have made it past page one. You, Sonny, and Dominic are the center of my world, and I would not be who I am without you.

Odds are that you picked up this book because you saw someone share it online, read a positive review, or someone recommended it to you. The success or failure of indie authors is largely a product of the community that supports them. I have an amazing community of Advanced Reader Copy (ARC) reviewers, authors that have helped me along the way, and fellow fantasy nerds. To the amazing people on the Indie Accords Discord, thank you. To the readers who took a chance on a debut author and agreed to review an ARC, you are irreplaceable.

Lastly, thank you, the reader, for deciding to read these pages. Without you, these pages are just a collection of words. You made them into a book. If I can ask you to help me take this one step further, please review this book on Amazon, Goodreads, and any other platform you might use. Reviews are the lifeblood for self-published authors. Reviews encourage others to give a book a try, and I want to share this book with as many people as I can.

Kaylo and Tayen will be back with No Safe Have, Malitu: Book Two.